THE VALIANT LADY

THE VALIANT
LADY

A NOVEL BY BRIGID KNIGHT

DOUBLEDAY & COMPANY, INC.

GARDEN CITY   1948   NEW YORK

First published, 1948, in the United States

PRINTED IN THE UNITED STATES

AT

THE COUNTRY LIFE PRESS, GARDEN CITY, N. Y.

FOR IAN AND ANDREW

THIS STORY OF A STRUGGLE FOR FREEDOM

IS MY TRIBUTE TO THE ENDURING COURAGE

AND UNFAILING FAITH

OF THE PEOPLE OF THE NETHERLANDS

FORE☩ORD

IN A LONG NOVEL ABSOLUTE ADHERENCE TO MATTERS OF PERIOD WOULD, I think, prove tiresome to the reader. Therefore, while endeavouring to portray faithfully the costumes, manners, and ways of the latter half of the sixteenth century, I have avoided the somewhat formal dialogue of Elizabethan times, and have ventured to express myself throughout in simple language, avoiding colloquialisms and peasant and county dialects. I have also used the form of a name most familiar to modern readers. For instance, Falmouth was Smithwick in Tudor days, but, as it seemed to me that the use of the old name would only tend to be confusing, I have used the later form.

To such authors as C. V. Wedgwood, *William the Silent;* Motley, *The Rise of the Dutch Republic;* A. L. Rowse, *Tudor Cornwall;* Claridge, *History of the Gold Coast;* J. E. Thorold Rogers, *Holland;* and E. L. Elias, *The Book of Polar Exploration,* I am particularly indebted, and it is only fair that I should state that many phrases and some conversations have been drawn almost verbatim from their pages.

BRIGID KNIGHT

CONTENTS

FOREWORD

ix

BOOK ONE THE FLOWING TIDE

PART I HOLLAND

3

PART II CORNISH INTERLUDE

53

PART III HOLLAND

58

PART IV CORNISH INTERLUDE

88

PART V HOLLAND

91

BOOK TWO THE TURNING TIDE

PART VI CORNISH INTERLUDE

113

PART VII HOLLAND

119

PART VIII   CORNISH INTERLUDE
123

PART IX   HOLLAND
127

PART X   GOLD COAST INTERLUDE
137

PART XI   HOLLAND
161

PART XII   GOLD COAST INTERLUDE
184

PART XIII   HOLLAND
193

BOOK THREE   THE GOLDEN AGE

PART XIV   HOLLAND
201

PART XV   CORNISH INTERLUDE
222

PART XVI   HOLLAND
231

PART XVII   CORNISH INTERLUDE
248

PART XVIII   GOLD COAST INTERLUDE
269

PART XIX   CORNISH INTERLUDE
276

PART XX   HOLLAND
279

PART XXI   HOLLAND
298

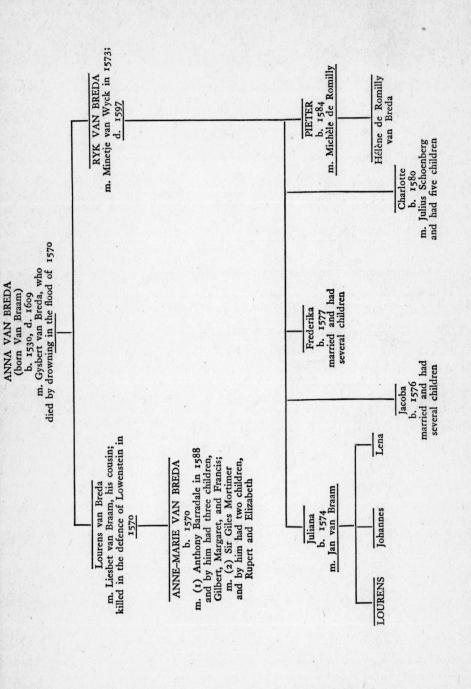

ANNA VAN BREDA
(born Van Braam)
b. 1530, d. 1609
m. Gysbert van Breda, who
died by drowning in the flood of 1570

Lourens van Breda
m. Liesbet van Braam, his cousin;
killed in the defence of Lowenstein in
1570

ANNE-MARIE VAN BREDA
b. 1570
m. (1) Anthony Barradale in 1588
and by him had three children,
Gilbert, Margaret, and Francis;
m. (2) Sir Giles Mortimer
and by him had two children,
Rupert and Elizabeth

RYK VAN BREDA
m. Minetje van Wyck in 1573;
d. 1597

PIETER
b. 1584
m. Michèle de Romilly

Hélène de Romilly
van Breda

Charlotte
b. 1580
m. Julius Schoenberg
and had five children

Frederika
b. 1577
married and had
several children

Jacoba
b. 1576
married and had
several children

Juliana
b. 1574
m. Jan van Braam

LOURENS   Johannes   Lena

BOOK ONE

THE FLOWING TIDE

PART I

ḦOLLAND

CHAPTER ONE

DEEP SILENCE ENFOLDED THE OLD FARMHOUSE OF OOSTERMEER IN North Friesland on a night in the spring of 1568 while Anna van Breda lay awake in her great bed built closetwise within the wall. Thinking sleep would not come to her that night, she climbed down the ladder to the floor and went to stand at the chamber window.

Her ward, Liesbet, and the two serving girls were with her in the house, yet she felt utterly alone, and an indefinable sense of impending trouble weighed her down.

She leaned a little way out of the window. Oostermeer lay before her in the benignant light of the full moon. She had grown to middle age amid the dykes and silver meers of this remote and watery province of the Netherlands and loved it well. She filled in from memory the details of the familiar landscape not defined by the moonlight, and saw stretching away before her the long avenue of poplars that now were swaying spires of darkness; to the right the roofs of the buttressed barns and the outlines of the neat garden were etched in a delicate tracery of formal design; dimly in the distance she saw the meadow and heard the turning arms of the windmill there creak gently; and the soughing of the wind in the trees and the cries of a belated gull came faintly to her as she watched and listened in the night.

A cat came velvet-padded across the floor and rubbed itself purring against her. Anna discovered when she bent down to fondle it that it was not one of the house cats. There was a little window left open in the larder off the kitchen and the barn cats entered there.

It was some time since the window had been put to its proper use, she reflected; and wondered with stabbing anxiety whether anything had befallen her husband Gysbert. In these dark days of oppression he was often away fighting the Spaniards at sea and on land, as were her sons, Lourens and Ryk: the younger boy, Ryk, sailed and fought with his father, while Lourens, the elder, who favoured her and had no love for the sea, was an ardent partisan of Orange and fought with the scattered bands of patriots in Friesland in this hour of national need.

Thinking of these matters, a wave of loneliness and longing swept over her.

"Gysbert, Gysbert," she whispered under her breath.

She felt she could no longer struggle alone, keeping her household of frightened women together and encouraging Liesbet to aid her in the gigantic task of allaying suspicion. Alva's spies and informers were everywhere and it meant death to every one of them if the activities of the Van Breda family were discovered. The ever-spreading tentacles of the Inquisition had now reached even their remote farmhouse. As the danger increased the part she and Liesbet played grew more formidable, and lately they had felt impelled to profess the Roman Catholic faith as an added precaution, although in secret they followed Luther. Anna shivered to think what would happen if the Spanish spies stumbled on the truth, for Oostermeer was the accredited headquarters of the patriots in the north. At Oostermeer her husband and her sons and the other members of the band met the Englishmen Richard Barradale and James Carey to lay their plans for surprise attacks on Spanish positions and Spanish shipping, and to hide in the secret cellar under the floor of the byre the powder and weapons of war bought in England with the money that came from the plunder of Spanish ships. They came under cover of darkness and left before dawn, so Anna barely spoke to her menfolk, although she was present at all their counsels. It was the hope of the Netherlanders that England would unite openly with them and make common cause against the invader; but the English Queen was wary and stayed her hand, trusting rather to diplomacy than to force of arms.

The burden was heavy; and unbearable if she dwelt too long upon its terrors. Her courage must be equal to the task. Anna drew back into the chamber and leaned her head against the wall near the window. She resolutely turned her thoughts from the terror of the time to Gysbert. Her feeling for him was so deep and abiding that she could conjure up a sense of his actual presence at will. When danger threatened, or when she was dismayed or discouraged, the thought of him brought with it a strong feeling that he stood close to her with his hand on her shoulder. There was great virtue in this casting out of her mind to Gysbert. Soon she felt quieter and calmer and, when she had climbed the ladder to her bed and settled herself, she fell at once into a heavy sleep.

Something stirred in the house. Anna woke instantly, every faculty alert. She lay rigid, barely breathing, in a concentrated agony of listening.

There was movement in the kitchen below her. She reached up for the thick woollen stockings on the shelf above her head and slipped them on. Her hand sought for the dagger beneath her pillow and found it. In her nightrobe and cap she slid like a trickling shadow down the ladder, moving noiselessly and stopping to listen after each step. She suspected that the one who had entered had not been to the house before because Gysbert or Ryk, Lourens or Jan Hattingh or the Englishmen would have given the signal ere now—three taps on the kitchen ceiling directly beneath her bed.

She glided forward and passed out of the room without sound. She had often practised descending the stairs and could get to the bottom noiselessly. The tension of her nerves was so acute that the air seemed like treacle and she felt she was thrusting her feet through it heavily and endlessly, pausing in between each step of her descent to listen.

There was enough moonlight coming in through the windows to prick out the open inner doorway of the kitchen in pale light. She summoned all her courage and approached it. Her spine tingled as she went forward wraithlike in her stockinged feet. There was a barely audible intake of breath in the room ahead as someone moved with less caution. Anna froze at the doorway.

Now began an appalling eternity of waiting. She knew that a stranger had entered the kitchen. He knocked into the furniture as though he were unfamiliar with its position. From where she stood she could glimpse a red-pink patch on the hearth and knew it for the glow of the peat fire beneath its film of ashes. A figure passed in front of the glow, blotting it out. She saw a man—and a Spaniard at that, she hazarded by his silhouette. He stooped and she saw his hand was pressed to his breast. She must have made a betraying movement as the bent figure at the fire stiffened into immobility. He also was listening.

The breathing of the man in the kitchen became noisy. He drew rasping, unwilling breaths as though he were endeavouring to restrain them and could not. Then he moved away from the hearth beyond Anna's gaze.

Her fingers closed like steel about the haft of her dagger. She raised her right arm and waited for the intruder to pass through the door. She would stab him as he came out, and God give her the strength to do it, as her life, and the lives of those asleep in the house, might depend on the sureness of her aim.

She thought he was moving nearer the door. She trembled; and braced her knees. God, God, she prayed, let me not fail. . . .

The blood beat in her head and drummed so loudly in her ears that she felt he must hear it. Years, a century, an age passed while they held their positions in the deathly silence.

The rasping breathing sounded much nearer. Suddenly there was a thud as though a body had collapsed on the floor.

Still Anna did not move. Perhaps it was a ruse to lure her into the room, she thought. She waited. There was a groan and then no further sound.

She stood waiting until her clamouring nerves could no longer bear the strain. Then she steeled herself to enter. She had no light, but there were unlit candles and a lantern in the kitchen. She saw a dark, huddled heap on the floor near the door. She crept near with the dagger in her hand. She grew bolder as the intruder did not move. She went swiftly past him and thrust a taper into the heart of the fire and, when it was alight, held it to the candles. Soon there was light enough to see clearly.

A Spaniard lay at her feet—one of Alva's men, and from his uniform, she judged he was an officer. His head was thrown back and he was unconscious. He lay in a little pool of water and there was blood seeping in an ever-widening patch on his doublet. She saw that water had dripped wherever he had moved. It was an easy surmise that he had been stabbed and thrown into a canal: the Netherlanders disposed of quite a few Spaniards that way.

She gripped her dagger firmly. If he moved she must slay him. A shuddering nausea swept over her, and again her knees trembled. She knelt down. It would be safer, she thought, to strike from that position.

She looked closely at the Spaniard. His olive-skinned face was drawn and shadowed and his moustachios showed soot-black against his death-like pallor. She noticed the greying hair at his temples. Her gaze travelled lower. She shuddered at the stain on his doublet; and at once steeled herself to mark where she must strike.

Above the heart . . . Where would that be? . . . Here. And then she saw a shadowy Cross, the arms of which intersected in the precise spot above the heart into which she must plunge her dagger.

A wave of superstitious terror swept over her. The Cross . . . the Cross . . . She looked up to see what had cast the shadow and saw a wooden Cross and their rosaries hanging from a hook on the dresser. They were there for outward show in case the priest called. The light from the candle shining behind the Cross had projected the shadow on the breast of the unconscious man.

Anna moistened her dry lips. It was an enormous relief that there was a natural explanation for the shadowy Cross. With this feeling of relief came flooding in the conviction that God was with her. He had indicated how she should make an end of the Spaniard.

The Spaniard groaned and opened his eyes. She was instantly on her guard. He saw her kneeling above him, the dagger uplifted in her right hand.

A flicker of fire came into his dimmed eyes; his lips curled.

"Why do you wait?" His weak voice rasped in sardonic arrogance. "Why not finish off what your compatriots have so inefficiently begun?"

Her nerves screamed out that annihilation was upon them if she did not act. Strike, her instinct shrieked, strike while there is time. . . .

Her fingers obeyed her insistent nerves; they gripped fiercely and the muscles of her arm contracted for the downward thrust. She glanced down to direct the shining blade. That glance was her undoing. The Cross . . . where the arms of the Cross met. The shadow on the blood-soaked doublet was still there.

The Cross . . .

The eyes of the Spaniard were fixed on Anna's face. There was a slight smile on his lips. He knows how to die, thought Anna. So brave men die.

"The Cross!" The cry was wrung from her.

The dagger fell with a little clatter to the floor.

"I will dress your wound," she said through pale lips.

The dark eyes of the Spaniard closed; he had fainted.

Anna rose from her knees and went for water and bandages.

The wound was deep. She cleaned and dressed it. He had lost much blood and she doubted whether he would live. She had removed his stained and sodden clothing and had rolled him in a blanket before he recovered consciousness again. He opened his lips to speak, but she put her hand on his mouth and shook her head.

"Do not speak. I shall give you a little water. And then you must try to get up the stairs with me."

He raised his hand and feebly removed hers from his lips.

"What are you going to do?" he muttered.

"I shall fetch the water," said Anna.

She rose to her feet and went for the water; but she found some milk in a bowl and brought that back instead. She slipped an arm under his shoulders and supported him while he drank.

"It is milk," she said quietly. "It will be better for you than water."

"I have had enough of water," he whispered; and there was a ghost of a smile on his lips.

"I dare say you have," said Anna drily.

They both smiled.

"Your pestilential canals," he said. "Fortunately the one I was thrown in was not deep."

"It would have saved me some trouble if it had been," said Anna fiercely. "Come, drink your milk."

When the bowl was empty he asked again: "What are you going to do?"

"I must think," said Anna. "I ought to have killed you. Now I cannot kill you in cold blood and you may exact vengeance for what was done to you this night."

"I was attacked in the dark: I did not see my assailants."

But that would not stop the Spaniards putting the population of the whole area to the sword, thought Anna. God in heaven, what was she to do? She moved suddenly, impatiently.

"You must stay in this house until your wound is healed. So much is clear," she said. "After that I do not know. I must think. I think better when I work. I will wash the floor and hide your clothes. That will be a beginning and perhaps it will come to me what I had better do."

She left him; and, having collected the pail and cloth, set to work to remove the telltale traces of his entry into the house. He watched her for a little while until he fell into a doze, a semicoma of weakness. He was roused by Anna's touch.

"It has come to me what I should do," said Anna quietly. "But there are certain things I must know. Firstly, are there any of your country-men near who are aware of what happened to you?"

"No," he answered in a voice alarmingly weak. "I was alone. I had a commission to execute and I was to follow my company in a few days."

"It makes it easier for me that you were alone. And how is it that you speak Dutch as well as you do?"

"I was once a page in the household of the Duchess Margaret," he said. "I learned the language in her service. But I know no Frisian, so I was glad when you spoke Dutch."

"We have connections in the south," Anna said. "No more now. Your strength fails. I shall help you to my bed. It is the safest place for you to hide. You must keep very quiet because there are two girls in the house who may betray your presence here, and I could not save you then. Can you get up the stairs, do you think? I shall support you."

"Why do you do this?" he whispered. "Is it so that you can hand me over to your Orangemen later? I can see no reason in it unless that is what is in your mind."

Anna's face grew wan and bewildered. She wrung her hands.

"You are a Spaniard and against us," she said. "I tend you when I could have slain you, and there would have been one Spaniard less to defile this unhappy country. They were right, those who stabbed you and flung you in the canal. And I am undoing their good woik. I may bring my household to the stake and have my house burned over my head."

"It is your choice," he said.

"How am I to know that when you have recovered from your wound and I have set you safely on your way you will not betray me or those who stabbed you?" she continued more hardly. "Have I the right to run so appalling a risk? It would have been better had I made an end of you while I had the dagger in my hand. I am a Dutchwoman, you are a Spaniard. Our countries are at war. We are enemies, and nothing can alter that."

"There lies your dagger," he said; and again his tone was arrogant. "There it lies, out of my reach, on the floor."

Anna shook her head.

"No," she muttered.

"Why not? It will settle all problems."

She looked across to the dresser and stretched out her hand to the Cross.

"That is why," she said. "The Cross. I have thought and tried to reason, but it all comes back to the Cross."

He turned his head and his eyes followed her pointing hand.

"Are you not a heretic then?"

She gave no sign of having heard him.

"All paths lead to the Cross in the end," she whispered, as though to herself. "We all come to the Cross, you and I, everyone. No matter how we will it otherwise, we must come to its pain and its benediction. I have no right to take your life, nor to send you forth to be slain."

As she said this her doubts fell away. While she was cleaning the floor she had pondered what she should do, weighing the consequences. There had been an element of cool calculation in her thoughts. It was plain that if she took the risk and harboured the wounded man it might allay Spanish suspicion. If the priest, Father Ramon, got to hear of it and reported the matter favourably, Oostermeer might escape observation and the farm would therefore be doubly safe as a rendezvous. On the other hand, if the Spaniard died and by some mischance it became known to the enemy she would be sore put to it to give a satisfactory explanation and Oostermeer and its precincts might be subjected to a rigorous search, and the secret cellar was an arsenal and discovery meant death. But as she spoke of the Cross she no longer weighed either the advantages or the disadvantages consequent on her succouring the Spaniard. She was upheld for an immeasurable moment of ecstasy by a strong sense of the abiding presence of God.

"What is to come of it rests with God," she said gently, looking down on the man on the floor. "I shall save you if I am able. Can you stand, do you think?"

"I shall try."

She knelt beside him and, exerting all her strength and rising with him, helped him to his feet. He leaned heavily against her.

"It will be all right," she encouraged him. "Hold onto the table while I put out the candles and leave the room in order."

The darkness seemed intense when she had snuffed the candles. She supported him with an arm about his waist. He felt her breath warm on his cheek as she whispered:

"Let us go now. And not a sound for your life."

Anna was on the point of collapse when they reached her chamber and she had assisted him to her bed. She tucked the covers round him and, crawling to a corner of the bed, sank down in exhaustion.

The reaction came; she began to sob soundlessly.

"God," she cried softly. "God, I am in such confusion."

Never had there been such disorder in her mind. She had put a Papist in Gysbert's bed who might denounce them all. Yet all human creatures shared the same God, the same heaven. Papist and Protestant were all the children of God under the sun, and it was not for her to discriminate.

The Spaniard slept restlessly, while Anna crouched at his feet.

As the first glimmer of daylight appeared she climbed down from the bed; she found a cloak and flung it about her and stole noiselessly down the stairs. She went out the back door and found the Spaniard's footmarks. These she carefully obliterated.

She was back in her bedchamber before the household stirred. She closed the door and leaned against it, breathing quickly. She remained there until her heart took on its normal beating. Then, when she was calm again, she remembered that the Spaniard had given her no pledge that he would not betray her. She had meant him to promise her that much at least, and she had implied it when she had spoken to him in the kitchen. The recollection that she had exacted no pledge was like a blow between the eyes. Cold with shock, she climbed up to the bed on the little ladder and looked at the Spaniard.

He was sleeping, but peacefully now.

ii

Liesbet van Braam, Anna van Breda's niece and ward, had lived at Oostermeer since she had been tragically orphaned in infancy. She was now seventeen years old and Anna, who had no daughter, looked upon Liesbet as her own child, and loved her dearly, as they all did.

Liesbet was an exquisite creature, small and fragile-boned and by no means robust. She was seldom actually ill but she was constitutionally delicate. Her skin was clear and flushed and so thin that the blue veins in her temples showed in twining traceries through its transparency. Her hair was of a rich gold colour, very thick and lustrous; and her eyes were huge and violet-blue in colour and vividly alive. She was by nature peace-loving and happy, with a sunlit serenity of mind that was her greatest charm.

Both Anna's sons were in love with their cousin; but from the first Ryk and Liesbet had been irresistibly drawn to each other, and now they were betrothed and planned to marry as soon as their lives were more settled.

So matters stood that spring morning when Anna, choosing a time when Elfrieda and Santje were busy in the byre, called Liesbet to her and acquainted her with the happenings of the past night.

". . . I could not think what to do," Anna explained, concluding her account of how the wounded Spaniard came to be in her bed. "And while I reasoned frantically it came to me that I had not the right to kill a man. And then there was not much to think about at all. Ach, Liesbet, I had not the heart to slay the Spaniard as he lay wounded at my feet, and, having spared him, I cannot bring myself to tell our people he is here. They will murder him. If we are careful he need learn nothing of what happens at Oostermeer, and when he leaves he may tell the Spaniards of our friendliness and they will not think to look for the patriot headquarters here. We shall be deceiving our men but great good to the cause may come of it."

"Be that as it may," said Liesbet, "you cannot have the murder of this man on your soul. We will keep the matter a secret and I shall stand by you whatever happens."

"What would I do without you, Liesbet, my heart?" said Anna warmly. "I knew you would see the matter through my eyes and I thank you for your understanding. It distresses me to implicate you; but I must have your help. I do not think it wise to speak of this to the maids. They are loyal, but it is possible that they may think their duty lies in another direction. They are aware that our people come and go in the night and on these occasions they are not summoned nor do we speak of the meetings. Therefore if they heard anything in the night they will attach no importance to it. We will take on the work of the house between us and send them out on the farm and they need never go near my bed."

"We shall manage. Do you think he will live, Mother?"

"Yes," said Anna. "He is stronger this morning. He told me his name— Don Rodriguez d'Esquerdes—and when you know a man's name he no longer seems a stranger."

Liesbet was the greatest comfort to her, Anna thought lovingly. She felt that she could speak of the wounded man to her as though he were a human being, and forget that she should hate him for being a Spaniard.

"Where shall we read the Bible, Mother?" asked Liesbet, pondering their difficulties. "If we go as usual to the closet behind your bed the Spaniard may hear us, and it would not do for him to discover that we are heretics."

"If we change the maids may be suspicious. It will have to be the closet, Liesbet."

Each day Anna read a chapter from the Bible to her household. It had been the custom at Oostermeer from her father's time.

"We can wait for the Spaniard to sleep and then read," said Liesbet. "There is no fixed hour so we can wait our opportunity. Your voice is low and will not carry through the wall."

"I shall leave it to you to go out at once and quieten the Spaniard should he make any sound," said Anna. "I shall keep the maids from following you. We shall need to be quick-witted."

"It is a risk, but one we shall have to take. Ach, Mother, what are we doing? All this plotting and planning, and for a Spaniard too! It is unbelievable; it is almost laughable!"

They looked at each other and smiled doubtfully. Then they put their hands on each other's shoulders and began to laugh, rocking with sudden, wild merriment. Anna sobered up quickly.

"All this for a Spaniard, as you say, Liesbet," she said. "It is absurd. But you have taken me out of myself and I think of you now. Ryk wishes to take you to Delft to the Van Breda relatives, or even to England after you are married. I like the idea, as Oostermeer is becoming too dangerous a spot for you. The Spanish soldiery are always about. Marry Ryk, Liesbet, and do not keep putting off the day. I long for half a dozen grandchildren and you keep me waiting."

Liesbet's laughter also died. Her eyes were haunted.

"What of Lourens?" she asked sorrowfully.

"You have chosen Ryk."

"I do not wish to leave you," said Liesbet. "If I remain here at Oostermeer when I am Ryk's wife Lourens will come home and I shall set the brothers against each other. I love Ryk; yet Lourens is part of my life. We three grew up together."

"You must come to it in the end, Liesbet. I know what it means because your uncle Gerard van Braam wooed me before I was married. I had to choose between him and Gysbert. I chose Gysbert, and I have never regretted my choice."

"You did not have to choose between brothers, and you were not all living beneath the same roof."

"Lourens has courage and he is no weakling," said Anna. "Do not belittle him."

"I do not belittle him; but it is not easy."

Lourens was very dear to Anna, dearer than Ryk; but the situation was getting out of hand and the longer Liesbet hesitated the greater the tension became. I shall speak to Ryk when he comes again, thought Anna; he must marry Liesbet and end it. Having made up her mind to this, her heart bled for Lourens, who would be bereft. She put her arms about Liesbet, this Liesbet who was made so small and so perfect that they all loved her. She drew her close to her.

"You will find a way," said Anna comfortingly.

iii

By the time a fortnight had gone by Anna and Liesbet were on friendly terms with Don Rodriguez d'Esquerdes. Although he was a Spaniard, they had discovered it was impossible not to like a man they had pulled back from death, particularly as he set himself to win their regard.

They felt sure they had successfully concealed his presence in the house. Anna shared Liesbet's bed and retired to it when the maids had gone to sleep; but she was restless and slept little. She was expecting some member of the organization to arrive any night and frequently she got out of bed and sat waiting in the kitchen. She feared the Spaniard might hear the voices of the men and she planned to arrange matters so that the next meeting should take place in the byre. If she told Gysbert that she thought spies were about it would be excuse enough.

As it fell out the next step was made easy. On a night when a light rain was falling a calving heifer kept Anna walking between the house and the byre. She sent Elfrieda and Santje and Liesbet early to their beds and kept her lonely vigil.

Shortly after midnight the rain ceased and the heifer calved. Relieved and reassured, Anna came out of the byre door with a lantern in her hand. She saw the dark figure of a man crossing the yard. She stepped out from the doorway and held up the lantern and by its flickering light saw Ryk.

"Ryk!" she called out softly and gladly to him.

"Mother! Why are you up at this hour?"

"The black-faced heifer has just calved. Are you alone, Ryk?"

He stood beside her with his arm about her shoulders, and the light of the lantern played on the wet earth at their feet and shone on the little pools of rainwater.

"No. Most of the band will meet here tonight—my father, Lourens, Uncle Gerard and Jan Hattingh, Richard Barradale and James Carey. The cellar must be cleared. There are great events afoot."

"So Count Louis of Nassau's campaign is to begin in earnest?"

"Yes, we are moving at last. You will hear all, Mother."

"Your news does not surprise me," said Anna. "There have been increasing numbers of Spaniards about and Groningen is strongly held. Alva will fight for every inch of soil in Friesland. Ryk, you remain here and tell the others to go into the byre. It is as well to meet there. The maids are trustworthy but they will speak under torture, and they must not know too much. There are Spanish spies where you least expect them. I shall go to the house and bring ale and food and whisper to Liesbet to keep the girls where they are."

"I must see Liesbet. How is she?"

"She is well and longs for you. When the business is over I shall call her. Are the others near?"

"They will arrive at any moment. We are coming singly. As you say, Friesland is full of spies."

"Wait here. I shall not be long."

Anna ran to the house and crept quietly up the stairs. She roused Liesbet by a touch on her shoulder.

"Wake up, Liesbet," she whispered urgently. "They are all here tonight. Get yourself dressed and keep watch. When the counsel is over I shall return and you must slip out to see Ryk. Here is my dagger. Scream before you use it. I shall be listening all the time. Keep Don Rodriguez where he is, and the maids. I must go now. Bless you, my heart."

They were waiting for her when she reached the byre. Ryk had slung the lantern on a hook and the byre was dimly lit. Anna set down the basket she carried and at once was in Gysbert's arms. She and Gysbert had been man and wife for more than twenty years and they were lovers still. Gysbert was a huge man, massively built. Anna was tall, but she seemed slight and slim beside him. Her youth was behind her but she was lovely still with a calm, grey-eyed comeliness. Under her stiff Frisian cap her hair that once had been ash-blonde was now silvery, so that it seemed hardly to have changed but to have taken on another degree of fairness. Her eyes were shining and her face had a radiant glow.

"You have been long away, Gysbert," she said.

She stood at his side and gazed round the circle of faces in the shadowy byre, smiling her greeting to her Frisian friends, and to her friends from over the sea.

"Much has happened," said Gysbert. "The Prince of Orange has declared himself and there is open warfare at last. Louis is here in Friesland raising the standard of revolt. He awaits the attack of Aremberg at Dam. We have been rousing the peasants in the north, and Lourens and

Gerard and Jan Hattingh are to go with them to join Louis's troops at Dam. Therefore we have come for powder and pistols and arquebuses and they must be got away tonight. And the rest of us go back to the sea to plunder Spanish shipping to get the money for arms and yet more arms."

"The last prize was rich," said Ryk. He sat on the edge of the manger and swung his legs. He was a handsome fellow with a gay, laughing face. "We captured a hulk off the Scilly Isles. She had a valuable cargo of silver and molasses, canary wine and five hundred reals of plate."

"The flow of arms can continue then," said Anna.

"Mynheer Barradale will see to that," said Gysbert.

"Buying arms in England and shipping them here is about all James and I can do," said Richard Barradale in execrable Dutch. He expressed himself with difficulty, although he understood fairly well all that was said. He was a genial man with a kindly face and a rich, deep voice, and looked what he was—an honest, bluff Cornish yeoman.

Lourens had stationed himself beside the heifer and her newly born calf. He leaned against the beast and fed her with trusses of hay. He shared with his mother a passion for Oostermeer. He had Anna's features and good looks and his father's massive build. He spoke now, and so impressive was his appearance and his firm voice that they all turned to look at him and he held their full attention.

"I have long wished to say that we must not neglect my mother's interests," he said. "If the Spaniards stumble on the truth of what happens at Oostermeer she will lose all, her life perhaps. I suggest that on this occasion, when the Spanish plunder is sold, an adequate sum be set aside in England in case she and my cousin Liesbet have to take refuge in that country. We may be killed and she cannot be left without some provision for the future."

"I have urged it before," broke in Richard Barradale. "If it is agreed I shall arrange it when I get back to Falmouth and give you an accounting."

"Do we all agree?" asked Gysbert.

Anna saw Ryk glance at Lourens and look away again. The jealousy between the brothers grieved her.

There was a chorus of assent.

"It should have been done long ago," said Gerard van Braam.

Anna spoke quickly. She did not wish them to quarrel about her, and it was a good moment to bring up the question of Liesbet.

"Things grow more difficult each day," she said. "The priest comes too often for my peace of mind. Last week some Spanish soldiers came. Liesbet and I were in the yard. Liesbet passed the time of day with them and smiled prettily, as she must. The men were bold and there was a change in their manner. They no longer try to conciliate. I shall stay on at Oostermeer and see the matter through; but Liesbet must go. I have thought——"

She paused, and her eyes rested on Lourens, whom she must wound. His hand was on the heifer's flank and he was frozen into listening rigidity. Their eyes met. Anna's were sad, the young man's hard. She knew that not until Ryk and Liesbet were actually married would he give up hope of winning Liesbet. She turned her gaze to Richard Barradale. He was a trusted friend. There had been religious troubles in England and Richard Barradale's wife had spent some years in Antwerp; there Richard and Gysbert had met and had sworn to work together against the tyrannical overlordship of Spain. With the accession of Queen Elizabeth better times had come and the Barradales had returned home; but Richard had remembered his days of adversity, and he and his son-in-law, James Carey, made common cause with the Van Bredas in their efforts in the cause of freedom.

"What have you thought?" prompted Richard Barradale gently.

Anna threw back her head with a decisive movement.

"Will you take Liesbet to your home tonight?" she asked.

"My wife would welcome her," said Richard Barradale. "Frances is lonely at Bodrugan with our small son Anthony, who is too young for company."

"I shall marry Liesbet at once," cried Ryk, leaping to his feet.

"It would be best," Anna said heavily. She was intensely aware of Lourens. She felt her words were molten, dripping like lead on his heart. Yet they must be spoken.

Ryk and Gysbert were smiling at each other. How alike they are, she thought. They lived on the crest of the wave, skimming the surface with gaiety and self-confidence, never giving a thought to the deeps concealed beneath the froth of change and adventure. And she loved them both, Gysbert with all the strength of her heart and mind. They were speaking.

". . . we will be married in England . . . at Dover . . . No, perhaps here so that my mother could be present. . . ."

And Richard Barradale's rich voice cutting in:

". . . leave it to Frances. She loves weddings. . . ."

Anna pulled her thoughts together.

"It is settled then," she said crisply. "And now to the real business."

There was much to discuss. Anna heard the details of the campaign that was planned in Friesland, and gave such information as had come her way as to the strength of the Spanish forces and their dispositions. She was given certain instructions to pass on to patriots in Groningen and elsewhere. Then the cows were herded in the far corner of the byre and the secret cellar was opened. When the stores of powder and weapons had been lifted out they were loaded on the carts that Lourens had assembled in the yard. The food was eaten and the ale drunk, and Anna had barely a moment for private conversation with Gysbert. Once, when she was handing the ale round, Gerard spoke to her.

"Anna," he said, "why do you not also go to England?"

"It is impossible," said Anna. "My work is not done."

"Someone else can take it on. You ought to leave before it is too late," Richard Barradale said. "The fighting in Friesland will be bitter. When it is over you can come back."

"I cannot leave Oostermeer," Anna returned quietly.

She felt Gerard's hand on her own.

"I shall watch over Oostermeer for you," he promised.

Gerard understood her deep feeling for Oostermeer. They were cousins and had known each other for the greater part of their lives.

"I must remain," Anna said. "Please do not try to persuade me, Gerard."

At last the cellar was cleared and the carts had left. Anna was careful and thorough in all she did. She climbed down into the cellar and swept it.

She went then to call Liesbet and send her to Ryk, who was in the yard waiting for her.

While she waited in the quiet house Anna's mind grew vivid with love and pity for them all. Through the window she saw the waning moon slipping through lacy folds of clouds; and the light in the byre was a pulsing flicker of flame in the dreaming dimness of the earth and the distant meer.

All save Ryk had gone to see the carts safely on their way. Some of them would be returning for a brief hour and then it would be quiet again. Ryk and Liesbet would marry and Liesbet would leave her.

Lourens. Anna remembered queerly the agony of his birth long ago. He was away with the carts but her thoughts of him were so tender that he stood warm and living at her side.

It had to be. Lourens should have Oostermeer. There was deep comfort in Oostermeer as well she knew.

iv

They gathered again in the byre when the men returned and now Liesbet joined them, and the house was left unguarded while they struggled to overcome Liesbet's unexpected opposition to their plans for her.

Liesbet, flaming and transformed, faced them with fierce fire in her violet eyes.

"I go to England and leave my mother here? Never!" she declared. "Whatever my mother's fate is to be, I shall share it. I am strong as she is strong. She will not falter or betray, and neither shall I. I stay with her. I shall not go and be safe on a farm in Cornwall. We shall see this thing through together, Anna van Breda and I. Mother, I shall not leave you. Do you hear me?"

In turn they pleaded, argued, and threatened; but Liesbet was obdurate. Time passed and soon it would be daylight and they must be gone. Liesbet would not yield for all Ryk's prayers and entreaties. In the end the men left and Liesbet remained. Lourens turned back and found Anna weeping in the shadow of the kitchen door. He put his hands on her cheeks and drew her face to his as had been his habit in childhood.

"I shall not go too far away, Mother," he said. "I shall get you both away in time if necessary. I have it all planned. Rely on me."

She stroked his hair and a passion of love welled up within her. Lourens laughed low, exultantly. Liesbet had not gone. She was not yet her brother's wife, and he would win her in the end.

It was morning now. Anna was in the kitchen. She had just kneaded the bread and her hands were sticky with dough and there was a streak of flour across her face. She put her hands on the table and surrendered herself to her dark thoughts. How is it all to end? she wondered. She had longed for Liesbet to go to a place of safety. It would have lightened her burden. There was this business of Don Rodriguez as well as the dread threat of a land given over to war. The weight of her responsibility bore her down. At last she roused herself.

"What am I doing?" Anna asked herself angrily aloud. "I must not weaken now."

She must not lose control when it was vital that an air of normality should invest Oostermeer. She dipped water from a cask on the kitchen floor and poured it into a bowl. She washed her hands and then changed the water and washed face. She straightened her cap and put on a clean apron.

Later, when Don Rodriquez slept, she called Liesbet and sent her to summon the maids for the daily reading. Life was to go on as usual. That way safety lay.

When they were on their knees in the closet there was a dull thud against the dividing wall. Anna felt the hair rise on her head and her frayed nerves almost betrayed her; but she continued to read in an even voice. She glanced at Liesbet, who stood up and went out.

The girl returned in a few minutes and said smilingly:

"There is no cause for alarm. I have looked through the house. I found a cheese had fallen off the shelf in your bed, Mother. It must have rolled against the wall. I put it back with the others. We think too much of the priest and his spies."

"I must have put the cheeses carelessly on the shelf," Anna remarked; and breathed a prayer of thanksgiving that she always put the cheeses to ripen on the shelf in her bed closet. She looked at the maids, but they appeared to have accepted Liesbet's explanation.

When they filed out of the closet Anna received a rude shock. Elfrieda turned and gave her a strange, hard look. And now Anna was certain that she and Liesbet had not been as successful as they had thought in their concealment of the presence of Don Rodriguez. If Elfrieda had had her suspicions there had been an opportunity of verifying them during the time they had been wrestling with Liesbet in the byre.

There was to be another shock that afternoon. She was assisting the invalid to walk in the chamber, to strengthen his muscles, while Liesbet stood on guard at the door, when she thought she detected something strange in his manner. She was very troubled. Liesbet had told her that the sound they had heard had been the impact of Don Rodriguez's fist against the wall. Liesbet had added that she had found him very disturbed and agitated and had had some difficulty in calming him.

"I would be happy to see a priest," Don Rodriguez said abruptly. "Could you not ask the father to come here at night?"

She had told him Father Ramon visited the house by day but she deemed it inadvisable to let him into the secret too soon.

A pulse began to beat in Anna's throat. She was convinced that he had heard them at their reading through the thin wall. She thought she understood why he had asked to see a priest. It was his intention to inform against them. She had nursed a viper in her bosom; but, God be thanked, it was not too late. Before God, she swore deep within herself, he shall perish by my hand before he gets the ear of a Papist priest. Somehow she managed to bite back the tide of words that boiled on her tongue; she must not put him on his guard. Her thoughts spun crazily, then righted themselves, and she was icily mistress of herself.

"I could not ask Father Ramon to come," she said, shaking her head. "His visit might give away what we must conceal. The maids may discover your presence."

A priest about the place at night! A cold shiver ran down her spine.

"I am a good Catholic," said Don Rodriguez. "I am here to assist in the uprooting of heresy in the Netherlands, and to such purpose that it will never spring again."

He at least is honest, thought Anna. But before she could answer Liesbet came up to them and laid her hand on Don Rodriguez's arm.

"We are good Catholics," Liesbet lied, gazing fearlessly into his eyes. "But do you not think that the Holy Church would accomplish more by gentler methods?"

Don Rodriguez's face was lined and strained. He was obviously struggling with some inward thought.

"It is a point of view," he said at last; and now he covered Liesbet's hand with his own.

Anna envied Liesbet her tranquillity. She herself was inwardly convulsed with a furious distaste for all the subterfuge and falseness her patriotism demanded of her. At heart she longed to be free of responsibility so that she might openly admit her faith and die for it, if need be, with other avowed Protestants.

"Let us talk of other matters," said Liesbet.

She told him then of the armful of lavender-pink Pentecost flowers she had gathered in the meadow by the windmill that morning; and of the black-and-white cow that had followed her, trying to nibble the bouquet; and of her clogs sticking in the mud so that each time she bent down to release them the cow snatched another mouthful.

Don Rodriguez laughed, and, still covering her hand with his own, told her in his turn how different he found the lush green land of the

Netherlands from the arid brown earth of sun-drenched Spain; and what a difference also in their cattle! There were bullfights in Spain but the polders and canals of Holland did not lend themselves to such sport. And the Holstein-Frisian, he said, was the most unsuitable of beasts for the arena.

Don Rodriguez did not again ask to see the priest. Indeed he was so unfailingly pleasant that Anna suspected him of deep guile. Thus two more weeks passed and Anna, brought more into contact with Don Rodriguez, discovered that she liked him very much. The month's confinement had changed him. He was quiet and very gentle. He told her he was a widower and had no family. Once when she was sewing she ooked 1) and found his eyes on her. Their glances met for a moment nd fell away. Ach, Anna thought sadly, he is only a man like other men, and he will make love to me if I allow it. Now she held herself aloof from him.

The three days before he left were days of almost unendurable strain. The work of the farm was awry because Elfrieda was not doing her share. She gave Anna an insolent stare when rebuked. Anna knew only too well why Elfrieda's manner had changed. What Gysbert and Ryk and Lourens and the rest of them would have to say to her about saving the Spaniard she did not care to dwell on just then; first things first, Anna told herself, exercising rigid self-discipline to keep herself from worrying too soon. The pressing problem was how to get Don Rodriguez away before the band returned.

The solution was the obvious one, in fact the only one.

"I saw Father Ramon this morning," she told him on the night before he left. "I informed him you were here, and of the circumstances that had brought you to my house. I asked him to find a horse for you to ride to Groningen tomorrow night, and to arrange some message to get the maids out of the way. It is settled; he will meet us in the thicket of poplars. You should be well on your way and out of this district before daylight, and then it should not be too difficult to reach Groningen."

He looked long at her. There was a strange blend of warmth, mockery, and tenderness in his eyes.

"I ask you the same question I asked you the night I arrived," he said. "Why do you do this?"

"I give you the same answer," she replied. "The Cross. We are all God's creatures, moulded and shaped by His own hand."

He saw that she had grown thinner and paler and there were signs of strain on her face, and dark shadows under her grey eyes. She was very beautiful with her skin fine and transparent and that air of wistfulness and fragility about her, he thought. And how lovely her hands were. . . .

The last night. Lying sleepless beside Liesbet, Anna wondered if she had acted wisely in seeking the aid of the priest. If Don Rodriguez chose to denounce them the priest could well be his instrument. She had been unable to divine what action Don Rodriguez intended to take. They had carefully avoided discussions on religion, yet, as a staunch Catholic, Anna knew that Don Rodriguez must hold that it was his sacred mission to destroy all heretics. She felt it would be as abhorrent to him to have her plead as it would be for her to humiliate herself. After all, he owed her his life, and she could not be positive that he had discovered their secret. She decided in the end that it would be best not to bargain, but to put everything for their destruction in his hand and let him use the weapon against them if he would. Anna understood Don Rodriguez better than she knew. Her psychology was extremely sound.

Anna did not close her eyes that night.

v

There were stars and a sickle moon in the great velvet-dark bed of the sky. Anna and Don Rodriguez d'Esquerdes walked across the meadow where Liesbet had picked the Pentecost flowers. The wide arms of the windmill were projected inkily black against the vast arc of the heavens. The arms turned unhurriedly in the breeze and creaked with tired gentleness.

When they came to the windmill Anna stopped.

"I shall wait here in the shadow," she said. "You must go on alone from here. Do you see the thicket of trees, yonder, to the right? You will find the good father there, and your horse. If by any chance he has failed us, return to me here. I shall be waiting. When I hear your horse's hoofs on the road I shall know you have gone on your way. Go now, and God be with you."

He took her hand.

"I shall never forget you," he said.

Anna struggled against an immense desire to weep. They stood there wordlessly, side by side, while he held her hand.

Suddenly she did an extraordinary thing. She slipped her free hand into her pocket and withdrew the dagger and held it out to him with the blade towards herself.

"You have no weapon," she said. "Take this."

Slowly he released the hand he held, his fingers clinging to it as though it were agony to let it go, and took the dagger from her. Then he dropped to his knees and pressed the dusty hem of her skirt to his lips. She felt his head against her knee; still struggled against that immense desire to weep.

"God be with you," she whispered faintly.

He rose to his feet and drew on the tasselled gauntlets Liesbet had given him as a parting present.

"I shall never forget you," he said again.

He left her then. He turned at the thicket to look back. The arms of the windmill were black against the sky. They formed a cross in the night. To him they were a symbol.

She stands at the foot of the Cross, he thought.

As his horse took the road its pounding hoofs seemed to him to beat out an endless refrain: She is released, she is released, they hammered into his mind.

For him he knew there was no release.

vi

As day succeeded day and the officers of the Inquisition did not appear to apprehend them Anna ventured to hope that Don Rodriquez would not denounce them.

Elfrieda announced that she was leaving. Thankful as Anna was not to have her surly humours to contend with, she endured agonizing moments when she wondered what tales the girl would spread abroad. As soon as Gysbert returned, Anna thought, she would tell him everything and seek his counsel. A new girl, Foukje, was installed in Elfrieda's place, and the household fell back into well-ordered smoothness.

News came of a great patriot victory at Heiliger-Lee, where Louis of Nassau, having lured Aremberg and his vanderas of Spanish veterans to the battleground of his choosing, had defeated them. Now Louis was entrenched before Groningen, which was strongly held by the enemy. Hope ran high in the breasts of the patriots. With God's help and the courage of the Prince of Orange they began to see a glorious end to their battle for freedom.

All went well, and Anna's heart lifted. Even Liesbet's disturbing item of news failed to depress her.

"I saw Elfrieda entering Jan Hattingh's house," Liesbet informed Anna after her return from the little village on the seacoast. "I wonder what tale she has told?"

"If she has told about Don Rodriquez we shall have Jan here before the day is out," said Anna. "Personally I would welcome having the matter brought out, although I would naturally prefer to tell Gysbert first. Jan will probably put it down to a spiteful invention on Elfrieda's part. However, if Jan does not come I shall visit him myself. I have messages from Groningen to pass on. I can judge from his manner whether there is anything on his mind."

When she called at Jan Hattingh's house a few days later she remarked nothing strange in his demeanour. She passed on certain information, and they parted on the best of terms. She returned and told Liesbet that if Elfrieda had told the story of Don Rodriquez's rescue Jan had apparently not believed her, as he had not mentioned the matter to her. Anna dismissed the incident from her mind and life at Oostermeer flowed on without interruption until the summer.

Once more Anna's serenity was disturbed, and miraculously restored in the space of a single morning.

She was confined to bed with a chill. As she lay dozing in her great bed she heard Liesbet and the maids enter the adjoining closet for the daily reading of the Bible. Now she could test whether the wall was soundproof or not, she thought. Liesbet began to read a Psalm. To Anna's horror every word came to her distinctly. This was worse than she had thought. Don Rodriquez could not have had the slightest doubt but that they were of the new religion. Anna flung aside the bedclothes. She searched feverishly along the wall for some crack or aperture. At last she found a long, wide crack near the ceiling. She had not known it was there. She could have made no more fatal mistake than to have continued to use the closet. Her error might well cost them their lives.

Back and forth her mind shuttled across the fabric of her doubts and fears. She forced herself to be calm. She reviewed the details of the last few days Don Rodriguez had spent at Oostermeer. That one so kind and grateful as he had shown himself should betray them was unthinkable. If she believed that, her faith in God and His mercy must crumble. She would not do him the wrong of thinking him capable of such perfidy.

Suddenly she was calm and at peace. It was as though a gentle hand had been stretched out to wipe away her confusion. A conviction that Don Rodriguez would not use his knowledge of the workings of their household against them came strongly to her.

Anna experienced a moment of ineffable bliss, of blessed benediction. The moment passed; and nothing remained save the warmth of that profound spiritual experience. She had no clear understanding of this transportation out of herself for a brief space. She felt a little bewildered, as a child might, who, having seen a bright light, finds it snatched away before he can grasp it.

CHAPTER TWO

The triumph of rebellion in Friesland was to be short-lived. The Duke of Alva prepared at once to exact a terrible retribution. An edict was issued banishing on pain of death the Prince of Orange, Louis of Nassau, and others who had taken part in the uprising against Spanish oppression. Their estates were confiscated and their lives were forfeit.

They faced disaster: the dread conviction slowly seeped through the demoralized patriot forces. Louis fell back before Alva until at Jemmingen he halted his forces and turned to face the troops of Spain, hemmed in between twelve thousand veterans and the river Ems.

In the north a sense of doom and despair settled on the land.

ii

Anna van Breda ran swiftly through the yard and entered the house at the kitchen door.

"Liesbet, Santje, Foukje," she cried. "Where are you?"

Alarmed at the urgency of her voice, the girls ran to her.

"We must leave at once," Anna said quickly. "The Spaniards are coming. There is just time. I was in the meadow when a messenger came from Lourens," Anna explained. "The forces of Louis are falling back and Lourens is with them. He will come when he can. He says the Spaniards are occupying every house along the route and Oostermeer is in their path. We must go at once. Lourens says we must follow the Ems and get a boat and cross into Germany."

"I shall go to my father's house," sobbed Santje. "And Foukje will go with me. Our house is far from the road. It is too small a house for the Spaniards to notice."

"We will go by your father's house and let him decide whether you stay with him or go on with me," Anna said. "You know what happens in this house, Santje? The patriots meet here, and if the Spaniards have found that out they will show us no mercy. Liesbet, collect what food you can find. And hurry, hurry . . ."

Anna ran across to the pigsties and let the pigs out. Then, calling to Santje, she began to drive the cows out of the byre.

"We must collect the calves and drive them to the farthest polder," she said. "And their mothers with them. The pigs can root where they will. The byre may be burned with the house and the cows in it if we leave them."

They herded the cattle through the gate and drove them down the avenue. The need for haste was great and they urged the beasts on, waving their caps and running with their skirts flying and their clogs pounding the dust beneath their feet. The summer day was hot and the sun shone down on them, glowing in the wide expanse of the cloudless heavens.

This is not possible, thought Anna as she ran. This cannot be happening to me. In a few hours Oostermeer may be in flames and I am running away. Ach, Oostermeer, Oostermeer . . .

The maids elected to remain at Santje's home and Anna and Liesbet made for the river. They walked all that day with frequent halts, for Liesbet tired easily and could not keep up. They went on during the early part of the night. At last, when they came to a thicket, Anna suggested that they remain there until dawn. She sat down and told Liesbet to put her head on her lap and try to sleep.

"Mother," said Liesbet, stretching up her hand and caressing Anna's cheek, "shall we talk? I cannot sleep."

"I see only the wretched people fleeing through the country," Anna said heavily. "That old woman, Liesbet, and the children. And we could not help them. Our homes are burning behind us. Did you see, Liesbet, the sky was red? I can smell the smoke. While we sit here Oostermeer may have been burned to the ground. I think of Lourens and the battle that is to be fought. May God bring him safely through and give us the victory. Ach, Liesbet, if you had gone to England in the spring and married Ryk you would have been safe."

"Forgive me, Mother," said Liesbet, weeping. "I could not come between Ryk and Lourens. I made up my mind that night in the byre that I would marry neither; but it would have been easier for you had I been dutiful."

Anna fondled Liesbet's cheeks.

"Do not cry, my heart," she said tenderly. "We will reach the river and cross it, and all will be well."

"All you think about is to keep me from falling into the hands of the Spaniards," Liesbet whispered. "If I had gone to England you would not have had this terrible responsibility."

"Hush, Liesbet. All depends on how the battle goes."

Anna knew a moment of panic. Liesbet should not fall alive into the hands of the Spaniards. Her dagger pressing into her thigh was a constant reminder of that. . . .

On the fourth day they reached the river. There had been a battle the day before. They had listened in terror to the far-off crash of cannon and had fled away from the noise of the conflict, hiding occasionally in thickets and in swamps, and crouching behind dykes. There was no boat. There was nothing for it but to go down-river and hope to pick up some sort of craft and cross over to sanctuary in Germany.

They walked on slowly for some time until Liesbet staggered and was obviously too spent for further effort. Their scanty supply of food had given out and they were hungry as well as exhausted.

Anna settled Liesbet with her back to a tree and prepared to forage for food. She had noticed smoke a little way back. It occurred to her that she might find food there.

"I am going to search for food," Anna said. "I shall not be away long. Stay here and rest."

She drew her dagger slowly from her pocket as she spoke.

"I shall leave this with you," she said.

Liesbet took the weapon from her without a tremor.

"You may rely on me to use this," Liesbet said. "The Spaniards shall not take me alive. Have no fear, Mother."

"You have courage far beyond your strength, Liesbet," said Anna, and could bring herself to say no more.

Anna went into the thicket, moving with the utmost caution, gliding from tree to tree. There was a hut still smouldering in the heart of the trees. There was no one about. She ventured into the tiny yard and searched and found nothing.

As she returned empty-handed she saw the Spanish soldier. He was edging towards Liesbet through the trees.

Anna glanced quickly about her to see if he had companions; but she saw no one. This soldier had probably fired the miserable hut and had returned for plunder.

Anna slipped her feet out of her clogs. She shrank behind a tree and watched him, her feet sinking into the slimy morass.

The Spaniard was stealing quietly from tree to tree, drawing nearer Liesbet. Anna picked up a short, broken branch of a tree, which was thick and heavy. She crept behind the Spaniard, gaining on him. He had stopped and was stooping to peer through the trees at Liesbet when she struck him a blow on the side of the head. She struck again as he fell and, throwing aside her stick, leapt upon him. She knelt upon his shoulders and thrust his face into the mud, which sucked greedily round it.

Anna knelt on the Spaniard's back until he suffocated and lay still. When she knew he was dead she still held on. Afterwards she stood up and methodically went back for her clogs. Then she lurched to the nearest tree, held onto it, and was violently sick.

Liesbet was sitting tranquilly against the tree, the dagger in her lap, when Anna returned. She started when she saw Anna's face and rose quickly to her feet.

"Why, Mother, what is it?" she cried in alarm.

"It is nothing," said Anna with a great effort. "The little house was burned to the ground. I thought of Oostermeer also burning and in ruins. It was a shock. And I found no food. Liesbet, if you are rested, let us move on."

Liesbet took Anna's arm and they began to walk slowly along the river's edge.

"I hear something," said Liesbet on a sudden, sharp note of fear, stopping dead. "Do you hear someone moving, Mother?"

"Give me the dagger," said Anna; and now she also heard footsteps coming towards them along the path.

A man appeared some distance away. They stared, stared again unbelievingly, recognized him. Both cried out together:

"Lourens!"

And began to run stumbling towards him. Liesbet outstripped Anna. When Anna came up to them Liesbet was held closely in Lourens's arms and he was murmuring over her bent head in a passion of love and tenderness.

"Never leave me, Lourens," Liesbet sobbed, completely shaken. "Ach, Lourens, never leave me."

"I shall never leave you, Liesbet," Lourens promised, holding her closer still and resting his cheek on her hair.

Anna looked at Lourens as he raised his head. Her bloodless lips shaped the one word "Ryk?"

She saw Lourens's face set, grow cold and unutterably stern. He answered his mother, addressing the words to Liesbet.

"I shall never leave you, Liesbet," he repeated.

Anna bowed her head. The words were simple; but she knew Lourens had sworn a solemn oath there in the silence of the trees beside the flowing river.

iii

Lourens had food with him. They sat trying to eat while they listened to his dread news.

"All is lost," he told them. "The patriot army is broken and it will be years before we lift our hand against Spain. Those who did not perish in the battle were massacred. Louis has swum the Ems and is in Germany with the remnants of the troops. I fled along the river, seeking you."

"You have not been home then, Lourens?"

"I have no news of Oostermeer."

"What of the others—Jan Hattingh and my cousin Gerard?"

"Jan Hattingh was in the battle and escaped as far as I know. Uncle Gerard was at his home. He was wounded in the foot when we fell back from Groningen and could march no farther. Pray God we will find him. His house is far from the main road and may have been overlooked."

Anna glanced at Liesbet, who was leaning up against Lourens with her hand in his firm clasp.

"What do you propose we do now, Lourens?" asked Anna.

"Return to Oostermeer. If it is razed to the ground we will have friends in the neighbourhood and Uncle Gerard's house may be standing."

"We may find nothing at Oostermeer."

"Nevertheless, let us return home. You must not think or worry any more, Mother," said Lourens gently. "I am here to do that. You have been through a terrible time. Stay here with Liesbet. I think I can find a horse broken loose in battle for Liesbet to ride."

"I leave it all to you," said Anna gratefully; and felt as though the world had sloughed from her shoulders.

At last they were on the road to Oostermeer and entering the avenue, and the house was still obscured from their view. Anna walked with her head down, looking at the little thickets of poplar shoots at the bases of the trees. Lourens walked beside the horse on which he supported Liesbet.

They had returned home along a way grey with ashes, and the bitter smell of smoke had burned their nostrils. Each hovel and house beside the road was a gutted heap of rubble, and the village where Jan Hattingh lived was a smouldering ruin. Nothing, it seemed, had survived the holocaust in the wake of the victorious army.

Anna could not look upon the ruins of her home. She had lived most of her life on Oostermeer and her heart was deeply rooted in its soil. Her father, her grandfather, and her great-grandfather had lived in the old farmhouse and had prospered amid the vicissitudes of their troubled times. After the death of her only brother and his wife she had inherited Oostermeer, and Liesbet had been willed properties in Groningen. Now Oostermeer was gone. . . .

"Mother!"

Anna lifted her head and there was wild hope in her eyes. There had been an exultant ring in Lourens's voice. Serene and framed in its setting of trees she saw Oostermeer before her. Fire and outrage had not touched it. It was as though God had drawn an invisible line across which the marching feet of the invader could not go.

"Oostermeer," Anna cried. "Oostermeer."

She fell on her knees in the dusty road. She folded her hands and lifted her face to the heavens, now rosy in the light of the setting sun. With tears streaming down her cheeks she cried out aloud to God in broken, incoherent words in profound gratitude for the blessed miracle.

The farmhouse was in some disorder but nothing had been removed or destroyed. The Spaniards had been there, but they had left it as they had found it. Only when she saw the tasselled gauntlets of Don Rodriguez d'Esquerdes carefully set down beside a bowl on the dresser did Anna know why her home had been spared.

Don Rodriguez had passed by and he had done her this service. Lourens was away in the polder searching for the cattle, but Liesbet exclaimed at sight of the gauntlets.

"We shall say nothing now," Anna said. "Later I shall tell Lourens."

"I shall say nothing to anyone," said Liesbet. "In your own time you must tell."

Then they separated, each to her own task. Anna collected fodder and filled the mangers in the byre and when her work was done she sank on her knees on the floor. She was struggling against an overwhelming consciousness of guilt. God has blessed me indeed, and I have slain a man, she thought; and strove to calm herself to pray for mercy.

Afterwards she went to the house for a lighted lantern to hang in the byre. Lourens returned, driving a cow before him.

"I found old Rosa," he said cheerfully. "It was too dark to go on and search for the others."

"Lourens, I must speak to you," said Anna desperately, looking white and distracted. She felt she must tell Lourens at once about Don Rodriguez and the Spaniard she had slain in the thicket. The burden was too much for her: he must share it.

Lourens misunderstood her.

"I shall marry Liesbet as soon as possible," he said.

Anna was unprepared for this. She passed her hand wearily across her brow.

"No," she managed to say. "You must wait. Liesbet does not rightly know what she is doing. This last week has nearly killed her; she is not strong. You must do nothing until she has recovered and until Ryk and your father return."

"I shall speak of my father now."

"No," said Anna, shaken into firmness.

"Yes; and for once you will hear me out. You love my father, and you are happy together; but, Mother, do you realize what I have felt for you struggling on alone here when my father was away at sea? He left you more often than he needed."

"I shall not discuss your father with you."

"As long as I can remember," Lourens continued, not heeding the interruption, "he has left you for months, at times for a year. The clearest memory of my childhood is going with you to the dyke near the sea and playing there while you scanned the sea and watched for the sails of his ship. You would watch and forget me in your longing for him to come home again. I can remember taking your face between my hands and pulling it down to my face and calling to you until your thoughts came back from watching the empty sea."

"I have had no more to endure than any other Frisian woman whose husband is a sailor," said Anna proudly. "Be silent, my son."

"Ryk follows the sea as my father does. Liesbet will have the life you have had if she marries him. She has a great heart, but she is not robust and will never stand the strain. I shall marry Liesbet and she shall watch for no sails on the horizon."

"I implore you to wait, Lourens."

"I shall wait no longer. What is that?"

They turned sharply. There was someone fumbling at the latch of the yard gate.

"I shall go and see," said Lourens. "Wait here."

Anna heard Jan Hattingh's voice. She waited for a few minutes before she joined the men in the yard. They were talking in low tones, standing near the gate.

"Ach, Jan," said Anna. "The village——"

"Hush," cautioned Lourens, laying his hand on her arm.

"Your husband has been wounded fighting in Zeeland, Anna van Breda," said Jan Hattingh abruptly. "He is lying ill at Rotterdam. I shall take you there in my boat in the morning."

He turned away and began to walk down the avenue.

"Jan, Jan," cried Anna, running after him.

Lourens called to her to come back.

"What is it, Lourens?" sobbed Anna. "He is so strange in his manner. Ach, Gysbert——"

"Let Jan be, Mother. He is half crazy. He is at Uncle Gerard's. Jan's home was burned. His wife and daughters slew themselves. Terrible things happened in the village."

"Lourens!" She was aghast.

He gathered her in his arms and held her closely to him.

"I shall go to Rotterdam tomorrow," said Anna at last.

"Liesbet and I will be married when you return with my father," he said.

"I can do no more; perhaps it is for the best," said Anna.

They stood in silence until Anna sighed. She put up her hand and touched Lourens's cheek caressingly.

"Nevertheless, I bless you both," she said.

iv

Anna was on her way home with Gysbert. She sat on the deck of the little ship, while he lay beside her. She was preoccupied, trying to decide when she should tell him about Liesbet and Lourens.

"Anna, do you know of what the wind from the sea puts me in mind?" Gysbert asked, taking her hand and stroking her fingers.

She would not think. She would tell him another time. He had so nearly died, and it was enough to live in the happy present.

"What, my dear?" she asked.

"Your hands. The first thing I was aware of when the fever left me was the feel of your cool hands on my face; feeling them, I wanted to live."

She laid her fingers against his cheek. He knew again the stirring of his blood at her touch. That was the abiding miracle and mystery of Anna. His passion for her had never wearied. He was as much in love with her as he had been on their wedding day.

"I shall be with you always now, Anna," he said. "This leg will hinder me, but not much, and I am lucky the cannon ball did no greater injury. I shall never leave you again, Anna."

"Gysbert," she cried joyfully, her face alight with love.

"There were times when Oostermeer seemed a prison to me," he confessed. "That was when the sea called and I had to go; but I shall turn farmer now, Anna. My wanderings are over."

He rolled over on his back and looked at the clouds and thought they were like a flock of woolly sheep straggling up from the sea. Already he was thinking in terms of the farm, he reflected, smiling to himself. Anna must often have been lonely, he thought. When his nostalgia for the sea had proved too strong for him he had left her. But he had always returned and she had received him back joyfully, and life had been sweet because of the beloved woman at his side. He had sailed into calm water. He lay staring at the blue sky and the drifting white clouds and every now and then he lifted Anna's fingers to his lips.

Anna was too happy to break in on this bliss with all the problems of Oostermeer. The little ship sailed slowly and they knew no one on board her. She could not sail slowly enough for Anna. She felt she wished the voyage to have no ending.

But it had to end; and one morning she saw the little quay and Jan Hattingh standing on it waiting for them. They were near home: she could delay the moment no longer.

"Gysbert, my dear," she said. "I am afraid I have some news which may distress you. Lourens and Liesbet may be married. Lourens spoke of it before I came away."

Gysbert turned to her in consternation.

"But what of Ryk?" he demanded. Ryk was his favourite.

"Ryk was away and Lourens was here when Alva invaded," she said, struggling to explain and unhappily aware that she ought to have taken her time and gone into the matter in detail. "It seemed the only thing to do."

"Ryk must be told."

"We must find out whether they are married. Liesbet may have refused," said Anna wretchedly.

"There is Jan Hattingh. I shall ask him as soon as I get on shore," said Gysbert.

When they landed Anna left Gysbert talking to Jan Hattingh and went in search of a cart to convey them to Oostermeer.

The drive to the farm in the jolting cart was a nightmare. Gysbert's newly healed leg obviously pained him. He sat pale and withdrawn with his face turned from Anna, not speaking. Jan Hattingh had had a long conversation with Gysbert, as she had been some time bargaining with the owner of the vehicle. Gysbert was bound to have heard of the sacking of Friesland, and the pitiful village, with huts and shacks rising from its ruins, was a sight to depress any man. It was no wonder that Gysbert was appalled, she thought. She ought to have prepared him for his return instead of selfishly refusing to cloud those perfect days at sea. She saw her error clearly now.

The silence became intolerable.

"Gysbert," Anna said timidly, putting her hand on his knee, "are Lourens and Liesbert married?"

"They were married three days after you left."

"Jan told you what had happened in the village?"

"Yes."

"I ought to have prepared you for this home-coming."

"I do not wish to speak," said Gysbert.

Anna's hand was still on his knee. He had not touched it; he had not seemed to notice it was there. He loved her hands and never before had he failed to respond to any demonstration of affection from her. She felt as though he had slapped her in the face. After a moment she withdrew her hand and laid it with its fellow in her lap. She stared down at it, white-faced. Gysbert had taken the children's marriage hardly indeed.

She looked about her at the flat landscape. In the clear light of day a few weeks after Alva's march through it the ruin and the desolation of the countryside caught her by the throat.

It is because I killed a man that this is happening to me, thought Anna. The blood of this one soldier cries from the earth for vengeance.

Dear God, be merciful, she prayed in deep anguish, for the need was great and I could not do otherwise.

The rest of the journey to Oostermeer was accomplished in absolute silence.

v

Lourens had done well. He had collected the cattle and some of the pigs, and there were hens and ducks in the farmyard again. A month after her return to Oostermeer with Gysbert, Anna was in the dairy washing a mound of yellow butter. She was thinking of the bitter day of their home-coming, and that first night when Gysbert had said his stiff knee would not permit him to climb up the short ladder to their bed.

"Of course," she had said, not comprehending his meaning at once. "I should have thought of it. We will sleep in Ryk's bed. It is near the floor and will be easier for you."

"I shall sleep alone."

Those words still rang in Anna's ears. They had broken her heart but they had steeled her pride. It was unforgivable that Gysbert should treat her thus because Lourens had insisted on marrying Liesbet. Everything was wrong: Liesbet, coming to herself, was deeply unhappy, as was Lourens. Ryk did not come home. Anna had not attempted to discuss their children's affairs with Gysbert. She was intensely aware that he misconstrued her silence and blamed her for all that had happened. Her pride was a barrier between them which his unuttered censure did nothing to lessen.

She had wondered whether he had heard that she had sheltered Don Rodriguez d'Esquerdes; but she had dismissed the idea. Apparently Elfrieda had not betrayed her as she had thought. All the band and her neighbours treated her as they had always treated her. Jan Hattingh was certainly strange in his manner, but he had suffered greatly and it was understandable that he should be morose and withdrawn. Anna knew the temper of her countrymen: if they suspected her of dealings with the hated oppressor she would most certainly have known it by this time. It could only be the matter of Lourens's marriage. If she could put that right it would be a blessed relief because she longed to tell Gysbert about those weeks when Don Rodriguez had sheltered there.

A shadow fell across the table and the great bowl of butter. Lourens stood in the doorway. He and Gysbert had been out late together the night before and she had been abed when they returned. She saw at once something was amiss. She put down the butter pat and came to him.

"What is it, Lourens?"

His face was pale, and he looked as though he had not slept.

He took her face between his hands and kissed her—her brow, her eyes, her cheeks, her lips.

"I am joining the patriot forces again," he said, the words tumbling out one after the other. "I shall probably not be fighting much in Friesland. I shall come back sometimes. I am leaving at once."

"But, Lourens, when did you decide this?"

"Take the greatest care of Liesbet, Mother," he said distractedly.

"You know I will."

He seemed beside himself. Anna could make nothing of the change in him. He lifted her hand and kissed it, and let his lips run up the arm she had bared for the butter washing until they rested in a long lover's kiss in the crook of her elbow.

"Remember always how I love you, my mother," he said.

"Lourens!" Anna breathed, kissing the top of his head.

He dropped her arm and, without looking at her, started through the door. He rushed across the yard to the house as though he did not trust himself to say any more.

She stared after him in utter bewilderment. She put her fingers to the curve of her arm where his kiss was still warm. She stood thus, quite still, trying to penetrate the mystery of Lourens's sudden demonstration of affection.

"Ach, he is leaving Liesbet and can't bear it," she said aloud, her brow clearing.

vi

Later that same day her cousin Gerard van Braam came to visit her. Lourens had already left and she and Gysbert were sitting in the living room in the afternoon sunshine. Liesbet was somewhere out of doors. They sat there, not speaking.

Gerard walked in unannounced. He had brought with him a basket of eggs and a posy of flowers culled from the pastures. It was unlike Gerard to give flowers because he was not given to such gestures. Anna was deeply touched.

"I understood from Lourens he was leaving today," Gerard explained his presence. "Therefore I came to see you. Alas! My son is dead, but I know what it means when a son leaves the house."

"How kind you are, Gerard," said Anna. "Thank you. I shall empty the basket and put the flowers in water. I shall not be long."

When she returned the conversation fell automatically into farming channels. Gysbert took no part in it.

"The white sow had a litter of eighteen piglets," Gerard volunteered.

"That is splendid," said Anna warmly. "Surely it is a record litter?"

"I heard of a sow once that had twenty-four," said Gerard meditatively. "But she overlaid some."

He stroked his short, tidy, grey-streaked brown beard. He had an honest face and steady blue eyes. He was a well-built man, soberly clad. He loved to talk to Anna. Now he was well launched, and he told her in detail of the calves he expected in the winter, and where he planned to build a larger barn. At last he said he must get back for the milking and took his leave of her.

Gerard rose, and Anna rose with him. He stood awkwardly beside her, searching for some little word to convey the warmth of his regard. He thought of Gysbert sitting there in silence, of Lourens leaving his young wife for some distant battlefield, of Anna herself, who stood alone and forlorn. He could find no word. He was a countryman and had no graces and pretty phrases. Blushing to the roots of his hair, he lifted Anna's hand and kissed it. He had never before done such a thing.

A wave of happiness swept over Anna. How kind he was, how understanding. Lourens must have told him that Gysbert had taken the marriage hardly.

"You have spread roses at my feet, dear Gerard," she said gently; and her smile was very sweet.

Ach, Anna, his cousin, was a gracious woman, Gerard thought. She had a word for every occasion. He was lifted out of himself. He was a plain man and a Calvinist to boot, but he soared to a plane of unimagined eloquence.

"If I carpeted this room with roses, Anna van Breda, it would not be enough," he said.

He was startled by his own utterance. He seized his empty basket and went quickly from the room, leaving Anna gazing after him with a glow on her face and her eyes misted. Dear Gerard . . .

She was very moved. In the space of that one day Lourens and Gerard had broken through their natural reserve in an unprecedented fashion to express their affection for her. She herself ought not to be lacking in understanding. She must try to put things right with Gysbert. Now, while her heart was warmed, she must try. She turned impulsively to him.

He had moved from his seat and was standing looking out of the window with his back to her. She went up to him.

"Gysbert," she said pleadingly, "please speak to me."

He said, not turning his head:

"Ryk was in the village last night. He would not come to the house."

Anna's outstretched hands dropped to her sides. Gysbert would never be reconciled. It was the end.

She went blindly from the room into the late afternoon sunlight. She wandered over Oostermeer, not seeing where she walked.

Liesbet, her eyes tear-drenched, found her in the meadow where the windmill stood and, with kind and loving words, led her back to the house.

CHAPTER THREE

The morning was as stormy as the night had been. It was the first day of November 1570, and for a week and more the northwesterly gale had been piling up an incalculable weight of water along the low land of the

Netherlands where the encroaching sea, as yet held back by long, broken ridges of sandy dunes and man-made dykes, gnawed at the fragile coast.

Anna stood at the farmhouse window and saw the darkness lift. She read in this continued assault of wind and wave the end of Oostermeer; perhaps Holland herself must come to lie beneath the surging sea.

The first light shone wanly on the turning arms of the windmill. There were gesticulating figures on the dyke beyond the meadow. Distance and the noise of the gale muffled the thunder on the beaches.

Her mind beat bruisingly to the muted rhythm of the waves, swinging between two hopeless poles—battering itself at the one end on the grim reality of Alva and the Inquisition, at the other on the threat of the sea. Alva struck at the life and liberty of the nation, while the sea clamoured for that and more, demanding the very land the Netherlanders had reclaimed from watery chaos. In this moment Anna believed that her countrymen and her country, she herself and her family, were doomed to destruction by God and man. As she plumbed the depths of realization, the scene before her shrouded itself to meet her mood. The immense horizon was compressed; the long avenue of poplars was no longer a quiet lane of peace and shadow. The trees were straining in dreadful urgency towards the succouring house, slim wands of stress, fluid in the tempestuous wind.

In the passage behind her there was the sound of a dragging step and the tapping of a stick. Instantly Anna's drooping shoulders squared. She was standing very upright when Gysbert came in. She might permit herself a moment of weakness when she was alone, but she had no wish that anyone, above all Gysbert, should know when she was near the end of her courage.

Gysbert came up to her. She did not turn. She felt his fingers on her arm, seeking her hand, and a sob came into her throat. It seemed an eternity since he had made that gesture and she had not ceased to love him. Although they did not exchange a word she knew his was a gesture of reconciliation, and her eyes smarted with sudden, stinging tears. The pressure of his hand increased, and the unmistakable sense of his compassionate love came flowing in to her.

At last he said her name:

"Anna."

Now she too could speak. She said slowly, and a little brokenly because she was near tears:

"I sent a message to Ryk three days ago by Jan Hattingh."

"I also sent word to Ryk when I saw this was no ordinary storm. I asked him to get you and Liesbet to England. You will be cared for on Richard Barradale's farm. It can be arranged."

"Ach, must we go, Gysbert?"

"There will be nothing left here, Anna. The sea will sweep the house and the lands away. Mistress Barradale will welcome you, Anna. Her daughters are married and she is a lonely woman. She speaks Dutch in a fashion so you will not feel you are with strangers," said Gysbert, framing his sentences disjointedly, aware that the utterances of hours must be compressed into a mere matter of minutes.

"Let Liesbet go. I do not wish to leave you," Anna said.

"Liesbet needs you more than ever now."

"Yes," she acknowledged with a heavy sigh. "Come with us, Gysbert. I cannot go without you."

"I must remain to see what happens here."

She wanted to cry out that he must put every consideration aside and think of her; but their reconciliation was too new, too brittle, to stand the strain of her heartfelt resentment.

He drew her near him so that her shoulder rested on his arm. He turned a little so that he faced her. He held her chin between his fingers and looked into her face. He noticed her pallor and the taut strain of her skin across the temples.

"I have been so unhappy, Gysbert," she said, her love for him rising up within her.

"I too have been unhappy," he said. "I have been living in a terrible dream."

"There is something I must tell you," she said quickly, while the words burned in her mind. "I sheltered a Spaniard here before Alva came to Friesland. I have not mentioned this to you, but I have wondered if others have."

"I knew the Spaniard had been here, Anna."

"Why did you not say you knew?" she demanded, stiffening.

She saw the look of unutterable pain in his eyes.

"Why did you not speak, Anna? I have lived in this house with you for two years, waiting for you to tell me why you took in the Spaniard. Anna, there have been hideous doubts in my heart. I could not be sure you were not betraying us; but now, looking into your face, I know you have not failed us, although the Spaniard escaped, and your house was spared."

"You have had such thoughts of me!" She was outraged.

"Many lives depended on what happened here at Oostermeer," he defended himself. "We could not take the risk. We changed the rendezvous for the few of us who were still able to meet. Ryk and Richard Barradale go now to Delft to my people there, when they cannot meet at Dover."

"Why did I not speak before! I wanted to that afternoon Gerard came."

"I had to watch you and not betray that I was doing so. Anna, my patriotism was tried high that afternoon when Gerard came. Yet I had my appointed task. I spoke to you of Ryk because I did not wish to put you on your guard."

She was appalled that he could deliberately have misled her.

"Ach, Gysbert," she cried, stricken. "I concealed that the Spaniard had been here, not because I had wronged you or the cause we strive for, but because I doubted my religious convictions." She had not encountered Don Rodriguez again, but disquieting rumours had reached her that he was in the south, the most rabid of the Inquisitors. "I had intended to speak that afternoon but I thought that if the children's marriage had so embittered you there was no hope of your understanding about Don Rodriguez. I could have slain the Spaniard—I had the dagger in my hand to do it; but God put it in my heart to do otherwise. Let me tell you now. I have longed to tell you these past two years."

"Yes, my beloved, you shall tell me; but not now. There is no time. Just one thing, Anna. While we live and can speak before the flood is on us I want you to know that I believe utterly in you. And I understand that Lourens had to marry Liesbet. I told Lourens that. I said that although I regretted the injury he had done his brother I accepted the fact that the circumstances were cruel, and there had been no other way. Tell me you forgive me, Anna. You have more to forgive than you know. There was a meeting in the village to decide what should be done and you had your defenders. I was not one, Anna."

A great light flooded Anna's mind. She had penetrated to the meaning of the great kindness of Lourens and Gerard.

"Lourens and Gerard spoke for me?" she asked.

"Yes; those two. It was a bitter day for me, Anna, when my first-born left the house so as not to be under the same roof as his father. He comes back to see his wife, but he will have none of me. And Gerard: I thought he would have struck me. Yet at the time I felt I had my stern duty to perform."

"Tell me afterwards, Gysbert. I must know it all."

"Do you forgive me, Anna?"

"I love you," she answered.

"My dear heart."

He held her long in his embrace. At last he released her.

"Anna, my love, we waste precious minutes," he said. "All is in order in the boat. We can be away in a moment if Ryk does not get here in time."

"If I had not kept silent!" Anna clung to the blessed moment.

"Hush, we will talk later. I shall light the fire if you will rouse Liesbet. We must eat and be ready for whatever is to happen."

"The dykes will not hold much longer?"

"I do not see that they can. There are still the polders between us and the sea, but when the first big break comes the dykes will snap like packthread."

"Our life here is over. This house, this farm will be ending. Yet when the sky was red with the burning farms and villages as Alva marched, it was left untouched. Oostermeer was spared for this—to be destroyed by water and not by fire," Anna said piteously, but without tears.

"It is not for us to say, Anna."

How empty of comfort his words were, he thought. He held her closely in his arms.

"Last night," he said, "I came to you. I got as far as the ladder of your bed. And then I remembered how I had wronged you, and I went away. I thought how much better it would have been for you if I had let you marry Gerard and then you could have lived your life peacefully. I left you and went off to sea. And now in the end, Anna, when I wish to be with you and never leave you, God sends the sea to me and we may have to part. It is my punishment."

"My life with Gerard van Braam might have been more settled," she answered. "But I would a thousand times rather have had my life with you. The anxiety and the separation do not weigh against what you have given me. I love you. When we are together it makes up to me for all the loneliness. I have had happiness with you such as I could have had with no one but you."

A light came into her face, and her eyes from clear grey were blue-grey, changing like the sea at the turning of the tide, Gysbert thought. It had been those eyes of hers that had called him away from the sea in the beginning.

He kissed her on the brow.

"Anna," he said, very moved. "My wife, Anna."

She put her hands together, long finger tip to long finger tip, and lifted them to her breast and bowed her head over them.

He looked down on her smooth shining hair where it showed at the sides of her cap, at her slender hands, folded like a gull's wings.

" 'When thou passest through the waters, I will be with thee; and through the rivers, they shall not overflow thee: . . . Thus saith the Lord, which maketh a way in the sea, and a path in the mighty waters,' " she prayed in a quiet voice.

She lifted her eyes and they exchanged a long look.

"That was always my prayer when you were on the sea," she said. "And now it is also my prayer while we wait for the sea."

Suddenly she was very calm. Come what may, she was back in her old relationship with Gysbert and she was happy.

"Each time I came home," he said with a tender smile.

"Yes," she answered. And added quickly as though she forced herself to break the conversation that held them: "I shall go to Liesbet now. This is a hard time for her."

She went from the room and his eyes followed her through the dark oblong of the doorway in the passage. He went then to the kitchen to get the fire going. When it was burning brightly Liesbet and Anna came in. Liesbet, moving heavily, insisted on preparing the meal and Anna agreed that she should. She wanted a little time for thought. Gysbert had already seated himself and she sat down also, facing him across the fireplace. She drew the peat smoke into her nostrils, and its pungent familiarity gave her a painful feeling of happiness. She looked about the low-ceilinged room with its red-tiled floor and whitened walls, lighted by the grey coldness of the morning and the dying flicker of the horn lantern Gysbert had forgotten to put out. Through the window she could see the straining trees shivering against the leaden sky, the tattered clouds flocking like demented sheep before the driving wind; and in the warm kitchen the pictures of Gysbert sitting motionless opposite her and of Liesbet moving about were indelibly engraved on her mind.

Gysbert was looking at Liesbet. He was thinking of Lourens and he was pitying him, and blaming himself bitterly for his share in Lourens's troubles. Lourens came home so seldom, and since Liesbet had been with child he had had the most exaggerated fears for her safety. And Lourens's forebodings seemed likely to be fulfilled, thought Gysbert, for the child was expected soon, and the flood threatened at any moment to overwhelm them. It would be wise to look at the dyke once more, he thought; and, putting his hands to the sides of his seat, he pulled himself to his feet. He gathered up an armful of loaves to put in the boat as he passed it.

He limped slowly to the dyke. When he got there he could see the advance the sea had made during the night. There were little rivers in the fields and already a shallow tide swirled below him. Ryk could not come, and they must save themselves. He went back to the house as fast as his lameness would permit.

"If you are ready, Liesbet, I think we had better eat," he said when he was in the kitchen again. "The dyke will not hold much longer. The last watchers have gone. All our preparations have been made. Come, Anna, eat if you can. God alone knows what lies before us."

The end came very suddenly. The wind seemed to have increased and was still keeping steadily to the northwest. They were grouped about the table, and Anna was looking about her and wondering what more they could put in the boat, when they heard the roar of the water as the dyke gave in half a dozen places.

Liesbet screamed and put her hand to her mouth; Gysbert stumbled and clutched at the table, half turning it over so that the crockery fell. A broad stream of milk overflowed on the floor and Anna saw Liesbet mechanically reaching for a cloth to wipe it up. She caught her arm.

"It has come! The dyke has gone," she cried, shaking Liesbet's arm. "The milk does not matter now."

In a daze of horror Anna saw that the cats were not attempting to lap the spilt milk.

"Anna, Liesbet, come," Gysbert shouted.

Liesbet looked wildly round. Then she stooped and picked up Anna's favourite tabby and put it under her cloak. They ran towards the boat in the bitter wind, Gysbert and Anna taking Liesbet's arms when she did not keep up.

"Ach, must we go?" said Liesbet through pale lips. "Could we not stay here and—and get it over?"

Anna felt rather that way herself. If her life had to end she would like to die here on Oostermeer. Nevertheless she said as they struggled towards the boat:

"This is no ordinary flood, Liesbet. It will not help if we crawl onto the roof and wait for the water to go down."

"Come, Liesbet," Gysbert said gently. "We have a good chance of saving ourselves."

He saw in her face that she did not care whether she lived or died. Her unhappiness smote him anew.

They had not long to wait in the boat. First there was a little water, then a swirl of water, then a boiling tide broke upon them, tossing the boat like a shell, so that Gysbert had the greatest difficulty in keeping it from overturning. He struggled to balance the small craft until the water deepened and the boat rode more easily.

Around them the heaving grey sea carried on its crest the spoils of its ruthless passage through the land—upturned boats, bits of timber, gates and posts, trees and casks. Anything that was buoyant bobbed frenziedly in the spume and spray of the rising waters. The sea, the invader, was conqueror. Cattle and sheep, hens and pigs, struggled and went under as the water poured into the enclosing walls of the farmyard. Anna stared in wild agony at the fearful scene; and the last sound of her old life to ring in her ears was the piteous mewing of three barn cats that had climbed upon the roof and were silhouetted on the rim of the gable, their fur flattened by the wind.

"We dare not turn back," said Gysbert, noting the direction of her eyes.

Anna nodded. She faced resolutely away from the drowning house. She bent over her oar so that Gysbert should not see her face.

"We cannot save them all," she said, glancing at Liesbet, who held the tabby closely under her cloak, stroking its head so that it purred in her arms.

ii

Time wore on and Anna tried not to recognize the landmarks along their terrible route. She rowed mechanically in a strange world where the watery sun had not the strength to dispel the bitter cold. The wind blew like the wrath of God and drove them on. They passed near orchards and groves of trees where the branches swayed madly in the stormy flood. Once they saw a dark line of houses and a pointed tower, and the tops of pollard willows. The roofs of the houses and the trees and the tower were dark with swarming humanity. In the water lanes between the houses boats and rafts, and upturned tables pressed into service, plied to and fro. Dark blots kept appearing and disappearing in the waves, and Anna saw they were the heads of men and women and every kind of domestic animal battling for life.

They could not help. Anna could not bring herself to look at the rapidly submerging village. Suddenly Liesbet half rose. She pointed to where, a little to the right of the course they were steering, a young boy was clinging to a log with a child supported on his shoulders. The log floated heavily, half in and half out of the water, and the baby wailed as he held to his brother's head.

"Turn," said Gysbert briefly.

Anna shifted her grip and began to pull the boat round. They had great difficulty in getting the lad and the child on board. Liesbet took the child, and the boy, blue with cold, flapped his arms feebly across his chest on Anna's instructions to restore his circulation.

The boat went on through the shallow water, but more heavily now.

"How long have you been in the water, boy?" asked Anna. "And what is your name?"

"My name is Dirk," the child answered. "We have been in the water a long time. We got away from the house, but we struck a tree and the boat went over. I seized my brother. My mother did not come above the water."

Anna offered Dirk food, but he refused it. He collapsed sobbing in the bottom of the boat and Anna tried in vain to comfort him. At last he sobbed himself to sleep and she flung a spare cloak over him and went on rowing.

There were neither trees nor rooftops visible now, and the boat floated on over what must have been open fields before the inundation.

The boy awakened and relieved Anna at the oars. Although he pulled feebly Anna knew she must rest.

Twice they ate frugally and in the late afternoon they reached a flooded orchard. Gysbert suggested that they should tie up, as they were well-nigh exhausted. There were derelict boats already there—fishing vessels and even ships of larger size entangled in the branches. Their position was dangerous; but they stayed there, swinging in the flood waters, while the afternoon passed and the short November day drew to its close. They sat in their places in the boat without speaking, and the child Liesbet held in her arms moaned and whimpered. At last the dying child quietened, and they huddled down in a speechless, tragic stupor of exhaustion.

Anna moved first. In the fading light she could see a boat with its side ripped open drifting by, keel up. The child began to moan and struggle. Anna crawled over to Liesbet. She uncovered him and looked into his face. He was very ill and she doubted whether he would survive until morning.

"Let me have him for a while, Liesbet," she said.

She went back to her place and Dirk leaned against her, and she wrapped her cloak around him and his dying brother.

The sounds of the trees being torn up by their roots continued around them, and in the darkness the eerie gurglings and their eldritch echoes added to the horror and the misery of their situation. In the night Anna chafed the child's feet and spoke every now and then to the others. Liesbet fell asleep, and Dirk. In the intervals when the child in her arms was not crying, Anna dozed. During one of these snatches of unconsciousness the boat broke from its moorings and began to drift. Only Gysbert was aware when this happened. He knew his utter helplessness, so he spoke no warning and prayed that the others might sleep on.

The uneven motion of the boat roused Anna. She did not at once take in what had happened because she felt the child limp in her cramped arms. She put her cheek to his face and a sob came into her throat when she knew he was dead.

Gysbert spoke in a low whisper.

"Are you awake, Anna, my heart?"

"Yes," said Anna in a stifled voice.

"We have floated free, Anna, and God only knows where we are. Speak softly so as not to waken Dirk and Liesbet. As near as I can judge, it will not be daylight for at least another hour. We must drift now and put our trust in the Almighty."

"The child is dead, Gysbert," said Anna.

"Are you sure?"

"Yes."

"My poor Anna. You must slip him over the side before it is light."

"Ach, no, not yet," she pleaded, and began to weep.

"Anna——"

"Gysbert," she said presently, "this is the second time in little more than two years that I have held someone dead between my hands. This brings back the first time. I have not told you about that other time—I have told no one. It was when Alva came. I fled along the Ems with Liesbet. We had no food so I left her in a little thicket by the river and I went back to a burning farmhouse to see if there was a hen, eggs, anything to eat. The soldiers had gone. I found nothing. As I was returning I came upon a Spaniard. He had seen Liesbet and he was edging towards her through the trees. I found a stout stick and I crept up behind him. I struck him and he fell. I leapt upon him and held his face in the mud, kneeling on his shoulders and pressing down his head. I knelt there and forced him into the thick mud until he suffocated. And then I still held on until I was quite sure he was dead and could not call his fellows. I went back to Liesbet then and pretended nothing had happened. It had all taken place very near her, yet mercifully she had heard nothing. The muscles in my arms ached and my knees shook and I could feel the dying struggles of the Spaniard in every nerve of my body. I had killed a man—I, who had never been able to kill any creature, not even a chicken."

Her voice failed abruptly, and she was silent.

"Give me your hand, Anna," said Gysbert.

She held out her hand and he groped for it and his fingers closed over it.

"I have never ceased to love you, Anna. I shall never leave you," he said.
He had said that on the voyage back from Rotterdam, Anna remembered. She had longed that he should say it all the years they had been married. Please, God, save us, she prayed. This time it surely would come to pass that they would never again be parted either in the spirit or the flesh. It *must* come to pass; she willed it.

"Say those words again, Gysbert," she whispered.

"I shall never leave you, Anna."

Reluctantly their hands fell apart and they waited for the darkness to lift. When the first pale light glimmered over the water Gysbert moved.

"Give me the child," he said softly.

Anna obeyed him; and put her empty hands to her breast and bowed her head over them. She wished to pray, but her mind was as empty as her hands. She looked up quickly when she heard the slight splash the body made over the side and cried out. Dirk stirred and sat up. She saw a lock of smooth yellow hair hanging through a hole in his red cap. She stared at it and her mind seemed able now to take in only the one small thing—the yellow lock straying through the rent in the red cap. Then she saw that Liesbet was awake and looking about her, searching for something. Liesbet's eyes met Gysbert's, and he nodded in answer to her unspoken question.

"Yes," he said. "The child died in the night."

"Ach, why did I awake!" cried Liesbet.

Anna stared again at the yellow lock of Dirk's and tried to push it back through the hole in the red cap.

The boy burrowed his head against her knees. Anna stroked his head. Only this boy left of a whole family, she thought.

And now it seemed to her that the desolation was complete.

iii

They passed by a town and saw men in boats plying between the sunken houses, taking people off the rooftops and saving those drowning in the water. They knew their safety depended on their keeping clear, so they steered away from the town, fighting desperately against the current.

Anna set her teeth and rowed mechanically. She was deaf and dazed with exhaustion and did not hear the shouting far behind them. She was facing Liesbet and was appalled to see how ill the girl looked.

"There is a boat making for us, Anna," said Gysbert.

"Some message, perhaps," Anna said through stiff lips. "Help may be coming."

A man in the oncoming boat shouted. Liesbet lifted her head with a sudden, swift movement and stared eagerly ahead. Then she stood upright in the bobbing boat, balancing herself with her arms outstretched. A light broke through the pallor of her face and her eyes shone as though there were a lamp behind them. She was uplifted, transported in a blaze of happiness. Anna ceased rowing and gazed at her, fascinated by the miracle of her spiritual quickening. As she looked at Liesbet she knew that Ryk and no other was in the boat behind her.

"Ryk," called Liesbet. "Ryk."

Her voice rang vibrant and joyous across the water.

Anna turned and saw Ryk. He was not looking at her or his father. He saw only Liesbet.

"Liesbet," Ryk cried.

He stood in the prow of his boat and he and Liesbet stretched out their hands to each other across the water; and the wind caught Liesbet's cloak and unbound her hair and blew them out behind her in banners of gold and black; and once again her face had youth in it and springing life. Anna forgot how chilled she was, how cold was the light that poured down on the waste of water and the wild scene and, with tears running unheeded down her cheeks, she remembered Ryk and Liesbet in their happy childhood. There was a radiance in the two stretching out their hands to each other that lent greatness and grandeur in their hopelessness and warmed them all.

Ryk reached them. He stepped into their boat.

"Father, Mother," he cried. "Thank God, I have found you."

"I knew you would come if you got my message," said Gysbert, trembling. In his heart he had not believed they would be saved.

"The storm is about over, Father. Help is coming. The Seigneur de Billy is sending out boats, and the troops from Groningen are doing all that can be done."

"Ryk," said Anna. "You see how it is with Liesbet? She must have help at once. We can wait our turn and drift in this boat until the water goes down; but she cannot wait. What can you do for her, Ryk?"

"I can go back to my ship at Harlingen and then make for Delft or Rotterdam."

"Yes, that is sensible. How did you find us, Ryk?" Anna asked.

"I went home," said Ryk.

"How was it there?" asked Gysbert, looking at Anna as he put the question. His compassion was a silent bond between them. Anna's house, Anna's lands, he thought. He doubted whether Ryk would have found one stone upon the other.

"The sea was over it," said Ryk.

He stood now at Liesbet's side in the rocking boat. He remembered how the fallen poplars and the house and the farmyard had looked under water. He had thought himself bewitched as he had gazed unbelievingly down and had seen under the few feet of water the blurred outlines of the roofs and walls as in a clouded mirror. He had rowed in a state of dreadful distraction over the shadowy, drowned house where he had been born, seeking Liesbet and his parents, torturing himself with the thought that they had been trapped within by the avalanche of waters. At last he had remembered Gysbert's boat and had known that his father would have found some way of escape from the engulfing sea.

Oostermeer has ended, thought Anna, and the waters are over it.

"Liesbet must be cared for," she said. "Your boat is small, Ryk, and I doubt whether you can safely take more than Liesbet and the boy. Get them away to safety. We will wait."

"I cannot go without you," said Ryk. "Help may not come."

"Could we not keep together in the two boats?" Liesbet asked.

"We are tired," said Gysbert. "My leg hinders me and your mother is exhausted. We could not keep up, and Ryk must hurry. It will be only a matter of time before we are rescued."

"If you can reach the town you will not have long to wait. Many people have been taken off," said Ryk in a troubled voice.

"Your mother is right, Ryk. You cannot take us. Liesbet, get into the other boat. And you also, Dirk. And God be with you," said Gysbert firmly.

"I cannot leave you," Ryk pleaded distractedly.

"There is nothing you can do but leave us," Anna said quietly. "We will row at once to the town. When there is dry land again we will meet. Liesbet, take great care of yourself and your babe. Ryk, I put Dirk in your charge. Keep him with you and treat him as your own. He is alone in the world. Go now, my son, and God bless you all."

Liesbet looked long at Anna. Their friendship and their trust in each other was deep and abiding. She caught Anna's hand.

"You are right, Mother," she said. "I must go. My time is very near. Tell Lourens to come to me at Delft. And thank you. I shall not forget. Pray God we may meet again soon."

She broke down and wept.

"Help her onto your boat, Ryk," said Gysbert.

Anna saw Liesbet and Ryk and Dirk move onto the other boat through a mist of tears. Liesbet still held the cat under her cloak. Ryk came back and she felt his arms about her.

"Ach, Mother, follow us. Try to keep up," he said.

"We cannot, Ryk, and you know it. Be merciful and make this no harder than it is. Good-bye, my son. God have you all in His keeping."

Then they were alone, she and Gysbert. They looked after Ryk's boat as it drew steadily away from them, growing smaller and smaller as they watched it.

The sun came out for the first time that day. The flood was a tide of dark gold, the sky a vast arc of purple and blue shot with light.

They saw the receding boat, a black speck on the horizon.

Suddenly the burnished surface of the water dimmed, and with magical swiftness the sun set.

They were alone, facing whatever might arise together. And, being alone with Gysbert, Anna rested on her oars and told him how it had come about that Don Rodriguez d'Esquerdes had found sanctuary at Oostermeer.

iv

She had told him all.

"I ask your forgiveness, Anna," said Gysbert in anguish.

"I should have spoken," she said. "It is I who ought to ask forgiveness. Out of my stubborn silence came our misery. That night you did not come to my bed broke my heart, but it steeled my pride. I had meant to tell you all when you had fully recovered."

"Jan Hattingh told me the day we came home."

"Elfrieda went to him?"

"Yes."

"Her accusations were malicious enough, I'll be bound."

"Elfrieda betrayed you; but she went too far. She insisted that the Spaniard was in your bed and that you slept with him. That you had sheltered a Spaniard for some reason unknown to him Jan Hattingh might have believed, but that you slept with the fellow was too much. He told Elfrieda that her tale was a fabrication and warned her not to repeat it. Poor girl, she had little opportunity because she was killed soon afterwards when Alva came to Friesland. There is not a man who doubts your integrity as my wife, Anna. It has ever been my proud boast that I have the fairest and most faithful wife in all the provinces. But later Oostermeer was spared by the Spaniards and then Jan Hattingh changed his opinion. Facts were against you."

"You had a meeting," said Anna, speaking jerkily in between her strokes at the oar. "What was said?"

"Ryk and Lourens, Gerard, Jan, and I met. Hard things were said that night, Anna. Lourens stoutly defended you. He insisted that you should be asked what had happened. He said that you had done your spying among the Spaniards so well that you had deceived them into thinking that you were on their side. He reminded us that there never had been a flaw in the information you had got from the priest and others in Groningen. And you had risked your life to do your work so well. He suggested that the priest had sent the Spaniard and you had not dared refuse. And Gerard: if I had not stated that I did not believe that you had bedded with the Spaniard I think he would have struck me. I feared Gerard that night. He said you were no betrayer. He came nearer the truth than any of us: he said you were tenderhearted and that was probably why you had spared the Spaniard. But Ryk and Jan and I would have none of their reasoning. The vote went against them and Lourens and Gerard were put on oath not to disclose what had been said to you. And I undertook to watch you, Anna, to my eternal shame."

"Lourens and Gerard came as near telling me as their oath would permit," said Anna. "I see it now."

"That countryman, Gerard," said Gysbert. "I can hear him now: 'If

I carpeted this room with roses, Anna van Breda, it would not be enough.' I have never been more insanely jealous or more unhappy than I was that afternoon. Ach, Anna, it was a hard struggle not to weaken and take you in my arms and tell you all, my heart. Let us begin again. I was beside myself. Anna, if I could recall these past two years!"

How he had hurt her. If he spent the rest of his life on his knees before her it would not be penance enough. He remembered the sad day of his home-coming and the long nights when he had occupied Ryk's bed.

"I cannot bear it, Gysbert," said Anna brokenly.

"Anna, greatly as I have loved you, I have always failed you."

"Do not let there be talk of forgiveness between us," she said. "It was also my pride that brought us to this pass. I ought to have made you speak. I see now how little a thing is pride, how great a thing is love. Gysbert, I care for you as I think no woman ever cared for a man before —you have all my heart. Come then, my dear, and let us go on together and there shall be no yesterday. I swear it."

"Anna, you are too good to me."

"There may be little of life left," she answered gently. "There shall be no yesterday. That is how it shall be."

"There shall be no yesterday," he said.

v

"It will soon be quite dark," said Gysbert. "We must try to reach the town."

They were rowing steadily towards the dimly visible rooftops. Night set in as they reached the first house. Anna longed to stand upon the solid earth again. They could just discern the lane between the buildings on either side. The lapping and the gurgling of the sea sounded threateningly loud as they rowed up the narrow channel, and the splashing of the oars was only one of the many sounds in the confusion of the terrifying night.

"We must make for the tower at the end of this row," said Gysbert. "We ought to be seen in the morning if there is no one about now."

"The rescuing boats appear to have gone," said Anna. She was so exhausted that her mind emptied itself of everything except an intense desire to be on the tower with Gysbert, with the terror of their hazardous passage through the houses behind them.

"I can't go on," she whispered. "I am tired, tired."

"To the tower," said Gysbert hearteningly. "Row, Anna, my beloved."

"Yes," she muttered through her teeth. "Yes."

And bent doggedly to the rowing.

She felt each pull at the oar must be her last. She caught her lower lip between her teeth and bit down hard. She was aware of the noise of the sea on every side. Its rushing and racing and menacing noise pushed out all thought. The accursed sea. She knew she was losing consciousness.

She bit her lip again and tasted the saltiness of blood. She pulled at the oar with the last of her strength. She must go on. Just a little while longer. To the tower, to the tower . . .

The boat plunged forward at the last stroke, plunged and crashed rendingly on some hidden wall. Anna leapt up as it overturned. She found herself in the icy water. She groped for Gysbert, for the boat, for something firm beneath her hand.

vi

Anna clung to the rim of the tower. She had called out to Gysbert, but he had not answered. She gripped the stone edge with both hands and felt the water dragging her down with the weight of her sodden garments. Her thoughts swirled confusedly like the currents that crisscrossed that false sea. She saw her life ending in misery and ruin and her unhappy country lost in the flood that had swept down from the unpredictable ocean to uproot, obliterate, destroy.

After some time her mind cleared and she had a brief vision of Oostermeer. With the unquiet sea lapping round the top of the tower she saw as in a mirror the buttressed barns with their lichened roofs, the avenue of trees, the neat garden and the fields of Oostermeer set about the drowned house that showed enlarged, pressed a little out of shape, and yet stood stone upon stone in a blurred enchantment under the moving grey tide of the North Sea that covered it.

She was alone, clinging to the tower in the wild, windy night. Alone with the sea she had loved and hated alternately all her life, so that she had not known whether love or hatred was the stronger. That was settled now. There was no longer a doubt. She hated the sea that had taken Gysbert from her, had brought him back, and now irrevocably had claimed him; she hated the sea that had turned from its ancient way to destroy in a day the toil of generations. And hating it, she would meet her death in it. She could not live without Gysbert. It was easy to let her numbed fingers slip. It was cold, and her fingers were already dead. There was no need to go on with her life, to drag out what remained of it in a strange place among strange faces. And the sea had taken Liesbet and Ryk and Lourens for all she knew. She was too tired to care, and she did not want to care in the barren, stormy future. If they lived, let them shape their lives. They were grown and beyond her. No one is indispensable, she told herself, putting up a defence for her longing for oblivion.

Exhaustion clouded her mind and her thoughts drifted. From the chaos of her tired thinking one recollection came back startlingly clear. She had forgotten for a while but now she remembered that some of the band of patriots had not trusted her. They had dared think her a traitor to the cause—Gysbert, Ryk, Jan Hattingh, and the legion of Van Bredas in the south, she supposed. They had dared to think it. Anna grew hot with anger, half submerged as she was in the water. She would prove to them that she was no renegade. She would live to prove it. One does not escape so easily just when one wishes, she thought. She set her teeth. Slowly, and with sullen determination, she began to lift herself over the edge. After some minutes of anguished effort she succeeded in dragging herself clear of the water and collapsed in a limp heap on the top of the tower.

vii

The new day dawned and Anna van Breda was alone, alive and fully conscious, on the top of the tower.

The isolation caught her by the throat. She felt as though she stood at the edge of the world in the expanse of dark water.

She saw the tide was ebbing fast. The shallow sea was dwindling as the flood began to be sucked back into its original marshes.

Looking out over the grey waters, Anna knew a strange peace. She saw in her survival the symbol of the survival of her people in their mortal struggle with Spain. Not forever would there be an Alva, an invading sea, a land lost beneath the engulfing tide. Her life was of no value in itself, but it was of value in the collective endeavour of the nation. The struggle was for each and all. She would go wherever she was needed, do whatever was required of her, and not slacken in resistance until from the soil of the Netherlands, watered by the blood of patriots, sprang the flower of freedom.

She stood at the edge of a new existence. Perhaps she would look upon unfamiliar faces, dwell in unfamiliar places. Yet she was resolved with her heart in the ruin of the flood to go on. She would set her face unflinchingly to the unknown future, firm in her belief that the Netherlands would one day be free. It had needed the spur of her ready pride to get her out of the water; but now her faith in God sustained her. She had forgotten herself, her doubts and her fears. A serenity came to her with this faith in God and the future. She would move in the full tide of her country's history and not stand as a spectator on the outer edge of its flow. She would live her life in the present and whatever there might be in the future, and put the past behind her until the passing years transmuted bitterness and loss into cherished memory.

Anna stood tall and unbowed, her ravaged face lifted to the grey sky. The depth and breadth of the ruin wrought in her was in her face.

Now she saw there was a band of silvery light where water and heavens met. Hope stirred in her heart, and she thought of her own small life. When the sea turned again to its accustomed way it might be that she would live at Oostermeer again, building it up from its foundations.

Be that as it may. The fight was on: she would struggle and she would rise.

Now she saw, almost without surprise, a boat a long way off and heading her way.

CHAPTER FOUR

The cowl was in the way of his eyes. Peering from behind De Ruyter's broad back, Lourens van Breda could see little else but the great fire of turfs. He moved his head cautiously and the commandant came into his line of vision.

So far all had gone well. They had gained access to the quarters of Commandant Tisnacq in the fortress of Lowenstein without incident. There had been a tense moment at the gate when the four Orangemen, in the garb of mendicant Grey Friars, had craved the hospitality of the castle. Their arrival had plainly caused some surprise, as with the floods and frosts travel was a matter of the greatest difficulty in that hard weather. They had stood at the gate awaiting the return of the guard, not knowing what the next step must be. The commandant, however, had wished to see them and they were accordingly admitted to his presence.

Their remarkable good fortune held, for the escort withdrew, leaving them alone in the apartment with Commandant Tisnacq and his wife. They stood there in single file, and in their monks' cowls and gowns they were like waiting birds of ill omen.

The commandant addressed De Ruyter.

"You are welcome to this fortress," he said. "Your blessing, Father."

"Do you hold this castle for the Prince of Orange or the Duke of Alva?" De Ruyter demanded peremptorily.

"I recognize no prince save Philip, King of Spain," declared Tisnacq haughtily, drawing back.

De Ruyter shook the cowl from his head and while the words were yet warm on the commandant's lips he drew his pistol from the folds of his gown and shot him dead. The slain man's wife began a dreadful screaming, and hard on the pistol shot a wild and startled clamour broke out in the thick-walled fortress.

The masquerading friars ignored the shrieking woman. They flung back their cowls and threw off their hampering gowns and stood swords in hand, awaiting the attack. The plan of De Ruyter's devising for seizing the fortress of Lowenstein by stratagem seemed to have every chance of success. While the Spaniards rushed hither and thither in panic and confusion they began a piecemeal destruction of the garrison, and soon were masters of the place.

De Ruyter mustered his small band and posted them, each man in a key point of the castle. In a few hours at least a score of his men would appear, and reinforcements were on the way. He knew he must consolidate his success and be firmly in possession before Alva knew the fortress was lost.

Lourens van Breda was De Ruyter's right-hand man and most to be relied on. He was accordingly posted at the gateway. Lourens had fought that night with the strength and ferocity of ten men.

In the faint light of the waxing moon Lourens van Breda paced to and fro at the main gate. The light shone wanly on his helmet and breastplate of steel, and on the cold steel of his long pike. On the land side there was the silence of the flooded fields; on the water side there was the murmur of the two mighty rivers, the Waal and the Meuse, at their junction at the outward walls of the fortress, built as it was on a narrow tongue of land.

He paced to and fro with only his thoughts for company. He thought of his mother and of Oostermeer; of Liesbet, his wife, and he longed to know that she had not been frightened and unhappy when the sea took her. She had been so carefree as a child at Oostermeer. And how beautiful she had been with her transparent skin with the waves of pink flushing her cheeks, and her hair golden and thick with a faint perfume always about it.

What the Spaniard spared the sea claimed, he thought; and his heart burned with the hot bitterness of youth.

ii

On the next evening at the hour of sunset Herman de Ruyter climbed to the top of the castle, from which vantage point he could command an excellent view of the surrounding country. Flood and frost were sealing down the activities of both Spaniard and partisan of Orange. There were now thirty stout Orangemen in the castle and all depended on whether Alva or William of Orange first sent reinforcements.

A man came up and stood beside him on the top of the castle. It was Lourens van Breda.

"No reinforcements coming up as far as I can see," said De Ruyter. "Do you see anything?"

"No," returned Lourens. "I think it is as impossible for the Spaniards as it is for our own men."

"You never know. I do not trust a Spaniard. They attempt the impossible. We must be vigilant."

Herman de Ruyter looked out to the cities of Gorcum and Dorcum and over the frozen, flooded fields. Then he looked at Lourens van Breda. He thought Lourens had changed out of all recognition since the time of the flood. His face had a set, strained look. But he was very young and the young got over tragedies. It was merciful how much of suffering the young forgot, thought Herman.

"We stand fast here," said Herman de Ruyter in his rough, rich voice. "We have made a beginning. By God's grace not a Spaniard will be left alive in all the provinces before we are much older."

Lourens van Breda did not share his leader's optimism. The Spaniards were a mighty foe, well trained and well equipped. Although the partisans of Orange fought with a ferocious tenacity and a devotion to their prince and their cause that neither death nor disaster could shake, soldiering was new to many of them. There was De Ruyter, their leader, in private life a drover, he himself a farmer, their comrades in arms drawn from every rank and occupation in the country. At this time it seemed to Lourens that God stood back from them. But he tried to avoid thinking too much: action was all he craved, and under Herman de Ruyter he knew there would always be plenty of that.

He would not think now; he turned away and began to descend. With his foot on the first step he paused, his senses arrested by the uncanny lighting of the snow in the sunset glow. The sun was red and it had dyed the heavens with the same angry hue; the snow on the roofs of Gorcum and Dorcum was red, and red were the frozen fields and the glassy canals. A land bathed in blood . . . Lourens stood transfixed till the sun dipped suddenly out of sight and a grey pall shrouded the scene.

He shivered then; and without a word to De Ruyter he disappeared down the narrow stone steps.

De Ruyter shook his head. Van Breda was a changed man with his long and disturbing silences, he thought. He took one last long look around him. There was no body of men moving up to the fortress walls. The Spaniards, used to a softer climate, would doubtless think this ill weather for bold manoeuvres, he decided.

It was cold in the frost up in the watchtower. Herman de Ruyter descended, and soon a solitary watchman appeared and patrolled the tower top, stopping to survey the flat landscape at short intervals.

But neither friend nor foe was to be seen.

iii

But the Spaniards were to attempt the impossible. They laid siege to the fortress, breached the wall with cannon, and forced an entry. The Spanish force was numerically overwhelming and, despite their heroic resistance, the tiny garrison was slain or captured with the exception of De Ruyter and Lourens van Breda. Now the slain lay in a heap and the sorely wounded had been dragged back.

"To the doorway," cried De Ruyter. "Cold steel now, Lourens."

"Steel it is," gasped Lourens.

They fell back on the doorway of the inner court, and shoulder to shoulder barred the entrance. From the clustered mob of the Spanish came a wolfish cry as they saw their prey at bay.

The two in the doorway prepared themselves for the final assault. Lourens's nerves steadied and he was firm and resolute. De Ruyter's face was terrible and transfigured, transformed into the face of a living vengeance. To them this was no present struggle against fearful odds but the embodiment of the deathless striving of every Netherlander for freedom. The coming death struggle was a thread in the design for ultimate victory; and there was an involuntary hope that was itself a prayer to turn the issue that was in the mind of God alone.

"They come," shouted De Ruyter; and now the last battle began.

The Spaniards attacked fiercely. Only these two dogs of heretics left. The two in the doorway fought as men possessed. Lourens's helmet was dented by a great blow from a sword and his face was bloodied.

The enemy pressed home the attack. When the first wave of the assault had been beaten back De Ruyter found himself alone. Lourens lay at his feet; but it was only a moment before his body was seized and dragged away. Again the Spaniards closed in on the solitary figure in the doorway. De Ruyter could not keep count of the men who fell beneath his slashing sword. The faces kept changing, dark faces with grinning lips above bared teeth. Take that, Spaniard, and that, and that; and his sword was hot and wet in his grip. Now he felt it grow heavy in his hand and he knew that his life was leaving him in a red tide from his many wounds. But they would never take Herman de Ruyter. He had sworn to himself that they should not, and he had provided a means of escape from them. He retreated slowly into the hall. He raised his bloody sword for the last time above his head and brought it crashing down on the shoulder of the Spaniard who pressed him closest. He felt the keen blade sink deep and, letting go of it, he feinted as though he would dart through the open ranks of his attackers; but, before they could see his design, he seized the lantern and bent low and lit the charge to the train of powder he and Lourens had laid on the floor many hours before.

The train was alight and the flames ran along the line of oil from the overturned lantern. Too late the Spaniards saw and began to huddle and squeeze to the door; but while De Ruyter laughed and flung his arms above his head in a triumphant invitation to death the roar of the explosion came and the tower sprang into the air.

The fortress was lost; the sounds of strife ceased. A flame shot upwards and a dark pall of smoke drifted over the water.

PART II

CORNISH INTERLUDE

WILD WEATHER HAD SET IN OVER ENGLAND. ALONG THE COAST OF Cornwall the wind, spray-laden, howled and tore at the land, and the storm-tossed waters of the Channel roared out to the boundless ocean. Privateers and merchantmen and the Queen's own ships lay side by side in Falmouth harbour; and the little fishing boats had long before reefed their sails and scudded to its safety.

The wind blew down the mile-long street of Falmouth, shrieking along it as it wound narrowly beside the harbour and round many corners, blustering up the hill to beat tempestuously upon Arwennack House, the home of the Killigrews; and then on to Bodrugan, the farmhouse of Richard Barradale, built on the height above the hamlet.

For more than a week the storm had raged. On this morning in November it showed small sign of abating. Anthony Barradale, ten-year-old son of Richard, fought his way against the wind to the headland. He stood at the wall of battlemented Pendennis. From where he stood he gazed up at the castle and saw the arms of the Tudors above the entrance to the round keep. The wind whistled through his hair, and the wild music of a host of gulls sounded in his ears above the crashing of the heavy swell.

He hoped his father was sheltering in some port and would not venture home; and he wondered if he were not perhaps with Ryk van Breda. All that had to do with Ryk was somehow exciting and mysterious, and although Ryk seldom appeared at Bodrugan, they often spoke of him; and from the stray facts Richard Barradale had disclosed Anthony had woven many threads into the warp and woof of the Dutchman's existence.

The storm fascinated him. Was it raging as fiercely all over the world? he wondered. Was Ryk battling against it also in the seas round Holland?

The wind knew the answer to that question. Just then it was sending

the tempest-driven seas along the beaches and dykes and sweeping on
and over the flat coast from Flanders to Friesland.

While Anthony Barradale thought of him Ryk van Breda was leaving
half-submerged Rotterdam behind him and was attempting to navigate
his ship through mountainous seas across the North Sea to Dover, while
the wind howled and tore at the vessel, and threatened every moment to
keel it over in the troughs of the gigantic waves.

ii

The wind beat against him, and the gulls wheeled and circled, struggling in the storm.

Anthony Barradale was a sensitive, intelligent boy. He half closed his
large eyes against the wind, and their glinting grey-green brightness was
netted behind thick lashes. He was a lonely child, having been born
many years after his sisters, Nan and Sarah. Nan was James Carey's wife
and her twin sons were but six years younger than himself; and Sarah
had married Martin Thomas, a distant kinsman of the Killigrews.
Anthony had been his mother's constant companion, and in many ways
was older than his years, and given to long spells of silence and imaginative thinking.

The wind is free, the boy thought. The wind in my hair is freedom.
It was a word that was often on the lips of men and women, and at
Bodrugan, when his father was home from the sea and the long-necked
Dutch glasses were filled, the toast was always "Freedom." Once before,
on a very different day, he had thought he knew what freedom was. It
had been on a morning in mid-August when a golden rain of sun had
fallen on the walls of Pendennis Castle. He had gone to watch on the
headland, hoping to see his father's ship put into the harbour.

He remembered that morning in vivid detail: the sun had shone on
the castle of St. Mawes on the opposite headland, and on the Carrick
Roads and the dark, wooded reaches of the Fal, encircling the harbour
and the bay where three tall ships, stripped of sail, rode at anchor, their
masts and spars a filigree against the cloudless sky.

A gull had swung on motionless wings at the rim of the headland and,
after a long moment, had plummeted like a stone down to the sea. He
had run to the edge of the cliffs and had seen the gull wheel up and away.

His mind, fickle as the little wind that was beginning to stir the grass
on Pendennis headland, took in the reality of the sun and the sea. He had
seen a Tudor ship slip from the mouth of Falmouth haven and had
watched her until she was clear of the harbour, and had smiled to see
her hoist her coloured sails and stand away to the Channel, gaily bobbing
on the waves. She is a pretty sight, he had thought. A toy ship, a dream
ship, a free ship . . .

A free ship . . . An abstract notion had suddenly been translated into
living reality.

The sea gull had returned. He had seen it swinging again on motionless wings at the rim of the headland, a pattern in dazzling white against the sky. Its beauty brought tears to his eyes.

In this certainty of sea and sky there had been nothing illusory or dreamlike. The sea gull was the realization of a dream. It was free, eternal.

At last he knew—or thought he knew—what freedom was.

iii

On a cold damp evening later in that same November Anthony Barradale sat with his mother in the winter parlour. There was a log fire blazing and candlelight, and shadows on the rush-strewn floor. But the leaping fire had not its usual attraction, as his mind was concentrated on his mother, who paced to and fro, wandering from window to window. The storm had spent itself and his father had not returned.

He saw her lift the curtain and peer into the darkness. He wondered idly how many watched the sea from their windows; the little hamlet of Falmouth had a vibrant life, for it was rumoured that much smuggling and a little wrecking gave zest to the lives of the inhabitants of the grey houses and twisted alleyways down near the sea and the clamouring gulls.

Anthony knew for certain that there was at least one other woman looking out over the dark sea even as his own mother was, and she was Lydia Wilson, Tom's mother. She dwelt in a filthy hut on the steep slope beyond the Manacles, rearing Tom in squalor and in idleness. Anthony and Tom were great friends and, in spite of opposition from his mother and interference from Big Ben Trevenna, the cowman, their friendship increased. Big Ben Trevenna had not a good word to say for Tom, and he had less time for Lydia, who lived in deplorable dirt and, so it was alleged, knew more about smuggling activities than she should, and was always first on the beach when a ship broke up on the Manacles and came drifting shorewards with the tide. The charitable said her troubles had turned her brain, but Big Ben would have none of it. He gave out that she dabbled in witchcraft, and he had proof of it, he said. The last time she had been at Bodrugan begging from Mistress Barradale he had seen her cross the yard mumbling and threatening because she had not got all she sought, she having been most immoderate in her demands. And that selfsame night two cows had sickened in the byre, and the next day the cream would not turn into butter. . . .

Frances Barradale was still at the window. Anthony forgot his dreaming and went to her. He caught her hand and attempted to draw her to the fire.

"The sea will bring him back, Mama," he said comfortingly.

"He has been gone so long," she murmured.

Richard was more than a week behind his time, she thought, and the storm was over. All day she had moved in the shadow of a vague dread and her anxiety never slept. Richard's life was always at stake. He carried news of Spanish activities as well as arms concealed in bales of wool to Dutch ports, and she lay sleepless night after night, wondering what fate might be meted out to him should he be captured by a Spanish ship. As the struggle in the Netherlands against Spain increased in severity she had watched the links that bound them individually, and as a nation, to the people of Holland forged one by one. On a not very distant day, so Richard said, the chain would be complete, and the English and the Dutch would be united in the face of the common foe.

Unknown to her that night, while she stared into the fire and lost herself in long, troubled reflections, a new link was being formed which was destined to bring the house of Barradale into closer contact than ever before with the war-torn land across the North Sea.

iv

The hound that had lain quietly all evening at their feet by the fire stirred. He stood with cocked head, listening; and soon he padded to the door and put his front paws on it, whining eagerly.

"Rollo never does that unless he hears Father," Anthony said, getting up to open the door. "He is wrong for once, I think."

"If he should be coming, Anthony!"

The faint promise of surcease from anxiety was blessed. Anthony had not the heart to extinguish the light in his mother's eyes. He opened the door wider and looked out into the hall.

"I shall go out and see whether Rollo is not right after all," he said.

And that was how it came about that the front door of Bodrugan stood wide open so that light streamed out in a welcoming glow when Richard Barradale fumbled at the latch of the farmyard gate, impeded by the bundle in his arms and the leaping hound at his side.

He was barely through the gate when Anthony ran up to him; and slipping, and sobbing with joy, and making her way as best she could through the mud, Frances reached him at last.

"Richard, Richard," she cried, clinging to his arm as though she would never release it again. "I did not think you would come home on a night like this."

The household had just realized that something was toward. Doors slammed and feet sped down corridors and voices were raised. In the midst of the clamour Richard Barradale announced unconcernedly:

"I have brought you a daughter home, Frances. Here she is, take her. Anna Maria van Breda, born on the North Sea and christened at Dover."

Frances was a nerve-racked, tired woman, but she loved babies. She gathered the bundle Richard thankfully thrust upon her gently into her arms. And heading the procession, for the entire household seemed to have poured itself into the yard, Frances Barradale carried the child into the house. For no reason at all, save, perhaps, the stupefaction of astonishment, for the servants were an insensitive mob, silence abruptly shut out the hubbub at her heels as Frances set her foot over the threshold. In that electric quiet with the faint light of the lantern flickering in the wind, and hemmed in by the circle of staring eyes, Frances Barradale drew back the shielding cloak from the child's face.

It was sweet to hold a child in her arms again, she thought, gazing down into the red, puckered face of the sleeping infant.

Anna Maria van Breda opened her eyes and began to whimper, not caring about the light and the lack of motion after her rude tossing in Richard's unaccustomed arms.

"Hush," crooned Frances, beginning a gentle rocking. "Hush, you have come home, Anne-Marie."

So Anna Maria van Breda came to Bodrugan by Falmouth.

PART III

ḤOLLAND

CHAPTER SIX

GERARD VAN BRAAM HALTED AT THE NORTHERN WATER GATE OF DELFTS-
haven to get his bearings. He saw at once the tall, graceful
spire of the New Church at Delft, seven miles away, marking where the
city stood behind its heavy walls. And from here also he had an unim-
peded view of the broad mouth of the river Meuse which, widening
gradually between Delftshaven and the shores of Brabant, flowed in and
out of the maze of small islands which lay between it and the sea.

With the pointing spire before him Gerard van Braam began to walk
along the path that followed the river. The day was fine and windy, and
the clouds scudded swift and loose across the heavens. In the clear
patches of sky the pale golden light had a luminous quality and it
glimmered behind the clouds. On either hand the flat fields were patterned by intersecting drainage ditches, and the windmills, pumping
the water from the fields over the dyke, gave out protesting creaks at
the pace at which the wind forced round their arms.

He walked on; and his thoughts ran ahead to Anna at Delft. Jan
Hattingh had told him she had asked to be taken there after her rescue
from the top of the tower at the time of the flood, as she had hoped
Liesbet would be there. He knew he would find her at the house of
Matthias van Breda, her brother-in-law. He wondered sadly how much
she had learned of the fate of her family. He was the bearer of hard and
heavy tidings. Lourens had been slain in the defence of the fortress of
Lowenstein; of Ryk and Liesbet there was no news at all; at Oostermeer
the walls and foundations of the house stood firm, but the fields were
under a foot of water and it would take years for the salt to leave the
soil, so that it might be arable again. He did not know if she would
marry him—he dared not hope she would; but in any event it was too
near Gysbert's death to talk of marriage. He had contrived a couple of
crude rooms in the old farmhouse of Oostermeer and he had come to
offer her all the help and comfort in his power if she cared to return to

what was left of her home. He would work for her; there was nothing great or small he would not do for her. While he lived, Gerard vowed, she would not lack a friend.

He had been to Delft but once before, he remembered, and that had been when his cousin Anna was a maid and he had hoped to win her. He had been a widower for years and of his children only one daughter survived and she had taken in little Jan, the two-year-old child of his only son. His son and his son's wife had fallen victims to the Inquisition, for they had been, as he was, ardent Calvinists. It was only in the matter of religion that he differed from Anna, Gerard thought as he walked along. She was a Lutheran, and the Lutherans were altogether too lax and tolerant in their views, he held. His life had not turned out as well as it had promised. After all the years he had no more than a daughter and a small grandson and a holding of land under the floodwater. In other ways also he seemed to be precisely where he had been that long time before—on the road to Delft with Anna once again at the end of his quest.

When the sun was about to set he neared the ancient walls behind which clustered the gables and rooftops of Delft. Approaching through chequered squares of garden plot and pastureland and orchard, he entered the city at the South Gate. He walked quickly along the old Delft street, flanked on either side by lime trees between which the canal flowed. He looked out for the brick-walled Old Church with its lancet windows and its perilously leaning slender tower. The tower still inclined at a considerable angle towards a house on the opposite side of the canal just as he remembered it. He stopped to look at this two-storied dwelling, surprised that the slender leaning tower had not yet fulfilled its threat and crushed it; but the westering sun shone tranquilly on its red-tiled roof and bathed its plain brick walls in rosy light.

Gerard wondered who lived in the shadow of the ever-menacing tower. From its appearance the place seemed to be some cloister or religious house, but, as it was separated by a spacious courtyard from the street, he could not satisfy his curiosity, and there was no one at hand to tell him that sometimes the Prince of Orange made the old house his headquarters.

Gerard kept on his way up the street until he came to Matthias van Breda's dwelling. The sun dipped suddenly behind the rooftops and the stone bridges spanning the canal cast wavering, mysterious shadows on the water; and boats and barges moored to the mossy canal walls lay in uncertain pools of darkness.

Beyond the cloistered house he found Matthias van Breda's door. He knocked loudly at it. And fell back a pace when the door was opened to him by Anna's son Ryk.

ii

On the morning of the day that Gerard had walked to Delft Ryk had walked into the living room of his uncle's house where Anna was wiping down the blue wall tiles. She had thought him dead. She stared unbelievingly at him. She saw a young man, tall and upright, who held himself with dignity and assurance. His fair moustache and beard were newly cropped and he had thrust the ends of a crimson scarf in at the neck of his leathern doublet. His eyes were blue-grey as her own were.

Until Ryk spoke Anna stood rooted to the spot, the damp cleaning cloth clutched in her extended hand. His voice broke the spell that held her motionless and she ran to him with inarticulate cries of joy. They did not speak at first. Ryk led her to one of the lovers' benches near the hearth and they sat down, she still holding the cloth. He took it from her and threw it on the floor. And then, with the fresh coldness of the spring morning coming in at the open windows, they exchanged their news. She told him his father and his brother were dead and explained the manner of their death; from him she learned that Liesbet had died in giving birth to a daughter. Ryk told her he had been delayed at Dover. While he was speaking Anna listened and watched the boats and barges gliding by on the canal. She saw the first green was showing on the lime trees. Men poling their barges in midstream shouted to others walking along the stone-paved way and hauling laden ones; children at play beside the canal laughed and skipped; there was life and light outside this room where she and her son sat side by side steeling themselves against a destroying sense of loss.

Ryk's tone changed, was more urgent. Anna caught at her sorrowful thoughts and listened to him.

". . . Lourens was always on your side. Mother, remember of him that he maintained his faith in you when we doubted. I have felt this so much since you told me he is dead."

"I shall remember," said Anna, thinking with grievous sorrow that Lourens and Liesbet and Gysbert, and possibly Gerard, were dead. She thought particularly of Lourens, but her mind did not spring to the fearful closing scene of his short life in the fortress of Lowenstein. She often saw him in these days as a small child at Oostermeer. Once on a day long ago she had taken him to play on the sea side of the distant dyke. He had searched for shells among the battered piers when the tide was out, while she scanned the sea for Gysbert's boat. The tide had been on the turn. When a long time had passed she had called out to Lourens to hurry back onto the dyke as the waves were coming in; but he had laughed and remained below until the last possible moment, and only then had he climbed back to safety with the flying spume breaking over him as he climbed. Lourens was dead. He had gone forth untouched and undefeated, and death had come to him in the flush of his youth before he had known age or disease, or weariness or disillusion. It was a fine setting out, this death in battle; and sober men had come to her in Delft to tell her how gloriously Lourens had died. She treasured their words proudly, but in her secret heart she could never think of Lourens as a valorous soldier: she saw him always as a gleeful barefooted child, braving the galloping horses of the incoming tide. Lourens was dead, but he had left a daughter behind him. . . .

"Tell me more of Liesbet, Ryk," she said.

"We could not save her," said Ryk harshly. "I told you all there is to tell: the seas were too high to get to Rotterdam or anywhere along this coast, so I steered for Dover. Liesbet was taken ill before we reached England. There was a sailor who had some knowledge of childbirth. He helped her. I was there. Shortly after the baby was born Liesbet died and we buried her at sea. Richard Barradale was sheltering from the storm at Dover. When the weather was better he took the child to Falmouth to his wife."

Anna put out her hand and covered his. The martyrdom of Ryk was engraved upon his face. He had aged ten years while he spoke. Anna's imagination filled in the details of the picture his short, bald sentences had outlined. She saw the smoking lanterns swinging against the walls of the tiny cabin as the ship pitched in the tempestuous seas; saw Ryk directing the feeble light over Liesbet while the seaman assisted her in her difficult labour. To see the woman one loved die like that was something a man could never forget. Anna's mind winced away from the pain of it.

"While we speak of Liesbet," Ryk said, the strange lines of premature age still on his face, "all my life I shall remember how you bade her go with me without question when we met in the flood. You had no thought to prevent trouble in the future, although you knew I loved Liesbet and she loved me, yet she was my brother's wife. Had you no thought in your mind that perhaps I should not give her up again?"

"You owe me no gratitude on that score, Ryk. There would have been no trouble in the future had Liesbet lived. The answer to all you have said was in Liesbet herself. There was no evil in her. She could be trusted in a thousand situations, no matter how equivocal. You ought to have known that."

"Perhaps I knew it," he said. "We were together all the time while we crossed to England. She stayed with me while I was at the helm and we spoke of everything. She told me about the Spaniard, Don Rodriguez d'Esquerdes. I did not realize then that those few precious hours with her were to last me for the rest of my life."

"We must look forward now, Ryk, you and I."

For the moment he had forgotten that she too stood alone.

"Yes," he acknowledged.

"When will you be going to England to bring Liesbet's babe to me?"

"Do you not think it would be as well to leave her where she is until you get back to Oostermeer again, Mother?"

"When will that be?" said Anna with a heavy sigh. "I think you are right. She will be better cared for where she is."

"She did not seem to be a sturdy child," said Ryk. "We had her baptized at Dover in a hurry. I gave her your name, Anna, and Liesbet's mother's name, Maria. It was Liesbet's wish."

"Three of us survive," said Anna. "You and I and Anna Maria. Perhaps we three can give an account of ourselves. My generation will not see our country free of the Spaniard, I do not think; but yours will, and Anna Maria at least will live part of her life in peace at Oostermeer. I have one important matter to settle here and then I shall go back to Oostermeer and see what can be salvaged there. And what are you going to do, my son?"

"There is always the sea. I am needed where I am."

"You must marry, Ryk."

He frowned in sudden distaste.

"Think it over," his mother urged. "You must come to it sometime, and I should be sorry if we should be wiped out as a family."

"That is sensible," he agreed.

"I have no bride in view," she said with a faint smile. "You are free to do your own choosing. Now I ask you to forgive me for presuming to speak to you in this way. Ach, Ryk, in these days there seems to be no time for anything—not even for private griefs."

"You are right," he said.

"I long to return to Oostermeer," she said, "but I cannot do so until I have cleared myself here in Delft."

"What do you mean?" he asked absently, wondering if she realized how complete the devastation in the north was; she always spoke as though it would be an easy matter to re-establish herself at Oostermeer.

She pushed her arm impatiently against the tiles.

"I mean that once and for all time I shall put an end to insinuation and suspicion in this house, to whispering behind my back and talking in riddles to my face," she said fiercely. "It took a flood to unseal your father's lips, and the good Lord knows what it will take to settle the doubts in the minds of your aunt and uncle. I am thought to have dealings with the Spaniards even now. That is the idea in this house, although I must say I have not noticed it outside of it. I came here broken and bereft and your father's brother took me in. But watching eyes follow me everywhere. All the suspicion starts here. I am determined to bring this thing out into the open. You know from Liesbet that I could not kill a fellow man in cold blood, and because that man happened to be a Spaniard it appears that I am answerable to every member of the Orange party because I put a wider interpretation on Christian charity than either a Catholic or a Calvinist does. I was condemned unheard. Only Lourens and Gerard spoke for me."

She was pale and shaking with suppressed passion.

"Mother, I shall never forgive myself," said Ryk, appalled at this departure from her habitual calm. "I shall explain everything to Uncle Matthias and Aunt Getruida. I can do that at least."

She broke in on his self-reproach.

"It is over, Ryk," she said. "I am sorry I gave way. You do not know what it has been like in this house without a friendly face."

"I should have come sooner had I known this," said Ryk.

Before the morning was out he had spoken with his aunt and uncle Van Breda; and now in the late afternoon he sat alone again with Anna and they spoke quietly of their plans for the future. While they sat in the growing darkness of the living room there was a resounding knock at the outer door. They both rose up in their seats and listened. The knock was repeated.

"I wonder who it can be?" said Anna.

"I will go and see," said Ryk.

"I shall light the lantern. I did not notice how dark it was getting," Anna said.

She went out for a lantern but Ryk did not wait for her to bring the light. He was back in the room with another man by the time she returned. Anna held the lantern high to see who had come in with Ryk.

"A friend has come to see you," Ryk said.

Now, as the faint yellow beam grew stronger, Anna saw the well-remembered face of her cousin Gerard.

CHAPTER SEVEN

They were gathered together in the tiled living room, and now Anna determined to speak her mind and let out the angry bitterness that had been fermenting inwardly for months.

They began by discussing the topics that coloured everyday conversation—the recent flood, the Inquisition, the seizing of the Spanish treasure in the English ports and of the reprisals Alva was bound to exact. But these topics were not inexhaustible and a constrained silence fell on the group of five seated round the table.

Anna rose out of her seat and leaned forward over the table and looked directly at Getruida. Her hands were pressed palms downward on the cloth.

"Let us be done with this trivial talk," she said, speaking with quiet deliberateness. "Matthias, Getruida, I ask you to state what it is that you have against me. Ever since I came I have been watched and followed. When I leave the house I am accompanied by someone, when a stranger calls to see me Getruida is always present. I congratulate you, Getruida on your good management. If there had been a traitor in your midst there could not possibly have been any leakage of information. Do you consider I am that traitor?"

There was absolute silence. Anna looked round the table, meeting their eyes in turn.

"Speak," she demanded.

Getruida van Breda opened her mouth to speak but before she could utter a word her husband broke in nervously.

"You have this wrong, Anna," he said uneasily. "We have been no more than solicitous for your health."

Anna beat her hand impatiently upon the table.

"The time for evasive speaking is past, Matthias," she told him. "Gysbert told me I was suspected of having dealings with the Spaniards because I sheltered one at Oostermeer. Gysbert knew the truth of it before he died. And Ryk told you this morning. Did you find his explanation satisfactory?"

"We find it hard to credit," said Getruida van Breda.

"I do not doubt but that you would," returned Anna coldly. And added: "Does your wife speak for you, Matthias?"

"No," answered Matthias with a stoutness Anna knew he would rue in private when Getruida had him at the mercy of her flailing tongue.

"Thank you, Matthias."

"I am sorry," said Matthias. "I ought to have spoken and cleared the matter."

"I am a plain woman and I see things as they are," said Getruida. "If we are to be quit of Spanish domination we must exterminate Alva's men whenever they fall into our hands. The man you saw fit to nurse back to life had been left for dead by our men. Then again you say you are no Catholic, but you are loose in your religion——"

"Gerard quarrels with me also on that score," Anna interrupted. "I stand for religious toleration and freedom of worship for all. And I do not believe that it is the will of God that I should slay a wounded man."

"Not even a Spaniard?" said Getruida meditatively, and there was a world of menace in her tone.

"No."

"I am against you there," Gerard said. "It was ill done. You should have handed the fellow over to us."

"You would have killed him," said Anna.

"Without a doubt."

Anna appealed a little wildly to Gerard.

"Gerard, you have known me since my childhood. Do you believe that I could succour the Spaniard and yet be true to my people and my religion?"

"Yes, I believe you could," said Gerard. "On the face of it, Anna, it was a strange thing to do."

"There is more to this than we know," said Getruida.

Anna turned swiftly to confront her.

"That is as you think," she said.

"No man can serve two masters," observed Getruida.

Gerard saw a flush rise to Anna's face, saw it recede again, leaving her very pale. He arose so suddenly to his feet that the bench he had been sitting on overturned and fell with a clatter to the tiled floor.

"This house is no place for you, Anna," he said. "Come back with me to Friesland. If there is nothing in the north save the friendship of a few, it is better than remaining here. I shall stand by you, Anna. You will not struggle alone."

Anna smiled with great sweetness and extended her hand to him.

"So speaks my friend," she said. "And I thank you."

She dropped Gerard's hand and again faced Getruida.

"However, I stay here," she said clearly in a voice that cracked like a pistol shot. "I shall stay here until this matter is settled."

"You will go," said Getruida. "You can do less harm in the north."

"For decency's sake Matthias cannot refuse to shelter his brother's widow," said Anna. "Matthias, will you turn me out?"

"No," said Matthias. He was caught between the grinding stones of two women of strong character, and so desperately pinched between them that there was no way out but an open declaration. His wife and his sister-in-law had always disliked each other, and the shock of their acknowledged conflict shattered him.

"Then I stay," said Anna; and she drew herself up and met Getruida's dark gaze unflinchingly.

Gerard's heart throbbed, seeing that proud bearing. They had thought to bring her to her knees, his peerless Frisian princess, but that, he knew, they would never accomplish. He knew the women of his blood better than they did. His heart cried out that he would be lonely in the north without her, but his pride acknowledged her right to remain.

He looked at Getruida, trying to read the thoughts behind the pallid heaviness of her face. The years had not dealt kindly with her, he thought. The faint down that had darkened her upper lip as a girl was now a decided moustache; the eyes were hooded by drooping upper lids, and from the corners of the eyes two heavy lines ran down her sagging cheeks; her lips were thin and bloodless; her body was gross. It came to him that she was cruel and hard and insanely jealous. And, thinking this, he was suddenly desperately anxious that Anna should not be near her.

Getruida van Breda had been sitting motionless with her eyes downcast and one swollen, purple hand placed above the other on the edge of the cloth. Now she raised her eyes and looked directly at Anna.

"You are very sure of yourself," she said hardly. "Did you think of the consequences that might arise when you set free the Spaniard?"

"That point need not be discussed," Anna observed coldly.

"Do you know where he is, or what he has done since?" Getruida persisted.

"I have heard rumours."

"I shall tell you facts," said Getruida; and Gerard noted the feline cruelty of her lips.

"There is no need," Ryk interposed swiftly.

"Let her speak," said Anna.

"There is no officer of the Inquisition more thorough in the extermination of members of the new religion than Don Rodriguez d'Esquerdes His name has become a byward for infamy and cruelty," said Getruida "I hear this from my sister in Brussels. He has become the terror of the south."

"No," cried Anna. "Ach, no."

"Nevertheless, it is true," said Getruida.

"My mother could not foresee that this would happen," said Ryk, coming to Anna's defence. "You cannot blame her."

"She succoured this wolf of a Spaniard."

Gerard's voice broke in on Anna's horror and confusion.

"The ways of the Almighty are inscrutable," he said. "In the fullness of time we shall understand. Anna, come back with me to Oostermeer."

"It is quite plain," Getruida said. "It is God's punishment for Anna's presumption. But perhaps Anna ought to stay. At least I can see that she spares no more Spaniards if any come her way."

"I shall stay," said Anna, drawing herself erect in dull defiance.

Only Gerard knew how near she was to defeat. She stretched out her hand in a blind gesture to him.

Through the numbing mist of shock Anna saw clearly and unexpectedly Oostermeer as it must soon be looking in the spring, with the poplars in first leaf and the flower-studded meadows, with the soaring larks' singing and the lazy turning of the arms of the windmills, and the wide sweep of sunlight on the glittering meers.

All that beauty was passing from her. Her fingers gripped Gerard's in an agony of realization.

ii

One morning when the lime trees were fragrant with blossom above the smoothly flowing canal Anna returned with her basket of vegetables from beyond the city walls.

She had almost decided to abandon the stand she had made and return to Gerard and the friendly north. Getruida excelled in sadistic cruelty and, although Anna had strength of mind enough to resist her attempts to undermine her fortitude, she was fighting a losing battle against her inward torment that she had mistaken God's purpose in saving the Spaniard.

As she neared the Old Church an impulse came to her to enter and seek relief in prayer. So she set her basket down by the canalside and went in. The light came in through the lancet windows and lay in golden patches on the dim, cool floor. Anna sank down on her knees and tried to compose herself to her devotions; but her mind was blind with misery and she could not shape her thoughts.

There was no virtue save in sincerity, she thought; and she got up from her knees and went out again to collect her basket, as there was always plenty to be done in her brother-in-law's house, and the morning was passing.

It was then she noticed that a man had begun to cross on one of the stone bridges spanning the canal. She knew as soon as her eyes fell on a little white pug dog trotting at his heels that it was William, Prince of Orange. All Delft knew that dog.

He had been in residence at the Prinsenhof, the old abandoned convent of St. Agatha, but a few days and, although it was his wont to give entrance and audience to all, Anna had not yet seen him so close. She put the basket down again and respectfully waited for him to pass.

As it was with her so it was with him, she thought, watching him walk towards her. They were both passing through their darkest hour.

As he approached her Anna looked into the face of this prince who had become the rallying point in their national life. She saw a man, simply dressed in a loose surcoat of grey frieze, over a leathern doublet, wearing riding boots with turned-down tops and woollen stockings showing above them. A spotless ruff encircled his neck. He wore a felt hat on his head and his moustache and beard were closely cropped. Although the spare outlines of his face were haggard his expression was open and gentle.

William came to a halt before Anna. The white dog flung himself down on the cool paving stones and panted, for the June day was warm.

"Good morning."

The Prince was addressing her. Anna had heard that it was his custom to speak with the people he met in the streets of Delft, but she had not expected him to speak to her. She bent her knee and dropped him a curtsey beside her vegetable basket.

"Good morning, Your Highness," she replied.

She met the gaze of his dark, deep-set eyes and on the instant she was quite at her ease. There was an abounding humanity and a warmth of understanding and no bitterness in those eyes. This was a rare man, a great prince.

"You have been beyond the walls early," he remarked.

"I like to go for the vegetables," she said with a faint smile. "I am a countrywoman and I feel I am home again."

"You are from the north?"

He missed nothing: the accent, her dress, the austere beauty of her young-looking face framed in white hair beneath her cap. She could not be forty, he decided. Actually he was a little out in his estimate. She was in her forty-first year.

"I am a Frisian."

"From what part of Friesland?"

"We had a farm near Groningen. My husband was drowned in the floods last November and everything was swept away, so I came to my brother-in-law, Matthias van Breda."

"His son is one of my guards," said William.

"Yes, Johan. You may also know of my late husband, Gysbert, and of Ryk, my son, and of my other son, Lourens, who perished at Lowenstein," said Anna. "Gysbert and Ryk held your commission to cruise against Spanish commerce. They flew the lion of Nassau."

"I know your son Ryk. And I have been told of Lourens's heroic death. Are you returning to Friesland, Mevrou van Breda?" he asked.

"I am not yet free to go back. I have a loyal and devoted cousin who will reclaim my land for me. I must remain here."

"Your heart is in Friesland," he said with conviction.

"And yet I remain in Delft! It is a long story, Your Highness; and I take up your time."

"There is a seat under the lime trees. If you would care to tell me you will find me a good listener."

"I must not weary you with my personal troubles."

"I want to understand this unhappy people," he said; and there was sudden vehemence in his voice.

They sat side by side on the bench by the canal. The blown blossoms drifted down from the lime trees to be borne away in the flow of the water. Seldom interrupting, leaning a little forward with his elbow on his knee and his chin resting in his cupped hand, William listened as Anna told him fully of her life in Friesland, of her family, of Don Rodriguez d'Esquerdes. All the time he gazed at the flowing water and not at her.

". . . now you will see what has brought about my present unhappy situation," she said when she came to the end of her story. "I feel I must remain here under the eyes of those who suspect me until such time as I am cleared. It is a point of pride, if you will. I deem it no more than an adjustment of self-respect. I should never know an hour's happiness again if I did not vindicate myself. And, while I wait, hardly a day passes that some news does not come of fresh horrors of Don Rodriguez' contriving. To think I spared this monster when I had it in my power to destroy him! And yet at the time there seemed no alternative but to help him."

"You could not know he would thus scourge the south," said William gently.

"I was so sure of my faith at Oostermeer," said Anna, and her voice sounded tired and despairing. "I could not slay the Spaniard because I felt it was against all I believed in to murder him. Afterwards I thought I had been right in thinking that, for I appeared to have changed the heart of Don Rodriguez. He spared Oostermeer. I believe in freedom of religious worship; I believe that God intends us all to live together in brotherly union."

He said with extraordinary intensity:

"Do many think as you think?"

Anna heard his voice lilting on a cadence of hope; saw his face shine as a light was lit in his sombre eyes. A wave of happiness engulfed her and she cried out, sobbing in her joy:

"I was not wrong then?"

"No, you were right."

"No one, excepting yourself and Liesbet, my daughter-in-law, now dead, has said that. Because they love me a few believe in my personal integrity. Others have no word base enough to use of me—'traitor' seems to them too light a word."

"You were not wrong," he said, "but you are ahead of your time, thinking as you think, and, what is more, putting your convictions to the test. In a day or an age that neither you nor I shall see there will be religious toleration and freedom of thought for all. The fanaticism of the Calvinists almost wrecks my plans at times, and I am immeasurably uplifted to know that a Frisian woman has boldly stepped out on the broad road of toleration. You will understand what our aims must be: we must respect each other's religious beliefs and see that the common cause is the national cause; we must unite against foreign domination; we must ensure liberty of conscience for all the people of the Netherlands. And you are the first woman I have met to put this ideal to the proof."

"Talking to you has set me on my feet again," said Anna. "I can go on. The future is in the hands of God, but in the end all will be well; of that I am certain."

"Yes, in the end. . . . But this bitter present. Why in God's name must this unhappy country be thus stricken?"

The cry was wrung from him.

"Perhaps, Your Highness," said Anna with such burning sincerity that her words were purged of all taint of flattery, "perhaps it is so that your presence may shine the more brightly in the darkness of our night. There is a splendour to a star when there is only one shining in the sky."

He was very moved.

"I would that I might lead the people forth, but I am still in exile. I am here at great risk, for, should I fall into Spanish hands, I shall be haled before the council to answer a charge of high treason with the block my inevitable end. Although I have friends here and there I can stay with safety but a short time in the Netherlands."

"The resistance movement grows, Highness," she said. "It will not be long before you can test its strength and cross the Rhine openly, never to leave this land again. This is the darkest hour for you. The strength of the provinces grows apace. We shall throw off the yoke if we can but unite."

"Ah, therein lies success or failure. If we can unite."

He thought of the mighty and inarticulate force that was arising against Spanish oppression and Spanish contempt and knew that if it were not continually being decimated and disrupted by the discord amongst the Netherlanders, by the local and personal jealousies which rent the petty political life of the cities, it would be a force at once articulate and irresistible in its mightiness. And to him was assigned the task of harnessing that divergent and tremendous tide of resistance. All had gone so ill with him and the cause to which he had dedicated himself that he doubted whether so colossal an undertaking would prosper under his unlucky hand.

The answer to his dark thoughts fell from the lips of the Frisian woman at his side.

"God will give you the strength, Highness," she said, "and the people the will to unite."

With such steadfastness did she utter the words that the wariness that repeated disaster had instilled in him was dispersed.

"So be it," he said devoutly.

They parted, he to return to Dillenburg and an exile that was no more than a breathing space between forlorn lost battles and the clash of a mighty and victorious struggle in the future, she, with her basket and hope beating high in her heart, to Matthias van Breda's house, facing the limpid canal.

CHAPTER EIGHT

The year 1572 was a momentous time in the history of the Low Countries. The steadily increasing resistance of the Netherlanders on sea and on land began unmistakably to mark the beginning of the end of the overlordship of Spain.

Elizabeth of England, hard pressed and ever anxious to avoid war with Spain, had at last agreed to close the English ports to Dutch shipping. De la Marck and his Sea Beggars, having failed to obtain their customary supplies at Dover, starving and hard beset by the weather, sailed up the Meuse and, by a fortuitous set of circumstances, succeeded in capturing the important seaport of Brill. De la Marck flew the flag of Orange from the fortress and declared in the Prince's name that he was there on the soil of the Netherlands to free the people from the hated tenth penny tax and to make an end of the tyranny of Alva and his Spaniards.

Fresh successes crowned the unrelenting efforts of the Dutch in their struggle for freedom: Louis of Nassau seized Flushing and on every side the spirit of revolt blazed forth and the people, hungry and workless, demanded the Prince of Orange, and Alva was sandwiched uncomfortably between De la Marck in the north and Louis of Nassau in the south.

On the eighth day of July 1572, at the head of a considerable army, William of Nassau, Prince of Orange, crossed the Rhine at Duisburg.

The Estates of Holland elected him stadholder. However long and hard the road, William was never to fail or to forsake the people who trusted to him for deliverance. The stage was set and the curtain went up on the scene of an epic drama—the drama of a small people, faithful to the ideal of freedom, and heroically rallied to resist Spanish despotism. William of Orange was to go steadfastly on to the end of his life, although the end of the struggle was not then in sight. The curtain was not to be rung down on the unceasing struggle until 1648, when the Treaty of Münster was to bring the eighty years' war against Spain to a glorious conclusion.

ii

Thus it came about that the familiar figure of the Prince of Orange was often seen in the streets of Delft as that fateful year drew to its close. He sometimes entered the houses of the people and would drink a draught of beer from a blue earthenware mug with them. He rapidly became a local as well as a national figure, and, enhanced by the simplicity of his life and his habits, the surpassing greatness of the man came to be widely recognized.

As the months passed and the seasons succeeded one another in peaceful Delft Anna's persistance won her a grudging place in her brother-in-law's household. Matthias befriended her, timorously at first, but more boldly after it became known that the Prince had once seated himself beside her and had publicly conversed with her for at least half an hour. Getruida held aloof, unimpressed by the favour that Orange had shown Anna. She continued hard and unbending and was unbelievably spiteful in small ways; but Anna's growing popularity in Delft brought her many defenders, and even the tale of the rescue of Don Rodriguez often provoked no more than a comment that the action had certainly been ill advised, but assuredly not traitorous.

Chief among Anna's admirers was Michiel de Noot of the bodyguard of the Prince. He was a middle-aged widower of pleasing fortune and appearance and whenever the Prince was at the Prinsenhof he came round to the house of Matthias van Breda when he was not on duty. Anna loved to draw him and young Johan van Breda out in conversation, which she always directed in such a manner that they would tell her of the sayings and doings of the Prince. William had become the surety for final good for her. She learned of the magnificence of his resplendent youth at the imperial court of the Emperor Charles; of his life in his own palace in Brussels; of his confiscated estates in Brabant. And now she knew him as a prince without his royal revenues, stripped of wealth and station, and yet immeasurably the greater for the vast sacrifices he had made, his faith in himself secured by the knowledge that the people looked to him to support them in their coming ordeals.

Now Haarlem was beleaguered. De la Marck's force, advancing to its relief, had been attacked by a strong detachment of Spaniards. The battle had been fought in a whirling snowstorm and had ended in the rout of the Dutch, and Ryk van Breda had been ordered by De la Marck himself to make his way at once to Delft to inform the Prince of the disaster.

The interview with the Prince had been a shattering experience. Ryk left his presence and stumbled on through the falling snow to his uncle's house. Spent and battle-stained, unutterably weary, he found the door of Matthias's house and, not pausing to knock, opened it and entered quietly.

The door of the living room at the end of the short passage was ajar. Ryk pushed it wider open with his toe and stood motionless, recovering himself, and taking in the scene before him.

The only light in the large room came from a lantern fixed to the wall. The room was full of moving shadows that took their shape from the flickering of the flames in the hearth. An atmosphere of drowsiness and tranquillity invested the blue-tiled apartment. The light of the fire was reflected rosily in the tiles and on the burnished surfaces of the brass objects about the hearth; in the semi-darkness it illuminated a helmet set down on the table and shimmered on the cuirass of a tall soldier sitting on a bench with his back against the table; it showed Ryk his mother sitting on the lovers' bench beside a young girl; it was merciless to Matthias and shone full on his lined face and white hair and danced on the glaze of the blue mug he held in his hand; it missed out Getruida altogether, for she sat in complete shadow and only the grey pallor of her face showed up in a strange way, like a wan moon in an uncertain dusk.

Michiel de Noot, with his eyes on Anna, broke the silence which had held the little company and had given Ryk an opportunity to calm himself.

"I must be getting back," he said. "There will be news any time now."

"It may be that Haarlem is saved," said Anna.

"It would be difficult to distinguish friend from foe in weather like this," the girl at Anna's side said.

Ryk noticed her particularly now. He liked her gentle voice. She was fair-haired and fresh-complexioned. She was a little nervous, he saw, for her small, square hands kept clasping and unclasping themselves on her lap. She cannot be a day older than sixteen, he decided, and wondered who she was.

"One finds out fast enough, Minetje," Anna commented. Ryk saw the shadow on her face as she added: "I wonder whether Ryk was with De la Marck's troops today?"

"I can find out for you," said Michiel de Noot comfortingly. "In fact I shall return to the Prinsenhof at once, and that will give me time to make inquiries before I relieve the man on guard. But do not worry, Mevrou van Breda, your son will be all right."

This was a fitting moment to announce his presence, Ryk thought; but he stayed quietly where he was, for he was fascinated by the little scene being enacted before him. He was beginning to be aware that many currents crisscrossed beneath that apparently serene surface.

Michiel de Noot was concentrated on Anna; his eyes barely left her face. Ryk realized with something of a shock that his mother was free to marry again, and that there was a man—or men, he mentally corrected himself, for there was his uncle Gerard to be considered—openly anxious to win her. He saw Anna through new eyes. She was beautiful still and there was always the magnetism of her boundless energy. She had an all-embracing sympathy. Perhaps that is really the secret of her attraction, Ryk thought, this infinite interest she has in her fellow creatures.

Anna rose from the lovers' bench.

"That is very good of you," she said, addressing Michiel de Noot. "And thank you."

There was a little smile on her lips. Ryk saw all the eyes in the room 'were fastened on her as she stood there with the light of the fire playing over her tall figure—Matthias's with kindly regard, De Noot's with adoration, the young girl's with affection, and Getruida's with a blank inscrutability.

Getruida moved impatiently in her dark corner, and from the pallid circle of her face her voice issued sharply:

"You are overanxious, Anna. Ryk was probably not with De la Marck at all."

It would be a pleasure to prove her wrong, Ryk thought. Now was the moment for a dramatic entry. He pushed the door open and stepped into the room.

In an instant they were all on their feet and Anna was at his side.

"Ryk!"

"De la Marck's force has been routed," Ryk said at once. "A thousand were slain and many taken prisoner. I brought the tidings to the Prince."

Anna's hands were exploring his limbs.

"Only the stains of battle, Mother," he said. "I am unhurt."

"Can Haarlem hold out, do you think?" Anna asked.

"As long as supplies can reach the city it will not fall."

"Haarlem can hold out only as long as the ice lasts," said Michiel de Noot. "If the blockade is not broken before the thaw sets in there is little hope for Haarlem."

"The Prince will send help," said the girl Minetje.

"You cannot send what you have not got," said De Noot. "If Louis of Nassau can come with an army all will be well."

"I leave it to the Prince," said Ryk.

He caught the eye of Minetje and she smiled shyly at him.

"This is Minetje van Wyck," said Anna, drawing the girl forward. "Her grandfather's house is but three streets away."

"Your father is Cornelis van Wyck?" Ryk asked her.

"Yes."

Inconsequently Ryk's thoughts went back to a conversation he had had with Anna in this very house. She had told him he ought to marry.

Perhaps his future wife had just been presented to him. His mind instantly conjured up a vision of Liesbet, but he banished it.

The girl before him was sweet and fair. After the exhaustion and frustration of that bitter day he felt as though he had stepped out of an unquiet world ringing with the noise and clamour of battle into another filled to the brim with light.

He smiled brilliantly at the rosy-cheeked daughter of Cornelis van Wyck.

iii

Michiel de Noot wished them all a good night and left. Matthias walked with him to the gates of the Prinsenhof. Ryk escorted Minetje van Wyck home, and thus the two women were left alone together in the living room.

"And so to bed," said Anna conversationally to Getruida as she moved about putting things in order.

Getruida vouchsafed no reply. Anna was accustomed to her sullen silences and generally paid no heed to them; but she found Getruida's unfriendliness irksome tonight and wished that their relationship might be more pleasant.

Anna longed for home. It would be happiness indeed to go back to Oostermeer. Gerard was a vile correspondent. He wrote on an average twice a year and his letters were laboured and curiously blank. Anna gathered that the semblance of the old house had been built again on the original foundations, that the soil was still too impregnated with salt to produce good crops, that Gerard continued in good health, that his grandson was growing into a clever, sturdy boy. Beyond those meagre facts she knew nothing of the conditions existing in the north. As soon as Ryk was settled she would return and see for herself, Anna decided. It would be easier if he married; then there would be a woman to care for him. He had seemed to like Minetje, so perhaps something might come of the attraction, she reflected. And then she would like to know Haarlem was free. She hoped these two events would not be long delayed because she had no desire to marry again, and Michiel de Noot was not the man to give up while she was still in Delft. Michiel turned a conveniently deaf ear to her repeated refusals to marry him, but he would not be free to follow her to Friesland and that would put an end to his importuning. At Oostermeer Gerard might have the same inspired notion, Anna thought; but he was an understanding man and would never seek to persuade her against her will. I shall go north to Gerard, she thought. Dear Gerard. If I tell him I do not wish to marry again he will understand. He always understands. He is as the shadow of a rock in a weary land. . . .

Getruida's voice broke in unpleasantly on her thoughts.

"De Noot is always here," she remarked.

Anna lifted her head sharply. Now the fantastic battle was to begin.

again. She must not allow a scene to develop, she cautioned herself. She was tired and absent-minded, and in no mood to exercise patience.

"Johan introduced him to the house," Anna countered swiftly.

"That is not why he comes."

The frail thread of Anna's forbearance snapped. She would tolerate no more of Getruida's insinuations.

"What do you mean?" she demanded on a hard note.

Getruida did not answer. Her smile was indescribable—thin-lipped, crooked with malice and horrid suggestion.

"What do you mean?" Anna repeated.

Anna had enough sanity left to turn away when Getruida's face showed her enjoyment of the scene that was brewing. This would happen to-night, Anna thought, when her mind was at ease about Ryk, and she had been happy thinking about Oostermeer and Gerard and Michiel de Noot. She had almost given way, but now, perhaps, she would be able to hold out until Ryk and Matthias returned and by their presence put a bridle on Getruida's tongue.

"Michiel de Noot does not propose marriage, does he?" said Getruida, addressing Anna's resolutely turned back.

"What do you suppose?" Anna retorted.

"As he cannot possibly marry you, I must think what I think," said Getruida. "In his position he could not marry you. You seem to have forgotten that your reputation went with the Spanish don."

Anna faced about. She walked to Getruida's chair and stood in front of it, looking down upon her tormentor.

"He has heard the story of that from me," she said.

"You no doubt have your own way of telling it," Getruida said. "But De Noot is no fool. He will ask himself why a Catholic and a Spaniard leaves a house unburned when his orders are to burn the property of heretics, why he leaves a heretic alive to continue in heresy when he is pledged to destroy all heretics. Michiel de Noot is an experienced man. You will not deceive him. There is only one possible reason why Don Rodriguez spared Oostermeer and you and your household." Getruida half rose in her seat and brought her face nearer to Anna's. "You were alone with that man for weeks, Anna. I put it to you that he owed you for something other than his life. What man will marry you now, Anna?"

Rage gripped Anna. She seized her enemy's shoulders and held her with fingers that bit through the flabby flesh.

"I see now I need not have stayed," Anna said with quiet yet terrifying vehemence, her fingers probing like iron points deeper into Getruida's shoulders. "You will find mud to stir in the clearest pool. You made me feel I must remain here because my patriotism had been questioned. That was a reason that men might understand. Now, because this charge has been discredited, you attack my honour as a woman. You are evil, Getruida. Your thoughts befoul your home."

"He won't marry you, Anna. Michiel de Noot takes no Spaniard's leavings," Getruida jeered. "Take your hands off me."

"Take those words back," said Anna.

Getruida smiled as only she could smile.

"I could kill you," said Anna.

"You could," agreed Getruida. "It was different with the Spaniard, wasn't it? You could always put him in Gysbert's bed."

"Will you be quiet?" Anna cried.

She pushed Getruida into her chair and, holding her down with one hand, held the other over her lips, gagging her more or less effectively. Getruida wrenched at the hand that clamped her mouth and succeeded in dragging it away.

"What is it like to sleep with a Spaniard, Anna?" she gasped.

She had overdone it. The spell was broken. Anna saw too late that once again Getruida had forced her into a detestable scene. Their words and their actions had been distorted and unreal, images conjured up in Getruida's lonely, jealous mind, and she had unthinkingly played up to that unbalanced envy. She was ashamed of herself for having been so easily beguiled, and relieved now that she realized that she need never attach much importance to anything Getruida might choose to say.

Anna did a wanton, reckless thing. She laughed and said with deliberate mockery:

"That you will never know. You ought to be more attractive, Getruida, and then you could find out at first hand."

"You don't deny it, then?" Getruida panted in her excitement.

She is mad, Anna thought; and was instantly sober.

"You have always been envious of me," she said. "And that envy is still the cause of all the trouble. When we were young we both wanted Gysbert. I married him and you took Gysbert's brother. And now that I am a widow and free to take another husband if I choose the old jealousy has arisen. This is very ugly. I shall return to Oostermeer as soon as I feel I can leave Ryk. I know there is no reason for me to stay here. You have set me free, Getruida. I ought to be grateful to you."

"Adulteress," muttered Getruida.

Anna received the epithet calmly.

"I strongly advise you not to repeat that word to anyone—particularly to Michiel de Noot. He'll either duck you in the canal or ask the Prince to say a word to you. I imagine the Prince would be on my side and not on yours. This affair is best kept between you and me. Have sense enough to perceive the truth of that, if you can."

There was the sound of the front door being opened.

"Matthias and Ryk have returned," Anna urged. "You will do what you will do, I suppose; but for pity's sake let us keep these indecencies to ourselves until a happier time."

Both women confronted the men smilingly as they entered.

"And so to bed," said Anna, genuinely smiling as she said it, recollecting that those had been her precise words before Getruida had launched her astonishing attack.

Suddenly her spirits soared. Ryk was with her and would be safely under Matthias's roof for one night at least; she felt she had Getruida's measure at last; and it was undeniably refreshing at her age to have two men very keenly interested in her even if nothing was ever to come of their devotion; and soon, very soon, perhaps, she would go home to Oostermeer.

Ryk looked long at Anna. She was not young, yet tonight her face had the radiance of youth in it. Was it her unconquerable spirit shining through? Was it because she was in love with Michiel de Noot? He could not answer his own questions. He did not understand her in the least and for that reason he was all the more enchanted. It seemed to him that she would never grow old or dull.

When quiet had settled on the house Anna lay awake. She was happily planning what she would do at Oostermeer. Her return seemed so near —almost within her grasp. Towards morning, with that thought uppermost in her mind, she fell into a restful sleep.

iv

In the spring Ryk and Minetje van Wyck were married, and beleaguered Haarlem was cut off from ice-borne supplies by the early thaw. Erratic communication with the starving city was maintained by means of carrier pigeons. Before mid-July William's attempted relief had failed and Haarlem fell.

Anna was still in Delft. Minetje was expecting a child and Ryk was away with the Sea Beggars. That summer was a black time for William and his supporters, and there was a general feeling of depression among the Orange party. As matters stood, Anna felt she could not leave. She moved to Ryk's tiny house beyond the square and waited for the baby to be born, and prayed that better days lay ahead for them all.

The tide of defeat had flowed fast, but it turned almost as quickly. The Sea Beggars intercepted the Spanish silver fleet and Alva's armies, impatient and unpaid, mutinied. The duke, however, soon had the situation under control and sent his son to invest the Orange city of Alkmaar. The blockading Spaniards were forced to retreat when the sea, flooding over the land from the breached dyke, swept over their encampment. Finally the naval battle at Enkhuizen on the Zuider Zee ended in a decisive victory and Alva's admiral was captured and his fleet scattered. This victory established the ascendancy of the Netherlanders on the sea and was to lead to Alva's recall.

Early in the New Year Anna's second granddaughter, Juliana, was born. When the child was a month old Ryk returned for a few weeks. He had recently called in at Falmouth harbour and had spent several days at Bodrugan and had seen how well his niece, Anna Maria, had fared in the care of her foster parents. They called her Anne-Marie, he told his mother. Anna Maria was a lively child, full of grace, and spoke English so fluently for her tender years that he had been amazed. Anna listened raptly to all he had to tell her of the granddaughter she had never seen. Anna asked him whether Anna Maria and her cousin, the infant Juliana, were alike. Ryk answered emphatically in the negative. Both little girls were fair, he said, but there the resemblance ended.

In these days Anna's thoughts dwelt lovingly on Anna Maria in far-away England. She made a frock for the little girl, measuring it on a neighbour's child who was nearly four years old. When Ryk touched at an English port again she meant to send it to her granddaughter at Bodrugan. And she decided to send a message to Richard Barradale to ask him if he would teach Anna Maria the little Dutch he had so that she might have some smattering of her mother tongue. Her thoughts of the child tinged her plans for the future. She would live at Oostermeer with Anna Maria for company, and Gerard and his grandson as part of the household. Perhaps the two young creatures might marry, she thought, her plans striding away with her. Yes, she determined, as soon as the country is more settled Lourens's daughter shall come home.

She often smiled to herself while she worked and dreamed of the future. She and Anna Maria would have a good life together at Oostermeer. Of that she had no doubt whatsoever.

CHAPTER NINE

As it neared the sea the Rhine spread out into a network of fine streams and, built in the web of these natural waterways, Leyden, the fairest city in the Netherlands, rose up in the midst of broad and pleasant pastures and the villages and orchards of a peaceful countryside.

The hated Duke of Alva had been recalled and had been succeeded by Don Luis de Requesens, who forthwith set himself the task of bringing the stubborn Netherlanders to heel. He therefore resorted to arms and the Spanish forces, under Valdez, went to blockade Leyden.

The citizens met the crisis with resolute courage, trusting, under God, to their own valour, and to William to save them from surrender. Nor did they leave the issue to God and William of Orange in vain. Although they were completely cut off from their friends, contact was maintained by pigeon post, and occasionally pole vaulters, familiar with the lie of the level countryside, hopped over the canals and ditches and carried messages to the beleagued city under cover of darkness. In reply rockets were sent up from the ruined tower of unknown antiquity which occupied a commanding position in the heart of Leyden.

The Spaniards threw an impassable ring of steel about the city walls. They wasted neither men nor ammunition but sat down to await the outcome with confidence, for well they knew that famine and plague would soon do their work inexpensively for them.

In June William the Silent opened the Estates of Holland at Rotterdam. He put before the assembly the scheme he had devised for the relief of Leyden. He proposed that the dykes should be breached and the sea called in to float a fleet of canal barges over the twenty-two miles of submerged land to the gates of the city. It was a forlorn chance that would entail the loss of crops and cattle, of fields and homes and villages. The Estates agreed to William's desperate remedy, and of that decision was born the soul of a people.

The cities were as islands in the flood and in Delft and elsewhere the homes of both rich and poor alike were filled to overflowing as the refugees with their possessions on their backs, or conveyed in any sort of vehicle, continued to arrive from the flooded countryside.

On an evening in that fateful summer Anna stood on the city wall and saw the grey, greedy water of the sea licking up the land and sending long foamy fingers to slither sinuously through the fertile plots of cultivated soil hard by the walls. Residents and refugees had gathered on the walls to watch in spellbound fascination the sea, at their invitation, pursuing its ancient way.

Among them was the burgomaster of Delft, whose own farms and orchards were in the process of being swallowed up by the flood. It was a fitting moment for exhortation.

"My friends, better a drowned land than a lost land," he said, addressing the people in a firm voice. "The price required of us is paltry indeed if we are to be rid of the Spaniards, and if Leyden is saved. May the ocean reach to its walls and drown every Spaniard gathered there!"

The rest of his peroration was lost in the cheering. The burgomaster spoke for them all. There was not a man or a woman on the walls who did not feel that on the issue about to be tried in their sister city depended the future of the country, the fate of generations yet to be born. No longer was this merely a religious struggle: it had become a national affair.

ii

The summer wore on in sultriness and frustration. The winds and the tides seemed on the side of the Spaniards. The waters ate with agonizing slowness into the twenty-two miles that stretched between Leyden and the sea, creeping over the pastures of Schieland and Delftland, reaching Rynland, and at last were halted at the Landscheiding, the great bulwark erected across the land to guard against an accidental inundation of Leyden from high tides and burst dykes. Here the dammed waters rose to within a foot and a half of the top of the barrier, yet could not force a way over.

While Nature and the season lent their aid to Valdez plague and famine were rife in Leyden. But the siege was unwaveringly endured, for in their burgomaster, Adrian van der Werf, the citizens had a leader worthy of the cause of national freedom. Inspired by him and their own stout hearts, the strong bolstered the weak, and the citizens of Leyden maintained a firm front, although they were almost at their last gasp. They hurled defiance at the encircling enemy from battlement and tower, and bore with unflinching disdain the derision of the Spaniards, who deemed it an impossibility to bring the ocean so far for the relief of the starving city.

Early in September Michiel de Noot sought out Anna in Delft. He had come by barge from Rotterdam. He went at once to Ryk's house. Minetje informed him when he got there that Anna had returned to Matthias van Breda's house. She stood talking to him with a crowing infant in her arms, while young faces looked over her shoulder to take stock of the stranger.

"Why did she move back there?" Michiel de Noot demanded, not a little disturbed. He had never exchanged a hard word with Getruida van Breda, but he instinctively disliked and distrusted her.

"With this flooding my parents and my cousins came in to Delft from Schieland. My grandfather's house is crowded so I have taken in some of my relations," Minetje explained, pressing the baby's fat hand against her cheek. "At the time they came Mevrou van Breda was taken ill, and a woman was needed in the house to care for her. Therefore my mother-in-law went back. Now, although Aunt Getruida's sickness has passed, she remains because she feels we are overcrowded here. One day soon I hope we shall be in the same house again."

"I have news of your husband," Michiel de Noot told her. "He has just arrived from Zeeland and sends you greetings. He says he will come home at the first opportunity even if it is for no more than a few hours. And he wishes me to take back word of how you are all keeping."

"We are very well. And Baby Juliana is a picture of health as you can see," said Minetje proudly. "She has six teeth, but she makes no attempt to talk. There she is a little backward, perhaps, but otherwise she is very forward."

"Speech will come," said Michiel consolingly, extending a finger to brush the child's plump cheek. "Wait until she grows up! She will talk too much then. It is a way women have."

A chorus of giggles broke out behind Minetje. There were plenty of juvenile cousins, Michiel thought, backing away from the door. He went quickly down the short, shell-strewn path. He wished to see Anna. He hoped that when things were normal and Ryk was home with his young wife she would marry him. She would grace his fine house in the Hague one day, perhaps, he thought. That house, mirrored in the placid *gracht*, was too large for him alone now that his children had gone to homes of their own. He liked to picture Anna clad in rich, glowing silks, mistress of a patrician home. She would be in her proper setting. Despite the money and jewels and plate he had given for the cause he was still a comparatively wealthy man. He was glad of it because he had a strong desire to pour all his treasures at Anna's feet. And, with his wishful thinking to speed him on his way, he was soon at the house of Matthias van Breda.

Anna herself opened the door. He was no tongue-tied lad, but at sight of her words and thoughts fled. He bowed and entered and not a word did he utter. When they were facing each other in the blue-tiled living room, she with a warm, wide smile on her face, he felt completely at ease and happy.

"You are pleased to see me, Anna," he said.

"I did not know I could be so pleased to see you," she answered.

"You have changed your mind then?"

"No, but you are my dear friend, and I rejoice to see you."

She rebuked herself inwardly. It was not to be wondered at that Michiel de Noot renewed his suit with ardour every time he met her, for she seemed to encourage him without meaning it. She must be more casual, Anna told herself severely, a little colder. But she had been so delighted to find Michiel at the door, and it was her nature to show her feelings. . . .

"Friendship is not enough, Anna," Michiel said firmly.

"I still have no more to offer, Michiel."

"My beloved Anna——"

"Hush," she said. "Do not let us go through it all again. I promise you I have not changed my mind."

"One day I hope you will, Anna."

"Did you come just to tell me that?"

"My love for you is always uppermost in my mind," he said. "Therefore it appears first. But, as it happens, I have two messages for you from Ryk."

"You have seen Ryk!" she exclaimed.

"Indeed I have. He has become so wild and fierce-looking that he is a Sea Beggar among the rest."

"There is much to avenge," Anna observed.

The Sea Beggars had the reputation of being the foremost in ferocity and in nautical skill. They made it a rule never to give nor to take quarter and in their hearts they kept the flame of hatred and revenge against the oppressor at fever heat. It was from this fanatical but fine and tested material that William had built up a useful navy, and the Sea Beggars were the founders of the subsequent greatness of the Netherlands as a seafaring power.

"He has come with Admiral Boisot from Zeeland," Michiel explained. "The Sea Beggars have arrived in force to assist in the relief of Leyden. If the wind will blow and the tides run high enough, Anna, the Prince's design may yet be accomplished."

"Has the Prince recovered from his fever?" Anna asked.

"He is better. He so nearly died, Anna. If he had perished, with him would have perished the hopes of a nation. He lives in dread that Leyden will yield, not knowing that help is near."

"It is a miracle of courage how the people have held out for so long," said Anna. "They die of starvation and disease in hundreds daily. There is not a dog nor a cat nor yet a blade of grass left within the walls of Leyden, they tell me. But, Michiel, did Ryk give you no message for me?"

"The messages from Ryk were the reasons for my visit, and you have had to ask for them," he said. "I am to tell you from him that your granddaughter Anna Maria, in England, does very well and has blue eyes like your own; I am to give you his love; and I am to tell you to take the boy Dirk into your care if he should not return from the attack on Leyden."

"Dirk? I thought he was sure to be with Ryk. He has been on Ryk's ship ever since we rescued him at the time of the flood."

"Ryk thought he ought to be sent to some safe place. He is with the Widow van Zijl in Zoeterwoude. She has a brood of young children and is well known in the village, so you should have no difficulty in finding her."

"The past comes back," said Anna. "I have not set eyes on Dirk from the day of the flood, although Ryk has told me from time to time how he fared. When the Spaniards have gone I shall seek him out at Zoeterwoude."

So much had happened since the time of the flood in Friesland that the disaster had seemed a thousand miles away; but the mention of Dirk had sufficed to bring back as though it had happened yesterday the time she had lost Gysbert.

"That is all behind you, Anna," said Michiel de Noot gently.

She was aware of his arm about her. She leaned her head on his shoulder.

"I thought I was beginning to forget," she whispered.

"Come to me, Anna. Let me comfort and cherish you. I shall never fail you, my beloved Anna."

She lifted her hand and laid it against his bearded cheek. He moved it to his lips and kissed her palm.

"I know you would not," she said softly. "But, Michiel, please, I do not wish to marry again."

"We could make something of life together."

"No, my dear."

"Obstinate one, we grow no younger."

She moved away from him. She was thinking of Gerard waiting faithfully in the north. No, she could not choose between them. Also when she considered putting anyone in the particular place Gysbert had always had in her affections she knew it simply could not be done.

"I am sorry, Michiel," she said quietly. "But it is still no."

He flushed in sudden anger.

"You will not marry me, you will not let me go. If I were half a man I'd walk out."

"The choice is a free one," she observed.

He laughed helplessly.

"You have me every time, Anna. I love you for what you are. I should never be content with a lesser woman, having known you."

"Is that an appeal to my vanity, Michiel? I am both vain and coquettish, I think. I hardly know myself sometimes."

"No," he said with surprising perspicacity. "It may seem like it, but vanity and coquetry are weapons too petty for you to use. Your great need is for loving companionship. You are always giving out warmth and vitality to others and you must get some of it back. And then, of course, you can never bear to hurt anyone, Anna."

"I think you are too kind to me."

"No," he answered. "I could never be too kind to you. All this is really my fault. I know you still love the memory of your late husband. I don't want to believe you do and I try to make you think you have forgotten; but I saw in your face when I spoke of Dirk that memory was still fresh and green. I would give the earth, if I had it, if the years could be put back and you and I could start our lives together."

"Do not speak like this, Michiel," she begged. "It was better when we laughed and played with love. This goes too deep and finds old wounds."

"I see where I stand," he said soberly. "I shall not speak of love again; but if ever you would wish me to you will find I have not changed."

"I shall remember," she said; and her smile was grave and sweet.

"You have almost made me forget that I came to Delft on the Prince's business."

"Am I permitted to know?"

"It is the Prince's dread that Leyden will not know how near help is. The dykes are cut, a fleet of barges laden with food is ready to sail in the wake of the Sea Beggars. We wait only for the wind and the tide."

"Have messages been sent?"

"I have sent two for him by the difficult way—by canal and by jumping the ditches on a long pole. I have a third letter from the Prince and I am seeking a means of getting it to Leyden."

"I know a way," said Anna, and the blood began to beat in her throat with hidden excitement. "It is so simple it has every chance of success."

"What is it?" he asked with interest. He had a great respect for Anna's ideas. He had never known her wild or foolish in action, and he was certain she would always be resourceful and practical in an emergency.

"I will take a message," she said.

"You?"

"Listen," she said, leaning towards him, her face flushed and eager. "I have a plan. It will be easier for me to get within reasonable distance of Leyden than it will be for a man, as he must move by night. I shall take my countrywoman's basket and fill it with eggs and butter and go on a visit to my foster son, Dirk, at Zoeterwoude. It is hard by Leyden. And when once I am there it should not be difficult to get the Prince's letter delivered. An arrow over the wall would do it. I shall make a neat hole in one of the eggs and take out the yolk and the white. I shall put flour in the shell to make up the weight and with the flour the letter, and seal it again so that you would not tell that egg from the others in the basket."

"Zoeterwoude is held in strength by the Spaniards."

"As a woman with a basket of produce I shall get into Zoeterwoude without difficulty. I shall go by boat and take a roundabout route."

She outlined her plan still further. She saw indecision, anxiety, love expressed in his face in rapid sequence. When she had finished speaking she dropped her eyes and waited to hear him refuse to let her go. He would be too fearful to permit her to hazard her life. She felt very sorry for him, but characteristically she waited for him to come to his own decision.

Michiel de Noot was in the throes of an inward conflict. He had the wit to see that, fantastic and impossible as it would be for most women to carry through such an undertaking, Anna had the ability to accomplish the mission coolly and with some hope of success. There was something about her that gave her power over him and over others. He was superstitious about her. He had the belief that there was a star set in her brow and that she would be fortunate. He thought of William of Orange, spent by fever, waiting in the heat with the steaming swamps of Rotterdam about him. The rockets had not gone up from Leyden steeple. There had been a false rumour a week back that the city had surrendered. Although the Prince had stoutly refused to credit the news Michiel had been alarmed at the heightening of his fever. If no news came that Leyden intended to stand firm he feared for the Prince's life. Yes, he would let Anna venture, for he was convinced that some unseen influence guided her aright. The rockets must go up. His course was clear before him.

"Meet me in the guardroom of the Prinsenhof an hour after sunrise tomorrow," he said. "And have your egg prepared."

"Michiel!"

She breathed his name in ecstasy. Her face was aflame with animation and vivid with joy.

"You will get through, Anna, I feel certain," he said.

"In this moment I love you, Michiel," she said. "No, not gratitude. I would not reward you with so paltry a feeling. In a way I can't explain, you seem part of myself. I can also leap to a decision. You have freely given me an opportunity for which I have prayed ever since that miserable business of Don Rodriguez d'Esquerdes."

"Win through, Anna," he said sternly to cover his emotion. "I have trusted you with much."

"The rockets will go up from Leyden steeple," she vowed.

At the time he was impressed and uplifted by her tone of quiet confidence. Afterwards, when he was alone, he was suddenly assailed by a legion of fears. His mind was filled with all the stories of Spanish atrocities he had ever heard, and his dread of what might befall Anna magnified the most horrible of them a thousandfold. He had been mad to agree that she should try to outwit the soldiery of Valdez. She had bewitched him. The scheme was impossible. He had fancifully thought a star was set in her brow to prosper her; but if she essayed this hazardous undertaking a constellation would not save her.

He almost went back to her to stop her. It came to him that if he retracted he might lose her regard. When she had voiced her reason for wishing to make the attempt he had seen how it must present a means of vindication if she still smarted for the misunderstanding about the Spaniard. There was nothing for it; she must have her chance.

He passed the night on his knees at his bedside, praying to Almighty God to keep her from harm, and to keep him from holding her back. Heavy-eyed but calm, he awaited Anna in the guardroom next morning. They discussed the route she should follow and he gave her careful instructions in case there should be a reply from Leyden other than the usual signal.

He kissed her cheek in farewell and did not accompany her beyond the gate. He watched her walk along the canal until her fine figure dwindled in the distance.

He returned to Rotterdam that same day to watch with William of Orange for the flash of rockets from Leyden across the far, flat plain.

CHAPTER TEN

They were besieged. Day after day the citizens of Leyden went up to their ancient tower to see if the ocean had come over the dry land to their relief. But the weather vanes continued to point to the east and the retarded waters crept forward with appalling slowness. As she approached Zoeterwoude Anna saw the besieged mount to the ramparts and raise the standard and knew the city still held out.

She hid her boat in a clump of alders by the canalside and moored it securely. Then she walked into the village with her basket, and, having knocked at a cottage door to inquire where the Widow van Zijl lived, went slowly along the little street until she reached the place.

A tall lad was stacking peat in the yard of the widow's house. His head was uncovered and she saw he had flaxen hair. He was well grown and strong. It must be Dirk, she thought.

"Dirk," she called softly to him over the wall.

He looked up and saw her. He stared at her vaguely for a moment, and then recognition dawned in his eyes.

"Mevrou van Breda!" he exclaimed. "Do you bring me news of my captain?"

"You mean my son Ryk?"

His face was answer enough to her question. It lit up at the sound of the name.

"Have you come from him, mevrou? Am I to be allowed to join him on his ship?"

"As soon as Leyden is relieved," said Anna.

"He said I was too young to help in the relief of Leyden," burst out Dirk indignantly. "I can man a barge with the best of them. Look at me. I am as strong as a grown man."

"So you are, Dirk; but there are other ways of helping. Ryk has often told me how he relies upon you. And I am here as there is something he feels you can do."

The boy came up to her and laid his hand on her arm.

"I am ready. There is nothing I will not do," he said earnestly.

"Hush," said Anna. "This is very secret. Is there anyone near? And can we be overheard?"

"I can see over this wall in every direction, mevrou. You may speak without fear of being overheard."

"I will tell you quickly what Ryk says you must do," said Anna. "It is all in one sentence: serve the Prince."

"He does not need to tell me that."

"Listen. I have a message from the Prince which must reach the burgomaster of Leyden as soon as possible. Do you think you can get it into the city somehow or other before many more hours have passed?"

"There is an easy way," he said. "And it is safe. The Widow van Zijl does the laundry for the officers in the fortress of Lammen near the city walls. I shall go there presently and ask if there is any soiled linen and look about me. And when it is dusk I shall go again and I should be able to get the Prince's message over the wall, tied to a stone. If it is dark enough I may even get right under the wall and call to one of the sentries. You may leave it to me, mevrou."

"The message is in a letter in an egg. I shall give you the egg as we walk towards the door and no one will know we have exchanged anything."

"The good widow is with us," Dirk said.

"Do not say anything, not even to her."

The Widow van Zijl was bending over her washtub and the little kitchen was full of steam and the clamour of five young children. Anna introduced herself and afterwards the widow went back to her laundry and Anna set about preparing a meal for them all.

In the evening Dirk went to Lammen for the second time that day. With messages being delivered to Leyden from three different quarters it was inconceivable that none should get through. Perhaps this very night the rockets would go up and the suspense would be over.

She would go home in two days' time, Anna reflected. She wanted to stay for a short time in order to see something of Dirk.

Before Dirk returned from Lammen the rockets went up from the tower of Leyden, carrying their message of no surrender across the plain. The flashing of the rockets from nearby Leyden caused some commotion in Zoeterwoude. People ran from their houses, and the Spanish garrison lined up in the square, and in the midst of it Dirk returned.

The widow stirred the embers and heated a bowl of broth for the lad. Then she went out to put the clothes to soak against rubbing them through in the morning. While she was thus engaged Anna managed to question Dirk as to how things had gone.

"There was no difficulty," he said. "I waited until it was really dark. I crept up to the walls and hailed the sentry and threw the letter, which I had tied to a stone, at his feet. And I was here in Zoeterwoude with the washing when the rockets went up, so the message must have been delivered."

"There were three messages and a deputation," Anna told him. "Any one of the messages may have got through—it might well be that yours was the one. That we shall know when Leyden is relieved."

She spoke to the boy, drawing him out. It was obvious that Dirk worshipped Ryk. Anna hoped Ryk would have a son. There were only girls in the family so far. She leaned forward and stirred the embers again as the heat sank. One day she would sit enjoying a peat fire at Oostermeer with Anna Maria opposite her. She wondered if the frock she had made for the child had been a good fit.

Gazing into the red heart of the fire, she formed mental images of the peace and quiet of her life in the future. She would leave Delft very soon and go back home and make Oostermeer a fit place for Anna Maria. Gerard would have done wonders, she knew, but the hand of a woman would be needed. The years of her exile were over.

The glowing peat took on shapes of faëry—squares and cubes of lambent heat, tall towers of scarlet thinly barred with black. She gazed into the crimson heart of the fire and dreamed her dreams. Dirk saw she was far away from him and her surroundings, lost in thoughts he could not follow. He no longer spoke although he watched her. And a sense of peace was with them.

The square of red-hot peat crumbled and disintegrated into grey ash. The red glow faded, the fire castles fell.

Anna shivered, reading in the dying fire the death of her hopes.

She rebuked herself at once for her folly. There was no room for superstition, for vague belief in signs and portents in the thrusting, stirring times she lived in.

But not all her reasoning could recover her mood of happy contemplation. Oostermeer and her hope of living there again seemed to have receded into the shadows beyond her reach.

PART IV

CORNISH INTERLUDE

CHAPTER ELEVEN

WHILE ANNA VAN BREDA SAT STARING INTO THE PEAT FIRE THERE WERE rockets flashing out at sea on the west coast of England. A vessel had come too near inshore and lay with her back broken on the Manacles, sending up signals of distress.

Anne-Marie was very wide awake. She had her nose pressed against the windowpane and was looking out to sea and the lights flashing there. Anthony Barradale was with her. They were alone there together.

"It is a pity you are a girl, Anne-Marie," Anthony said. "If you had been a boy we might have gone down to the beach with the servants. Only Mother stayed."

Anne-Marie had not yet arrived at the stage of easy conversation. She did not reply, so Anthony went on speaking.

"I shall stay with you," he said. "Are you frightened?"

"Stay," said Anne-Marie, reaching for his hand. She pressed her nose still flatter against the pane, for just then another rocket had flashed redly in the dark night.

"The ship is in a line with Lydia's house," said Anthony. "She is a witch, you know, Anne-Marie, and draws ships onto the rocks when she wishes."

"Tell me," said Anne-Marie comfortably, not knowing what a witch was.

Anthony drew on his imagination and the maids' gossip.

"No one ventures near her house after dark," he said. "She will put a spell on you if she finds you. She holds intercourse with the Devil, and there are unearthly noises and muffled hoofbeats as the Devil rides his horse round and round her hut, and strange lights bob to and fro. Ben Trevanna says I am never to go anywhere near when the sun has set."

"Yes," said Anne-Marie on whom this recital of horrors had obviously been lost. Anthony bit his lip. She was so understanding that he never could remember what a very little maid she was.

"I wish you would grow up, Anne-Marie," he complained.

He fell to thinking. He was connecting up this shipwreck and others with the tales of bobbing lights round Lydia Wilson's shack. He had heard tales of the wreckers, and he wondered suddenly if Lydia were more wrecker than witch.

"There goes another," he exclaimed as a rocket flared.

"I saw it," cried the little girl. "Pretty, pretty."

At that moment Frances Barradale entered the nursery.

"Anthony," she scolded. "You have not got that baby out of her bed! She ought to be asleep."

"The noise woke her and I heard her and came in. And there were the rockets going up," he explained. "Will the ship break up, do you think?"

"I could not say," answered Frances.

"Do you think she was lured onto the rocks by a light from the land?" he pursued.

"Of what are you thinking, Anthony?" His mother's tone was guarded.

"Of Lydia Wilson," he said slowly.

"The currents are treacherous, Anthony. One wants a lighthouse on these dangerous points to warn shipping not to come too close inshore."

"I wondered whether Lydia wove a spell or showed a light."

"Neither," said Frances crisply. "You must have been gossiping with the servants, Anthony. Lydia's no more than a simple, unfortunate woman. Now, no more of lights and shipwrecks. Anne-Marie ought to be asleep. Come to your bed, my pretty, and I shall sit with you until you fall asleep. Go back to your room, Anthony, and put shipwrecks and lights and Lydia out of your mind. You imagine too much, my darling."

Frances Barradale noticed how Anthony kissed Anne-Marie's soft hand and brushed his fingers against her cheek. He had an extraordinary affection for his foster sister, which did not surprise her at all, for all at Bodrugan loved the little girl. She hoped that affairs in the Low Countries would take decades to settle down, as she could not bear the thought of parting with Anne-Marie. Now that Ryk was married and had a daughter of his own, perhaps the Van Breda family would be content to leave her at Bodrugan. It was disquieting, however, that the Dutch grandmother showed signs of taking an interest in the child.

When the children were asleep Frances Barradale watched at the window. Anthony is no longer a child, she thought. What had put it into his mind to suspect that strange things happened at Lydia Wilson's hovel? She must watch him closely, she decided, and try to discover what precisely he knew. She and Richard had known for a long while that Lydia's house was a meeting place, and a place of concealment, for smugglers; had known that Big Ben Trevenna was hand in glove with the woman and deliberately spread abroad tales of witchcraft and satanic goings on at the little cottage above the Manacles to cover the real activity there; had known that Sarah's husband, Martin Thomas, was head of the organization of smugglers operating in that area.

Frances wished that she did not know all these things. The burden of knowledge and responsibility was too much, and she always had a fear at the bottom of her heart that one day Richard would be dragged in willy-nilly. Her thoughts were dark, as dark as the night, for no more rockets were going up and the sea had claimed its prize.

PART V

ħOLLAND

CHAPTER TWELVE

IT WAS ONE THING TO GET INTO ZOETERWOUDE AND ANOTHER TO GET OUT of it, Anna discovered. In the first place her boat was not where she had left it in the clump of alders, and, secondly, the Spanish troops had gathered inwardly towards Leyden as the Landscheiding was taken and breached. And the congestion of soldiery grew worse as William's men successfully carried the Voorweg, the two main dykes left between Leyden and the oncoming sea.

Event pressed on event. Distant gunfire and the blaze of burning villages showed that Boisot was on his way; but, when Dutch hopes ran highest, the contrary wind blew again towards the east and the unwieldy fleet of barges settled in the mud of Rynland. Within Leyden itself the hearts of the starving citizens, uplifted when Boisot's salvos of artillery had been heard, were cast down to the depths as the news of the foundering fleet was obligingly relayed to them by the Spaniards around their walls. And this same sea that with capricious cruelty delayed the relief of the city also kept Anna marooned in Zoeterwoude. A boat was essential, as the flooded and muddy countryside was impassable and the only means of reaching Delft left open to her was by canal.

As Zoeterwoude grew daily more crammed with Spanish troops Anna resigned herself to the inevitable and settled down to life at the Widow van Zijl's. She was at the washtub one morning when a knock came at the door. The widow went to answer it. A Spanish sergeant was there and he demanded to know how many men she could accommodate as, with the abnormal increase of the garrison, the soldiers' quarters were hopelessly inadequate and there would have to be billeting in the village.

"I could take in one man," Anna heard the widow say. "I must keep the kitchen clear for the washing. I do the laundry for the garrison at Lammen, and other washing besides."

"You must take more."

"It is impossible. I am a poor widow with a brood of hungry children to support. We shall starve if I do not work and if the kitchen is always full of men I shall not be able to wash."

"Washing or no washing, four you must have," the sergeant stated authoritatively. "We would never find quarters for the men if we took any notice of excuses."

"The house is very small as you can see for yourself."

"I shall look round."

Anna had barely time to plunge her arms into the suds before a sergeant of the garrison stood before her.

"Who is this woman?" the sergeant demanded of the widow.

"She is my friend."

"You do not live in Zoeterwoude," he said. "I have never seen you before. Who are you?"

The sergeant came right up to Anna as he spoke. She thought quickly. It was too dangerous for anything but the truth.

"My name is Anna van Breda and normally I am a resident of Delft. I am a widow. I have come to stay for a time with my friend, who has also recently been widowed. I wished to help her. She is poor and must work very hard to keep her family. I brought her eggs and butter, for I know things go hard with her sometimes."

"So you come from Delft?" said the sergeant. "And Delft is the nest of your Prince of Orange. From Delft, you said?"

"Yes," said Anna firmly, and hoped she had not turned pale.

Suddenly the sergeant changed his mind about her. She looked handsome and harmless enough and he wanted room for his men.

"Well, get back to Delft then," he bawled surprisingly. "This is no time for visiting. We want soldiers in your place in this house. You get back to where you belong, and at once. A little water won't do you any harm. You Dutch are used to it on every side, anyway. And when you get your feet wet, mind you curse your Prince of Orange."

He laughed at his jest, and Anna smiled and did not dare catch the widow's eye.

"I shall leave at once," she said meekly, thankful to have got so easily out of what might have proved an awkward situation.

Her ready acceptance had been a mistake, she saw at once when a look of suspicion came over the sergeant's dull face.

"From Delft," he muttered. "Perhaps the captain ought to look into this."

"As you wish," said Anna, her heart sinking.

"When did you come?"

"About a fortnight ago."

"Were you not challenged?"

"No. And I did not expect to be challenged. It is of no consequence if a countrywoman like myself comes and goes."

"The matter requires investigation, I should say," the sergeant affirmed stubbornly. "I still do not understand how you just walked into the village and no one stopped you. Where were the guards?"

"I am in your hands, and I feel sure I shall be able to give a satisfactory explanation to your captain," Anna said.

The Widow van Zijl was looking at her. Anna saw she was holding one of Dirk's shirts and instantly she understood that he must not be implicated.

"I have some washing to deliver," said the Widow van Zijl. "I shall soon be back."

She did not wait for the sergeant's permission but went out of the room. She has gone to warn Dirk to keep out of the way, Anna thought.

It was an awkward moment. Anna began to rub the clothes with industry, leaving it to the sergeant to make the next move.

Now that they were alone the man gave her a long, appraising look. Anna caught his eye and smiled. A show of friendliness might not come amiss, she thought. And the longer she could keep him with her the longer Dirk would have to get clear of Zoeterwoude. Anna knew where the lad would go: he would seek out Ryk, settled in the mud of Rynland with the rest of Boisot's men. Ryk had tried to keep Dirk out of the worst fighting but it seemed it just had to be that he would be in the thick of it.

The Spaniard returned her smile and then looked round for a stool on which to sit. He sat down near the hearth and began to confide in Anna.

"I have been in this place for months," he told her. "And, believe me, you are the handsomest Dutchwoman I have seen in all that long time."

"I am not so young," Anna countered stolidly, slapping a soapy garment down on the board and rubbing it with vehemence.

"You wear very well, if I may be permitted to say so, mevrou."

He twirled his black moustachios and it was plain that he considered himself a dashing fellow. So this is the way of it, thought Anna, and forced herself to smile charmingly.

"I thought there was something different about you the moment I set eyes on you," he went on. "You are quick and graceful where the other women are slow and heavy."

They fell into conversation, which beguiled a little time. The Spaniard was often complimentary and Anna, going as warily as possible, adroitly avoided his overtures. He had not mentioned bringing her before the captain again. After some minutes she decided he was quite at home with her as he had arrived at the grumbling stage, and she was experienced enough to know that men only grumbled when they felt at ease with a woman, and she did not suppose a Spaniard differed vastly from other men in that respect. Not that she had an extensive knowledge of Spaniards—Don Rodriguez d'Esquerdes had been the only man of that nationality she had ever known, and in the end he had proved an absolute enigma. She dragged her thoughts back to the disconsolate sergeant astride his stool, and heard the latter part of his tirade against his lot.

". . . I have had the worst of fortune in this canal-ridden land. I ought to have achieved advancement long ago but jealousy has always kept me down—and interference. And after all these months here a higher-ranking sergeant from outside has superseded me, and I have been given the ignominious job of billet hunting. And to think of the months I have wasted in this little village, waiting for famine and plague to open Leyden's gates for us. Another week and the city would have fallen."

"Another week," Anna murmured. A great deal could happen in a week if the winds and the waves fought for them, she thought.

"And there's another matter," went on the sergeant, still full of griev-ance. "We were going to enter the city and put every man, woman, and child to the sword to cure them of their obstinacy, but now something different has to be arranged to rob the simple soldier of his pleasures. The fall of Leyden is to be an example to all heretics and they have to be weeded out as soon as the city is ours. The Inquisitor who can scent a heretic ten miles away has arrived to deal with them, and after the sorting out the city can be sacked. After all these months round the walls of Leyden to sort out Catholics and heretics at the last! Let them all perish together. It comes to the same thing in the end."

Anna bent her head over the washing.

The sergeant added as an afterthought:

"You are a Catholic, of course?"

It had come. For years in Friesland she had lied about her religion. It had been a matter of patriotic necessity in those days. Now she was free of that obligation. Anna raised her head.

"No," she said clearly. "I am of the new religion." And met his eyes boldly.

"Aha, brave one," he said, and smilingly he rose and approached her. "That was what I liked about you—your spirit. You are a heretic then, but not a snivelling one. But we will keep this little matter a secret, shall we? You're much too good-looking a woman to burn. It has never wor-ried me whether a woman be Catholic or heretic as long as she be fair. I have been lonely in this place and if I billet myself in this house and keep you here things might be much worse. What do you say, beautiful one? Let Don Rodriguez d'Esquerdes burn and torture the skinny heretics in Leyden. You shall escape him. I shall see to it."

"Don Rodriguez d'Esquerdes," Anna repeated, blanching to the lips. "Don Rodriguez d'Esquerdes."

"His name strikes terror to your heart, I see."

"I know him," Anna gasped, too shattered for thought.

"You know him!" the sergeant exclaimed, checked abruptly in his amatory advances by the expression on Anna's face.

Anna could not recover herself. At the back of her mind she had known she must meet Don Rodriguez again. She was aware of the sergeant's staring eyes. Still she could not speak.

"This matter needs investigation," said the bewildered fellow, stupidly falling back on what he had said before.

Anna made a great effort.

"I knew him in Friesland," she volunteered. "It was some years ago."

"You had better tell me more," he threatened blusteringly. To think he had almost come to terms with a heretic with Don Rodriguez d'Esquerdes about! He had had a narrow escape, but mercifully the woman had given herself away in time.

"There is not much to tell," said Anna. "He was attacked and injured. He came to my house and I nursed him and set him on his road again when he had recovered. And that is all."

"Don Rodriguez in the house of a heretic! I don't believe a word of it; but you will have the opportunity of telling him this preposterous tale to his face as he is here in Zoeterwoude."

"Nevertheless, it is true," said Anna.

"There is something very suspicious about your being here at all," the sergeant pursued. "I'll wash my hands of the whole business. I shall take you along to the captain. I came to find quarters for the men, not Dutch spies. Come with me at once."

"May I put a few things together?"

"Come as you are."

There was no help for it. She could gain no more time. Anna dried her hands on her apron, undid its bands, and hung it neatly on a peg.

"I am ready," she said.

And walked ahead of the Spaniard out of the house into the golden light of the September day.

ii

It was late in the afternoon before Anna saw Don Rodriguez d'Esquerdes. She had spent that long autumn day in the guardroom of the small Zoeterwoude prison, awaiting her summons to appear before the Inquisitor.

Don Rodriguez d'Esquerdes did not look up as Anna entered with the guards, although her clogs clattered on the stone floor. He was concentrated on some parchmentlike papers on the table, beneath which his booted legs stuck out stiffly. Anna stared at the top of his uncovered, grizzled head.

He knows I am here, Anna thought, and he cannot decide how to greet me. She felt more hopeful and confident now. If there was a loophole perhaps she would discover it through him. Once she had saved his life. . . .

"Leave the woman and wait in the anteroom until I call you. I wish to examine her alone," said Don Rodriguez, still not looking up.

The guards saluted and withdrew. There was a short silence. Don Rodriguez began to flick the stiff sheets of paper on the table sharply between his forefinger and thumb, the papers making gritty sounds like falling gravel. At last he raised his eyes and regarded Anna.

"Again it is you," he said.

Anna's heart sank as she saw his face. He had changed almost beyond recognition, and his eyes were terrifying. They were the coldest eyes she had ever seen. There was a strange blankness in them as though they were made of dark glass and there was nothing but emptiness behind them. It came to her that he was no longer altogether sane. A tremor of fear ran down her spine.

"Yes, it is I, Anna van Breda," she answered faintly.

"I would have known you anywhere," he said.

His eyes were fixed icily on her.

"Why are you not in Friesland?" he asked.

"It is the will of God," she answered. "The flood swept away my home and my husband was drowned. I live with relatives in Delft."

"Why did you go from Delft to Zoeterwoude?"

"To visit my friend, the Widow van Zijl."

"When I knew you, you did not visit washerwomen. Why should you change your ways now?"

"You forget the flood," Anna pointed out. "All I had I lost. My circumstances are very different."

"Have you no sons to support you?"

"My elder boy Lourens was killed, and the younger is married. Lourens married Liesbet. Do you remember Liesbet?"

A flicker of warmth came into Don Rodriguez's eyes.

"Yes, I remember her. What of her?"

"She died at the time of the flood."

"She gave me a pair of gauntlets," he said.

This was not the ordeal Anna had expected. Her heart lifted. He was each moment becoming more normal and reasonable. She said with deep feeling:

"You left those gauntlets in the kitchen at Oostermeer. I thank you from the bottom of my heart for sparing my home."

Her words had a startling effect on Don Rodriguez. He rose up in his seat and made passes in the air as though he warded off something. Anna shrank back from him.

"The judgment was God's," said Don Rodriguez harshly. "What I spared in my weakness He thought fit to sweep away. I fell into mortal sin when I disobeyed my orders and did not burn Oostermeer and destroy you and your household for heresy. Liesbet was not spared; but you were. You were left for me to destroy."

He advanced slowly round the side of the table towards Anna, who retreated until she stood with her back to the wall. When she could move no farther she waited quietly for him to come up to her, steeling her quivering flesh into rigidity.

"God in His mercy has given me a second chance," he told her, staring into her face. "It was my holy mission to root out heresy and I was false to my faith when I failed to denounce you. I have paid for that omission in suffering. I admitted my error and I have tried to atone by rigorous searching out of heretics, and the tortures I have devised for the guilty are ingenious beyond anything the Inquisition had contrived before me. Yet it availed me nothing. Above the wildest shrieks of the tortured I heard your voice; through the smoke and the flames of their burning I saw your face. You were the archheretic among them and I had let you go free. I knew God's punishment for me: no matter what measures I took to stamp out heresy, it was no reparation for the wrong I had done. Only when I had brought you to your doom should I be at peace with my conscience."

He lost control of himself. His face went livid and he raised his hands and brought them up to Anna's face, flexing his sinewy fingers.

"You will be tortured and burned alive," he shrieked. "It will be a slow torture and a slow burning. Slow as can be. You are a strong woman and you will not die easily. Confess! Confess!"

Anna pressed back into the stone wall until her shoulders were bruised. The dull pain in her back brought her to reason. As she could not escape there was no sense in trying to push through a wall and she might as well put a good face on it, she decided practically. And was immediately herself again. She thrust out her hand and pushed Don Rodriguez away and stepped into the centre of the room.

"I am a follower of Luther," she said clearly. "If that is what you want I freely confess it."

Her action calmed him. He lowered his hands and no longer menaced her.

"Shall I tell you why you escaped me before?" Don Rodriguez said more quietly. "I am incapable of gratitude, but I admired you. You have an indestructible spirit. It is a pity you are not a Catholic; you would have made a good one. That night when I left Oostermeer and you waited at the foot of the windmill I pictured you standing there with the windmill arms a cross above you. It was a symbol. It was the Cross to which I was bound. I struggled that night with my conscience all the way to Groningen. It was my duty to denounce you; and I failed. You have been a torment and a torture to me from the hour I blundered into your house and now, at the end, I am still in dark confusion of mind, whereas you are free in spirit. I can see in your face you are free. You are in the light while I sit in darkness. I do not understand why this should be; but I do understand that God has given you into my hand and this time I shall not fail."

"If the spirit is free, the body is of no importance," said Anna. "It is no more than a shell."

"The body is a betrayer," he said. "It can be made to suffer and to weaken the spirit. I have yet to examine you. I shall do so later."

He raised his voice and shouted a command. Almost at once the guards were in the room again.

"Take her to the cell at the foot of the steps. Put a double guard in the corridor. The woman will be examined later under torture," he said.

Anna bit her lip and struggled against a wave of faintness. She felt hard hands gripping her arms and in a moment she was out of the room and her swimming senses were slowly clearing.

iii

The cell was small and dank and there was a narrow aperture in the wall which let in a thin slit of light. The masonry was domed so that in the centre of the cell Anna could stand upright, but at the sides she had to crouch as the ceiling was too low. An unspeakable odour of corruption rose from the floor. As soon as the heavy door had been locked behind her Anna stumbled over to the aperture through which the pale light of late evening flowed. Stooping, she pressed her face to the oblong of air, gasping because the stench from the floor was almost overpowering.

There was a sound at the door but Anna did not move. The guard put an eye to the grating and peered into the cell. It was remarkable how each prisoner in turn made straight for the air vent, he thought, and crouched there until he fell from exhaustion.

The evening light faded and night came on. Anna could see nothing except a blank wall, but at least one knew whether it was night or day. Now it was night. There was a breeze, and gusts of pure air fanned her cheeks. Her mind was dulled. She was concentrated on not moving. If she could keep quite still and not shuffle her feet on the floor the dreadful vapours would not rise. Each time a guard passed her door the thought came to her that she should rush to the grating and asked to be released; but she had wit enough left to perceive that such a plea would invite the mocking ridicule of her tormentors and not improve her condition. She must fix her mind on not moving. To fall down on that reeking floor was to perish. She braced her fingers, finding purchase for her clinging grip on the uneven faces of the stones of the cell wall. Once, deliberately, as the hours wore on and she found herself barely conscious, she rubbed the fingers of one hand on the stone so that the pain should keep her clinging like a fly in that huddled attitude with her face to the air.

There was not a muscle that did not ache. Long shivers ran up and down her body with the effort of holding her unnatural position. Perspiration started to her forehead and ran down her face. She set her teeth, struggling against a mortal weariness. It came to her that this must be the first stage of her torture.

There were periods of blackness, almost of unconsciousness. Each time when she came back to an awareness of her surroundings she found that by some miracle she was still clinging tenaciously to the air vent.

Hours passed but she had no consciousness of time. She was roused suddenly from her apathy by the crisp crack of gunfire, quite near at hand, it seemed. The guards began an animated discussion at the far end of the corridor.

Anna felt her knees give under her. She made a superhuman effort
and braced herself, trying to take some of her weight on her elbows. She
relapsed into partial unconsciousness again and only the will to keep her
face to the air kept her swaying on her feet. She was brought somewhat
to herself by the sound of the key turning in the lock. The heavy door
swung open behind her.

She would not turn or release herself from the agony of her cramped
position. It was the next stage of the torture. They were coming to pull
her down onto that obscene, ordurous floor as she had not collapsed into
its filth. All her life she had been fanatically clean. Don Rodriguez knew
that. It was the worst thing they could do to her, thrusting her into this
vile spot. But they should not pull her to that floor. She would hold on.
. . . They would have to break her fingers to loosen her grip. . . . Oceans
of time broke over her tortured body.

Someone entered. She gasped and choked as the foulness reached to
her at the aperture. There were footsteps behind her. Her fingers were
steel prongs clinging to the wall.

"Anna!"

It was Don Rodriguez d'Esquerdes himself. He had come in person to
drag her down to that loathsome floor. She felt his arm encircle her waist
and braced every muscle for resistance.

"Come away from here," he whispered urgently, his arm supporting
her. "Quickly. There is no time to lose."

This was the continuation of the torture, Anna thought. He had said
that he had some ingenious devices and this certainly was one of them.
It was a ruse to get her off her guard. She would not relax.

"I have sent away the guards," he said. "Come, Anna."

She made no answer. He wrenched her suddenly from the wall and
staggered with her out of that fetid place. As he released her she collapsed on the floor of the corridor. As she lay there she saw him lock the
cell door and hang the keys carefully on a peg. He is very neat, she
thought remotely, leaving it all tidy for the next one. . . .

Anna forced herself to her knees, to her feet. She was free if she could
find a way out of the prison. There was only Don Rodriguez to overcome.
Like a creature at bay, she backed against the wall, waiting for life to
come back to her cramped limbs.

"What do you want of me?" she managed to whisper.

"Here is water," he said, and handed her some in a beaker. "I am
releasing you. You must go at once. There is a door at the back of the
building. Leave Zoeterwoude and on no account return."

He is really mad, thought Anna. It is a trap, a way to get me to the
torture chamber without a struggle.

"Do you not hear me, Anna?"

"I hear you," she muttered.

"Time is short. Are you able to walk now?"

She went up to him and clutched his arm.

"What fiendish jest is this?" she asked. "Is it a new way of introducing victims to the torture chamber?"

He covered her hand with his own and his face worked uncontrollably. The horn lantern on the wall flickered and shadows leapt tormentedly from floor to wall, from wall to ceiling; and their own shadows, long and grotesque, reached up the corridor in swollen, shapeless bands of black.

"The Dutch are attacking not far away," Don Rodriguez said. "The garrison has been called out. I sent the guards away on a pretext. In the confusion you should be able to get away. There is no one who dares question me."

"You give me my life," said Anna, trembling.

"As once you gave me mine."

She looked closely at him. His face was drawn and ill-looking but something of life had returned to his eyes. He met her gaze steadily. At last he lifted her hand and held it in his own.

"Your hands were always my undoing," he said. "They are so beautiful."

"I understand," said Anna, barely heeding him and answering the question in her mind. Don Rodriguez had come to himself. He had been in a dreadful dream and he had awakened from it.

"No, you do not understand," he contradicted her gently. "I have failed again. Tonight I had determined you should be taken to the torture chamber, tomorrow you were to be burned at the stake. I was about to send the guards into the cell for you when the commotion began. Then, to my horror, I discovered how happy I was to find that there was a way out for you. I stayed alone until I had fought it all out with myself. Then I sent the guards to report at Lammen. The battle between me and my conscience is over. I have lost it. Twice over I have failed in my duty and I am doomed to everlasting perdition. The chance to atone was given me and I have not taken it. Anna, I cannot harm a hair of your head. Again you escape me, as you always will escape me, no matter what the circumstances."

"What will you do?" Anna asked. "What is to become of you?"

"I shall resign from the position I grace so ill," he returned with a faint smile. "And the rest, I suppose, will lie with the Chief Inquisitor."

"Come with me," said Anna.

"That is impossible," he said. "With one or two exceptions I am the most hated man in the Netherlands. And where would we go?"

"To Friesland," she said. "The ruins of Oostermeer are still standing, and that is the one spot on earth I can truly call my own."

"Would you hide me there again?" he jested.

"We will think when we get there," she answered soberly.

"We talk like children," he said. "And underneath you are very practical. You are a strange woman, Anna. You combine the shrewd wit of the peasant with the hands and heart of a princess. Where did you get your hands, Anna? And your proud carriage? I never knew a woman walk so well. Even in clogs you walk beautifully."

"Far back in my ancestry on my mother's side there was a baron," she said, falling in with his mood and talking of unimportant things when matters of life and death were at stake. "Even for a baron he was debauched and we are very ashamed of him as an ancestor. We prefer the peasant stock."

"I prefer the enchanting blend," he said gallantly. "If I were half a man I would go with you to Friesland and see what would happen. But I am a Catholic first, and then a man."

"Forget all that and come."

"I think you know I must not."

"Yes, I know," she said. She smiled at him and her face was soft and sweet. "I know our lives can never be lived together. But this much I promise you: wherever I go, whatever I may hear ill of you, I shall always think of you only as I personally have known you."

"That is how I would like you to remember me."

"You are at peace now," she said.

"Yes. For years I have played a cruel part, trying to make others suffer for what you should have suffered perhaps. I see I was wrong. I am at peace at last. Come now to the postern. Soon it will be too late."

They parted at the little gate in the wall. Don Rodriguez watched Anna slip away like a shadow. When he could no longer see her he sighed and shuddered.

It was as though he passed from life to death.

iv

The night wore on. Anna slipped her feet out of her clogs. She washed them in the first stream she reached and, carrying them in her hand, walked along the muddy canal bank out of Zoeterwoude.

There was noise and confusion everywhere. Spanish oaths and low growling tones from Dutch civilians, shouting in both languages, sodden blows on solid flesh, were the strange accompaniments to the din of the night. She could not think what was happening. She determined, therefore, to make her way with all speed towards the distant, irregularly coughing guns which might lead her to Boisot's men, and perhaps among the Sea Beggars she might find Ryk. There was the tang of smoke in the air from a far-off burning village, and there were farmsteads on fire close at hand. It was terrifying to be alone in the mystery and violence of the night.

Anna began to run. She did not fear death, but she had a tremendous urge to live her life to the end. She wanted time to work out the problem of Don Rodriguez and, above all, she longed to reach Delft and to speak just once more with the Prince of Orange and ask him what he made of it all.

Anna ran until she approached the clump of alders where she had left her boat. She might find another boat there. She found nothing and, although she had not expected such good fortune, the disappointment left her with a tired, flat feeling. She sank down by the canalside. She saw the silvery gleam of the water sweeping its gradual way into the lifting darkness, the alders glistening; and in the distance there was always the urgency of guns and shooting flames. . . .

Anna put an arm over her eyes. If only it can be peaceful for one minute, she thought, I shall be able to go on. She went on sitting there and must have dozed.

She was dragged abruptly from her short-lived sleep by a new conglomeration of sounds. There was a babel of angry, shouting voices, a clashing of steel, the rush and clatter of running feet in the village she had left behind her.

She staggered to her feet and gazed wildly about her. She saw the night was almost spent and soon the day would break. Now there was clamour and confusion behind as well as before her. It flashed through her mind that Boisot's men were attacking in two places. There was still no gunfire coming from Zoeterwoude, so perhaps they were taking the village by surprise and using daggers and pikes in a hand-to-hand combat, while the main body of the Spanish troops had been drawn off to meet the distant challenge. If that was so she would meet the Sea Beggars sooner than she had thought. As she was caught between two fires she decided to return to Zoeterwoude.

She walked slowly. When she came to the outskirts of Zoeterwoude there seemed to be no fighting. Ahead there was a clattering river of sound as an ever-growing throng of people in clogs ran swiftly over the cobbles. They all ran one way, screaming. She had not realized there were so many people in Zoeterwoude. They must all have left their houses, old and young, rich and poor, to run in the streets. She caught sight of a thin stream of women coming in from an alley and began to run towards them to find out what was happening. But she was too weary to catch them up and they were too eager to notice her. Anna followed them, running as quickly as she could, stumbling every now and again as her clogs slipped on the cobbles.

Once she was brought to her knees. She put her hands down and rested on them for a moment. She had not known one could be so tired and live. She saw now that a windmill was alight. It burned fiercely like a great candle. Its arms were whirling in the wind.

"The wind," Anna cried aloud, getting to her feet. "The wind."

The wind was in the northwest, in the right direction. The miracle of a favourable wind and a high tide was to be vouchsafed them. Leyden would be saved as soon as the pent-up waters could be blown through the gashed dykes. It was the fitting end to the sleepless, untiring energy of William, the Prince of Orange.

The flaming arms of the windmill were turning. Joy filled Anna. She looked about her, but she was alone. The shouting and the screaming ahead were demoniac. Musket shots rang out for the first time. And, as if the first shot had been the signal, the arms of the windmill ground to a standstill as the mechanism burned out, and stretched themselves in a fiery cross against the brightening sky.

Anna gathered up her skirts and fled on with the strength of great fear. As she turned into the principal street she saw with horror that the crowd had converged on the prison, that Spanish soldiers, the last of the garrison, were firing spasmodically from the low ramparts, that the shouting mob of men and women was heaving like a sea at the wide-open gates.

A piercing, exultant howl burst from the mob. And the waves of humanity fell bubbling back and forth.

V

Don Rodriguez d'Esquerdes also saw with great clarity the windmill burning beyond Zoeterwoude. He saw the flaming arms turn swiftly in the stiffening wind.

His life was about to end. A wild, white, featureless sea of faces confronted him. His captors held his arms and prepared to thrust him out to the mob.

The burning arms of the windmill were suddenly transfixed and a fiery cross stood out against the sky. In the last minute of his life he thought it had been given him to read the riddle of existence: he, all men, lived more for the long time they should not see than for the little they held of time.

He motioned them to take their hands from him. He stood for an instantly bodily free, and released also in his mind. It was over, this was the end.

He advanced unfalteringly towards the waiting people; felt clutching hands; and went down under the death-dealing clogs.

CHAPTER THIRTEEN

The dusk of the autumn evening descended. The gables and trees and rooftops of Delft rose above the walls in the beauty of muted colours, which faded each moment as the light failed.

In the dimness of the approaching night Anna secured her boat. She made her way at once to Ryk's house to change her soiled, stained garments before presenting herself at the Prinsenhof. She passed unnoticed through the deserted streets as the citizens were in their houses, and the canals were silent beneath their flanking trees.

When she reached the Prinsenhof she gave her name to the sentry and was admitted almost at once.

The Prince was seated at a paper-strewn table. He was wearing a close-fitting skullcap, and the immaculate whiteness of his ruff seemed to accentuate the lines on his face. It was plain he had been very ill.

Anna curtseyed at the door and came forward into the room as he motioned her to advance. She was dressed as for a great occasion in a dark silk dress. It was her best, the only frock she had at Ryk's house. It was plainly made and well cut and her white cap and white ruff set it off to perfection. She stood before the Prince, her hands clasped lightly in front of her.

"Pray be seated," he said.

"I can tell you, Highness, that Leyden holds out and that the wind blows from the northwest and the waters are rising fast," she said. "But in truth I am no accredited messenger. It was for a private reason I sought you out. If you have not the mind to hear me now, please tell me. Perhaps, Highness, some other day there will be time to tell you of my trouble."

"I have a few moments at my disposal," he answered. "I should like to hear what you wish to tell me."

Anna sat very upright in the chair that had been placed for her. She felt she might lose her composure and break down in wild tears. She stared at the floor until she was certain her voice would be steady.

"You have had a long day, I think," William said gently. "I am in no hurry."

She made a quick, nervous gesture with her hands.

"If you will bear with me I shall tell you from the beginning when I went to Zoeterwoude," she said in a low voice. "If I do not make myself clear, please check me."

She told him then in detail of all that had befallen her since she had left Delft and of the events that had led to Don Rodriguez's shocking death at yesterday's dawn.

"I am calm now, Highness," she finished. "Yesterday in Zoeterwoude they thought me mad. While the crowd was tearing Don Rodriguez limb from limb I was on the fringe of it. I beat with my clenched fists on the back of the man in front of me and demanded to know what was happening. He told me the accursed inquisitor was paying his debt to the Dutch people in full. I cried out that they should desist, for he had shown me mercy and kindness. I screamed and was as demented as anyone there. Afterwards they led me away. They thought I had lost my reason. It seemed strange to them that I, the woman they had set out to rescue from a hideous death, should be the only one to plead for the Spaniard."

"How had they known where you were?"

"Dirk, warned by the widow, fled to Boisot and there discovered my son Ryk. It was decided to save me if possible. The plan was simple— a small detachment of Sea Beggars was detailed to burn a village and to fire guns and to behave in every way as though a big attack was impending. The feint was successful. Most of the Spanish troops in Zoeterwoude went to meet an attack which threatened and did not materialize.

With the garrison out of the way the villagers of Zoeterwoude and the neighbouring hamlets stormed the prison in order to set me free. Don Rodriguez told them he had set me at liberty. They did not believe him. They slew him, and I was there, shrieking in his defence, and I could not save him. He made the supreme sacrifice for me."

William the Silent had been sitting with his elbow resting on the table and his head supported in his hand, listening to Anna's story. Now he raised his head. His dark eyes were full of a great compassion and a great understanding.

"Mevrou van Breda," he said, "you have come to me because you do not understand why the guerdon of Don Rodriguez should have been a dreadful death. Against his conscience he had always been your friend. When he has died this brutal death you ask yourself why God permits these things to happen. Is not this so?"

She inclined her head.

"I have not been able to pray since it happened," she said very low. "There is a veil between me and what I once believed right."

"If you lose your faith in God you lose all. The ways of the Almighty are His own. We do our best to further His kingdom on earth to the limit of the powers He has given us, but we do not presume to read His mind. Mevrou, do not think of yourself as an individual, think of yourself as one of many. Other feet have trodden your hard road, other hearts have cried out from the depths against seeming injustice."

"Yourself," she whispered. "Yourself for one, Highness."

She looked into his eyes, full of memories and melancholy. She slid from her seat to her knees and put her folded hands on the table.

"I have been presumptuous," she said.

He shook his head.

"No," he said. "Do not feel that. I would I could counsel you, but it is my belief that each man or woman works out his or her own salvation in matters of faith. I am here in Delft at this moment because my faith cries out in the future of God and our cause. My trust is complete. I feel that much is left us, that it is man's high destiny to build himself up again, to undo wrong, to be of resolute courage. I cannot make your road plain before you, but in itself hardship is not always to be dreaded. It is a welder, a shaper of destiny and character in both men and nations. It has its uses. Shall I tell you my thoughts?"

"Please," said Anna. She rose to her feet and stood with her hand resting on the table.

William left his seat and began to pace to and fro. He came to a halt before her.

"I shall go back a long way," he said, "to a mistake made many centuries ago—an error of judgment, you might term it. I think of the history of the early Romans. When their empire was at its zenith they gave the people free corn, free games; they made life too easy. Do you know anything of the early Romans, mevrou?"

"No, Highness," she answered, smiling, "except that the roads they made in Friesland formed the first dykes."

"Well, it was as I have said. Too much was done for the Roman people and I have always contended that nothing saps moral fibre so fast as to have things made too easy. It is against the spirit of man. If the Romans had been given hard work on good terms, a share of responsibility, there would not have been that decay of a virile nation, I think. In the Netherlands we struggle and we fall; but we arise again. We, the Dutch people, are going forward together through the darkness, stronger for our bitter struggle, united as never before. I believe we shall go steadfastly on until we achieve our freedom. Now, for a moment, do not think of the nation: think of yourself. So much has happened, so much is still to happen, that you cannot go on without faith to the end. Believe me, we are enriched by our struggle. So face your problem. There is glory in the sternest hour, and joy also, if you keep your faith alive."

"I see why the people follow you to the death," she cried out, uplifted. "If I were a man it would be my glory to march with you."

He smiled into her shining eyes.

"That is better," he said. "And I see why Michiel de Noot allowed you to go to Zoeterwoude."

"You knew about that?" Anna said in amazement.

"Naturally. I berated him soundly when he returned to Rotterdam and told me on what dangerous mission he had sent you. It was too late to stop you, so there was nothing to be done. By the way, when the guard told me you were here I sent word to Michiel that you had returned safely. There will be no man more relieved of anxiety in Delft than he tonight. If I may be permitted to give you some unsolicited advice, you should marry again. Companionship means more as one grows older."

"I have thought of it," Anna answered simply. "But, you understand, I loved my late husband dearly, Highness. If faithfulness were only a physical thing to me I should have remarried; but it is also a thing of the spirit, so there it is."

"It is a pity," he said.

"There is something I wish to say to you," Anna went on. "It is that Leyden will not fall. Yesterday morning I saw the sign. A windmill burned like a fiery Cross in the sky. The favourable wind blows and the sea creeps to the city walls."

"Please God you are right," William said fervently.

Anna saw the shadow of an immense anxiety on his face. Being the woman she was, it was impossible for her to achieve any great degree of objectivity, but at least she could sink her troubles for a little while in admiration of the courage of a great man who bore on his shoulders the colossal burden of a nation's existence. She said impulsively, her heart wrung by the unspeakable weariness of William's drawn countenance:

"I shall pray that Leyden will be saved."

"That settles your problem then."

"Perhaps. I shall pray for Leyden and then the veil may be withdrawn."

"I may see you in my private chapel. There are continuous prayers for Leyden in all the churches."

"I shall attend; and I thank you from my heart for your words tonight," said Anna.

William bowed his head. He seemed lost in thought. After waiting a little while Anna thought she ought to leave him. She curtseyed and began to move towards the door. He lifted his head as she reached it.

"Remember," he said quietly, "all passes—even pain."

The words came as a benediction to Anna. She felt the tears burn behind her eyelids. She curtseyed once more and passed through the door.

Michiel de Noot was waiting at the gate for her. She saw him through a mist of tears. Wordlessly she took his arm and they walked into the rising storm with the tops of the trees straining in the wind and the water in the canal lapping against its banks. At Oostermeer, thought Anna, clinging to Michiel's arm, the gulls would wheel and scream as the weather worsened and ride out the gale as they often had before, as she would ride out the storm of her torment. The Prince had promised it.

The moon struggled out from the tattered clouds and its wan light poured down upon the dark water at their feet and showed them the sleeping, storm-swept city.

CHAPTER FOURTEEN

A continuing storm, furious in its strength, swept the land. On the first day of October the tempest-driven waters of the North Sea poured through the open sluices and the breached dykes.

Within two days the stranded fleet of barges was afloat and on its way to Leyden. It sailed at dead of night when the storm was at its height. To the terrors of the tempest were added the sounds of such strange battle as the cloaking darkness permitted; cannon coughed and flashed; and here and there, like torches, blazing buildings lit up the wild and watery wastes. One by one the Spanish outposts were engulfed and obliterated by an enemy barely seen.

Thus the first night of the month wore on, and the next day, until on the eve of the second of October, Leyden was in sight. At dawn on the next morning the final assault was to be made, as now only the formidable fortress of Lammen interposed its bristling batteries between the relieving fleet of barges and the beleaguered city. And it had been arranged that the citizens would sally forth with men and arms and join with Boisot in the attack on Lammen.

That last night was a night of exceptional darkness. Throughout the long hours of waiting the besieged, the Sea Beggars, and the Spaniards in their fortress, strained their eyes to detect any movement. In the midst

of their suspense a portion of the city wall, undermined by the water, fell
with a deafening crash. Hearing it, the people of Leyden prepared for
death, thinking the Spaniards were upon them; the Spaniards in their
turn thought the assault had begun and now, in the terror of the night
with the wild wind and rain and the ever-rising sea about them, they
forgot that Valdez saw no reason why they should not fight in the
water as the Dutch did. The unpredictable sea was lapping at their last
bastion. The dread of the unknown overcame them. Soon along the last
crumbling dyke strange lights appeared and strange sounds were heard.
Boisot, holding his Beggars in leash and keeping his unwieldy barges
afloat as best he might, waited for daylight to solve the problem of noise
and swaying lights. So the night wore on in an atmosphere of dread and
nerve-tingling expectancy.

Day broke upon the desolate scene. From the fortress of Lammen
came no sound or stir of life; in the city of Leyden, with its wall between the Cow Gate and the Tower of Burgundy fallen in the false
sea, no living thing moved.

In one of the foremost of the barges sat Ryk van Breda. The silence
was mysterious and frightening. His tired mind conjured up impressions
of sack and slaughter. And Dirk had been lost. He had disappeared from
the barge during the night and it seemed certain he had been slain or
drowned during one of the hard-fought engagements along the route.
Ryk loved Dirk; he felt as though he had lost his own son.

The light grew ever stronger. Suddenly a murmur rose from the
anchored fleet of barges that swelled to a deep-throated, jubilant roar.
Ryk looked up and saw a solitary boy on the deserted ramparts. The
boy waved his cap frantically. It was a red cap such as Dirk usually
wore. Ryk recognized Dirk and, standing upright in the barge, hailed
him across the water.

All was plain: in the night the Spaniards had fled to safety along the
last dyke, abandoning their arms, their fortress, and the protracted siege.

Now there was no impediment. Boisot's fleet swept on to Leyden. As
the gates of the city swung open to receive food and friends Dirk, soaked
to the skin and laughing, pulled himself aboard Ryk's barge. He was
back where he wished to be.

ii

On that same day, which was a Sunday, a service was in progress in
the little chapel of the deserted convent which was William's home in
Delft. William, his household, and many of the townsfolk were deep
in their devotions when the sentry quietly pushed open the chapel door
and tiptoed up the aisle. Anna, on her knees at the back, looked up and
saw Johan van Breda hand a missive to Michiel de Noot, who passed it
on to William.

Heads lifted and there was a rustling of stiff, Sunday clothes. All eyes were turned on the Prince as he opened and read the despatch. It was from Leyden. They saw that on his face; and the news was good; they saw that also.

William passed the pages up to the pulpit and the minister read aloud to the tense gathering the message they contained. All was well. Leyden was saved. The prayers of intercession became the prayers of thanksgiving, and while they still knelt in thankfulness the bells of the city rang out peal upon peal to spread the glad tidings far and wide. Leyden was saved.

Tears ran openly down Anna's cheeks. The Cross in the sky had been a true sign of grace. She was free. She had already told Matthias and Getruida that she was returning to Oostermeer. The web of her life, woven first in Friesland, now here in Delft, had been rich with incident, its pattern dominated always in recent years by her strange encounter with the Spaniard. But the pattern was imprinted and the mould destroyed; she was free to go back to Friesland where, please God, the thread could spin on in peace and content to the end of her days.

She rose quietly and went out. She walked to Ryk's house to tell the glad news to Minetje, who had not been at the service because of the baby.

She took her time about returning to Matthias's house. The bells were still pealing and an atmosphere of exultant joy pervaded Delft. She had reached the canal and was nearing Matthias's home when she first became aware of something amiss. People were issuing from the door of the house; women were running, and men passing in and out of it. Anna picked up her skirts and began to run also. She pushed back a little crowd at the door and spoke to a woman who passed her.

"What has happened?" she asked anxiously.

"Thank God you have come. Your sister-in-law has had a stroke. Poor woman, she is like to die. The surgeons are with her, letting blood."

Anna entered the living room. A fair number of the citizens of Delft seemed to have crowded into it. They stood against the walls and looked in at the windows, while Johan van Breda and Matthias, both haggard with shock, stroke to keep them back so that the surgeons might have room to move.

They had stretched Getruida out on the floor almost where she had fallen. Anna gazed in horror into the livid, distorted face with its glaring eyes.

She raised her eyes from Getruida's terrible face and looked at Matthias.

"You will not leave us now, Anna," he appealed to her. "You see what has happened."

Anna's first feeling was of anger. She had been caught again before she could break free and return home. Now she must stay. The thought struck her very heart and she grew white to the lips. Now, strangely, she had the selfsame vision of Oostermeer she had had when she clung to the rim of the tower in the flood. She saw it as in a mirror—the buttressed barns with their lichened roofs, the avenue of trees, the neat garden and the fields, set about the drowned house that showed enlarged, pressed a little out of shape, and yet stood stone upon stone in a blurred enchantment under the moving grey tide of the North Sea that covered it.

She looked again at Getruida. She knew instinctively it would be a long time before she could return home. Event crowded upon event to keep her back.

There was nothing to do but remain. She gathered her strength together to answer Matthias's appeal.

"No," she said clearly in the silence that lay upon them all, "I shall not leave you now, Matthias."

And, her mind reverting at once to her vision, it seemed to her that the grey waters of the North Sea flowing over Oostermeer had grown turgid, so that she no longer looked down and saw the house.

BOOK TWO

THE TURNING TIDE

PART VI

CORNISH INTERLUDE

CHAPTER FIFTEEN

TWO BOYS WALKED IN THE SHADOW OF THE DEEP CORNISH HEDGES where the toadflax buds thrust out between the honeysuckle and the lush ferns. The warm wind of that summer twilight blew the scurrying clouds across the sky; it blew against their tanned cheeks and dappled with light and shadow the grey stone cottages and the green fields above which the sea gulls wheeled.

The boys talked as they walked, stirring up the dust and the fallen leaves with their feet. They were Anthony Barradale and Tom Wilson on their way to the cliffs, to lie there until the moon came up and watch on the off chance that the smugglers would be busy through the night.

Poor Lydia Wilson's strangeness was now almost madness. There had been a wreck which she was known to have engineered and her long-lost son had been one of the drowned men washed ashore. This preyed upon her mind and greatly changed her.

"The smugglers meet at your house," said Anthony. "I have long suspected it."

"That is about the size of it," Tom admitted.

"Big Ben Trevenna spreads the tales of sorcery and witchcraft to keep folks away. I know it all now, Tom."

"You'll wish you hadn't thought to find out what goes on," said Tom. "It doesn't do to know too much round here."

When the image of the moon quivered in the sky Anthony lifted himself a little over the cliff edge and looked down on the sandy shore pricked by rock points, while Tom laid a restraining hand on his shoulder and whispered that he must take care not to be seen.

Far below, to the right, the white ridges of the incoming tide marked the creek that bit deep into the land. All vestige of cloud had gone from the heavens and the moonlight was clear and bright. Men on the sands were dark shapes and their voices came up to them above the noise of the sea. From two boats with furled sails the smugglers were rolling barrels and throwing out bulky packages that surely were kegs of brandy, barrels of rum, and parcels of silks. Surmise was easy, for it was for those goods the villagers looked.

The moon shone on. At last the business of unloading was done and the ponies were brought out from the shadow of the cliff. The kegs and packages were slung under them and then began the climb up the precipitous path. Anthony knew each turn of that path as it wound along the face of the cliff. He leaned forward eagerly and at once felt Tom's rough hand jerk him back to their place of concealment under a clump of furze. He lay still again, waiting for the line of bearded men on their shaggy, hardy ponies to pass by. He felt he would know them all, as they were the fishermen and the villagers he saw every day. And a sense of power came to him. He would learn the best-kept secret of Falmouth and he would honour that unsuspecting trust. Well he understood how much depended on the loyalty of all parties concerned. In the abstract he thought well of smuggling: his mother had once explained that it was the poor man's easiest means of supplementing a meagre livelihood. He had grasped that smuggling was not for people like themselves who could afford to buy goods through the usual channels, but the case of fishermen and miners and the like was very different, for they lived in dire poverty.

Anthony hugged the thought to himself that now he would have a close link with these hardy folk. Lost in his reflections, he was taken by surprise when the head of the first pony showed itself. In a moment he was studying the faces of the men riding by. He knew them. They were all Falmouth men, and he had often seen them on the quays and walking down the alleyways. The line had almost passed by. There was something very familiar about the last man. He looked closely at him and his pleasant reflections received a rude jar.

The last man of all was Martin Thomas, Sarah's husband.

ii

Anthony Barradale so seldom went away from home that the week he had spent in Sarah's house seemed more like a year. Richard was absent and Frances Barradale had gone to Plymouth to mind the house while Nan was abed with her fourth child, so he had been sent to Sarah's.

It was quiet there in the lonely farmhouse on the slope of the green hill. Martin Thomas was an indifferent farmer; he cared only for his horses and his ponies, and the fields lay fallow. He and Sarah were jolly company and their two young daughters, to whom he was uncle, amused him. Yet, after a week there, Anthony longed for home.

He had been asleep for an hour or more when he awoke suddenly with the feeling that something was happening in the house. He lay under the covers, listening intently and wondering what could have given him that impression. Then from the dining room came the sounds of laughter and the clinking of glasses. There was a lively stir about the place, and doors opened and shut again.

In an instant Anthony was out of bed. He tiptoed down the short passage and peeped in at the dining-room door, being careful not to show himself.

The room was full of men and the table groaned under a load of food. He knew the men who were gathered there. Almost to a man it was the same company that had ridden up the path that evening when he had watched with Tom. The thought that Martin should be in with the smugglers distressed him.

He ran considerable risk of being seen if he remained where he was. Holding his nightgown tightly round him and treading cautiously, he retraced his steps and went back to the room in which he slept. He climbed out of the window and walked round the house. There were horses and ponies tethered everywhere in the farmyard, and the night air was alive with the clinking of bits. Through the open windows of the dining room shouts and laughter came to him as meat and drink were plied. While he struggled with his thoughts someone came out of the house. A voice spoke.

"Come on, then, come on," it said in a deep growl. And there was the sound of a pony moving and a girth being tightened. Then the small, dull thud of a man's weight on the saddle, and the click of moving hoofs as the pony walked out of the pebbled yard.

Anthony moved and stood in the shadow of a rick. Ten minutes later another man came out, mounted, and rode away. At intervals men came out and slipped away. Anthony remained where he was; he was determined to wait until he saw what Martin did.

The back door had been left open. The night was close and warm. Anthony yawned and struggled against drowsiness while he watched the light from the open door. He sat down and leaned his back against the rick. It was a comfortable position and invited sleep. He opened and shut his eyes with conscious effort.

The square of light was partially blacked out as two figures appeared in the doorway. Sarah and Martin, thought Anthony, wide awake on the instant. He watched them embrace and he heard Sarah say:

"I shall expect you back before the night is over."

"I should make it comfortably in that time."

"Is all well tonight?"

Anthony shivered at the unease in her voice.

"Of course; don't think otherwise."

"I shall wait up for you, Martin."

"No, go to bed."

Martin put his arms about Sarah. Anthony heard Sarah catch her breath in a sob. He heard Martin say:

"It will be all right."

Then Martin was in the saddle and his pony was picking his way to the gate. Sarah stood motionless with her hands pressed to her heart, listening. Anthony heard her sigh heavily; then she went back to the house.

He waited for her to enter and then he ran like a hare across the yard. He climbed back through the window and was in bed feigning sleep when Sarah came into his room. She stood at his bedside.

"Anthony," she called softly. "Anthony."

Her voice sounded forlorn, but he lay still, not trusting himself to deal with the situation. He felt Sarah's hand move lightly here and there on the bedcovers. Then her fingers rested on his forehead.

"How sound the children sleep," she murmured.

She left the room and moved about the house, putting out the lights and clearing the platters. At last she went to her bedroom. She paced up and down there. To the accompaniment of the endless procession of her soft steps he fell into an exhausted sleep.

He seemed barely to have closed his eyes when he was awakened by the sound of rapidly beating hoofs. He started up in bed as he heard Sarah open her door and run out of the house.

He ran out behind her, his bare feet making no sound. When he reached the back door she was already speaking to a horseman at the gate. Even in the moonlight there was a glorious familiarity about the bulky figure astride the horse. He did not need to hear the voice to know his father had come.

"Father," Anthony cried softly in relief and joy.

At once he pressed his hands to his mouth. The instinct for caution was stronger than his natural desire to hail his father. Anthony remained where he was in the shadow of the house.

"Is Martin here, Sarah?" Richard Barradale asked.

"No, Father."

"Where is he?"

Sarah did not answer.

"Quick," said Richard Barradale. "Speak. I know all about Martin being in with the smugglers, so you need conceal nothing. Information has been given and the searchers have baited a trap. I came into harbour with the preventive men. They have been following the boats from Rochelle, and they expect to find hogsheads of wine and brandy somewhere in Cornwall in the next few days. Poor crazy Lydia has told them everything, even to giving up forty ankers of brandy she had hidden in the thatch. The preventive men are guarding the approaches to her cottage and the King Harry Passage in case some get away. There are fifty of them out tonight; they are armed and mean business. Now, Sarah, where are they meeting? Is it at Lydia's?"

Every word came clearly to the shivering child.

"Yes; at Lydia's, Father."

"There may be time to stop them. I'll be off at once."

"The preventive men may already have surrounded Lydia's house, and what of you, Father?"

"If they have, I have reason to be riding that way. It is on the road to Bodrugan, and I shall say I called at your place first to see my boy. In fact I am the only man around here who can ride past Lydia's and have no questions asked."

"You will be careful, Father?"

"There is nothing to fear except that I may be too late. Kiss Anthony for me."

Richard stooped to kiss Sarah and rode away at a gallop.

Sarah leaned on the gate and sobbed. Anthony went to her.

"I heard it all," he said. "Oh, Sarah, do you think he will get there in time?"

"I pray he may."

He sensed her dependence on him. The events of the night had reversed their relationship in some way. She no longer seemed wiser and older than he was. He assumed control without thinking.

"Do not cry, Sarah. You ought to go to bed. There is nothing we can do. Come on in, Sarah," he said.

He took her unresisting hand and they walked back to the house. They went to their beds and occasionally they called out to reassure each other when the long hours of waiting seemed unbearable. Neither slept and it was a relief when dawn came greyly in at the windows.

iii

Not long after daybreak Martin's pony galloped riderless into the yard with two ankers of brandy in the sling under him. Sarah ran out of the house and Anthony followed her, but she had the sling and its load off the pony before he came up with her.

Now that there was need for action she was calm and practical.

"Put that pony in the stable, Anthony," she said crisply. "Rub him down, he's all in a lather. And I'll attend to this." She stirred the kegs with her foot. "This has happened before. Martin and Father will be here directly."

"Why?" demanded Anthony, who did not follow her reasoning.

"It is an old trick," explained Sarah, stooping to pick up the sling. "If you are pursued you send your horse off home with the load and dodge about a bit yourself. And you've no contraband on you if you are caught. It's my responsibility this end to hide the stuff at once, which I am about to do. And if you can make that pony look as if he hasn't been out of the stable all night it will be so much the better."

Sure enough, Martin Thomas walked in laughing an hour later. As he left Lydia's he had been pursued. He had hidden in the first thicket he came to when he saw he was bound to be overtaken and had lashed the pony and turned his head homewards and had known he would get safely back with his load. When the preventive men had reached the spot he had shouted and they had dismounted to search for him. He had slipped away and they had argued themselves into a tangle and in the end had done nothing but patrol solemnly up and down where they were. And he had finished the journey home on foot.

"Where is my father?" Anthony asked him.

"He met us at Lydia's house. He got there with the news before the preventive men. Half of us took the stuff and the rest took nothing. We with the loads had to get home by devious routes while the others were to ride openly to King Harry Passage and draw the preventive men away on a wild-goose chase. Your father went with them, Anthony. He's probably at Bodrugan now after a lively night of galloping about."

"Could I not go home?" asked Anthony.

"I will ride with you in the afternoon if he does not come," said Martin. "We must not appear to be hand in glove, you know."

At noon there was news of Richard Barradale. In racing down the precipitous track that led to King Harry Passage his horse had fallen with him and he had broken his neck, a white-faced farmer told them. His body lay at Bodrugan.

Neither Anthony nor Sarah cried out when they heard what had befallen Richard. Anthony saw Sarah's face grow grey, and he himself felt the cold breath of desolation in his soul.

It was unfortunate that Martin Thomas took upon himself the task of Anthony's welfare. He blamed himself bitterly for having indirectly been the cause of Richard Barradale's death and he wished to make such reparation as was possible. Thus for some years—and they were impressionable years—Martin and Sarah saw much of Anthony and had the run of Bodrugan as Frances Barradale, broken by Richard's death, cared little what happened.

As the years went on life changed at Bodrugan. The house was no longed sober and quiet. Sarah and Martin were often there for weeks at a time. They kept open house for all who cared to join in their revels and then the house rang with the shouts and the songs of gay company. As Anthony grew older he automatically entered into partnership with Martin, and smuggling and near piracy seemed to come naturally to him as a profession; and he began to enjoy his life too early. After a successful foray it was highly satisfying to get back with money to spend and gifts to give; and smuggled wine and brandy bought an easy popularity.

Thus it fell out that Anthony Barradale was fairly on the road to becoming a reckless, freebooting fellow when Ryk van Breda decided that it was about time he called upon his niece Anne-Marie.

Of that visit to Bodrugan much was to come.

PART VII

ḣOLLAⱤD

ON A COLD, DARKENING NOVEMBER AFTERNOON IN 1583 RYK VAN BREDA saw his mother there beyond the windmill. She was ploughing the meadow, and the scraping of her wooden plough and the crying of the greedy gulls were the only sounds of life. As the blunt share scored and twisted the dank earth the wavering furrow grew and stretched itself into a long trail ending in the grey mist rolling in from the distant sea.

Anna had tied an old piece of sacking over her clothes, and her clogs were heavy and shapeless with clinging mud. Weather and hard manual labour had tanned and roughened the skin on her face and hands. She ploughed firmly and carefully, and Ryk stood watching her from the side of the windmill. He could see her spirit soared within her in the ploughing of that bleak and lonely meadow.

He stepped out and hailed her. Anna paused in her toil and looked his way. When she saw who it was she stood upright and held out her arms.

Ryk came to her and they embraced.

"Mother, what is this!" he exclaimed. "If I had known you were to do such heavy work I would not have let you return to Oostermeer. What is Uncle Gerard thinking of to allow it?"

"Allow it! Gerard! I am being wilful, that is all. It is your misfortune to find me ploughing on the only occasion I have tried. The idea is my own entirely. Gerard is away in Groningen for a week. He says nothing will grow in this meadow because of the salt in the soil; but I think otherwise. After all, the flood was thirteen years ago, Ryk. You can help me plough and sow if you have a few days to spare. Did you see the house, Ryk? It is almost as it used to be. It is a perpetual miracle to me that so much was left of Oostermeer after the waters receded. I have to thank Gerard for much, Ryk."

"I thought I was dreaming when I saw the house," said Ryk. "It does not seem to have changed."

"The poplars have yet to grow tall and sturdy. I have been happy here these last few months."

"Come back with me to Delft, Mother. Life is hard and rough here," said Ryk, unconvinced that the picture was as rosy as she painted it.

"No," she said, shaking her head. "I am happy here. I work, I live in the present, I plan the future, and I have taken ten years off my age since I came home. When this field I am ploughing springs green I shall see its growth as a renewal of hope, and a pledge that life will be good and the people will be free. I do not mind poverty."

It was true. She did not mind being poor: it was nothing very grievous, a transient affliction. Never had she been in better health or as happy as she had been this short while in Friesland. She was richer in physical vigour and clearer in mind, and there had been deep joy in taking up her comradeship with Gerard again. They were achieving much together. No weariness stopped them, no lack of money or lack of labour hindered them. Side by side they improvised, toiled, schemed with the few guilders of the butter money, and together they were shaping the well-loved farm after a particular design again.

The improvement not only of her land but also of Gerard's occupied them, so they were very active, being in two places at once, as it were. In the years she had been held in Delft Gerard had done very well by himself; but it was plain how much better matters shaped under her hand as well. They were a good combination and worked with zest towards the final reclamation of the sea-ravaged land.

In the end Anna had remained in Delft for almost thirteen years. For most of that time Getruida had been a bedridden invalid. Anna had tended her and had kept Matthias's house, somewhat grudgingly at first, it must be admitted. When Matthias had died four years before his stricken wife Anna had continued to nurse Getruida faithfully and with a willing heart. When death finally came to the partially paralyzed woman she and Getruida had made their peace. After the death of his parents Johan van Breda had taken unto himself a wife, and in the year 1583 Anna had achieved her home-coming.

The years in Delft had been full and eventful. Ryk and Minetje had had four daughters by the time she left—Juliana, Jacoba, Frederika, and Charlotte, the last little girl being named for the third Princess of Orange, Charlotte de Bourbon. Ryk had acquired no riches, although now and again, in between his maritime engagements in home waters, he had captained ships of merchants in Amsterdam on trading ventures, which invariably yielded fabulous profits to the owners and meagre ones to Ryk; but then he was no business man as Gysbert had been before him. Minetje had developed somewhat disappointingly. She was at variance with life because God had sent her daughters and no son, and her temper did not sweeten, although many people were at pains to point out that the wife of William the Silent had produced six girls in seven years and thanked God and rejoiced.

William's third marriage had turned out most happily and Charlotte de Bourbon was a loving and beloved wife. There had been in this period the Act of Federation between Holland and Zeeland which was to be the nucleus of the Dutch Republic. Spain had annexed Portugal and a price had been put on William's head. In the spring of 1582 his life had been attempted and he had been sorely wounded. Although he recovered, his beloved wife, Charlotte, took a fever and, weakened by the strain and worry of her husband's illness, had died in a few days. Finally in the spring, in the year that Anna left Delft, William had married for the fourth time, taking to wife the virtuous widow, Louise de Coligny. Anna had thought at the time that the Prince certainly lived up to the advice he had given her on the wisdom of seeking companionship in marriage; but it was difficult for him with a brood of young children and the hardships of his arduous life.

At the end of all these matters she had come home.

Anna put her hand on Ryk's arm.

"Do not distress yourself, Ryk," she said. "Do you not see how hard work agrees with me? Have you ever seen me in better health?"

"No," he admitted. "You seem very well indeed; but still I do not like it. Ever since the flood your life has been spent in service to others. I would like to know you were having an easier time."

"It will not always be so hard," she said, pleading for Oostermeer. "Gerard's Jan is a fine lad and soon will be old enough to help more."

"I came to see you about Anne-Marie, Mother," said Ryk, coming abruptly to the point. "I have just returned from Falmouth."

Anna's face was vivid with interest.

"How was Anna Maria? I mean Anne-Marie. I must learn to pronounce her name in the English manner."

"She is very well; but I do not like the way things are going at Bodrugan. Since Richard Barradale's death Sarah and Martin Thomas are often at Bodrugan and they are a roistering couple. Anthony Barradale has come under their influence and as far as I can make out is a wild young blade, ever away on some mysterious business at sea. Richard was a privateer, but his son is no less than a pirate from all accounts. When I arrived at Bodrugan Anthony had just returned from a foraging expedition and the house was given over to wild carousal. Bodrugan is no place for a young girl. I spoke with Mistress Barradale on the score of Anne-Marie, and she assured me that I had come at a bad time and that Bodrugan was not always as I had found it. When the young people were away it was quiet and orderly, she said; and she told me Anne-Marie was properly brought up and had acquired some skill in reading and writing and fine needlework."

Liesbet had excelled at fine needlework, Anna remembered. Across her mind flashed that unforgettable impression of Liesbet in the boat. She saw her clearly, standing upright with her arms outstretched to Ryk, and that look of unearthly radiance on her face.

"Is Anne-Marie like her mother?" Anna asked.

And saw by the look in Ryk's eyes that he also was remembering Liesbet as she had remembered her.

"Anne-Marie will be very lovely someday," Ryk said after a pause. "She looks like you."

Anna felt the warmth from her heart rush to her cheeks at the caress in his voice. Her eyes misted. She had thought only Gysbert could charm her by an unexpected compliment, and here was Ryk with the same divine enchantment in his tongue.

"She grows more like you every time I see her," Ryk went on. "Lourens also favoured you, Mother."

He raised her stained hand to his lips. He is becoming courtly in his ways, Anna thought. The wandering life and mixing with all degrees of society taught airs and graces her own parents would have scorned.

"It has always seemed best that Anne-Marie should stay where she was happy and well cared for," Anna said. "In England there is not the horror of the Spanish soldiery; also I have so little to offer her. We may have been wrong to leave her at Bodrugan for so long. She could have shared our lives, no matter how reduced our circumstances."

"You could not possibly have had her back while you were nursing Aunt Getruida," said Ryk. "But now it would be as well to bring her over to Holland. She might end by marrying young Barradale, and it would be a disastrous marriage for her. If you wish she could live with Minetje and the children."

"Do you think it will be too rough at Oostermeer?" Anna asked anxiously. "She may end by loving the old place as I love it."

"She has been finely brought up," he said. "But then you were and you can turn your hand to anything, if need be."

"We shall try bringing her here first," said Anna. "If she is unhappy she can go to Delft."

"It will not be an easy transplanting for Anne-Marie," said Ryk. "She barely speaks Dutch—she understands more than she speaks. She knows French and English. This will seem an alien land at first."

"Instinct is a sure thing. Her roots are Dutch, and she will soon feel at home."

Anna fell into a reverie. She was excited and stirred to think Anne-Marie was to live with her at Oostermeer. She had always fretted, having one of her blood so far from her; but now that was being put right.

Anne-Marie would help at Oostermeer and do the lighter work. She might come in time to love the farm. It was possible that she and Jan might marry and the Van Braam family would once again come into its own at Oostermeer.

Anna's lips moved in a smile, and her eyes travelled the wavering furrow that was lost in the wraithing mists from the sea.

PART VIII

CORNISH INTERLUDE

CHAPTER SEVENTEEN

ANNE-MARIE BY-PASSED PENDENNIS CASTLE AND WALKED TO THE TIP of the headland. She had escaped early from her lesson at the vicar's and Mary had not arrived in time to escort her home. She promised herself one look at the sea before she went sedately back to meet the maid on the way.

The December seas were wild and rough with the clamour of falling surges and the crash of whipping spray upon the rocks. Anne-Marie's slim figure was buffeted by the wind, and its tearing at her body seemed to pluck some of the confusion out of her mind. Uncle Ryk had come to take her to Holland to the grandmother she had not yet seen. The possibility of solitude and strangeness in her new life disturbed her. She knew but one Dutchman and he was her kind uncle Ryk; but everyone in Falmouth was a friend. She came grimly to the point with herself: she would miss Anthony Barradale more than anyone or anything. He was all that really mattered. He had been her only playmate and she saw the world through his eyes; he was her world and she wanted no other.

Yesterday she had been a child. She had grown up overnight on learning that she was to leave Bodrugan. If Anthony knew he would keep her from going. It was the greatest misfortune that he had gone to Plymouth to consult James Carey on a matter of grave family business. They had expected him hourly at Bodrugan, but he had not come. It was possible he had arrived during her absence. As she thought this Anne-Marie turned to set off homewards.

She saw Anthony. He was standing close behind her and had been watching her.

"I dared not breathe, Anne-Marie," he said, "in case I blew you over. You were on the very edge."

"Anthony!" she exclaimed. "You have come back! Have you been to Bodrugan?"

"Yes; and I spent an hour with your uncle Ryk and heard the most melancholy news; and then bribed Mary to wait under the hedge while I fetched you home. I watched you come here and I followed you. Of what were you thinking while you stood at the cliff edge?"

"That I must leave you," she said directly, her eyes darkening with pain.

"I shall never give you up," he said so positively that her heart leapt within her. "I did not speak to your uncle; I wished to speak first to you. You must not leave Bodrugan—you must be my wife someday. I cannot lose you. It is impossible for us to marry now. You are very young and your uncle would not permit it, I feel sure. Also I must get my affairs in better shape before I can ask you to share my life. Your uncle has ideas about my affairs as well. One way and another I have had an unpleasant afternoon, Anne-Marie."

"Are the affairs so urgent?" she asked.

Anthony put his arms about her.

"Very urgent," he said. "I must speak like this to you sooner than I had intended, Anne-Marie, because there may not be another opportunity. Poor Mary will freeze beneath the hedge, for I shall be a long time talking."

He felt her tremble within the circle of his arm as he drew her closer to him. He looked down into her oval child's face, with its dark blue eyes and golden hair, and saw the clear milky skin with a faint pink bloom in the cheeks, the throat smooth and white and delicately veined, the rise and fall of her immature breasts.

"You are so precious to me, Anne-Marie," said Anthony.

He released her suddenly and they stood facing each other, both very pale.

"You will wait for me and have faith in me? Promise me that," he said.

"You know I will."

"It was here on this headland of Pendennis that I thought I knew what freedom was," he said bitterly. "Experience has taught me there really is no such thing. There is always pressure from somewhere—one's family, one's lack of means——"

She knew these sudden changes of mood of old.

"Tell me," she said sweetly.

"It all began with my father's death——"

"When Martin began to advise you," finished Anne-Marie with a sagacity beyond her years.

"You have lived at Bodrugan. You are aware of what Martin and I do for a living?"

"Smuggling. But there is no disgrace in that, is there?"

"It is not for us. Nor yet is piracy."

"I did not realize you were as deep in with Martin as that."

"Martin is not to be blamed."

"You are not very old now, Anthony. You were no more than a boy when you began. Give it up."

"It is not as easy as that. I am in debt all over the county. I have only just learned to what extent. Some time ago I began to look into accounts myself as there seemed to be a perpetual shortage of money. Martin has no business head, and Mother and Sarah cannot add a row of figures, so I took my troubles to James. It was a shock when I discovered how I stood financially because my sisters' portions have not yet been paid, and lately it has even been necessary to mortgage Bodrugan. James was very helpful and he rather rebuked himself for having let me and feckless Martin make such a muddle of affairs. While in Plymouth a wonderful chance to recover was offered me. When I've put through the enterprise I'll take out a letter of marque and become a respectable privateer, and we shall be married."

"What is this enterprise you are about to undertake, Anthony?"

"A voyage to the coast of Guinea and thence to the Spanish Indies."

"To put in hand a voyage to Guinea betokens a slaving run, does it not?" she asked slowly.

"Yes, but the profits are huge, and one run would clear me."

"Are you in such sore need of money, Anthony?"

"I mortgaged Bodrugan to finance this venture."

"I have some money. There is quite a deal of it, I understand. You may have that."

"It is your dowry from your relatives in Holland. No, not a shilling of it will I touch."

"If we were wed you might."

"If we were wed!"

A wave of high colour flooded the milky pallor of her face.

"That day will come," she said with a proud smile. "Anthony, do not endanger our future. Abandon this venture."

"It is too late, Anne-Marie."

"I do not like the thought of slaving. It is wrong to enslave even a savage."

"Negroes are Negroes—cattle. It does not mean anything to them to be transported to another part of the globe to work on a plantation."

"I am afraid you are just talking, Anthony," she said sternly. "We have spoken of the slave traffic before and you deplored it; and now you are for it."

"Necessity admits no abstract theorizing," he muttered.

"They are human beings," she said angrily.

They had fallen into a childish quarrel as they sometimes did. Anne-Marie's face was flushed and her eyes sparkled with anger. She had temporarily forgotten why they were standing there on the cliff in the wild weather.

Anthony said sadly:

"Are we to mar our last few minutes together with a pointless quarrel, Anne-Marie? We may not meet for years."

"Anthony," Anne-Marie cried, cut to the heart.

He fell into earnest pleading:

"Let me go this once, Anne-Marie, and I swear it will be my first and my last slaving venture. I have already invested my share in three good Plymouth ships and it is too late to withdraw. I promise you there will be no more slaving for me after this."

Child as she was, Anne-Marie knew her Anthony and his weaknesses. She was impulsive and always ready to yield where she loved. Her heart could, if it were given, despise facts and refuse to be moved in accordance with reason. She knew the slave traffic was wrong, but she loved Anthony too much to argue farther.

"Go then, Anthony," she said sadly.

In the fading light he saw her face was white and strained and it bred in him an anger against himself. And the wind seemed to blow more strongly and the sky was darker, and the sea crashed with violence on the rocks below.

"Not ever again after this, Anne-Marie," he vowed with fierce remorse. "I wish I had not told you I loved you. You ought to marry some more stable person."

She brushed his compunction aside with a quick, characteristic movement of her hand.

"I wouldn't have understood it if you had not told me you loved me," she said. "Besides, I knew it, and I have always loved you. Whatever comes of this, it is right that we should have spoken."

"I love you," he said.

"I love you," she answered. They stretched out their hands to each other and smiled into each other's eyes.

Anthony did not trust himself to prolong that agonizing moment. If Anne-Marie had had a few more years to her age a runaway marriage would have settled their problem. She was a child still. She was shyly drawing away her hands. . . .

"We must go," he said, clutching at his fast-slipping scruples.

"I love you," she said again.

The wild surging of the sea was in her ears as she said it, and the rushing of the wind. Whenever I hear the sea and the wind, she thought, I shall be with Anthony. . . .

This was their coming together and their parting. The minutes were flying too fast, flying steadily, uncontrollably. Soon they would be apart; but now they were together, standing silently side by side.

I must remember this, I must remember this, thought Anne-Marie.

And sought the shelter of his arms as the wind came weeping in from the darkened sea.

PART IX

HOLLAND

CHAPTER EIGHTEEN

IN THE NORTH THE PEOPLE WERE JUBILANT. TOWARDS THE END OF JANUary 1584, William of Nassau's fourth wife, Louise de Coligny, had given birth to a son, and, after the vicissitudes and trials of the prolonged struggle against the Spanish oppressor, the birth of the child seemed an augury of better days to come.

In Groningen the occasion was celebrated with gaiety and fireworks. Anna had taken her granddaughter Anne-Marie to stay for a week with Gerard's relatives in that town. She felt that the hard cold winter might prove dull for the girl, and the joyful occasion of the birth of a Count of Holland seemed a fitting time to introduce Anne-Marie to her friends and relatives, and to provide some amusement and diversion as well.

The week in Groningen was an interesting experiment. Anne-Marie's moving story and the fact that she had been reared in England attracted considerable attention; and her immaturity promised great beauty at a later time. She also had poise, and a vivacity which was unusual in girls of her age and upbringing. When she threw off her reserve she was charming. There would certainly be no lack of suitors for Anne-Marie, for she had created an impression in Groningen on her first introduction to such society as it boasted that was quite remarkable.

Back at Oostermeer after a week of festivity and some shrewd observation of Anne-Marie on Anna's part, Anna was unexpectedly afforded a glimpse of what her granddaughter really was like and it warmed her heart. Anne-Marie set herself to entertain the two who had remained on the farm and had missed the fun and the feasting—Gerard and Jan. She came vividly to life and, with a gay spontaneity, in her bizarre mixture of languages, described the highlights of the week.

You are rich in kindliness and thoughtfulness, thought Anna, loving Anne-Marie. Gerard and Jan were good and devoted and as true as steel, but they were slow and heavy and undeniably dull. Few charming young girls would have put themselves out to entertain them, and Anne-Marie had created no small stir in Groningen, and, what was more, she was fully aware of it.

That same night of their return to Oostermeer Anne-Marie came into Anna's great bed in the wall. She did not perch at the foot of the bed as she usually did, remote and isolated. On this night she sat beside Anna. Anna drew the covers over her knees and she caressed her granddaughter's slim feet, and there was a feeling of intimacy between them which had not been there before. Without preamble Anne-Marie began to tell Anna about Bodrugan; she had had almost nothing to say on that score before. She told about wild scrambles in the Cornish hills with Anthony Barradale and Tom Wilson; about wreckers and smugglers and the mystery of Lydia Wilson; about Frances Barradale; and much about Anthony.

This was the first time since her arrival that Anne-Marie had taken her into her confidence. Anna prayed earnestly that she might be given the perception not to blunder and interrupt the establishment of a friendly and loving relationship between them. She must move carefully and kindly and encourage the absolute breaking down of Anne-Marie's reserve. Therefore she drew the girl out and talked to her of Bodrugan, and, after some time, when she felt she dared move onto new ground, she introduced another topic.

"Was Oostermeer as you thought it would be?" she asked.

"No, not altogether. I had been warned that Holland was flat and full of dykes; but I had not realized how flat it would be, and how large the sky would look."

"Do you like being at Oostermeer, Anne-Marie?"

She sensed a hesitation in Anne-Marie. Had she probed too deep?

"A house is a home, and a place to live in," answered Anne-Marie, speaking slowly and evidently choosing her words. "I like Oostermeer as much as I like Bodrugan; but if I speak truly, I would be happy anywhere in the world as long as Anthony were with me."

Now she must tread warily indeed, Anna thought, praying for guidance. One false move and the finely set balance would be shattered. Her hand caressed Anne-Marie's feet more lingeringly. She decided that she would leave the talking to the girl and so she said noncommittally:

"One is always devoted to the friends of one's childhood."

"One day I hope to marry Anthony," Anne-Marie declared almost defiantly. "I have promised to wait for him while he sails to Guinea to make his fortune."

The chances were that Anthony might not return from Guinea, Anna reflected, and, with the resilience of youth, Anne-Marie would get over his loss. He might well fall into the hands of the Spanish or even the Moors, or he might suffer shipwreck, thought Anna, dispassionately cataloguing the misfortunes that might overtake this trying young man. . . .

"When he returns we shall discuss it," said Anna; and wished Jan van Braam had been born handsome, gay and fascinating; then, perhaps, Anne-Marie might forget the other. When first she had set eyes on Anne-Marie, Anna had doubted whether anything but disaster would come of a marriage between sober Jan and Anne-Marie, as they were so alien in temperament. Still, time would show. . . .

"You do not mind then?" Anne-Marie asked, and Anna knew by the tone of her voice that a great deal depended on how she answered that question.

"We will leave the matter open," said Anna. "When he returns, if you are still of the same mind and devoted to each other, and if he has means enough to support you, I shall put nothing in your way."

She heard Anne-Marie's swift intake of breath in the darkness.

"Oh, my grandmother!"

Anna said spontaneously from her heart:

"If you care so much for him I pray that he will return. But, Anne-Marie, I want you to be a child still. Do not run to meet the future: troubles come fast enough."

It struck Anna that she had not said the obvious thing—that Anne-Marie was too much of a child to bother herself about a love affair. For her years Anne-Marie was very mature mentally, and she had been long enough at Oostermeer for Anna to have come to understand her character. Anne-Marie was of the constant type. If she carried an image in her heart it was there forever, as it was with herself. How often had she not gone to the distant dyke when Gysbert was away at sea, hoping against hope that she would see his ship put in at the haven? In her turn Anne-Marie loved a wanderer on the seas, also a man charming and unstable and inevitably attractive to the steadfast, enduring type of woman. If history were to repeat itself, as it seemed it might, Anne-Marie might also be a lonely watcher on an English shore.

"I will be a child still," Anne-Marie promised. "As long as you know and understand about Anthony. Uncle Ryk is not in the least sympathetic."

"He is very sensible," Anna commented. "But we will leave it all to time."

"Yes," Anne-Marie agreed.

"I have a great deal I would like to talk to you about," said Anna. "I want you to know something about your mother and your father. And once there was a Spanish don here at Oostermeer. But all that tomorrow and in the other days, for you are very tired, my little one, and must go to sleep."

Thus began a treasured companionship. Anne-Marie was no longer a stranger. By degrees Anna told her all that had happened in the stirring and tragically splendid years. And Anne-Marie poured out in her broken language all of her life at Bodrugan and her farewell to Anthony. Anna listened, and sometimes she followed what the girl said, and sometimes her thoughts were worlds away, and sometimes she felt, This is my life all over again.

By the end of the winter, when she had got to know what went on in the mind of Anne-Marie, she knew she must in time give Anne-Marie to Anthony Barradale. And knew also how greatly she would miss her when the parting came.

ii

In the spring Ryk came to Oostermeer. The first person he saw issuing from the kitchen door was Anne-Marie. He halted in surprise at the sight of her. She had grown much taller and was beginning to fill out. In her neat cap and her full skirts she made a pleasing picture. She was a digni-fied child. His own daughters were not so fair, he thought. He had four girls now, and he hoped the next child would be a son, or Minetje would not be pacified.

"A brisk wind blew me here and an even brisker one must take me back," he said when they had exchanged greetings. "And how is my mother, Anne-Marie?"

"She is very well. She is in the byre and I am on my way with a pail." She spoke Dutch quite well, he noted.

"Do you like it here?" he asked curiously. "Do you not long for England?"

"This is my home," said Anne-Marie with great self-possession. "And I love my grandmother."

Ryk noted also the quiet evasion of a direct answer. He regretted the coolness that had sprung up between himself and Anne-Marie since he had been instrumental in removing her from Bodrugan.

"I am glad of that," Ryk answered.

"If you wish we ought to go to the byre," said Anne-Marie.

Ryk carried the pail and walked with Anne-Marie to the byre. He turned over in his mind how best to approach his business with Anna. He wished to go on another voyage. His financial position was bad. His ever-increasing family swallowed up his earnings, and Minetje was pregnant again. She refused to let him sail unless Anna came to stay with her in Delft while he was away, and therefore he had come to Oostermeer to persuade his mother to fall in with Minetje's condition. There was also another matter on his mind: he had called in at Plymouth and had gone to the Careys' house. James had given him a letter for Anne-Marie from Anthony, and Ryk, after much deliberation, had come to the conclusion that the faster Anne-Marie forgot that graceless scamp the better for her. Accordingly he had destroyed the letter unread. He thought of this now with a strong sense of guilt. He had felt he wanted a more stable and settled life for Liesbet's daughter than Anthony would give her. At the time he thought he had acted for the best; but now he was not so sure and regretted his action. He started when Anne-Marie, with a simple question, drove straight to the heart of his troubled conscience with unconscious and devastating effect.

"Have you been to England lately, Uncle Ryk?" she asked.

"Yes," he answered. "I went to Plymouth."

"Did Anthony leave a message for me with James Carey?" she asked. "He said he would let me know when he sailed for Guinea, and I was to send word to James if I wished to get in touch with him. That was our arrangement."

"He left no message," said Ryk firmly.

He hated the falsehood, but, as he was so involved, he saw nothing for it but to lie with hardihood.

"Has Anthony sailed?" Anne-Marie asked her last question.

"He had been gone a month when I put in at Plymouth," Ryk said.

And saw with compunction how pale and shadowed her face was.

iii

When the evening meal was over Ryk broached the subject that was uppermost in his mind. They were gathered about the table with him—Gerard and Jan, his mother and Anne-Marie. There was a little pause in the flow of the conversation. They were expecting him to announce the purpose of his visit, for one did not lightly travel so far in the cold spring days. So Ryk began, and very difficult he found it.

"You have heard of Hans Grobbelaar of Amsterdam, Mother?" he asked.

"I know him by repute," Anna said. "He is a wealthy shipowner, if I remember rightly."

"Yes, he owns several ships," Ryk confirmed. "He wishes me to captain one of them to the west coast of Africa."

Anne-Marie leaned forward with shining eyes.

"Uncle Ryk, you may have news of Anthony!" she cried. "The west coast means the Gold Coast, does it not? And that is where he has gone."

Their eyes were on Anne-Marie, but she was too absorbed to notice.

"Yes, one of the ports of call will be on the Gold Coast," Ryk said.

"He may have left for the Indies," said Anne-Marie. "But you will hear of him."

"A slaving trip, is it?" Jan said disparagingly.

"Yes, a slaving trip," said Anne-Marie, immediately on the defensive. "And I hope he has a prosperous voyage, what is more."

What an unfortunate attitude for Jan to assume, thought Anna in distress. To belittle Anthony was to send Anne-Marie fervently to his defence. And Jan again rushed on to his doom. . . .

"But you are against slavery, Anne-Marie," he said.

"Yes," Anne-Marie agreed, "but that has nothing to do with it."

She gave no further explanation, but relapsed into proud silence.

Ryk's venture also involved a slave run to the Spanish Main. He had no intention of stressing that fact. He would dwell instead on the trading side of the enterprise. But he felt thoroughly uncomfortable. He broke an awkward pause.

"I am to get a good share of the profits this time," he said. "I think I should close with Hans Grobbelaar's offer if I can possibly arrange to do so."

"What is in the way of your accepting?" asked Anna.

"You will remember that we moved to a larger house last year, Mother," Ryk explained laboriously. "It is really too much for Minetje to cope with. She has the four little ones and another on the way. We hoped, Mother, that you and Anne-Marie would pay a visit to Delft and stay in our house to be with Minetje while I am away. I could sail then with an easy mind."

Anna looked down at the table and wondered what answer she could make. There was so much to be done at Oostermeer, and, above all, she had no wish to leave her home again. She had barely had time to settle down. . . .

She looked up at last.

"It is a big decision to make, Ryk," she said. "I want to think it over in the night and I shall tell you in the morning. How long do you expect to be away?"

"The best part of a year, Mother."

"A year, or the best part of it, is a long time," said Gerard, who did not in the least like the idea of Anna going to Delft.

"That is why I cannot leave Minetje alone," said Ryk.

"In the morning, please," said Anna, holding up her hand.

She turned the conversation to politics and kept them to that safe topic until it was time to retire for the night.

Ryk and Gerard talked on by the dying fire when the others had sought their beds.

Gerard van Braam seemed to have arrived at the static stage of life. Ryk could not remember his ever having looked any older or any younger. He was no more grey than he had been when they had met in Delft after the flood.

"I regret so much having to ask Mother to leave Oostermeer, especially after the years she has struggled to get back home," Ryk said. "I wish there were another way open to me."

"Is it essential that you undertake this voyage?" Gerard asked.

"Absolutely. There is no money on either side of the family now, and I have many children, and there must be provision for my mother's old age."

"She has Oostermeer."

"You no more than scrape a living here."

"In a few years Oostermeer will bring in a good living," said Gerard. "We have survived the worst, and the easier times lie ahead. It is hard for Anna to leave home."

"You think she will agree to stay in Delft for a time?"

"Yes, she will go to Delft."

"What makes you so sure?"

"I have heard people discussing your mother, wondering why she has power over us. Some said it was her beauty, others her manner; but I have known Anna long enough to disagree. There are many women more beautiful, many more charming. I think it is because she has a genius for the right moment—she knows when to submit, when to stand fast. That is a gift which is rare, Ryk, and she has it to perfection. She will go to Delft, for she sees she has no alternative: you have a wife and a large family to support. When Anna is put in that position she does not rail or argue. She makes up her mind and there is no bitterness ever to remember in anything, and for that reason one comes back gratefully again and again, and Anna has become a pleasant, reliable part of one's life."

"I hope Minetje has a son this time, and mother will have a man to work for her in her old age."

How he harps on the theme of Anna's old age, thought Gerard, somewhat nettled. And Anna was by no means so old. He hoped Jan and Anne-Marie would marry and there would be young blood to carry on the land; but the two did not always agree, which worried him. . . .

"Well, the morning will show," said Ryk, yawning.

They also retired, and silence fell on the old house.

iv

Anna dreamed that night. Usually when morning came she had forgotten her dream, but on this occasion the impression of it was vividly in her mind when she awoke. She rose early and went out. She walked away from the house in the spring morning. She saw that the sea gulls had come in from the sea and the meer. They were hovering above the windmill and the dyke and the flat fields. The scene before her was unreal compared with the clarity of the dream that was still fresh in her mind.

This was her dream: she stood in the kitchen at Oostermeer. There was a sense of quiet and familiar peace in the room, with a fire flickering and casting its rosy reflection on the crocks and platters on the dresser. A door faced her. She opened it on a room she had never seen before, a large, pleasant room, with open windows looking out upon a wide sweep of fields and trees and meadows, and in the background was the silver sheen of the meer. A feeling of happy content was on her. This is a room I had not known was in my house, she thought, I must use it more often; it is a lovely room.

She walked between the avenue of young trees for a short distance, then cut across to the field she had ploughed and sowed with Ryk's help. As she walked on the quiet peace of her dream left her. She was distressed about Ryk. He was changing, and for the worse. She had seen his face when Anne-Marie and Jan had quarrelled over the slaving venture and she had realized that Ryk also was about to participate in the same grim traffic; but he had not made this plain. Minetje's incessant grumbling was at the root of the change in Ryk, she thought unhappily. She did not see that she could help him. There were some things one had to work out for oneself, she reflected, and Ryk would have to thresh about until he learned the truth of that. Yet she must leave Oostermeer for his sake, and take Anne-Marie with her to Delft.

She had no wish to leave. On this spring morning, with its cloud and shadow, and the vast, variable sky arching over her, she must take her last look at the familiar scene. She had been happier these few months at Oostermeer than she had been since Gysbert's death. And, to crown her happy days, Anne-Marie had come to give her rare companionship.

Her thoughts turned to the years she had spent in Delft. She remembered very clearly an autumn evening when she had sought in her extremity to throw the burden of her personal problems on the overburdened shoulders of a great prince. Strangely had he aided her, giving her no counsel, making nothing clear save the glory that lay in righteous conflict, the greatness of the eternal struggle against darkness. She had asked him to show her an easy way, but he had shown her a thorny path, inviting her to forget her little woes. Her thoughts dwelt lovingly and with deep gratitude on William, the prince and father of the Dutch people. It was a lesson she had not forgotten, and the remembrance of it even now brought its balm.

The blue and cloud-patched sky was mirrored wherever water lay— in pool or stream or gently flowing canal. Sunlight and shadow played on willows and alders and the lush green grass, and, as if to round off the impression of all-pervading light and shade, a herd of black-and-white cattle was moving out to pasture. She had come to the meadow by the windmill. She saw the springing lines of green where Gerard had said no blade would grow. She had been ploughing that field when Ryk had come to tell her Anne-Marie was to return.

The pale green spears of wheat were thrusting up through the rich earth: there would be a good crop. She had been right about the fertility of the meadow. From her small success in the cultivating of that square of land she took a line to matters of greater moment. She felt better days lay ahead when the dark tide of war would be rolled back from them and the nation should come into its own.

She would go to Delft as Ryk wished. It would not be for long. She had had time enough to see the corn spring through the earth with its glad autumnal promise: she had seen it. It was her moment of reward as the welfare of her son was essentially the end of her striving.

She was almost light of heart when she opened the kitchen door and found Gerard, usually the first in the household to be astir, tending the fire.

V

Soon she found herself sitting facing Gerard across the hearth, where once she and Gysbert had sat. Now, as then, the pungency of the peat smoke burned her nostrils.

She rested her chin on her palm and gazed into the fire. She lifted her head at length and gravely regarded Gerard. She made him an astonishing offer, and made it so suddenly and unexpectedly that he was completely taken by surprise.

"Would you care to marry me, Gerard, when I come back from Delft?" she said.

"Anna!"

"I have always felt that was your wish," went on Anna, giving him time to recover himself. "Possibly I was mistaken."

"You were not mistaken."

He hesitated, searching for words.

"It has long been my dearest wish to have you for my wife, Anna," he said at last. "But I am at a loss now because I do not understand what prompted you to make me your offer."

"I thought of Gysbert," said Anna. "When I came in and you sat in his chair time was pushed back nearly fourteen years, and I saw the whole thing through your eyes. And there you have it."

"A momentary impulse, Anna! Fie on you! It was your thought of Gysbert that came first. You care only for him still."

"Yes, that is so. I would not deceive you, Gerard."

"Was there no other reason?"

"I am going back to Delft," she said. "There is another man I am bound to see when I am there, Michiel de Noot. Once I might have weakened and married him, but nursing Getruida was my duty and I had no inclination for Michiel and a sickbed both together. It will be different now, and of you and Michiel I like you the better."

"Years ago I would have been content with however little you had to give me in the way of love; but now I have learned wisdom. I see you as a painting in oils. When you are close to the canvas the colours are crude; but go back a little and stand away from your picture and view it objectively, and it has become a thing of beauty, a perfection of the painter's art. I see you best, my Anna, standing away from you. My emotions would blind me if I were too near you. I would want more than you could give me. I should be jealous. I have no wish to mar the abiding tie of friendship that is between us by straining after too much. Ach, Anna, you are dear to me."

"I meant no sacrificial offer," said Anna. "I think too highly of you for that."

"Your first thought was for Gysbert," he reminded her, smiling.

"So it was," admitted Anna, smiling back at him. "Gerard, I am so muddled."

"And so you go to Delft again. Ach, Annetje, do not be away so long this time. I miss you sorely."

"Ryk's ship will barely have dropped anchor when I shall be sending a message to Jan Hattingh to stand by with his boat to bring us home again," she said.

"Ryk has changed," commented Gerard.

"It is a temporary change, I think," said Anna sadly. "There is the perpetual struggle for money, and Minetje is not much help to him. But, Gerard, there are two very fine points to remember—Ryk is good to Dirk, and he is loyal and kind to his wife. I must help my son. All these matters may right themselves with a little patience."

"Anne-Marie will enjoy herself in Delft, bless her," said Gerard.

"We dote on the child, do we not?" said Anna. "We must beware of spoiling her."

"When I look at her I remember you as a child, Anna. You are as like as two peas in a pod."

"I see Liesbet in her," said Anna.

They drifted on to quiet discussion of their particular interests. Around them the farm came to life and they were drawn into the bustle of essential work. The girl came to clean the kitchen and Anne-Marie went to the dairy; Gerard went belatedly to open up the byre while Anna and Jan collected the pails for milking.

Later, when she brought the foaming pails of milk to the dairy, Anna noticed how pale Anne-Marie was, and how drenched her eyes looked, as though she had wept the night through.

Anthony had set out on his long voyage and had left her no message, Anne-Marie told her. She voiced the fear that filled her: she did not doubt Anthony's deep and lasting affection, never would she doubt that, she said; but often she was afraid that from some false sense of his own unworthiness he might think it would be best for her if he went out of her life, and this might be his way of seeking to serve her.

What ill service Anthony did the child, thought Anna in anger, looking into Anne-Marie's white, pinched face.

She longed that there should be neither time nor space, so that Anthony and Anne-Marie could see each other as they were in that moment.

And resolved, if need be, to cross the North Sea to England one day, to look into the matter.

PART X

GOLD COAST INTERLUDE

CHAPTER NINETEEN

THE LITTLE FLEET OF THREE ENGLISH SHIPS LAY OFF THE SHORES OF the Gold Coast. With furled sails the blistered hulks of the vessels rose and fell in the dull opaqueness of the sea. Palm trees straggled in an uneven line beyond the fringes of the surf, and peeping out between them were little thatched excrescences of a beehive shape, betokening the presence of a native village; and the Negroes were to be observed moving up and down on the sandy beach on which nests of canoes were drawn up beyond the reach of the tide. Over all there was a steaming haze with the hot grey heavens arching overhead.

In the breathless, tropical heat of noonday the crews of the anchored vessels, sweat-drenched, moved under awnings of matting. They toiled, bringing up the merchandise from below and stowing away in the ship's boats certain offerings for the Chief and the headmen of the village. These gifts consisted of a generous supply of crude liquor, bales of brightly coloured linens, a basket of basins, spoons, and cheap mirrors, and an assortment of glass beads. As no welcoming canoe had shot through the breakers and headed their way it was plain that coercion and tact would be needed if the trading venture was to be successful. The boats were therefore setting out from the ships in the afternoon to establish a friendly basis for negotiations.

The diffidence of the inhabitants was not unexpected. It was well known that the Portuguese, established in their fortress castle at Elmina, dominated the local tribes, and, jealous of their dwindling influence in the teeth of counterattraction from English and French merchant adventurers, had forbidden any trading with the interlopers. This injunction was naturally evaded whenever possible, and the English and the French, and occasionally the Dutch, carried on successful, if surreptitious barter, obtaining pepper, gold, and ivory, and slaves in exchange for the commodities they had to offer. This was done under the very noses of the exasperated Portuguese, who exacted reprisals by confiscating the bartered goods, imprisoning or enslaving the natives, and vigorously attacking all foreign shipping within reach of their warships or their fortress.

The *Sylphide* rolled in the swell; her sister ships, the *Bluebird* and the *Diane,* were anchored a little astern. From the deck of the *Sylphide* Anthony Barradale looked out on the scene before him. So this was the fabulous coast of Guinea.

The captain, Lucas Mason, came up to him as he stood leaning over the rail.

"Well, what do you make of it, Mr. Barradale?" he asked in a deep, resonant voice. Lucas Mason was sturdily built, with powerful shoulders and a dark, pugnacious face. Sweat had matted the dark hair on his forearms into a damp mass, and, on his brow, a wet forelock stuck so closely to his streaming skin that it seemed to have been painted there. For the rest he was heavy-jowled and heavy-browed and when he scowled he had a look of ruthless ferocity; but he had humanity enough and was always just and impartial. Incongruously in his rugged, determined face a pair of bright blue eyes twinkled with a lively appreciation of everything that went on around him. His natural element was the sea, and he was invariably a miserable and besotted frequenter of taverns on land, a practice he abandoned the moment he felt his ship beneath his feet again.

Having had ample opportunity of improving acquaintance with Anthony during the long voyage from Plymouth, Lucas Mason had found the part owner a likable young man with sound enough views despite his sartorial elegance and finicking ways.

"But for the heat Guinea would be a good enough spot, I'm thinking," Anthony observed. "And Tom is set to go ashore and view it at first hand."

Tom Wilson had insisted on accompanying Anthony and had signed on as one of the crew.

"We have missed the rainy season and there's no relief from the steaming jungle vapours and the sun and the mosquitoes. If you and Tom are still of the same mind about going ashore with the boats you must see to it that you are back on salt water before the sun sets. But the mate has landed here before and he'll tell you the moment to leave."

"What trade do you think we'll do?"

"It is difficult to say. The Chief hasn't sent to welcome us, so it means, I should think, that he got into bad odour with the Portuguese after last year's trade with us and dare not; but the mate has a persuasive tongue. He knows some Spanish and a bit of Portuguese and a word or two of the coast language and he will talk the Chief into trading with us again. It's not the Chief that'll need the persuading as much as his old grandmother, Aba, the Queen Mother. She's the difficulty. She's an old crone who will never see a hundred again, I'll be bound. A bag of bones, she is, with a memory as long as her tongue, and why they haven't thrown her in the river—as I am told they do with their aged and useless ones—I cannot think. They're afraid of her. Even the fetish priests let her alone. If you can get some liquor into her you'll be able to open negotiations and she'll not interfere. Drink as little as you can of their wine. It's palm wine and it's potent stuff and it takes a seasoned drinker all his time to keep sober on it; and treat them civilly and with courtesy, for the blacks won't traffic if they be ill used."

"It is out of the question for you to accompany us, I suppose?"

"I cannot leave the ship because there may be trouble at any minute. If the Portuguese discover we are here they may have warships lying off Elmina and we'll be attacked forthwith. The mate will try to persuade the Chief or the headmen to come on board if there's gold to be exchanged."

"It is to be hoped that we will not be attacked while we lie becalmed here," Anthony said.

"That's where we are at a disadvantage. If the Portuguese can get their galleys up it will be awkward; but we must take the risk."

"With the attraction of the rich traffic it seems worth an attempt to gain a footing in this region."

"It's no climate for a white man. I've seen men die of the fever like flies in the winter."

"What the Portuguese can survive we can survive."

"When you've been ashore and have had your eyes opened we will discuss the matter again. You're here, safe and sound on this ship, but I'll wager you when you are on the shore things may look a little different. Nothing ever comes up to what you think it will."

There was wisdom in that last remark, thought Anthony, not taking up the challenge. His life had not worked out as he had thought it might. All that morning, with the promise of new adventure ahead of him, his thoughts had been overshadowed by images of the past. He knew why this was: he had been awakened at dawn as the anchor chain ran screechingly out, and as he lay in his bunk he had heard the gulls scream about the ship, and his thoughts had gone to Pendennis and Anne-Marie, and he had remembered as vividly as though he had seen it but yesterday the sea gull swinging on motionless wings at the rim of the headland, a pattern of dazzling white against the sky.

Thinking of the purpose of their voyage, he was suddenly and violently at variance with his life as he was living it. At heart he had no desire to enslave others, yet he found himself anchored off the shores of a strange land, whose inhabitants it was his intention to assist in taking away in chains to a lifelong captivity.

Anthony had compelled himself to stop thinking by an immense effort of will: it was too late now even for regret.

As though to thwart him in this stern disciplining of his wayward mind, all morning the gulls had wheeled and screamed about the anchored ships.

ii

The mate of the *Sylphide,* Roger Dunne, had impressed upon Anthony the importance of the rigid observance of certain etiquette, for much depended on the manner of their entry into the village of the Kormantins on their official visit to the Chief.

He had gone forward with ten sailors following a few paces behind him, the men bearing presents for the Chief, the Queen Mother, and the headmen. Some distance in their rear Anthony Barradale walked with a retinue of half a dozen seamen.

No sooner had they left the beach than the Negroes swarmed down from the village. Somewhat impeded by the mob that howled and danced before them, the two parties endeavoured to maintain their ceremonial march between palisades and compounds to the Chief's abode. A stalwart youth, black as ebony and glistening with oil, appointed himself guide and led the way.

Anthony walked with such dignity as he could command with the heterogeneous crowd leaping about him—men and women, naked pot-bellied infants, withered crones, scruffy goats, and bedraggled hens all stared and united their clamour.

The fantastic progress continued thus until the beating of a drum began and, as the rapid tattoo gathered volume and its signal became clear, the rabble miraculously assumed some order and fell in behind the white men.

As if to mark his arrival in the African village, a bird projected itself into the bizarre scene. No white sea gull this time, emblem of freedom, but a vulture, that, with bare, repulsive neck extended, flapped heavily down from the leafless bough of a dead cottonwood tree to gorge on a piece of goat's flesh left unattended in a compound.

Dunne was waiting at the gate of the Chief's compound. He disappeared within as Anthony came up. When he emerged again he and Anthony advanced together into a covered inner courtyard before the royal huts. Through the interstices of the palm leaves with which the courtyard was thatched the light of the afternoon glimmered, throwing a patterned trelliswork on the floor of trodden earth. As his eyes became accustomed to the gloom Anthony discerned the massive figure of the Chief near the entrance to the huts.

He saw a huge man seated on a stool of carved mahogany. He sat motionless with his arms extended and on them were golden ornaments so numerous and so heavy that the young men who knelt to support them swayed a little with the weight on their shoulders. Grouped about the Chief were the fetish priests, hideous in the panoply of their trade, and the headmen, ranged in a semicircle about their leader. On either side the Chief stood the bearers of the royal insignia.

A gleam of light showed in a corner and drew Anthony's attention.

He saw, seated on a stool of state with one female attendant behind her, a very old woman. From the waist downwards she was draped in a twist of scarlet and yellow calico. Above that she was naked and her withered breasts hung slackly. She wore a collar of gold about her shrivelled neck and her woolly white hair was dressed high and stuck through with gold ornaments. Her face was seamed and parchmentlike, and the greyness of extreme old age was on it. She sat motionless, scarcely breathing, and the gleam of gold that had drawn Anthony's gaze to her came from her arms. He saw they were encased in gold. At the wrists bracelets of heavy design gleamed yellowly and came up to the foresleeves of the same precious metal.

Anthony looked again at the Chief. He waved Roger Dunne forward to make his speech of presentation and while he was declaiming he looked closely at the Chief. He was a magnificent figure of a man, running to flesh, and the godlike proportions of his body were marred by a small and degenerate head, on which was placed a circlet of gold to proclaim his overlordship of the tribe.

The Chief in his turn made a speech of welcome. It was a long address and several times the Chief paused to allow Roger Dunne to interpret. The gist of it all was that there had been trouble with the Portuguese but, if the goods the English had brought out in their ships were to his liking, he was prepared to run the gauntlet and trade with them.

This was the signal that negotiations were about to begin in real earnest. There was a general stir and shuffle. A number of youths appeared with fans of palm leaves and began a steady swishing away of the flies. The Englishmen stolidly braced themselves to endure an hour or more of interminable bargaining amid heat and flies and the strong odours of sweating humanity in that enclosed space.

The Chief's wives appeared with pots of baked clay filled with palm wine and the liquor thoughtfully provided by Lucas Mason. Shrewdly calculating that the moment for debate had come as the pots emptied, the Chief began by asking whether the English vessels were adequately armed. Anthony assured him, through Dunne, that they were well able to defend themselves. Kwaku, the Chief, thereupon informed him that it was a moral certainty that they would be attacked as soon as the Portuguese learned of their arrival. There were four Portuguese warships anchored off Elmina, he said. He therefore advised that they should get on with the business in hand as expeditiously as possible so that the English could stand away from the hostile shores, as to delay was to invite trouble for all concerned.

In answer to the plea for haste Anthony asked for fresh victuals to be sent off to the ships at once; and added that they were seeking cargoes of gold, pepper, ivory, and slaves. They wished to take on board at least three hundred slaves.

Apparently the three hundred slaves Anthony had asked for presented a knotty problem, for Kwaku relapsed into sudden silence and seemed deeply sunk in thought. His followers also were silent and his wives ceased their soft jabbering among themselves.

In the quiet that descended on the stuffy courtyard Anthony sensed an ominous tension, which was brought home to him more sharply by the instant stiffening of the figure of the old Queen Mother. Both she and her handmaiden were as rigid as figures carved in stone. Anthony, a little fuddled by palm wine, but still clear enough in the head to remember that the Queen Mother had taken no part in the discussions, nor yet in the drinking, was aware that her aloofness from the ceremonial negotiations indicated a division between herself and her grandson, and that his request for three hundred prime slaves had precipitated some crisis. . . .

"You ask them if they have been to war lately," Anthony suggested to Dunne, taking the initiative when he found the prolonged silence too irksome. "The Chief did not refuse outright. He may have a likely parcel somewhere or other for disposal. They are thinking very hard about something."

Dunne put the question to Kwaku, who shook his head in denial.

"He says they have not been to war lately," Dunne translated.

The Chief turned to the headmen and the fetish priests and burst into vehement, rapid conversation. Whatever it was he spoke about, his words seemed to provoke mixed feelings in his audience, for some faces expressed doubt and unwillingness, while others showed ferocious joy. Throughout the heated argument which followed on the Chief's words the Queen Mother on her carved stool of state in the far corner remained tense and watchful.

At length, after some minutes of furious debate, Kwaku said to Dunne:

"Convey to the owner we may have three hundred young men for him. He will hear definitely in the morning. I have yet to discuss the matter with my elders."

At once a hubbub of conversation broke out. There was fierce quarrelling among the men, and some of the women were in tears. Only the old woman in the corner was inscrutable in her silence.

On the way back to the *Sylphide* in a native canoe Dunne told Anthony what the commotion had been about. Some of the excited gabble had been beyond him but he had managed to get the sense of the argument.

"This is the way of it," Dunne said. "It appears the ancient dame is the grandmother. Among the coast tribes descent goes by the female line. The old woman had twin daughters and each daughter became the mother of a son. So there have always been two factions, each with a strong claim to the kingship. Some years ago Kwaku's faction got on top and he was proclaimed Chief. There has always been a minority dissatisfied with his rule and several attempts have been made to destool him and to put Afori, the son of the other sister, on the stool. A few weeks ago there was a serious revolt in which Kwaku's side just managed to defeat the other. In the civil war—you may call it that, I suppose—

several hundreds of the opposition were captured. They are still held prisoner. And it was touch and go whether the old woman should be thrown into the river because she makes no secret of her preference for Afori's claim, as his mother was born a few minutes before her sister, and he is the better man, she declares. She was spared, however, much against the wishes of Kwaku, who knows she will stir up trouble for him as long as she is alive, and the last occasion well-nigh cost him his stool."

"Why did they not make an end of the poor old soul?" asked Anthony, in whom compassion stirred. A quick death was better than to dwell in isolation among her people.

"The fetish priests were against it; she is of the blood royal. There is some sort of juju about it."

"I take it Kwaku thinks he will wear his crown easier without three hundred young men of the opposition?"

"That is about right."

They talked on to the accompaniment of the chant the naked black boatmen sang as they thrust their short paddles through the waves with quick, chopping strokes, keeping to the rhythm of their song.

Darkness descended suddenly in those equatorial waters. The distance between the rolling ship and the mysterious shore seemed a wide gulf. The sounds of the sea reached out to Anthony as he paced the deck alone—the slapping of the waves against the hull, the cry of a belated gull, the sighing of the wind in the rigging, the voices of the sailors yarning in the forecastle. And, with the wind lifting his damp hair, he thought of the far green fields of Cornwall, of the ramparts of her cliffs where he had wandered with Anne-Marie. He sent his thoughts and his heart out to his love, watching the steel-dark sea under the purple sky.

CHAPTER TWENTY

As the sun, breaking clear of the horizon, flung across the rippling sea its first shafts of gold, the ships that had been shadowy before leapt into an actuality of crowded canvas; and, bearing down upon the anchored English vessels, the four Portuguese men-o'-war sailed in to the attack.

The watch on the *Sylphide* saw the menacing sails and shouted the warning. The trumpets blared out the alarm and anchors were weighed and sails were hoisted with a despatch that showed the crews were fully aware of the urgency of their situation; and, tacking to take advantage of the wind, the three English ships, with the *Diane* in the lead, headed for the open sea, manoeuvring for a running fight. Although they were still out of range of the enemy's ordnance it was soon apparent that the Portuguese had the faster vessels as the distance between pursued and pursuers lessened.

The *Sylphide* came on some way astern of her sister ships, and the Portuguese vessels sailed past in succession and poured their broadsides in at long range. Not much damage was sustained and the *Sylphide* held steadily on her course in the wake of the *Bluebird* and the *Diane*.

Anthony Barradale sought out Lucas Mason. He realized that to offer fight in the circumstances was madness, but to slip away without firing a shot was too ignominious a course to contemplate.

"Will we get away, do you think?" he asked.

"Not if the breeze continues to freshen as it is doing," said Lucas Mason gloomily. "They have the speed."

"We'll fight for it then," declared Anthony, action being more to his liking.

"The *Diane* and the *Bluebird* will put about to our rescue, and if we beat off the Portuguese we'll not do it without loss. The thing to do is to get away. After dark we can get clear, and come back later to finish off the trading; but it will be a tricky business."

"Look!" Anthony exclaimed.

The sun was well up in the pale sky. The four Portuguese vessels were drawing closer, manoeuvring to encircle the *Sylphide*. On the starboard bow the largest of the enemy was hoisting and furling sail and altering her course so as to lie directly in their path. The rigging swarmed with men, and the shouts of command came across to them, so near in was the vessel. The yells from the Portuguese came challengingly across the waves, and drew from the crew of the *Sylphide* a roar of defiance.

"To your stations!"

Lucas Mason roared out the command; and at once there came a broadside from the Portuguese which riddled the *Sylphide* and struck the mainmast. The men at the gun stations on the *Sylphide* replied with a salvo of cannon fire. The roar and rocking seemed to blow out Anthony's eardrums, and he staggered against the bulwarks as the ship rolled violently. The thick, choking smoke billowed between the vessels and momentarily screened them from each other.

While the *Sylphide* yet reeled from the concussion another of the Portuguese had sailed into position on the starboard and, without warning, a broadside from the larboard added to the confusion.

"Hold your fire!"

With a burst of exultation Anthony realized that Lucas Mason had exercised some restraint and had backed his cool judgment. The Portuguese broadside had fallen short, as the distance was still too great for their fire to be effective.

The smoke was drifting away and the surface of the sea rippled in response to the freshening wind. In wraithlike trails of white the last of the gun smoke cleared, and then a great shout arose from the *Sylphide* as it was observed that the Portuguese vessel was hoisting all sail and preparing to ram. The wind was with the enemy. The vast spread of canvas filled with the ever-stiffening breeze, and, cutting through the sapphire water, the whitened foam of her progress fell away on either side of the cleaving prow. Driven by wind and wave, the Portuguese man-o'-war, the voluptuous plumage of her sails at majestic stretch, swept irresistibly down upon them.

On the *Sylphide* the helmsman swung the helm hard about to avoid a head-on impact; and, as the vessel answered to her helm, the second Portuguese warship on the starboard, having sailed appreciably closer, got in a broadside with stunning effect, riddling the superstructure and bringing down the mainmast in a tangle of spars, cordage, and smouldering sails.

Thrown off her balance by the terrific force of the salvo, the *Sylphide* heeled over and for a fearful moment shuddered in every timber, slanted from bows to stern. Then, for yet another timeless moment, the stricken ship hung poised on the brink of disaster.

Anthony found himself clutching at the shattered bulwarks. He saw the blue-green translucent sea, the waves with curling crests glittering in the sun. The sudden lurch of the *Sylphide* blotted out the vision of the sea, and he was left to stare in unbelieving horror at a snarled mass of rope and canvas, at charred timber, at the bodies of two dead men who had been felled by the mainmast as it crashed on deck.

On the brink of the abyss the *Sylphide* righted herself and with a sigh in every joint and stay assumed an even keel.

Disengaging himself from the drifting tackle, Anthony stumbled over the barriers of wreckage.

"Stand by to repel boarders!"

Lucas Mason's stentorian shout shattered the unnatural silence that disaster had bred. It jerked Anthony abruptly from his daze. Mechanically he snatched the pistols from his belt and rushed forward to the bows of the ship.

There was no sequence in the happenings of the next few minutes. The Portuguese man-o'-war was on them. Defeated in her object of ramming the *Sylphide,* she shot past the bows and ran alongside. In an instant the grappling irons were out and the two vessels lay side by side in an embrace of death.

Under the blazing African sun hand-to-hand fighting was joined. The combat raged on both sides with unsurpassed ferocity. The crew of the *Sylphide,* on the defensive, thrust at the Portuguese with swords and cutlasses, with lengths of twisted iron and shattered spar when the weapons fell from their hands. At first the Englishmen were driven back to fight in and out of the disorder of their deck, slipping in the blood of friend and foe, stumbling over the bodies of the dead. In the heat the stench of blood and sweat and smoke rose fetidly from the littered deck, and the groans of the perishing mingled with the shouts of those soon to perish.

Anthony had fired his pistols. He flung them down and seized the cutlass of a dead man. He fought shoulder to shoulder with Lucas Mason, and they were joined by the mate, Roger Dunne, and finally by Tom Wilson. In between his lunges at the hard-pressing Portuguese Anthony stole a sidelong glance at Tom and saw he was grinning like a fiend, with blood streaming from a cut above his eye, which he wiped away every now and then with an impatient curse. The country lad was wielding a cutlass with a scythelike movement, Anthony noticed with cool detachment; and thought that what habit bred in a man invariably betrayed itself in a crisis. The deadly sweep of Tom's cutlass, steady, swishing, lopping off limbs as easily as he had cut hay at Bodrugan, brought back the memory of home and the green swathes falling before the mowers in the fields of Cornwall. His thought was a flash, a gleaming moment of truth and sanity. . . .

Now the Englishmen were taking the initiative. They were pushing the Portuguese back, little by little. The shouting quietened, and a deadly intensity of purpose held them all.

"Keep it up, men, and we'll have every man jack of them over the side," yelled Lucas Mason, his unceasing downward blows doing great execution. Under his breath he was muttering the foulest oaths, blasting the Portuguese to the hell they came from. Shouting, when he had the breath, words of encouragement to the battling crew. "Keep it up, men. There's help coming."

It was true. There was help coming. The *Diane* and the *Bluebird* had put about and had returned to the assistance of the slower *Sylphide*. Afraid to put in a broadside lest the shot should rake the stricken *Sylphide* over the Portuguese vessel, the *Diane* came close to the fast-locked ships, tacking again and again until it was obvious to the Portuguese that it was her intention to board them on the other side. A great clamour arose, and now the Englishmen thrust them back to their own deck more readily, and the fiercest combats raged about the grappling positions, for it was apparent to them that the Portuguese were anxious to disengage and they put forth superhuman efforts to prevent their doing so. With the assistance of the *Diane* they hoped to hold their prize.

Anthony caught the infection of this exultant enthusiasm. He tossed back the wet chestnut locks from his brow and clove a Portuguese from skull to chin. The sun blazed in his eyes and the steel blade threw back a blinding reflection as he wrenched it from the dead man. He laughed aloud and the lust of battle burned like fire in his veins.

They had reached the shattered bulwarks of the enemy vessel. With a shout of triumph, cutlass uplifted, Anthony leapt aboard, the three behind him. Immediately a fierce attack developed around them as the Portuguese tried to thrust them back. The mortal combat reached its height and a demoniac fury filled both contending parties—the Portuguese fought for the freedom of their ship through a living wall of the bodies of their foes; the English, carried away by the dread glory of the affray, pressed them back. The four, Anthony, Lucas Mason, Tom Wilson, and the mate, seemed to bear charmed lives. They had come through unscathed and now they surged on united towards the helm, their intention being to gain control of the ship.

A bloody path marked their progress to the wheel. Lucas Mason slew the helmsman where he stood, and the vessel, freed from control as the dead man loosed his grip on the wheel, careened wildly. There were splintering sounds and the joined ships rolled violently and then were wrenched apart, the shattered bulwarks reduced to matchwood. The *Sylphide* yawed away; a gap of troubled water showed between the ships; they were free of each other.

The significance of the crash came at once to Lucas Mason. He looked round, then, with his back to the dead man at the wheel, he and the three faced the pack of Portuguese who came on to the attack. Lips bared teeth in wolfish grins, and Englishmen and Portuguese fought in silence and like devils round the untended helm, while the ship swung back and forth, wallowing in the troughs of the waves. The Englishmen were pushed back, the helm was brought round hard, and the Portuguese vessel leapt forward, clear of the *Sylphide*.

Risking damage to the *Sylphide,* the *Diane* got in a broadside at close range as the Portuguese vessel plunged forward. There was a deafening roar, a rending crash, and the acrid smell of gunpowder hung in the hot air. The stricken ship lurched and reared, and the combatants on her deck were flung in all directions by the shock of the concussion.

Anthony struck his head with considerable force against the superstructure. Half stunned, he struggled at once to his knees, slashing blindly about him, determined to take as many of the enemy with him as time permitted, if die he must.

He was struck down from behind with some heavy implement; and felt consciousness ebbing in a dark wave from him.

ii

Long lines of palms grew along the beach hard by the castle of San Jorge del Mina. For a century this fortress at Elmina had reared its majestic bastions from the solid rock with the surf breaking endlessly at its walls, and the surging tides vainly battering at its foundations. It was surrounded on two sides by the sea, with strong defensive batteries commanding the roadstead; and it was equally well fortified from the landward side. Again and again it had proved its impregnability in the teeth of opposition from intrepid seafarers and merchant adventurers of many nations, who, attracted by the lucrative trade in gold and slaves, had sought to gain a footing in that far, equatorial land.

To Elmina, the scarred grey watcher of the surf-washed African shore, on the day following the naval action off the Kormantin coast, were delivered four prisoners from one of the three English ships. Of these four men two were sorely wounded, and stumbled from the beach to the castle supported by their companions and urged forward by the pikes of the escorting soldiers. Anthony Barradale and Lucas Mason were in poor shape indeed, while Tom Wilson and Roger Dunne had come through with bruises and contusions and minor scratches.

As the little band halted at the gate while the drawbridge was being lowered Anthony looked about him. He saw the ramparts and the bastions of the fortress shimmering in the glare, and, surmounting the impressive pile, the flag of Portugal flying from a lofty tower. He stared until the sun blinded him and he could see nothing for the smarting of his eyeballs. He was in a high fever and semidelirious from the blows he had sustained on his head. His vision turned inwards and, as in childhood, he saw again the images of certain events in his life. In a blinding flash he realized that Anne-Marie had spoken no more than the bare truth when she had assured him that she loved him and would wait for him—it was a physically blinding flash, for his sight returned and for an instant he saw the chrome-yellow sunlight on the frowning castle walls. And then darkness again, and an inward picture in his mind: he saw a wild, dark night at Bodrugan and his father giving Anne-Marie into his mother's arms. . . .

"Anne-Marie," he shrieked. "Anne-Marie."

But no scream issued from his swollen lips. Only the thinnest of cracked sounds came from his parched and contracted throat. Tom Wilson bent his ear to Anthony's lips, and only he could have recognized the barely audible cry.

"She is all right," he said. "She is sitting on one of them dykes in Holland Ryk was ever talking about, quite safe and as happy as you please."

Tom spoke soothingly as a mother would to an ailing child. The tone of his voice penetrated to Anthony's fevered mind if his words did not and he was quiet again.

Roger Dunne and Lucas Mason exchanged glances. They were aware that Anthony had the sunstroke and that his mind wandered on account of that and because of the injuries to his head; but they had not thought that Tom was in a similar state. Tom caught the look that passed between them.

"He's remembering, that's all. And my wits ain't wandering," he said bluntly.

"That's something to the good," said Lucas Mason. "We'll need our united wits to get out of this place once we're in it."

"It'll be the galleys for us, Captain?"

Lucas Mason nodded.

"The natives tell us it's the usual fate of French and English prisoners."

"I doubt whether he'll make a galley slave," muttered Tom, jerking his head at Anthony. "His sort'll never stick it."

"Anthony," said Lucas Mason, putting his hand on Anthony's shoulder. Anthony turned deep-sunk, unrecognizing eyes on him.

They had been exchanging these remarks in whispers under cover of their loud-voiced escort, who shouted and jested with such of the garrison as looked out upon them from the battlements. Suddenly a shout of command rang out and, with a rattle of chains and a reverberating thud, the drawbridge clanged across the moat, and the four prisoners and their escort were admitted within the thick stone walls of the outer fortifications.

For a gruelling hour in the guardroom they were interrogated by the commandant of the fortress. Roger Dunne acted as interpreter. Anthony, unable to keep on his feet, collapsed on the cool stone floor and knew nothing of what passed.

Later they were delivered to the surgeon, who looked at the setting of Lucas Mason's arm and approved it—the mate had set it with Tom Wilson's assistance on board the Portuguese ship, stretching it and putting it in splinters as Lucas himself directed. The surgeon applied a fresh dressing to the wound on Mason's shoulder where a cutlass had bitten to the bone, a task he performed with skill and care as prospective galley slaves were valuable, and the sea captain was a fine specimen of manhood, not to be permitted to die before he had worn himself out chained to the oars. Therefore he was deft and immaculate in his cleansing of the wound, for all too often tetanus set in and undid his work. Tom Wilson and Roger Dunne were in good condition and in a few minutes he had satisfied himself that there was little to do for them.

The three were marched out, while Anthony was left lying on the floor, muttering and turning in delirium. At the doorway Tom Wilson thrust past the guard and went back to Anthony.

"What's to happen to him?" he cried. "Dunne, you ask them."

The soldiers seized him by the arms and dragged him to the door while he fought and struggled.

"You'll do no good. Stop that," commanded Lucas Mason. "There's no sense in making matters any worse than they are."

Tom ceased his pointless resistance and joined his companions in the doorway. Dunne put his question. The guard cursed and struck him across the mouth. The surgeon, however, thought fit to intervene.

"He is to be taken to the sick bay," he said. "Your friend is in a high fever and will need skilled nursing."

There was nothing for it but to accept their captivity and to hope it would be less rigorous than they feared, nor broken by visits to the torture chamber—an unlikely contingency, as the galleys were constantly in need of rowers: few of the slaves stood up for long to their labour in the broiling sun with nothing to keep up their strength but a minimum quantity of the coarsest food and little or no hope of rescue or escape. In these conditions life was short.

iii

The dungeons were situated in the bowels of the castle. They were small and the walls were hewn in the rock upon which the fortress was founded. There was a single low, stout, nail-studded door to each cell, and at the far end a grating with heavy bars embedded in the masonry.

The prisoners endured solitary confinement, but they were not usually shackled. The reason for this seeming clemency was self-evident: the sea poured through the gratings when the tide was high and potential galley slaves in fetters might well come to a premature death by drowning if they were not free to retreat from the water.

The Englishmen were incarcerated in three dungeons, side by side. Before the day was out they had learned to fit in a few moments of whispered conversation from their gratings in the intervals of the passing and repassing of the sentries.

So resilient a thing is the human heart that hope revived, and soon two desperate pairs of hands wrenched at the bars of their prison, testing them, searching for the slightest flaw. It was Roger Dunne who felt a bar tremble under his touch, and guessed that some poor wretch before him had weakened it in its socket. He communicated his discovery to his companions, and wild hope and the desire for freedom crystallized abruptly in an aspiration so dazzling that it almost took their breath away. They might yet be free!

iv

In the darkest hour of the night the bar came away from the wall. Wet through with perspiration and the sea water, Roger Dunne stood panting from his exertions. He was aware of a quick intake of breath from the adjoining cell and knew that Lucas Mason shared his moment of triumph. Throughout the day they had planned their course of action and now it only remained to strip himself as naked as God made him and ease himself through the narrow aperture.

Once out of the dungeon, they had decided, he must swim to the far shore and endeavour to make his way to the Kormantins, walking at night and concealing himself by day. To be captured meant death, as the Portuguese exacted that penalty on runaway slaves, and, after execution, it was their custom to thrust the heads of their victims upon the spikes on the fortress walls, to act as a deterrent to any of the prisoners who thought in terms of escape. Roger Dunne, if ever he reached the Kormantin country, intended to use all his powers of persuasion to induce Chief Kwaku to lead an attack on Elmina and hoped thus to rescue his companions in misfortune.

The wave had ebbed; a greyness lighter than the blackness of the cell showed where the grating was. It was the moment. Roger Dunne dropped to his knees and put his head through the aperture. As the next wave came surging up he drew the rest of his body through and crouched, a free man, outside his dungeon.

He waited with his head above the water for the wave to be sucked down to the sea again. The instant this happened the faces of Lucas Mason and Tom Wilson appeared at their gratings.

"God speed you," whispered Lucas Mason. "I do not think they heard."

"Look for me in about a week with the Kormantins," said Roger Dunne under his breath. "Not sooner. Good-bye, Captain. 'Bye, Tom."

He was gone. They strained their eyes till the next wave came to watch him scrambling down the rocks on which their prison stood. When a wave had swept up and receded they saw the dark blob on the sea that was his head, and a flash as a white arm was lifted out of the water, as though a fish had leaped.

On the next morning a great commotion broke out when it was discovered that Roger Dunne had escaped. Tom Wilson was at once removed and sent on a galley for fear he should make a like attempt. Lucas Mason, being in no state to break prison, was left where he was.

Someone was brought to the cell Tom had occupied. Lucas waited for the sentry to march away. Then he rushed to the grating.

"Who is it?" he whispered.

"It is I, Anthony, Captain."

To his horror Lucas found that tears were gushing from his eyes. He had not wept for years. It was God's grace that no one was by to see him. He conquered his emotion.

"Roger Dunne has escaped. He is on his way to the Kormantins. He may bring help back. It is a very remote chance."

The heavy tread of the returning sentry sent him away from the bars back to a corner of the cell; and in intervals throughout the day they exchanged their news in whispers.

Time passed. Roger Dunne had been away overlong, Lucas told himself. He must have failed to reach the Kormantins, or Chief Kwaku had no mind to risk an attack on the Portuguese. Well, whatever it was that had happened, he knew he and Anthony would lie in their dungeons until they died. His arm was painful and he knew it was not knitting as it should, and, from such accounts of his state as he could glean from Anthony, he guessed the lad was in sorry shape.

Lucas entered upon a strange and selfless phase of his chequered life. He cheered and encouraged Anthony, and told him to sleep while he watched the incoming tide. They could not see each other, but sometimes they thrust their fingers through the bars and their fingers met in a forlorn contact.

Neither of them realized how time passed. They could not have said whether they had been confined for a week or a month or a year. They grew perceptibly weaker. A strong tie of love was woven between the rough, disillusioned seaman and the oversensitive, inexperienced young man. Although they kept the knowledge from each other, each believed that he would not see the sun again. Lucas prayed daily, for the lad's sake, that he would not be the first to die.

V

They were to see the sun again. They saw it on a perfect morning. The sea rolled in from the far horizon in a deep blue swathe, rippling and shimmering in the sun. The surf lay fine and lacelike on the gleaming yellow sand. Against the clear azure of the sky the palms showed darkly etched, their feathered crowns in perfect silhouette.

Anthony and Lucas, scarce able to stand, had been brought from their cells to the topmost gun terrace of the fortress, for what purpose they knew not. Behind them the armed guard brought their pikes to the salute as the commandant mounted the steps of the terrace, and remained stiffly at attention until he had taken up a position at the base of a cannon sunk in the masonry in the centre of the small amphitheatre of guns, whose wide iron mouths gaped through each embrasure. Anthony felt a sudden stiffening, a rigidity of nerves, in Lucas Mason's body. The thrill of some new horror was communicated to him. He turned his eyes to the far end of the terrace where the steps came up from the battlements and saw, standing between two soldiers, an emaciated wreck of a man who was Roger Dunne. His hands were bound behind his back, and he was barely recognizable.

Dunne was stark naked. His face was wild and haggard, and his eyes gazed blankly ahead from the cavernous hollows under a brow burned red-raw by the sun. Fever had yellowed his skin and his hair hung in a matted mass to his shoulders. He had starved and sweated away the flesh from his bones, and his gaunt frame was red and covered in sores from head to heel from the stings of mosquitoes and sand flies, the bites of ants, and general rough usage.

"Roger Dunne!"

The cry was wrung from Anthony.

The fixed stare on Roger Dunne's face passed and he looked at them.

The commandant began a long speech. When he had made an end of speaking there was a roll of drums, and when the last throb had died Dunne said:

"He says your fate will be mine if you attempt to escape."

Before he could say more a hand was clapped over his mouth and the soldiers began to push him forward to the centre of the terrace. Dunne shrugged himself free of the Portuguese. He walked forward of his own accord, so that the soldiers had no need to drag him. Across the terrace they went to one of the great guns overlooking the sea. Here ropes were produced and Roger's ankles were securely bound together, the long, trailing ends of his bonds being wound round and round his body until he lay like a mummy at the base of the cannon.

He made no outcry so they did not gag him. When they lifted him and began to secure him to the cannon's mouth Anthony realized what it was they intended to do. Roger Dunne was to be blown from the great gun. He was stunned and shocked into speechless horror, rendered all the more terrible by his own utter helplessness.

Anthony could not have cried out if he had wished. The scene, that like some inexorable nightmare was being enacted, he was to see as long as he lived as a dreadful dream. As he lay dying in the frozen splendour of a frosty night with the Northern Lights burning rosily for his passing the memory of that moment on the battlements of Elmina castle was to come back to him, so that all save his last breaths were to be panted away with that horror in the background.

The cannon was fired. Anthony felt himself falling away into bottomless darkness, felt the support of Lucas Mason's whole arm; and, with an immense effort of will, kept on his feet and marched back to his dungeon.

He lay unconscious in his cell for hours, while Lucas, crouched at his grating, watched the rising tide. He had resolved that he would not call Anthony when the water came in. Let the lad pass from stupor to death without knowing it. It was better that the sea should make an end cleanly and quickly.

vi

The gold mine on the hill at Abrobi had been worked for more years than the celebrated castle of San Jorge del Mina had stood. It had proved rich in alluvial deposits and a source of great wealth to the Portuguese. As time went on deeper penetrations into the earth were made, and badly shored-up tunnels honeycombed the heart of the hill. In that climate of heavy, tropical rainfall the earth was overladen with moisture and, as was inevitable, the riddled hill one day partly collapsed, burying a number of African workers.

The Africans read in the fall of the mine the vengeance of a malignant and implacable god, called a sasabonsum, who chose for his dwelling place either a silk-cotton tree or some place where the earth was red. The sasabonsum, moreover, had greater powers than he had yet been moved to exercise—he could also cause an earthquake. He had not yet been provoked enough to use this most drastic measure of vengeance; but he had been somewhat provoked and no African would set foot near the mine, and the work was at a standstill.

The commandant of Elmina sent emissaries to the chiefs of the tribesmen who worked as miners at Abrobi to see if the superstition could be overcome. The fetish priests decreed that the great sasabonsum could be placated if white men were sacrificed in the mine. The commandant thankfully accepted this way out of the difficulty and consulted his lists to see who the victims should be.

In consequence of these happenings Anthony, Lucas Mason, and Tom Wilson found themselves united once more and travelling into the interior.

The train was a long one and the three Englishmen were separated.

There were several Portuguese engineers, some soldiers of the garrison, and a hundred or more Negroes, who head-loaded the stores and machinery. For three days they walked through evergreen forests, skirting mangrove swamps where deformed and twisted roots started in writhing distortion from the fetid swamps, and where mosquitoes and midges bred in myriads. So dense was the growth of the vegetation that the sunlight rarely penetrated, and an unending twilight prevailed. All the while the heat was drawn up from the saturated earth where rotting leaves disintegrated and a miasmatic mist dispersed its vapours.

Only once did it fall out that the three friends spoke together on that long march. On the second evening, when camp was being prepared for the night, they saw their opportunity and seized it.

"Anthony," said the captain, "have you any idea of what this move means?"

"The commandant did not trouble to inform me of our destination," returned Anthony with a brave effort at humour. "But my reason tells me this trip is bound to have an unpleasant ending. I do not see the Portuguese taking us so far into the forest for our amusement."

"Well, you have survived, and in the cell I thought you were not likely to live the day sometimes. When the sea washed in you always came to in the nick of time and dragged yourself out of the water."

Mason moved his arm and Anthony noticed he carried it at a peculiar angle. The bones must have gone apart, he thought, as the fingers of the injured arm were swollen and purple. The captain must suffer with it, although he voiced no complaint.

"Your arm, Captain," said Anthony.

"You have an infection in it," said Tom.

"I can still get about, which is the main thing. A leg, now, that would have been very awkward," said Mason cheerfully.

"Nothing could be worse than the dungeons or the galleys," Anthony remarked.

Tom was not so sure of that. The galley slaves had told him dark tales of juju and superstition in the interior, and what a fetish priest knew regarding the refinements of torture.

"No," answered Tom, keeping his thoughts to himself.

A hand was laid on his shoulder and he was drawn away. No violence was offered him or the others and Tom wondered anew what lay behind the good food they were being given and the almost gentle handling they received.

Towards evening on the third day they halted at the approach to the Awoin village. To the west rose the little hill in which was situated the gold mine.

As the sun set a strange procession issued from the village to greet them. The people advanced dancing and leaping to the beating of drums and the wild pagan rhythm of throbbing tom-toms. Then came the Chief and the elders of the village with the insignia bearers carrying on high the tribal emblems. And finally, grotesque and hideous, came the fetish priests and the priestesses.

The Englishmen were not left to ponder the meaning of the appearance of the Chief at their halting place. They were made to join in with the howling procession, and now the long line of Africans faced about so that they looked up at Abrobi Hill, and the priests and priestesses were in the van, with the three white men in their midst.

Solemnly chanting now, the Africans went in an orderly train up the hill. There, at the end of a tunnel that had not fallen in at the time of the general collapse, the fetish priests entered the mine with the three prisoners, and following them down the long shaft came the wailing chant of the tribe.

When they had penetrated some way underground the three men were bound hand and foot and left lying on the stagnant floor of the shaft as propitiatory offerings for the appeasement of the outraged god. After long incantations and much writhing and twisting in ceremonial dance, the fetish priests withdrew.

At last the secret of the journey through the green twilight of the primeval forests was out: all that long night they three were to lie in the darkness, and at dawn the sacrifice of their blood was to make the offerings yet more acceptable to the Great One, the sasabonsum, who had his dwelling where the earth was red.

CHAPTER TWENTY-ONE

She spurned the carved stool with her foot. The raw mahogany had acquired colour and polish from years of use. The sun had been shining on its base all afternoon and she felt the hidden warmth of the wood touch her ankle.

She, Aba, the Queen Mother of the Kormantins, was old, very old. Today she had realized that she had run her course and must surrender to the years.

Lost in thought, she continued to press her bare foot and the side of her leg against the stool, drawing the heat into herself. She was very cold: she drew her cover cloth higher over her right shoulder, the golden bracelets at her wrist jingling against the foresleeve of beaten gold. At that moment the sun came out strongly between the leaves of the cotton tree and its rays lived in the burnished brightness of the golden ornaments with which she had loaded herself. She had put on so many rings of gold wire that her fingers were stiff as sticks; and her collar of gold was well-nigh choking her; and the chains of gold dripping in yellow brightness between her withered breasts had accentuated what she had wished to hide—her age and her uselessness. To add to her shock and misery the golden anklets had bitten into her bones all day, irritating the wound where once she had been galled by a too tight anklet in the days of her early wifehood, when she had been proud and plump.

She was alone in her private courtyard. They had all left her because her grandson, Afori, had been killed by a leopard while out hunting, and Kwaku, his power undisputed, had looked with disfavour upon her. The fetish priests had decreed at last that she should be cast into the river on the morrow; and Kwaku had made the scornful observation that, if she desired a less public death, the remedy lay in her own hands, and there were yet a few hours in which to cheat the tribe of its spectacle.

They had all left her. She was quite alone. She shivered with a nervous chill, cold to the marrow even in that humid atmosphere. Her blood was as thin as water. She was old, finished, her work taken out of her hands. If Afori had not met with this mischance she might have seen a man upon the stool of her ancestors. Kwaku had not the spirit of a mouse in his dealings with the Portuguese; he could take a valuable lesson from the Chief of the Awoin village. After the fall of earth in the mine he had demanded the sacrifice of white men to appease the fetish before he would send his young men back to dig gold for the Portuguese. And the commandant had accepted the condition without demur. Ha! There was a man for you. And Kwaku, a fool, a man of no wit or subtlety for all his fine apparel and rich stores of gold. Pah! thought Aba, her lips curling back from her toothless gums, rubbing her thin ankle reflectively up and down the stool so that the anklets jingled and jangled like castanets.

They had all left her; they all stood aloof, fearful of befriending one so unfortunate. As the god of the cotton tree stood aloof. She had sat in the circle of sacrificial stones and broken shards of pottery and had cried to the god to counsel her; but he had not heard her.

It was near sunset and a little heat and energy had returned to her. Quite unexpectedly, when she had decided that thought was beyond her, an inspiration came to her. It occurred to her that, although no human aid would now be given her, an appeal to a sasabonsum was a different matter. She would not petition the small god of the cotton tree—he had already turned a deaf ear to her plea—but he was an unimportant god and the help she needed could only be given by the Great One of the Abrobi mine, in the country of the Awoins.

But was it help she desired? Her thoughts ran on and their tenor changed. She no longer wished to save herself—she was old and death must come to all. She longed now to leave red ruin behind her. She wanted to provoke the sasabonsum to such frenzy that he would produce the greatest of all his catastrophes—an earthquake. An earthquake would shake Kwaku from his indecent complacency. Ha! If only she could arrange such a calamity!

All her life she had sought to appease and placate the gods. Mortal man did not dare work upon their resentment. That Aba's weary brain should have conjured up such a fantastic dream of vengeance showed how deep had been her plunge into despair. If she had to die, then she did not wish to die alone, and certain slaves and some of her followers must accompany her into the world of shades as was the custom. Aba leapt to her feet. She would celebrate her own funeral custom, and it would be a royal one with a multitude of people to walk with her on the other side of life.

Her thoughts ran in currents of red-hot excitement that burned in her veins. She translated them into action, removing her anklets and the bracelets and rings and tying them in a cloth to carry with her.

At the hour of sunset she slipped from the compound. Kwaku's men saw her tiny wasted figure pass between the palisades as she made her way out of the village. They thought she had gone to put an end to herself, and they let her go her way in lonely dignity, for once she had been a great queen, and they would have honoured her had Kwaku not seized the power.

The westering light lent a golden tinge to the green walls of the jungle. As she walked swiftly along a hunter's path in the forest Aba reckoned that she would reach the gold mine in Abrobi Hill at midnight. She had not decided in what way she would bring down the wrath of the god of the red earth; she would leave that until she reached his dwelling in the hill.

ii

She could not have set out under better conditions had she carefully planned the journey. The majestic moon, at its full, lent its light to aid her in her ascent of the hill. She had reached the mine entrance on the undamaged side and saw the dark mouth of the tunnel before her. Without hesitation Aba plunged into inky darkness and, feeling her way along the tunnel, walked on into the heart of the hill, stumbling sometimes over an inequality in the ground.

She had proceeded for some way down the shaft when she saw a faint light ahead of her. She came to where the shaft widened. The walls of this underground chamber, from which tunnels sprayed in every direction, were lined with props of local timber, and hung on a hook was a miner's lamp the fetish priests had left burning.

Upon the ground at Aba's feet lay the three white men, gagged, and bound hand and foot. A smile of almost childish delight drew back the aged woman's rubbery lips. Here at her feet lay the instruments of vengeance. She need look no farther for a means of enraging the god. If she robbed the Great One, the sasabonsum of the hill, of his prey, he would undoubtedly shatter the world with an earthquake to avenge the sacrilege.

Vengeance, shrieked Aba's soul, vengeance is mine. And her twisted, gnarled old hands began to fumble at the knotted cords of the white men's bonds, while the flame of the lamp on the wall flickered and flared convulsively, and the red earth seemed to rock as she knelt upon it.

iii

At the identical moment that Aba, the Queen Mother, entered the mine six ships dropped anchor off the Kormantin coast. The moonlight lay in silver splendour over the sea, picking out the tall masts, the furled sails, each rope and stay, in delicate detail as the dark hulls lay like sleeping beasts on the beaten silver of the sea.

The *Diane,* the *Bluebird,* and the battered *Sylphide,* sailing back to Madeira to refit and repair the damage of the action with the Portuguese, had met a small fleet of three Dutch vessels from Amsterdam, bound for the Gold Coast. They were in the command of an experienced and daring mariner, Captain Ryk van Breda. The ships' boats plied between the vessels and it was decided that the *Sylphide* could be temporarily patched up at sea, and the fleets should combine and return to the coast in strength in order to repulse any attack from the Portuguese warships; and while they were at anchor the carpenters could make the *Sylphide* sufficiently seaworthy to enable her to limp across the ocean with her sister ships.

On the Kormantin coast the palm trees stood sentinel-like, guarding the wide stretch of shining wet beach, for the tide was at the ebb.

A few minutes after midnight the first giant tremor shook the land and the sea, to be followed after a short interval by a second and then a third tremor, each shock a little more severe than the one that had preceded it. A strong wind arose. On the land sleepers turned uneasily on their mats and thought a tornado was blowing up, and wondered whether their thatch were secure, and fell asleep again. At sea the ships trembled and the sea stirred, and the men in their bunks half woke and wondered.

Then a mighty convulsion shook the land with a violence that was prolonged over several seconds, shaking the solid mass of the earth as a terrier might shake a rat.

In the jungle the giants of the forest crashed, their shallow roots tearing from the quaking earth and devastating whole areas in their collapse; in the native villages and compounds the huts and palisades folded up neatly and their occupants crept out into the terrifying darkness of falling dwellings and pale, spectral moonlight; in the subsidiary forts about Elmina the masonry crumbled and only a few fragments of torn and tottering walls were left; in the fortress of San Jorge del Mina the structure rocked on its imponderable foundations, its walls fissured in several places, and on the landward side the outer fortifications were rent in twain, the cannon leapt from their bases and plunged through the embrasures into the sea, yet it stood firm in its essential structure; on the sea a vast tidal wave rolled landwards with catastrophic suddenness. Of the six vessels anchored off the Kormantin coast five dragged their anchors and were borne some way towards the land, the sixth, the luckless *Sylphide,* disappeared beneath the wave and was lost in shallow water with every soul on board. In the roadstead at Elmina the Portuguese men-o'-war were washed ashore and beached in the yielding sand.

On the Abrobi Hill the tunnel and such of the galleries of the mine that had not fallen in at the first disaster collapsed. The supports slid from the tottering roof of the shaft, burying all beneath it. Great boulders and rocks rolled from the crest of the hill and lodged where once the entrance to the mine had been, sealing it so that it was completely closed and unrecognizable.

iv

The Dutch and the English vessels found they had suffered little damage when the day dawned and the horrors of the night were past. At high tide, with the aid of the ships' boats and the *Bluebird,* the lightest of the ships and the farthest out at sea when the disaster occurred, they were towed back to deep water.

As soon as they had set their ships to rights the Dutch and the English sent boats off to shore to find out how the inhabitants had fared in the earthquake. On the whole they found that matters were not as bad as they had feared. In some places villages in the heart of the jungle had been wiped out and many people had been killed by falling trees, but, although the tribes had scattered, there had not been much loss of life. In a fortnight, by dint of persuasion and bribe and a readiness to assist in the rebuilding of huts and compounds, by large "dashes" of nails and rope and a generous issue of trade rum, the Kormantins were induced to resume the interrupted negotiations. Soon all the vessels had their cargoes on board and were fully slaved. It had been a matter of no great difficulty to round up several hundreds of homeless natives.

Kwaku himself had lost his grandmother. She had last been seen entering the jungle, which had apparently swallowed her as no trace of her or her gold ornaments was to be found. If she had been eaten by a leopard, reasoned Kwaku, the gold ornaments at least would have been left. He mourned the loss of so much tribal gold most sincerely, but for the old woman he did not mourn at all. She had caused him much trouble all her life, and at the end of it she had not thought to leave her gold trappings behind.

The villagers and the fetish priests howled and rent their hair in Awoin. The wrath of the sasabonsum had not been appeased. The offerings had not been acceptable. The Chief mourned and Kwaku paid him a visit in his village of Awoin. There he learned that the three Englishmen who had been left bound within the mine when it fell in were three of the four seamen from the *Sylphide.* There would have been a fourth, he was told, if the commandant of the fortress of Elmina had not caused him to be blown from a cannon. Kwaku expressed his condolences and departed home to inform his friends, the Englishmen, what a terrible fate had befallen the four who had been carried away as prisoners at the time of the naval battle.

Ryk van Breda soon heard the news. All the way to the Indies on his first slaving trip he wrestled with his conscience. He did not care about this inhuman business of dealing in human flesh, albeit it was black flesh; but a man had to live and the slave traffic was highly profitable. Anthony Barradale's death was also on his mind. With a pang of self-reproach he thought of the beautiful child, Anne-Marie. It was settled now. She would live her life in Holland, and in time the years at Bodrugan would seem no more than a dream to her; as in time the jungle would creep up Abrobi Hill and cover it with long green fingers of creeper, with an impenetrable tangle of vegetation, with shrubs and trees, so that no man could tell what lay beneath the landmark of the lonely mound.

PART XI

ḨOLLⱭND

SHE SAW HIM WALKING BY THE WATERWAY WHERE THE LITTLE humped bridges spanned the canal and the slow barges drifted. It was early summer and Anna van Breda had been for some weeks in Delft with Anne-Marie. She was returning from the gardens beyond the city walls, and it seemed that she would meet William of Orange as she had met him once before with a laden basket. She had not seen him save in the distance on the happy twelfth day of June when his infant son, Frederick Henry, had been christened. She had remarked then how well he looked, and she had thought how apt was the device he had chosen on the occasion of the baby's birth: "Calm amid the raging of the tempest." The day of the christening had been a high day and a holiday in Delft.

Louise, the new Princess of Orange, reigned over more than her homely little court: she had made a home for her numerous stepchildren in the old nunnery with its sunny refectory and wide corridors, and its shady walled garden. At the Prinsenhof all William's children enjoyed a family life to the full, save only Philip, so long immured in Spain. It was as well that his home life was happy, for there were problems hemming William the Silent in and deepening the heavy lines on his face. There was that perennial trouble, the lack of money. The wealth that had come to him in his youth had long since been lavished on the cause of the Netherlands to which Orange had devoted his life, and he found himself constantly in debt and even faced poverty. More distressing to him still was the apparent collapse of his political aims. As ever, when they had stood together for a time, the cities and the provinces fell apart, and quarrelled and split themselves with party strife. Only the north stood loyal and firm, but, alas, the northern provinces were too small and poor to remain free if the south withdrew its support. Divided they fell, and no words of William's seemed to abate the petty bickering of the wayward cities that could not see their danger.

Anna saw the Prince stop to speak with a group of children playing on the cobblestones in the shadow of the lime trees, and throwing leaves and bits of twig to float away on the slowly moving waters of the canal. Then he continued on his way towards her. As he approached she observed that he was rather shabbily dressed in a worn doublet. He had not changed since she had last seen him. The mouth was firm, the eyes alert and kind. There was about him no evidence of pomp and circumstance, yet, to the most casual observer, there was about this middle-aged gentleman popularly known as Father William "the outward passage of an inward greatness."

His dark eyes lit up when he saw Anna.

She curtseyed; and wished with all her heart that Anne-Marie had accompanied her to the gardens that morning. She would have liked the Prince to see her favourite granddaughter. But Anne-Marie and Dirk had found some other occupation, and she had been thankful enough to have Dirk amused. He had done nothing but fret since Ryk had sailed. Ryk had refused to take the lad with him on the voyage to Guinea, which was proof enough to Anna that he had many qualms about the trading venture on which he had embarked.

"I heard you had gone home to Friesland," said William, smiling. "Delft has soon attracted you back."

She did not call him Father William. They were too much of an age for her to address him thus, she felt; and she preferred the more formal designation.

"My daughter-in-law has need of me, Highness," Anna explained. "Her husband is away on a long voyage."

"And how was the north when you left it? My dear, devoted north. Mevrou, if the south could stand firm as the north stands firm, life would be easier."

"The north was full of promise when I left," she said.

She did not speak of cities and provinces, which were matters too great for her, she thought; but she told him instead of the meadow she had sown with wheat in the autumn, of the green spears of vigorous growth that had thrust up through the earth in the spring. She told him of her simple farming problems and of how she and Gerard had solved them. And lastly she told him that her granddaughter, Anne-Marie, had left England and was with her even now in Delft.

He too spoke of little things as they walked slowly onward together. The long, pleasant summer days were usually so occupied with affairs of state that it was a pleasure to discuss the everyday interests of life. He spoke of the fruit in the walled orchard at the Prinsenhof; of the brilliance his son Maurice was displaying at the University of Leyden; of the companionship he enjoyed with his two elder daughters, Marie and Anna; of his sorrow at the prolonged detention of his son Philip in Spain; of the sturdiness of the six-months'-old infant, Frederick Henry; and, mingled with this pleasing gossip about his family affairs, he mentioned that it would seem that the Protestant cause grew apace. Lately a young man, who called himself Guyon, had come to him asserting that his father had been martyred for the Protestant cause at Dôle, and that he wished to serve him.

"This young man had come from so far," William concluded, "that I had not the heart to refuse him. So he has been sent on a message to France. He is a most devout young man, and wanders around with a Bible under his arm. Perhaps you have seen him in the church? He is very religious, it seems, and was always at his devotions when he was here."

Anna shook her head. She had not seen the young man; but he was not important. There were many young men to be observed deep in the discussion of religion, although all of them did not walk about with the Bible.

Thus lightly did they dismiss the subject of the young man, Guyon, who in fact was one Balthasar Gérard, who had sworn to complete the work Juan Jauréguy had begun. They walked and talked, the Prince, as always, kind and pleasant in all his ways. Neither of them gave a thought to the price of twenty-five thousand écus on William's head. It was impossible to think that danger lurked in peaceful Delft in those warm summer days, when the clear light of the sun flowed into every cranny and the enchantment of the cloudless sky lay over the quiet city and the shadowed waterways.

ii

All did not go well with Minetje, and Anna was sorely troubled. It was only the first week in July and it would be long before Ryk returned. She made Minetje keep to her bed and sent for the physician, who pronounced that the young woman was suffering from a low fever and prescribed rest and careful dieting. Minetje's baby was not expected for another two months, and Anna thought sadly that they might well anticipate difficulty at her lying-in.

Anne-Marie was very helpful and understanding. She had some skill in household matters and she was tactful in the handling of her four young cousins. Juliana loved her and was her shadow except on the occasions when Dirk took Anne-Marie with him in the boat when he went to Delftshaven.

Anna came to look for Anne-Marie's start whenever mention was made of English ships putting in at Delftshaven or Rotterdam. Anne-Marie always inquired whether there had been a message for her. Dirk, a very obliging young man, would visit the quays on these occasions, and once he returned with a letter; it was from Frances Barradale to tell Anne-Marie how lonely she was, and how she missed Anthony and herself. Anthony had not returned, she wrote, and there was no word of what had happened to him.

Anna saw how the girl fretted. When Minetje had been abed for a few days and it was clear that her indisposition would be long and tiresome Anna came to the conclusion that Anne-Marie should return to Oostermeer to help Jan and Gerard. With an ailing woman and four young children in Ryk's house it was no sort of life for a young girl. Accordingly she put it to Anne-Marie that it would be very hard on their menfolk if they were left too long to fend for themselves, and she suggested that Anne-Marie should go back north.

"I should like to go back," said Anne-Marie in her careful Dutch. "Although I am sorry that we cannot return together. But there is something that troubles me: here in Delft I have had news from Bodrugan, and soon I may hear that Anthony is home again. Will I get the message at Oostermeer?"

"If any message comes I promise you that Dirk will convey it north at once," said Anna.

Ach, the poignancy of the waiting of youth for a message that might never come! It wrung Anna's heart to listen to Anne-Marie.

"Oh, thank you, my grandmother," said Anne-Marie.

As always Anna found Anne-Marie's "my grandmother" very moving. It was an idiosyncrasy of the girl's, and none of the other granddaughters had thought to use the personal pronoun in that endearing fashion. Anna saw, just for an eyelid's flicker, like a door opening and shutting a long way off, an illuminating glimpse of the character of Anne-Marie. All her life, Anna saw, Anne-Marie would have the right touch, the sure instinct for the gracious word, the kindly thought. It was not a habit that one could acquire: one was born with it.

Thus it fell out that Anne-Marie returned to Friesland and Anna remained on in Ryk's house to help Minetje through her bad days.

iii

On the next Sunday Anna heard more about the religious young man, Guyon. Michiel de Noot and Jakob van Maldere, the master of the Prince's horse, called in to see her for a few minutes. Anna enjoyed these visits. Middle age had its compensations, she had discovered. One certainly achieved more freedom the older one became, and Michiel, as the tried friend and no longer the aspiring lover, she found delightful company. He and Jakob van Maldere made her rock with laughter, recounting the antics of the small, dusty, pious stranger, Guyon, at the porter's lodge.

"If you could have seen the little man this morning, Anna," said Michiel. "He borrowed a Bible from the porter because he said he wished to read a portion, as he was in no fit state to join the congregation in the church, shabby and travel-stained as he was."

"Then he hung round in the courtyard with the Bible, looking for a shady spot no doubt," Jakob van Maldere carried on the tale. "And he wandered around until the sergeant of halberdiers asked what he did there. And Guyon told him the same tale. And the sergeant reported the matter to the officer, and the officer carried it to the Prince, and there, the little man was suddenly an object of interest. He had achieved the highest importance. And lo! twelve crowns were forthcoming from His Highness' purse, and M. Guyon had his change of attire!"

"He has his crowns, and it is to be hoped he puts them out wisely," said Anna. "And did he then go to church?"

"No; nor did he read in the courtyard after he had had the Prince's gift, for the sergeant had had enough of him and turned him out. The last I heard of him, he was walking by the moat, reading the Bible and taking no heed of his surroundings, so that every moment it seemed he must plunge headfirst in among the slime and the ducks."

"It is just as well for the Bible he held to his course," observed Anna.

They asked her if there was news of her son Ryk. Anna shook her head sadly and said there had hardly been time. She was evasive about the object of Ryk's voyage: she did not wish the Prince to hear that he had set out on a slaving expedition. A little later the two men took their farewell of her and left.

In the porter's lodge there was a soldier who was checking over a little pile of crowns. He looked sheepish when they questioned him, but at last he admitted that he had parted with a pair of pistols to Guyon for the money. The little man had a long journey before him, the soldier muttered, and he was afraid he might meet with footpads on the way, and therefore he had sold him the small carabines. He had meant well and he hoped his superiors would not take exception to this little business transaction of his.

There the matter rested. Before two more days had passed this same soldier was to stab himself to the heart, having learned for what fell purpose the pistols had been bought.

iv

Tuesday, the tenth day of July 1584, dawned and life went on in its accustomed way in Delft. The slow barges slid down to Delftshaven; the lime trees dropped their leaves in the quiet canals; the children played on the cobblestones, calling out greetings to bargees as they drifted by; and at the Prinsenhof a nervous young maid polished the remarkable wooden staircase of the old nunnery. It had been pointed out to her by the gimlet-eyed housekeeper that a spider had actually spun its web across the sunken arch at the foot of the stairs—it had done it overnight then, the girl protested almost in tears, for she was very particular about dusting the arch although it was sunk deep into the wall and was completely in the shadow of the door. So on this fateful

Tuesday morning the young maid polished the staircase with diligence. There was light enough to see that she left no speck on the treads, as there was a window where the stairs turned sharply. As for the archway, she lit a lamp and shone it in the recess to make certain that not a single filament of the accusing web should remain.

All that morning William of Orange had been busy. He had been closeted with the burgomaster of Leeuwarden for hours, and when at half past twelve the trumpet sounded the dinner hour, the burgomaster remained to the family meal, at which William, his wife, and two elder daughters, his sister, the Countess of Schwartzburg, were present.

A distraught-looking young man pushed forward as the little company reached the door of the dining room. It was Guyon. In agitated tones he demanded a passport.

Princess Louise of Orange took fright at the pale, wild face of the young man. Like a shadow hanging over her and darkening her days was the price on her husband's head. And William was so careless. He would not take the most elementary precautions.

"Who is he?" asked Louise, putting her hand on William's arm.

"Merely a person come for a passport," said William, and added over his shoulder to his secretary who was standing not far off: "Do you see that one is made out for Guyon immediately, please."

"I have never seen so villainous a countenance," protested Louise, still fearful, and unconvinced that so extraordinary an individual could be about honest business.

The secretary disappeared with Guyon and they seated themselves at the table. The conversation quite naturally flowed in political channels. William was animated and merry and, following his lead, the little company kept up a cheerful spate of comment. The talk turned to Friesland. To William this was a happy topic. And who shall say that while he discussed the politics of Friesland he had not in mind the tall, white-haired Frisian woman whom chance had caused to cross his path on more than one occasion? She was a woman he, in particular, could not forget, as in her life and her actions she embodied the principle of tolerance, and tolerance was his life line in the stormy waters of conflict and enmity in which he struggled. She had seen a virtue in tolerance and a reward in kindliness. One individual did not make a nation, William saw all too plainly; but she had inspired the great hope that where there was one tolerant soul there might be others.

The meal ended. The Prince led the way from the dining room. In the vestibule without were various persons who had presented themselves at this hour to seek a brief audience with him. William spoke with certain of them and then began to ascend the stairs. He had reached the second step when Guyon showed himself, stepping clear of the shadowed arch. He raised a pistol and, at point-blank range, discharged three poisoned balls into the Prince's body, one of which passed right through him and struck the wall behind him. With an heroic effort William kept swaying on his feet. Jakob van Maldere, the master of the horse, caught him in his arms as he fell back and laid him swooning on the stairs.

"O my God, have mercy on my soul!" cried William of Orange as life ebbed from him. "O my God, have mercy on this poor people!"

So passed William of Nassau, Prince of Orange, "the wisest, gentlest and bravest man who ever led a nation."

v

Their Prince was dead. Amid the tears of a whole nation the tidings spread through the Netherlands, north and south, leaving the people desolate. In Delft an air of mourning enwrapped the city, and the sorrowing citizens spoke in whispers of the tragedy, and the children forgot their games with twigs and leaves and cried in the streets for the Father William who never would tread those familiar ways again.

Vengeance is sweet, and sorrow was to find its customary and terrible outlet in ensuring that the assassin should pay to the full for his hideous deed. Guyon—or, to give him his true name, Balthasar Gérard—had been captured and he had confessed freely, exulting in his crime. For seven long years he had planned to take the life of William of Nassau. He was an ardent Catholic and he felt the removal of this prince of heretics would see the true religion—as he saw it—triumphantly re-established in all of King Philip's possessions. Thus it was not astonishing that he should glory in his deed when haled before the examining magistrates in Delft.

"Like David," he exulted, "I have slain Goliath of Gath."

Nor rack nor torture could abate that exultation. Gérard's constancy in suffering amazed his judges, who pronounced a terrible death sentence, for alas, there was no compassionate Orange to plead for the wretch. The fourteenth day of July, when William the Silent had been four days dead, was the day appointed for the public execution of Gérard.

It was on this day that Mevrou van Wyck, mother of Minetje, came to Delft to accomplish a joint purpose—she wished to be present at the execution, and she desired to find out what progress her daughter had made under the physician's care.

It was yet early in the day when Anna saw her stout figure, encased in stiff black, walk up to the front door. Anna opened the door to her relative-in-law. The two women kissed, but with no enthusiasm.

"I am happy to be able to tell you that Minetje is better," said Anna at once. "The physician thinks that she will be well enough to leave her bed in another week. He is very pleased with her. It seems she was merely overtired, and the summer has been sultry."

They sat down on the benches near the window.

"It will be hot today," observed Mevrou van Wyck. "I am glad she is better. I never thought she ailed much. A fine day for the execution," she added with gusto.

Anna repressed a shudder.

"I have kept much of what has happened from Minetje," she said softly so as not to be overheard by Minetje in the next room. "I have told her the Prince has been slain and that they have captured his murderer. Beyond that I have said nothing. In her state she ought not to be alarmed."

"If she is better I do not see that it will hurt her to know. She might even come with us——"

"Ach, no," cried Anna, horror-stricken. "I shall not be present at the execution, and it would kill Minetje."

"I breed daughters tougher than that," snapped Mevrou van Wyck. "You are a strange woman, Anna van Breda. Do you not rejoice that the assassin is to reap the reward of his crime? Will not his dying shrieks assuage your grief? One would think you cared nothing that the Prince has been foully slain."

"I think of the Prince," said Anna.

An unbearable sorrow weighed her down. She arose and stared out of the window, seeing nothing. If he were but alive to walk the streets of Delft again, her heart cried out. If he were but alive . . . She was bereft and alone. Everything passed, the Prince had said once, even pain. At this moment it was hard to believe.

"The Prince would not have permitted this brutal execution," Anna said firmly when she had recovered herself. "It is an insult to his memory."

"I would not let the crowd hear that, Anna," advised Mevrou van Wyck. "You would be lynched. Did you not love the Prince, then, as we did?"

Truly some women spoke foolishly, thought Anna. She did not think it necessary to reply.

"You behaved just as strangely when the mob saw to it that the inquisitor got his deserts at Zoeterwoude," pursued Minetje's mother. "Your tender heart may get you into trouble someday."

"The Prince approved my behaviour," Anna said quietly. "He was the most gentle of men."

"Yes, he was too kind to those who did not merit kindness."

"Do not let us argue," said Anna. "By all means attend the execution, and I shall remain here with Minetje."

"She is no daughter of mine if she does not rejoice to see justice done. It is a shame that she is not well enough to go out."

"Mother!"

The voice came from the doorway of the adjoining room.

Both women started to their feet. They saw Minetje in her night robe, regarding them from the doorway.

"I thought I heard your voice, Mother," said Minetje. "Why did you not come in? It is so dull, and the children have been sent away for the day. I heard you speak of the execution."

"It was not meant for you to hear, Minetje," said Anna. "Gérard will be executed today and all will be over. Now go back to your bed, my dear."

"But I feel perfectly well," Minetje protested, "and it is so dull."

"And she looks well, what is more!" Mevrou van Wyck exclaimed. "I do not see at all why she should not be allowed up. And such a lovely day too. Her legs will get weak with all this lying in bed."

"She has done very well under the physician," Anna said patiently. "It would undo all his work if she gets up too soon. Have patience for only one more week, Minetje."

"I feel perfectly well!" Minetje exclaimed. "In fact I have felt well for days. And here all this is happening, and I lie in bed not knowing it."

"If you had been well, my daughter, you should have witnessed the accursed assassin paying the penalty of his crime," said her mother.

"But I am well." And Minetje stamped her foot.

"No, you are not quite well," said Anna firmly. "I beg you, Minetje, please go back to bed."

"I do not see why," whined Minetje, bursting into tears.

"There, and you shall not then," said her mother, going to her and putting a comforting arm about her shoulders.

Anna saw she was fighting a losing battle. She was thoroughly alarmed. She was convinced that the danger of a premature labour was by no means over. There was nothing for it but to find the physician and with him ranged on her side Minetje might be prevailed upon to rest for a few days more.

"I shall go for the physician," she said. "If he pronounces Minetje well enough to leave her bed that will settle it."

"The physician is overcautious," sniffed Minetje.

"You so nearly lost the child you are carrying," Anna reminded her. "The physician may be cautious, but he has saved you all the same."

"I am perfectly well," muttered Minetje mutinously.

"I shall not be long," Anna said. "Go back to bed just until he has seen you, Minetje."

Her back was turned for a moment while she found her outdoor cap. If she had noticed the look mother and daughter exchanged she would not have left them. As it was she hurried away with an earnest injunction to Minetje to keep quiet.

The physician was not at home and Anna was a long time searching for him in various likely places. She found him in the house of another patient. He came along at once but a considerable time had elapsed before they reached Ryk's house.

As they entered, the silence struck Anna like a blow. She looked around the place, but it was deserted. She returned to the living room where she had left the physician.

"They have gone out," she said in despair.

"I cannot answer for the consequences," said the physician.

Anna's head drooped. She wished Ryk had not put all this responsibility on her shoulders.

"She must have gone with her mother," she said at last. "I shall go after them and try to persuade Minetje to come home to bed."

"I will wait here," said the physician, who felt very sorry for her.

Anna returned in an hour's time. She had been unsuccessful.

"The streets are thronged," she told the physician. "I could not find them. Do not waste your time sitting here; I do not know what will happen."

"I cannot wait any longer; but send for me at once when your daughter-in-law returns."

Anna waited on alone in the silent house, while through the open windows came the clamour of the distant crowd. And a man was dying a hideous death.

Shortly after five Minetje and her mother returned, the younger woman supported on the arm of the elder.

At midnight Minetje was prematurely delivered of a son—a puny child, and Minetje's last, who from the hour of his birth had lavished upon him the idolatrous love of his mother.

CHAPTER TWENTY-THREE

Like great tired birds, white wings adroop, three ships slid into Amsterdam waters. The voyage to Guinea and the Indies, with its many hazards and its strange happenings, had been successfully accomplished. Ryk van Breda was back in the Netherlands again.

The vessels had not long dropped anchor at the Amsterdam wharves when Dirk, ever haunting Delftshaven for news, learned of Ryk's safe return. Back to Delft he went at once to carry the glad tidings, his urgent poling sending his craft shooting along the Schie.

While Dirk was on his way Anna sat alone in the kitchen of Ryk's house, nursing an infant on her knees. The winter had tried the delicate child and it was only by exercising the greatest care that they had kept Ryk's frail son alive. He had been hurriedly baptized when he was three days old and given the name of Pieter. It was astounding how he had survived his birth and seven months of life. Minetje, whom love made overanxious, was forced to leave the main care of the infant to her mother-in-law, as she had not the heart to handle him much. Now Minetje was putting the older children to bed, and Anna opened up the shawls that enshrouded the baby and chafed his feet before the blazing peat fire. The mite was always cold.

The child was asleep on her knees when Dirk burst into the warm kitchen. He was scarlet-cheeked and his blue eyes were round with excitement.

"He is back!" shouted Dirk. "All three ships have reached Amsterdam."

"Ryk is back! Minetje! Minetje!" cried Anna.

Minetje came running in, the staring small girls behind her.

"What is it, Dirk?" she exclaimed. "Is my husband back?"

"Yes; I heard this afternoon in Delftshaven."

"God be thanked," cried Minetje, bursting into tears of joy.

"If you agree, mevrou," said Dirk eagerly to Minetje, "I shall leave early tomorrow and meet the captain in Amsterdam."

"Yes," said Minetje. "And tell him he has a son. . . ." She hesitated. "But do not tell him how frail a boy he is."

"Be comforted, Minetje," said Anna. "This boy will live. He is slow about making a start, that is all."

Minetje came and stood over Anna and the babe and laid a hand on the sleeping child.

"Perhaps that is it," she said, snatching at the straw of hope. "I have waited so long for a son, Mother, and now I do not know whether God will let me keep him."

Anna put up her hand and drew Minetje's face down and kissed her cheek. Their joint struggle to save Pieter had brought them close together.

"I was looking at Pieter's little legs," said Anna. "I can see they are plumper. How peacefully he sleeps, Minetje!"

"Yes; it is a good sign, the physician says."

Minetje smiled tremulously down at Anna. Then, pushing the bevy of small chattering girls out before her, she left the room.

Dirk sat down opposite Anna at the fireplace. Anna smiled into his glowing face.

"So your captain has returned, Dirk," she said.

"Never again could I endure staying at home while he voyages to distant lands," said Dirk vehemently.

"He sailed on a slaving expedition, no less," said Anna deliberately. "That was why you could not accompany him. You are not the cabin boy, nor just one of the ship's company, Dirk. You are a member of our family, and Ryk, quite properly, did not wish to involve you in a venture he knew to be dubious."

"I can do what he does," cried the young man passionately.

Ryk must be an inspiring captain, Anna thought. There was devotion as much as hero worship in Dirk's cry.

"He does well to have scruples," she said. "And I should be very grieved if he did not show some conscience in his handling of you young creatures. I wish Ryk had not undertaken this particular venture; but there was a driving necessity for it. He needs money and I have none. We are, and shall be for many years, very poor in Friesland. But the life in the north is a good life, Dirk—and a better life altogether since Anne-Marie came."

"Yes," said Dirk simply. "I often think of her."

The young men all thought of Anne-Marie, Anna mused. And Anne-

Marie's thoughts revolved in an unbroken circle about Anthony Barradale. She sat up, stiffening suddenly. Ryk might have news of Anthony.
The young man might also have reached port.

"Ach, I do long to see my son," said Anna in a quivering voice. "He
has been away such a long time, Dirk."

"Only a few days now until you see him," said Dirk.

"I shall walk beside the Schie every day until you come," she said.

They were silent, thinking their own thoughts. The fire leaped and
flamed and held them in its languorous thrall. Peace was in the room
while a young man looked eagerly into the future, and a middle-aged
woman thought nostalgically of the past, and a sleeping babe slept on.

ii

Up and down the Schie the white and brown sails dipped and swelled.
Yet the boat she looked for was not there.

The winter sky was blue between the banks of cloud. The afternoon
sun was falling towards the low horizon, lending a blond vividness to
the polders on either side of the river and creating a pleasing effect of
light and shade over all the even contour of the land.

At last, when Anna had made up her mind that Ryk would not be
coming that day, his voice hailed her from a distance. He was standing
upright in a boat and he waved to her.

She ran to the river's edge and waited for the boat to come up to her.
Ryk must have arranged with Dirk what to do if they met his mother,
because the boat shot straight past to Delft as Ryk leapt from it and
landed on the bank beside Anna.

"How good to see you, Mother!"

He held her in a long embrace. She wept joyful tears unashamedly on
his shoulder.

"Dirk has told you you have a son?" she asked at length. "I wish you
all much happiness."

"I am so glad you were with Minetje. I am very grateful to you,
Mother."

They began to walk along the path to Delft.

"Pieter's birth has made all the difference to Minetje," Anna told him.
"I think there are some women who never come to their full blossom-
ing until they have borne a son. Now, Ryk, did your venture turn out as
well as you hoped?"

"Financially it has been very successful."

She sensed the reservation behind his statement. In his own time he
would tell her everything. They were only playing with words. . . .

"I am glad of that. And no more slaving, Ryk?" she probed delicately.

"So you knew," said Ryk. "I did not want you to realize that. Why
did you not speak, try to stop me?"

"Ryk," said Anna, "I have also had my dark days. I knew your need,

and the slave run to the Indies seemed the only way for you to earn
the money you must have. Once I did something I knew to be evil, and
I have prayed to be forgiven ever since. I slew a Spaniard at the time
Alva came to Friesland. He was creeping up to Liesbet and there was
no other way of saving her. I have told this to your father and now to
you. I slew the man, knowing I was committing murder. I did not speak,
although I knew you were setting off on a slaving run. I felt you had no
alternative."

"Why did you not say you had slain a Spaniard? Less might have been
said, perhaps, about your saving Don Rodriguez d'Esquerdes had that
been known."

"I kept the murder of the Spaniard a secret between God and myself
and I pray that God might forgive me because my need was sore. Now,
Ryk, no more slaving unless you are in an extremity?"

"Not if it is possible for me to avoid it."

Ryk no longer strove to conceal his feelings. Even now, standing on
the path beside the peaceful river, he could hear the moaning and the
long mournful howling of the Negroes in the holds. No, not that inhuman traffic again, he vowed. And now the shadow of Anthony's death
was on his mind and he must speak. He said:

"How is Anne-Marie?"

Anna felt a shock of anticipated dread. When she had looked into
Ryk's face she had glimpsed some hidden calamity. She forced her
tingling nerves to calmness, clenching her hands at her sides to aid self-
control.

"She is well, she is in Friesland," said Anna, and she could feel the
perspiration suddenly damp on her brow. "What of Anne-Marie?"

"I do not wish to meet her—not just yet."

"It has to do with Anthony Barradale then?" Anna forced out the
words.

"He is dead."

"Ach, no!"

"It may be a good thing he is dead," said Ryk swiftly, almost savagely.
"Anthony was wild. If he had lived she would have married him and we
would have lost touch with her. Perhaps it has happened for the best,
Mother."

She saw he was talking to convince himself.

"I thought so once, Ryk," she answered. "There was a time when I
should have been heartbroken if she had married him; but I know now
that his death is the worst thing that can befall the child."

"She is a child. Her affections cannot be deep-rooted."

"She is an unusual child," Anna said gently. "In many ways she is very
mature. Her affections go deep, Ryk."

"The marriage would have ended in disaster. Anthony was unstable."

"I have never met Anthony. I have seen him through your eyes, Ryk,
and through Anne-Marie's. He impresses you as a wild and worthless

fellow; yet I think you are prejudiced. Anne-Marie loves Anthony. I have lived long enough to know that such constancy as Anne-Marie's is never lavished on an unworthy object. Anthony may belittle himself, you may stress his weaknesses, but Anne-Marie sees him as he really is, and there is worth in what she sees. I have joined my prayers with hers that they might be brought together again. And now it is not to be."

"He was killed on the Guinea coast," said Ryk.

Anna's face was pale and drawn. She could measure the blank there would be in Anne-Marie's life by the blank there had been in her own life since Gysbert's death. They were of the same breed, she and her granddaughter, fated to mate with men weaker than themselves, and to be gloriously fulfilled in unusual ways by so doing. Ryk's voice, seeking reassurance, broke in on her thoughts.

"There is something I beg you to put right with Anne-Marie for me, Mother," he said. "It has been on my mind for more than a year."

"What is it, Ryk?"

How quiet her voice is, how gentle is my mother, thought Ryk. Although she had not touched him he felt as though her hand had smoothed his brow.

"It has to do with a letter," Ryk said, continuing with some difficulty. "Anthony left a letter for Anne-Marie with James Carey in Plymouth. I was given it. On the way across the North Sea I destroyed it unopened. I felt that the sooner the break between the young people came the better, so I took the law into my own hands and burned the letter. I regret most bitterly that I did so."

Horror dawned in Anna's eyes.

"Not Anne-Marie's letter!" she exclaimed incredulously.

"Anne-Marie asked me at Oostermeer whether there had been a letter and I gave her the lie direct," said Ryk wretchedly.

She turned away from him and looked at the river rippling by, remembering how Anne-Marie had fretted for a letter that never came.

"It was an ill thing to do, Ryk," she said, staring down into the water.

"Well I know it," he acknowledged humbly, waiting on her judgment.

Anna remained lost in thought for a moment or two. When she turned to Ryk her smile was very sweet.

"If I am to make a decision for both of us, Ryk," she said, "you must leave it to me to tell Anne-Marie about that letter. In my own time and in my own way I shall tell her. It is essential that you should stand well with Liesbet's daughter, so let me do it my way."

"I would always wish to stand well with Liesbet's daughter," he said; and the sweet, wild dream of his youth brushed his memory lightly, like the touch of a bird's wing in its flight.

"I shall go to Friesland at once," said Anna. "Anne-Marie must learn of Anthony's death from me."

"If you please, Mother. And I shall follow you later."

"No," said Anna quietly. "You must wait awhile. And you must be with Minetje. The baby does not thrive. Pieter will live, but he is frail. Minetje needs your help now."

"How was Pieter born so delicate?"

"Minetje was not well. There was the shock of the Prince's assassination. These things happen, Ryk."

"I wish I had known."

"You could have done nothing, Ryk."

"Anne-Marie is young. She will get over Anthony's death and marry some Dutchman. I can see it all working out well in the end."

"Perhaps. There will be no difficulty about finding a husband for Anne-Marie."

"She will be beautiful," he said.

"More than that," said Anna. "Beauty in itself does not mean much. Anne-Marie's chief attraction is that she is kind."

As you are kind, my mother, thought Ryk, his heart suddenly overflowing with his love for her. He noticed now that she was thinner and that her face had a spiritual quality he had not seen before. He said with quick compassion:

"You are tired, Mother."

"No, I am not tired. It is that I miss the Prince so sorely. I could count on the fingers of one hand the times I have had speech with him; but I miss him sadly now he has gone. Delft is strange without him. I shall be glad to be back at Oostermeer for a while."

Then, abruptly, as he knew he would never again have the courage, Ryk told her how Anthony Barradale had died. By the time he had made an end of his telling the sun had sunk below the horizon; and the church towers of Delft loomed greyly behind its ancient walls as they entered at the South Gate.

iii

When Anna reached Oostermeer she was greeted with cries of delighted astonishment by Jan and Anne-Marie, and more soberly by Gerard. Anna strove against her heavy-heartedness, but with scant success. She kept back the purpose of her immediate return, waiting until she and Anne-Marie should be alone.

When Jan and Gerard were busy in the byre Anna suggested to Anne-Marie that they should walk to the meadow by the windmill. That meadow was Anna's special pride. Had she and Ryk not ploughed the land and sown the seed? The harvest had been good, Gerard had told her with a twinkle, complimenting her on being a better agriculturist than he was.

The two women barely spoke as they trudged in their clogs to the meadow. Anna was aware that Anne-Marie suspected that something was very wrong. As they walked the twilight fell, and the evening light deepened to greyness, and the silence between them widened to a yawning gulf, that Anne-Marie's imagination sought to bridge with one dread surmise after another.

They heard the sounds of the farm more distantly, heard close at hand the cry of a benighted gull. The sough of the wind through the long grass on the sheltered side of the dyke came to them, and the rush and whisper of dead leaves as some bird or small animal moved in a drift of fallen vegetation on the wet ground. And overhead the sky was steel-dark and overcast.

At the windmill they halted, and the wide arms went creakingly round above them.

"What is it, my grandmother?" asked Anne-Marie.

And there in the meadow where once Liesbet had picked the Pentecost lilies Anna told Anne-Marie that Anthony was dead.

CHAPTER TWENTY-FOUR

The year 1585, which was also the year of Ryk van Breda's safe return to Amsterdam, was a turning point in the history of the struggle against Spanish tyranny, as England was now openly at war with King Philip, and the might of the Spanish fleet and the Spanish armies was divided. Philip did not prosecute the war against England with vigour at first, as he was busy preparing the largest armada that had ever put to sea, and his tardiness was of the greatest assistance to his smaller adversaries.

By the spring of this same year Frances Barradale and Lydia Wilson knew their sons had perished in Guinea. Frances Barradale lost what frail interest she had in life and cared not what became of her. Lydia Wilson, crazier than ever now, lived on in her wretched cottage, applying herself to the pursuit of religion as earnestly as she had once applied herself to wrecking and smuggling. To the great discomfiture of sea-faring men, she took to frequenting the Falmouth quays. She strove to convert every man who would stop to speak to her; and when she had no human audience she would harangue the gulls.

If Frances Barradale had no thought for herself and her condition there were two persons to whom she was the object of the gravest concern. James Carey, remorseful over having encouraged Anthony in his Guinea venture, set himself the task of paying off the mortgage on Bodrugan and supporting Frances Barradale in her old home. And in Holland Anne-Marie van Breda, her foster daughter, also pondered what help she could give.

One morning three months after Ryk had returned from his voyage Anne-Marie broached the subject that was in her mind, while she and her grandmother were washing the butter in the dairy.

"Anthony told me in what bad shape his affairs were before he left," said Anne-Marie without preamble. "If the venture failed he was ruined and Bodrugan would have to be put up for sale, as he had mortgaged the place to cover his share of the cost of the expedition to Guinea. If one of the English ships was lost the other two could not possibly have made good the loss no matter how successfully they traded."

"Yes," said Anna, methodically pressing out the water from the yellow butter and not looking at Anne-Marie.

"How much money do I own in my own right, Grandmother?" asked Anne-Marie with nervous abruptness.

"That is a question I cannot answer quickly. Your inheritance in this country is doubtful, owing to the Spanish occupation. Your mother owned considerable property in Groningen, which is valueless at the moment but may be worth something when we have rid ourselves of the Spaniards. There is, however, quite a substantial sum of money in England which is regarded as strictly yours. I cannot tell you the amount, but James Carey could give you an exact accounting. I understand there is more now than there was in the beginning, owing to wise investment. You must honour the Englishmen who have had the handling of it, Anne-Marie, for there never was a scrap of paper to prove it was yours: they have looked after your interests where they have neglected their own."

"I suggested to Anthony that he might use my money. I did not wish him to undertake the voyage to Guinea. If he had but yielded to my prayers!"

"Do not think that, Anne-Marie. It is as God wills."

"I have a proposal to make, Grandmother. If you permitted the money in England—or as much of it as is needed—to be used to clear the mortgage on Bodrugan and give enough to keep Mistress Barradale from want, I shall never claim any property that may come to me in Friesland. I wish this to be done if possible, Grandmother. It is something I can do for Anthony."

"It is a matter for the men to decide, Anne-Marie," said Anna. "I shall make one stipulation and that is that at Frances Barradale's death the advance must be made good by her heirs, or Bodrugan sold to pay back your dowry. Ryk ought to be coming soon and we can put the matter to him. I promise you I shall support you in this. You owe it to your foster mother. Anne-Marie, there is a question I have hesitated to ask you: would you like to go to Bodrugan for a time?"

Anne-Marie closed her eyes for a moment.

"No," she said clearly after a short pause. "I could do no good there because Mistress Barradale has lived too long in the shadows for me to reach her. There is too much to remind me of Anthony. Mistress Barradale gave up the struggle a long while ago, Grandmother."

"It is by no means a difficult thing to give up the struggle, in fact it is fatally easy," observed Anna.

"You did not give it up," pointed out Anne-Marie.

"I know how easy it would be to give up all the same," said Anna. "At the time of the flood I would have slipped from the tower had I not been so angry."

A smile came to Anne-Marie's pinched face. Her grandmother!

"I have never seen you angry," said Anne-Marie.

"I was very angry. Anger is the best antidote for weak-mindedness I know."

"I am glad you grew angry in time, my grandmother."

"So am I. It has been a good life although a hard one. You also have not given up the struggle, Anne-Marie. It is worth the effort to go on. I have proved it."

"The struggle would be more than I could bear if I went to Bodrugan," said Anne-Marie with sudden passion. "There are too many associations at Bodrugan. Anthony was so English, like England——"

"Yes," said Anna, trying to keep pace with Anne-Marie's rather muddled Dutch, and fearful of checking the unexpected flow of confidence.

"A man is like his country. It is natural he should be," went on Anne-Marie. "Cornwall is wild and rugged and unexpected. And Anthony has unexpected corners in his personality and there is always something new to discover in him. That is why I love him. This country is flat and carefully planned. Its smoothness helps me to forget a little, like a drug. But if I were to return the very stones in Bodrugan farmyard would cry out, 'Anthony, Anthony!' There was one stone in particular as you entered the yard. He called it Traitor's Gate because he said it was like the stone the Queen had sat upon when she was taken to the Tower in her girlhood. It was green and mossy and we often played there and wondered what it would be like to be imprisoned in a tower. And London seemed a million miles away. And if I went to Pendennis the wind would cry, 'Anthony, Anthony!' On Falmouth quays there would be the sailors we both knew and they would speak of him——"

The tears streamed down Anne-Marie's cheeks and she had no more words. She had exhausted her vocabulary and at the end she had cried out in English.

"Ach, cry on, my child," said Anna compassionately, taking the butter pat from Anne-Marie's hand. She held her comfortingly in her arms and then took her by the hand and led her away.

All that morning they talked and wandered over Oostermeer, while the butter was neglected in the dairy, and the barn cats licked at the tall yellow pyramid it made, and lapped the cream in the skimming bowls. And Oostermeer and Anna between them brought the first thin healing skin over Anne-Marie's hurt.

"I cannot believe he has gone," Anne-Marie cried more than once. "I feel I should have known the instant he died or ceased to love me. And I have had no such feeling."

"You must accept his death, Anne-Marie. If there was any hope I would let you cling to it; but there is not. There was the earthquake and the hill falling in and he under it."

"If I could but go to Guinea myself," said Anne-Marie. "I should search out the truth and find his body. Only then should I believe."

"That is impossible. Ryk made no mistake that time. He left no stone unturned to find out beyond any doubt. A white man could not move far in that country without every African being aware of his presence, Anne-Marie."

"Yes, I must accept it," said Anne-Marie dully.

"Ryk did make one mistake," said Anna. "I must tell you about it because it concerns you. Anthony wrote a letter and left it at Plymouth for you. James Carey gave it to your uncle Ryk to give to you and Ryk destroyed it unopened. Your letter came, Anne-Marie. I feel you ought to know that."

"Uncle Ryk destroyed my letter!" cried Anne-Marie angrily. "Oh, how could he!"

"He thought he was acting for the best. He sees now he was wrong. He is very sorry and he hopes you will forgive him. Anne-Marie, it made no difference to you. Your feeling for Anthony never changed."

"Nothing can change that. It will be all right about the letter."

They had reached the distant dyke where once Anna and Lourens had watched for Gysbert's ship. The sun shone on the dunes and in its reflection they were golden, and purple were the shadows they made. Behind them the canals gleamed, and the cows stood knee-deep in the lush pasture of the polders. The windmill lay behind them also, its arms in a cabalistic cross against the sky.

"It was here your father played," Anna told the girl.

Sitting there on the great dyke in view of the sea, she related the little everyday happenings at Oostermeer when Lourens and Ryk and Liesbet had been children. The morning went by and Anne-Marie recovered. She looked better and less strained, Anna thought.

Anne-Marie began to talk about Jan van Braam.

"He is very kind to me," she said. "He has been particularly thoughtful since Anthony died. He does not talk about the things I imagine he would wish to talk about, but is at great pains to think up conversation he feels might be pleasing to me."

"I hope you will always know much of the kindness of men," said Anna. "I have been fortunate that way. There was a conversation I once had with a man. For years it puzzled me why he should have spoken in the way he did. One day a great light dawned and I understood how kind and subtle he had been."

"What did he say?"

"Have you not had enough of my reminiscences, Anne-Marie? I have told you before about Don Rodriguez, and of how he set me free from Zoeterwoude prison at the time of the siege of Leyden. The conversation we had when he carried me from the dungeon was a strange one. I was not astonished at the time, but afterwards it seemed well-nigh incredible that we could have sustained such a conversation in such a place. Imagine the state I was in, Anne-Marie. I had been for hours in that cesspool of a dungeon and the foulness clung to me. Don Rodriguez wooed me as though I were a princess clad in silks and satins. I remember he spoke of my beautiful hands and he asked me where I got them. And I, in a daze, played my part and spoke my lines. The Van Braam ancestry came into it, and I recollected that there had been a dissolute baron some generations back. So powerful is the stimulant of suggestion, Anne-Marie, that I began to feel a princess among women. Courage and strength came back and I forgot the foulness of my condition. I was able to walk away and to think clearly. If Don Rodriguez had not set me on my feet in that subtle fashion I should never have struggled through. He built my spirit up and gave me back my self-respect, and so skilfully that it took me years to see through his device. When a man speaks in a fashion that seems strange to you, do not wait for as long as I did, but search for his reason at once."

"I know Jan's reason," said Anne-Marie.

"As a matter of fact I do too," said Anna casually.

Anne-Marie asked about the baron.

"He was an ancestor of my mother's." Anna went into family history. "My mother thought nothing of him, but I am not quite so Calvinistic in my views, and I have a fondness for him, although he was something of a villain. I'll tell you of an idea that came into my head this last time in Delft. It would not surprise me if Minetje began to take an interest in that selfsame baron. If Ryk makes a fortune she will think about a social position and arms on her carriage door and so on. When Ryk comes sheepishly to me to find out the quarterings I shall smile."

"Aunt Minetje would not be so silly."

"It would be a good thing for her to take an interest in something. She has her son now, and a social position is always an advantage, and she will not have the time to be dissatisfied, as she used to be. I learned a little of subtlety from Don Rodriguez."

Thus pleasantly they gossiped and beguiled away another hour. The sun was high when they rose to go back to the house. There was a meal to prepare and, with guilty starts, they wondered whether they had thought to shut the dairy door against the cats. . . .

As they walked up the avenue of young trees to the house Anne-Marie laid her hand lightly on Anna's arm.

"I know the reason for Jan's conversations," she said, and her voice did not quiver. "One day I shall marry him. But not for a long time."

"It is what I hoped you would do in the end."

Overhead the poplars shook and shivered in the spring breeze.

ii

In the new year Queen Elizabeth sent help to the Dutch land forces. In this year also Ryk van Breda set off on another long voyage. He was accompanied by Dirk and headed for the East, intending to slip through on a peaceful commercial enterprise while the Spanish and the English had at each other on the high seas.

Anna and Anne-Marie came and went between Delft and Oostermeer, and the life of the family in the city and in the north flowed uneventfully on. Pieter improved in health and at fifteen months began to stagger about on his spindly legs. He was still undersized and pale, but there was no longer the dreadful anxiety that he would die. Ryk's daughters flourished, the four of them, all very much alike. They were flaxenhaired, apple-cheeked, good-tempered, and of a build that promised to be buxom in maturity.

At Falmouth Lydia Wilson continued to haunt the quays and gained no converts to Protestantism; and at Bodrugan Frances Barradale wandered from window to window, scanning the sea and the passing ships, silent always, and wraithlike in her slimness. Martin Thomas and Sarah with their brood of children had settled permanently at Bodrugan to be with her. James Carey and a much sobered Martin had set themselves the task of restoring the fortunes of Richard Barradale's house. They thanked the Van Breda family warmly for their offer to secure Bodrugan for Frances Barradale's lifetime by the timely use of Anne-Marie's dowry, but they explained they wished to put the matter right themselves.

Meanwhile James Carey was calling in Anne-Marie's monies to return them to her family in Holland as, with Anthony's death, the link that had bound the child to them had snapped, and it had always been a point of pride with Richard Barradale's family to preserve Anne-Marie's modest dowry intact. But the final settlement would be delayed, Anne-Marie gathered, as the details were somewhat involved. James Carey hoped, however, to give an account of his stewardship before eighteen months had passed.

iii

Ryk van Breda returned in fine fettle early in 1587. He had eluded both Spanish and English in his long voyage, and had returned with a rich cargo of silks and spices and pepper from the East, and was well pleased with his venture as, on this occasion, he had managed to scrape together enough capital to buy a share in the enterprise, so he personally had profited.

Their changed circumstances were already apparent in Ryk's house in Delft. Minetje's gowns were more opulent, she had two servants, and there was a gratifying air of prosperity about the place. Ryk had promised his wife a fine house in Amsterdam if this next venture turned out well. A voyage was still in the process of being planned, and there was some discussion as to whether he should undertake another long voyage to the East or sail to the west coast of Africa for gold, pepper, and ivory. The voyage to Africa was undoubtedly shorter and less hazardous, and, to lend attraction to the African venture, the might of Portugal had been on the wane since Spain's victorious war against her, and the garrisons on the Gold Coast were less to be dreaded than formerly. While he and Minetje argued this way and that, and little Pieter climbed onto Ryk's knees and thrust his wizened face against his father's beard, Anne-Marie came unexpectedly to Delft and settled the issue.

Ryk had not seen her for some time. It was early in the afternoon when Anne-Marie opened the door and walked in and found them grouped in the living room.

Ryk stared at her as she entered; and he heard a swift intake of breath from Dirk, who was seated beside him on the settle.

She halted in the dark doorway, holding an enormous basket. She wore a black cloak from which the hood had fallen back to reveal her blond hair, waving back from a high, broad forehead. Her skin was particularly clear and fine, faintly tinged with pink in the cheeks, and her lips were scarlet and proudly curved. Her eyes were large and brilliant and very dark blue, with long dark lashes curling back from them, and brows etched in an arching black line above them. Her youth and vitality flamed; she was so very much alive that she seemed to fill the room with a new life as she stood tall and lithe in the doorway.

They were all on their feet, starting towards her.

"Anne-Marie!" Minetje cried.

"Aunt Minetje, Uncle Ryk, Dirk, children!" exclaimed Anne-Marie, putting down her basket and beginning on a circular tour of embraces, not omitting the overwhelmed Dirk. And then she explained that Anna was anxious to know what was to happen about Ryk's proposed voyage and therefore she had come to find out.

"Pieter, you have grown into a big boy!" cried Anne-Marie, dropping onto her knees and drawing the tiny child to her. "Your grandmother has sent you I don't know what in that great basket."

Her sparkling spontaneity reached out to them. She arose and Minetje helped her remove her cloak. She was plainly dressed in homespun and wore clogs, yet Minetje in her velvet dress seemed insignificant beside her. Anne-Marie glows like a jewel, thought Ryk. This superb creature might have been his daughter if Liesbet had married him that night at Oostermeer. . . .

"How is my mother?" Ryk asked Anne-Marie.

"She is well, as we all are. She longs for news of you and Pieter specially."

"All goes well with us," answered Ryk. "There is one slight difficulty and that is that I cannot decide whether to voyage to the East or to sail again to Guinea."

He saw the colour drain from her face. She has not got over Anthony's death altogether, Ryk thought; but, heaven be praised, she had forgiven him for destroying her letter.

On the next day when Anne-Marie came upon Ryk alone she told him why she had come to Delft.

"If I may make up your mind for you, Uncle Ryk," she said, "you will sail to Guinea."

"Do you still hope then, Anne-Marie?" he asked sadly.

"If I speak the truth, no, I do not hope. But I must make up my mind to live without Anthony and time passes. I have told Jan van Braam that, when I am sure beyond a doubt that Anthony did indeed perish on the Gold Coast, I shall marry him: My grandmother suggested that you might make certain inquiries on your next voyage to Guinea. If when you get back you can confirm that Anthony is dead I shall marry Jan."

"The business of the voyage is settled, Anne-Marie. I shall sail to Guinea at the end of the year."

"You will make the most searching inquiries?"

"I promise you I shall not leave those shores until I have absolute proof of Anthony's fate. I owe you that, at least, Anne-Marie."

"You owe me nothing, Uncle Ryk."

"It is very good of you, Anne-Marie," said Ryk. "But I have a tender conscience. It will be my happiness to find out for you."

So it was to be the Gold Coast again, Ryk thought, with the surf pounding endlessly on the sandy beaches, and the fringe of palms against the sky; where the sun burned its way across the heavens and the sea lay still and deep like dark sapphire.

PART XII

GOLD COAST INTERLUDE

CHAPTER TWENTY-FIVE

ANCHORED OFF THE SHORES OF THE GOLD COAST, WITHIN FIVE MILES
of the fortress at Elmina, three Dutch vessels lay becalmed.
They were separated from each other by about a quarter of a mile.
They had lain at anchor during ten days of haze and exceptional heat,
the ships' boats cruising up and down at intervals to see that no Portuguese warship bore down upon them unawares, as they lay in a curve
of the coast which, although it promised shelter if a tornado came up,
laid them open to a surprise attack. A successful week of trading with
the Shamas had been concluded. The holds were full, and the little fleet
awaited a fair wind to begin the homeward passage.

Ryk van Breda looked anxiously at the sky. Although it was intensely
blue with not a cloud in it he read something ominous in the haze that
hung quivering like a golden veil between the green, encroaching jungle
and the sea. There was the making of a tempest in that shimmering
heat.

He gazed moodily at the shore. The sands were brazen and the crawling tentacles of the tide sent long, tarnished fingers to mar their gleaming
gold.

He would have nothing more to tell Anne-Marie than what she
knew. Anthony was dead, and Abrobi Hill had reverted to the jungle.
The mine had not been reopened. The Awoins and the young men of
the neighbouring tribes had held out against the blandishments of the
Portuguese and had refused to disturb the fetish. Ryk had gone in person
to the village of the Awoins. The tribes he had met on his way were
friendly, and he was asked through his interpreter why the Dutch did
not build a fort on the Gold Coast, and he gathered that the inhabitants
were weary of the harsh domination of the Portuguese and hoped that
some other nation of white men would come to settle among them. At
the Awoin village Ryk had established beyond any doubt that the three
white men had perished at the time of the earthquake. There was no

more to be done for Anne-Marie. She would accept the evidence he put before her and marry Jan, and that would be the end of it. There was a recurring regret in Ryk's mind that he had judged Richard Barradale's son so hardly. The lad had been no more than a stripling when he had formed his adverse opinion of him, and had not had the chance to prove his worth; but regrets were idle, Ryk told himself, now that Anthony was dead.

ii

At noon the Portuguese galleys appeared round the curve of the shore. It was the hour of the siesta. It was also the time for the ships' boats to set out on their precautionary patrol of the coast. They had delayed, however, as the heat was at its fiercest. When the watch in the rigging of the leading vessel shouted the alarm the trumpets blared out and the crews, half drugged with sleep, began to stream onto the decks in that windless noon.

The galleys came on so fast that they were soon too close to be fired on with effect. The Portuguese were employing their favourite method of attack, which was to creep up to a ship's stern as she lay becalmed and helpless, and thus to take her at a disadvantage. Each galley carried a gun in the bows which could be used with great effect and no danger of retaliation as its position under the victim's stern kept it safe from the ship's guns. A number of harquebusiers and crossbow men in the sterns of the galleys were ready to press home an attack. As for the rest, there were eighteen oars on either side of the galley, to each of which three slaves were chained, and two stalwart galley masters, armed with whips, were ready to lash them to greater exertions.

Ryk's ship, the *Maaskerk*, had two galleys under her stern before the entire crew had got to their stations. Two cannon balls, fired at the closest range from the galleys, struck her and, as she shuddered under the shock, a rain of arrows fell on the deck.

Ryk van Breda rushed forward.

"Bring up the demiculverin, you ———," he roared, letting loose a flood of invective to rouse the crew from their first shock. He had not served a long apprenticeship with the Sea Beggars in vain, and Spanish oaths, intermingled with homely Dutch ones, whipped the sailors into action. "Get that demiculverin into position on the stern, and fire down on them. Blast them from the water. Are we to take all this and not defend ourselves?"

A shout went up from the crew. They had recovered from the paralyzing shock of the onslaught. The demiculverin was brought into action with devastating effect, killing and wounding many of the slaves, among whom, it appeared, there were both Englishmen and Frenchmen. As far as could be judged from the *Maaskerk*, the other vessels were similarly beset but appeared to be holding their own.

The broiling sun beat down upon them. Ryk was here, there, everywhere, shouting orders and directing the fire himself at times. On the whole the fight was not going too ill for the defenders, for the perspiring gunners at intervals got their fire well home—so well that the Portuguese were compelled to revise their strategy.

It was now observed that two galleys attacking the second of the Dutch vessels were pulling away from her, and soon it was clear that they were coming up to assist in the attack on the *Maaskerk*.

This put an entirely different complexion on the Dutchmen's brief complacency. Ryk, realizing that a rain of arrows would not prove effective against a combined attack, resorted to other means. On his instructions pyramids of cannon balls were built beside the bulwarks, and cutlasses and belaying pins put out in readiness to repel boarders. While Dirk and some of the crew were employed in carrying out Ryk's orders, the gunners, by a stroke of incredible fortune, succeeded in silencing the Portuguese gun in the bows of one of the galleys, which gave the men a breathing space in which to complete their preparations.

The reinforcing galleys were now within range of the *Maaskerk's* cannon. The galleys shot through the water and, having avoided the cannon fire from the *Maaskerk*, crept in to join the partially disabled galleys under the stern, one of which was practically out of the action, with half its oars shot away and the thwarts cumbered with dead and dying slaves, while the other had a high percentage of its crew killed or wounded, although the gun in the bows was fired at intervals, and the archers were still giving a poor account of themselves.

The battle was joined with great ferocity. The *Maaskerk* suffered badly and her foremast was carried away early on in the renewed fighting. The Portuguese raised a great shout of triumph when this happened, thinking that now surely they must take the ship. But Ryk van Breda had been in tighter corners and had survived fiercer battles.

"Let them have the cannon balls," he shouted.

A sudden deluge of cannon balls hurled by devils who showed themselves boldly at the bulwarks created confusion and panic in the galley crews. The chained slaves dropped their oars and, being unable to dodge the heavy missiles, many were struck and fell insensible into the bottom of the galleys. The galley masters, although the whip was mercilessly applied, were unable to restore order for some minutes, and for a short while it seemed as though their unexpected weapon might swing the tide of battle in favour of the defenders.

Ryk perceived that the moment had arrived to take the offensive. He ordered the demiculverin to be fired again.

The chief gunner and his assistant gunners, having run short of gunpowder, repaired at once to a pile of barrels which had been brought up on deck and placed under an improvised roofing. As the men stooped over the pile, the gunpowder, for some unknown cause, exploded. The chief gunner was killed outright, and the majority of his assistants were severely injured.

The disaster was observed by the Portuguese, whose crews had by this time been brought to some kind of order. Their guns roared from the bows and, to the horror of the accidental explosion on the deck was added the concussion of the enemy cannon. The deck was slippery with blood and a rain of arrows showered down upon it. Shattered by the renewed onslaught of the enemy, their ship reeling beneath them, for a fearful moment the remnants of the *Maaskerk's* crew gave themselves up for lost.

Ryk himself stood dazed, incapable of action. He had been very near when the gunpowder in the cache had exploded and the effects of the concussion had not yet worn off. He had been flung flat on his face by the blast and had recovered his senses to find Dirk laving his head and hands with water.

A voice came suddenly up to him from the sea.

"Do not give up. We are weakening also," shrieked an English voice from beneath the stern of the ship.

Ryk's heart gave a great leap and then seemed to stop. He had heard that voice before. For an instant to his reeling senses it appeared that he had heard a voice from another world. They were doomed; the voices of the dead were sounding in his ears. . . .

The shriek came again from the sea.

"Do not give up. It is better to die like a man on your own deck than to lead a dog's life as a slave."

Ryk rushed to the ship's side to look down upon the galley whence had come the voice. He stooped for a cannon ball and, regardless of his own safety and heedless of the shambles the deck behind him had become, poised himself for deliberate aim. Arrows fell about him.

Dirk had taken over the demiculverin. He was struggling with the charge at the moment Ryk showed his massive torso above the bulwarks.

In the galley directly beneath him Ryk saw a galley master bringing his whip down on the shoulders of a man down whose back the blood was running in streams. The slave's head was bowed. As he was being subjected to this fearful punishment Ryk came to the conclusion that it must be the man who had shouted to them not to yield. And, taking careful aim, he dropped the cannon ball on the galley master, who collapsed and lay groaning.

The face of the chained slave was uplifted for an instant and Ryk looked down into it.

"Anthony!"

All the breath in Ryk's body seemed to go out in that mighty shout.

At this precise moment Dirk succeeded in firing the demiculverin. The shot tore along the side of the leading galley, in which Anthony was, breaking nearly every oar down one side and cutting the craft practically in two pieces.

"As God lives we shall not surrender!"

The words had been spoken by one of the crew. They had all seized their bows and were pouring so close a shower of arrows down upon the galleys that Ryk trembled for Anthony, who crouched in a slumped heap over his broken oar in the foundering galley. And, as he stared down in agony, the slave chained with Anthony to the useless oar suddenly flung himself forward over the body of the crouching man, shielding him. Two arrows sank quivering through the barrier of his body.

The galley broke in two. Anthony and the two slaves were still chained to the smaller portion of the breastworks. Both halves began to submerge. The chained slaves, in a dreadful confusion of heavy, inert dead and writhing, shrieking living, were being sucked down in the vortex.

Ryk saw Anthony's face uplifted once more in his final struggle for life. He acted without thought. With a wild shout he climbed upon the bulwarks and leapt into the sea. As he came to the surface he struck out. And when he was clear of the agitated water he looked round. The larger portion of the broken galley had disappeared, and in the suck and eddy of its submersion the fragment of the breastworks was bobbing like a cork, and there was a man clinging to it, lifting his face out of the water. Ryk made for him, came up with him, and caught his head as he went under. He knew he was powerless and must himself be drawn under if he held on. All the while arrows fell about him and drifted away in the sea.

Three men's weight was on his arm—two dead slaves and the yet living Anthony. The water was coming away red as it flowed against Anthony's battered back. The shackles held. He could not tear Anthony free. The dragging on his arm was terrific, and for a moment of suffocation Ryk was pulled beneath the water. He fought his way up again and his fingers were so dug into Anthony's shoulder that he arose with him. Anthony's lips moved, but no words came. Again the dreadful suction began and Ryk strove against a dead weight. Gradually Anthony's face was pulled down and he saw it under water, the long chestnut hair floating like dark seaweed. He could do no more. He must release his grip or drown. It was the worst moment of his life.

Ryk felt himself being dragged down. He could not release his grip. His free arm was yet above the water when a rope struck it. Instinctively he stretched out his fingers and by some miracle seized hold of the rope. There was a great strain at the other end and Ryk felt that he was being lifted.

His head came to the surface again, and Anthony's unconscious face with the wet hair falling back from it. Now Ryk was aware that there was someone in the water beside him. A rope was secured round his body, and a rope round the wreckage. He felt himself hoisted, heard the muffled blows of an axe under the water; felt as though the weight of the world had fallen from him as he found himself floating with only Anthony's body in the grip of his cramped arm.

There were more ropes round him and round Anthony. They were being lifted. They were clear of the water and being drawn up the riddled stern of the ship, and there was a protective veil of arrows between them and the galleys, and from above the shouts and cries for vengeance were mingled with urgent appeals for haste and endurance, with prayers for deliverance. The clamour and confusion came distantly to Ryk, like the surging of a tempest in his ears: he was struggling in a void; there was a cessation of sound and sensation; and as they were hoisted over the bulwarks and received into the arms of the bloodstained crew, for the first time in his life Ryk fainted.

iii

Some long time after their unconscious captain and the wounded galley slave had been saved from the sea, the exhausted crew of the *Maaskerk* had seen that the ships' boats had put off from the vessel to the leeward and were coming to their rescue. The remaining galleys, by now in poor shape indeed, had pulled slowly away and the struggle was over.

That night the wind came up and, lending herself to it, the crippled *Maaskerk* slipped out to the open sea, shepherded by her sister ships. She sailed under part of her canvas, as the jury mast, at which the carpenters had toiled as men possessed all afternoon, was a frail affair, and likely to collapse at the slightest strain.

The sun rose over a white-crested sea and a moderate breeze carried the three vessels a stage farther on their homeward journey.

Before a week had passed it was plain that the *Maaskerk* must lie to for essential repairs. The vessels accordingly altered course and hugged the shores of the jungle-covered land and, when the wind failed and they were once more becalmed, they dropped anchor a mile from a wild and seemingly uninhabited shore.

Now, while the *Maaskerk* rang with the sound of hammers, with the buzzing of saws and the voices of carpenters and seamen, Anthony Barradale took a definite turn towards recovery, and Ryk knew he would live. Before the repairs had been completed Ryk had learned from Anthony how it was that he had been pressed into the galley service of the Portuguese on the Gold Coast.

iv

The actual escape from the mine presented no difficulty, so Anthony told Ryk. No sooner were he and Lucas Mason and Tom Wilson clear of the tunnel than the earthquake occurred. They threw themselves flat on their faces until the shaking of the ground was over. It was a remarkable night, with a bright moon at the full, and they were aghast to discover when they got to their feet that the rocks and boulders from the summit had fallen so as to block the entrance to the mine completely.

They concealed themselves in a depression in the ground, hiding in the dank growth. It was as well they had gone to earth, as natives ran by panic-stricken. They lay still, fearing to reveal themselves on such a catastrophic night. They waited for a time, hoping that old Aba would appear, although they were certain she had not followed them out and must have been buried when the hill collapsed.

They decided to walk south and hope to pick up an English or Dutch ship when they reached the coast. They had great good fortune on their journey through the jungle. The earthquake had scattered the tribes and in the ruins of huts they found coconuts and yams, palm wine and honeycomb, and were able to exist on this diet for several days. Only once did they encounter an African. They came face to face with a woman. She, apparently convinced that she had seen a trio of apparitions, fled howling into the bush. They were not molested, and, apart from the discomfort of heat and mosquitoes, they had not fared too badly on their journey to the sea. As dusk fell on a certain evening they reached the shore of an uninhabited strip of coast line. Lucas Mason judged they had cut down in between Elmina and the Kormantins. Here, on the desolate beach, fortune favoured them once more. They found a sound canoe washed up against a palm by the great tidal wave.

They determined to spend the night on the beach and set off on their voyage up and down the coast line in the morning.

In the distance they saw a light once or twice during the early part of the night. It was not steady and Mason had the notion it might have been a ship's light. If this were so it was conceivable that the vessel might be anchored at some trading town. They decided, therefore, to row in that direction as soon as it was light enough to see.

At daybreak they began to row. Soon they came to an inlet in the coast and saw on a tip of land a watchtower with a large black wooden cross in front of it. The little tower stood on a rock and beyond it a castle showed. They gazed upon the Portuguese fort of San Antonio at Axim, of the existence of which they were ignorant. The fortress had stood firm throughout the earthquake, although it had been much shaken.

No flag broke from the castle, so they could not be sure it was a Portuguese stronghold. They were certain they were not approaching Elmina; therefore there was a wild hope that either the French or the Dutch had built a fortress commanding the inlet to safeguard their trade.

They decided to act on the forlorn hope. They were suffering from the sun and their journey through the jungle on an insufficient diet. A man issued forth from the fortress, bearing a white flag in his hand. He was followed at a distance by a company of soldiers. He beckoned them to come ashore.

It was the moment of decision. And also a moment of dreadful doubt.

"We must assume they are either French or Dutch," said Anthony. "There is no need for a Portuguese to approach with a white flag. They are the masters on this coast."

"Can't make out from this distance," growled Lucas.

"Let us row nearer and find out," said Tom practically.

It was the counsel of desperation. They applied themselves to their paddles and brought the canoe appreciably nearer the shore.

Now they saw the man on the beach was a Portuguese. They tried to make off, whereupon the soldiers fired upon them. Lucas was killed, although Anthony and Tom escaped without a scratch. The canoe, however, had been badly holed and, in spite of their frantic attempts at scooping the water out with their hands, she began to sink.

So they beached the canoe and gave themselves into the power of the Portuguese.

The men from the fort recognized them as the three English prisoners from Elmina who had been delivered to the Awoins as propitiatory offerings for the appeasement of the sasabonsum. Amid much argument and gesticulation Anthony and Tom were taken into the fortress.

After another interlude of consultation the Portuguese apparently came to the conclusion that the escape of the human sacrifices from Abrobi would greatly increase their difficulties in obtaining labour among the superstitious tribesmen. A soldier who had a smattering of English questioned Anthony and Tom as to whether they had been observed or followed as they had walked through the jungle. The Portuguese seemed to be greatly relieved to learn they had successfully avoided the Africans. It was therefore reasonable to suppose that no African would be aware that the three men had not perished in the collapse of the mine. And Tom and Anthony were eventually drafted to the galleys instead of being hanged.

Of the three who had left Elmina only Anthony survived; Tom Wilson had died as he threw his body over Anthony's to shield him from the Dutch arrows. His death preyed upon Anthony's sick mind, and all Ryk's beguiling talk of Anne-Marie could not shake his depression. Once Ryk succeeded in lifting his mood for a short time when he told him that James Carey and Martin Thomas between them were repaying the mortgage on Bodrugan and supporting his mother, and that they had declined to use Anne-Marie's dowry for the purpose although they had been offered it. But Anthony's spirits were never more than temporarily lifted in spite of Ryk's persistent efforts to make him see the past in a less sombre light. It took an English ship to restore some of his natural buoyancy of spirit.

Anthony saw her on a day when the sea sparkled in the sun and a strong wind blew. She was scudding for home under full canvas. The dazzling sunlight gave her a glorious delicacy of outline, gilding her sails to a bright gold against the deep blue sky. The fair ship lent herself to the wind and passed effortlessly through the waves, as effortlessly as a gull in flight. For an hour and more Anthony watched her, and he lived again a summer morning on Pendennis when a little Tudor ship had slipped from Falmouth haven and cleared the harbour. He had smiled to see her hoist her coloured sails and stand away to the Channel, gaily bobbing in the waves. And there had been a sea gull in that picture. It had swung on motionless wings at the rim of the headland. In that certainty of sea and sky there had been nothing illusory or dreamlike. The sea gull had seemed the realization of a dream of freedom and eternity.

As though she were aware that she carried Anthony's thoughts with her, the English ship sailed on in sight of the Dutch vessels for several days. Each morning when Anthony saw her like some bright vision on the horizon he left his dark experiences a little farther behind him and dwelt instead on his youth at Bodrugan. In his thoughts he roved the secluded coves and rocky inlets of Cornwall; and his memories of Anne-Marie returned and brought their healing.

While the four ships sailed the northern summer seas a fifth vessel, outward bound, approached them and signalled that they should draw together. Tacking and manoeuvring on the calm Atlantic, the vessels drew into a rough circle, and ships' boats plied from one to another, conveying news of shattering import.

Philip's Great Armada had set sail from Spain on the twentieth of May, it being the year 1588. Four huge galleasses had led the hundred and thirty fighting ships of Spain, under the command of the Duke of Medina-Sidonia; but stormy weather and the want of supplies had caused the Armada to put back into Corunna again for seven weeks, and a fine stir this had created, for with the Spanish fleet mysteriously lost, no man knew at what point or at what time to expect an invasion. Indeed, the Queen of England, thinking that the threat was over, ordered the lord high admiral, Lord Howard of Effingham, to dismiss some of his ships; but he, putting no trust in the Spaniard, maintained the extra vessels at his own expense.

It was early in the month of July and now tidings had reached England that the Great Armada was once again under way. The vessel outward bound from England had thought to warn the traders to seek the shelter of an English port before the storm of the invasion broke.

Anthony, much recovered in health and greatly invigorated in mind, decided that he would remain with Ryk and go first to Holland and Anne-Marie before joining an English ship. Having arrived at this decision, he sent a message to his mother at Falmouth by the captain of the English ship, who was a Devon man, to tell her that he lived and would return to Bodrugan as soon as events permitted; and to his mother he entrusted the task of informing Lydia Wilson that Tom was dead and acquainting her with the circumstances of his death.

The ships separated in mid-ocean. Ryk van Breda, in whom the zest to get to grips with the Spaniards had awakened with renewed vigour, set all sail to reach a Dutch port as soon as might be, where he intended to abandon the *Maaskerk* and all commercial enterprise, and join the strength of a naval unit to play his part in the defence of the Netherlands.

Like scattered swans the little fleet of trading ships crowded on all sail, and, with their sunburnt canvas bellying in the wind, set urgent course for home.

PART XIII

ҺOLLAND

UNDER THE CROWDED CANVAS THE JURY MAST OF THE MAASKERK threatened to give way. Smothering his vast impatience as best he could, Ryk van Breda was forced to lag behind the other ships and let his vessel go steadily on at her own slow pace.

They were still out in the Atlantic when the Invincible Armada was sighted off the shores of England, and the greatest chapters in English history were in the making. The news that the long-expected invasion had begun was signalled from end to end of the land by a chain of bonfires upon the heights, of which one at least had not been prepared beforehand. It smouldered for a day and a night on the slope above Falmouth.

On the same day the Armada was sighted the English trader that had sailed with the Dutch vessels put in at Falmouth, having passed by the Spanish fleet in the dark. An aged woman with a Bible in her kerchief came up to the captain and asked him whether he stepped ashore a good Christian. The woman was Lydia Wilson. Thus she learned at once, for the second time, that Tom was dead. The news was years old and ought not to have sent her crazy; but it did. When the blazing beacons on the hills spread the alarm far and wide on that summer's night in July, smoke hung like a pall on the hill above Falmouth and drifted over the harbour, and it was seen that Lydia Wilson's poor cottage was on fire. By the time the townsfolk arrived on the scene the flames had taken well hold of the thatch and there was no quenching the conflagration. Of Lydia there was no sign then or thereafter. It was concluded that she had perished in the flames, although there were a few who declared that water and not fire was her element and expected her to reappear in some supernatural shape at a later time. While those of the townsfolk who lingered on and did not return to their watch by the sea stood around they heard explosions in the burning thatch, and blue flames ran in livid fingers down the walls as forgotten ankers of brandy added their alcoholic content to the blaze. The watchers, remembering Lydia Wilson's magpie habits, wondered covetously what other treasure besides good brandy was being consumed in the ancient thatch. For a few hours the fire at Lydia's was of more moment than the appearance of the Armada in English waters.

After the captain's message reached her Frances Barradale threw off her apathy and took Lydia's place on the quays, watching each boat and ship as she put in. Anthony was coming home: she had something to live for.

The battle was joined. The English and the Spanish fleets lined up, the Armada in a crescent formation, seven miles long. The English broadsides thundered out from the bodies of their warships, throwing the tall, unwieldy galleons of Spain back upon one another and casting the Spanish line into confusion. The Armada then bore down upon Calais, expecting to link up with the Spanish army under the Duke of Parma on the coast of Flanders.

Meanwhile at Tilbury the Queen of England put herself at the head of her troops, encouraging the captains and the soldiers by her presence and her words.

The Duke of Parma's tardiness averted the landing of Spanish troops on English soil. It had been decided that he was to cross with his troops from Flanders to England to join with the fleet under Medina-Sidonia. But Spanish strategy was not brought to nought by Parma's unreadiness alone. Drake made use of fire ships which were carried forward by a favouring wind and floated into Calais after dark. The vessels of the Armada had anchored close together and now, in the face of this new danger, they cut their cables and put out to the North Sea.

In Dutch waters the Sea Beggars had played their part. They had blockaded Spanish shipping in their harbours and were keeping the Duke of Parma from leaving Dunkirk.

As the campaign neared its crisis and the battle of Gravelines was about to be joined, Ryk van Breda brought his weary ship safely to Dunkirk.

ii

At the battle of Gravelines fearful havoc was caused among the argosies of Spain, caught as they were between the English broadsides and the shallows on the other side. As a contemporary wrote, "The Spanish ships are lying up and down the coast like birds without wings." The remnants of the Armada fled to the North Sea, where they were hotly pursued past Scotland.

Leaving Dirk aboard the *Maaskerk*, Ryk and Anthony joined one of the Dutch ships, and the Sea Beggars had the task of pinning down the land forces of the enemy. When four large Spanish vessels had been sunk the blockading Dutch were proved to be the masters of the situation. Now that it was clear that Medina-Sidonia was not returning but was intending to double back to Spain round the north of Scotland it was impossible for Parma to carry through his share of the invasion as planned. In these stirring days of fighting in the warm August weather the ultimate success of the Dutch in their long struggle for liberty against Spain was assured, and England was secured against invasion of her shores.

When the fighting was over and the maintenance of the blockade had settled down to a matter of routine, Ryk and Anthony sought permission to go a little way north. They found a small trading vessel about to sail to Delftshaven and boarded her.

Anna and Gerard and Anne-Marie were the sole occupants of Ryk's house in Delft. They had come from Friesland to be with Minetje. Minetje, however, declined to remain in Delft and be murdered, she said, so, taking her five children, she had retreated to her parents in the country and declared her intention of staying there until the danger was over.

Anne-Marie had gone as usual to the South Gate to glean the latest news from travellers coming up from the coast. She had heard of the notable victory at Gravelines, and on this particular afternoon a bargee delayed for some time to explain to her the tactics of the English sea dogs.

"They gave the Spaniards no chance to board," the bargee told Anne-Marie, expounding at some length to the prettiest girl he had seen for many a long day. "They hung round the Spanish fleet, pounding it at a distance, and hounded it down the Channel relentlessly. As for the flotilla of blazing fire ships the English loosed upon the Spaniards as they lay at anchor in Calais, why, that was a masterpiece! They are a boastful crowd, the English, and their insolence is unbounded, but we can be generous and praise them now, for their ships were few, and the argosies of Spain were a host and enough to frighten any man."

They had something to boast about, thought Anne-Marie, warmly remembering her Falmouth days. It was no wonder, she reflected, that the Elizabethan sailor believed himself superior not only to an individual foreigner but to any number of foreigners. Now there had been the defeat of the greatest Armada the world had seen to prove they were not mere vain boasters. She longed to hear the rough Cornish speech, see the Cornish men set off in their ships. Oh, Anthony, Anthony . . . Would she ever forget? Every day she longed for Ryk's return, and yet dreaded it, as he could not but come back alone.

"They would not have done so well," she said, struggling with her pain, "had not the Sea Beggars held Parma here."

"No, that is the truth. And I'll tell you another truth: the English may have the sailors, but we have the pretty girls."

Anne-Marie blushed and laughed.

"I must tell you they have both," she said. "I have been to England, you see."

"Have you? And when was that?"

"When I was a child," she said.

They spoke together for a while longer; but time waited for no man and regretfully the bargee continued on his way.

Anna and Gerard were alone in the house when Ryk came.

When the greetings were over and they had sat down Anna asked where Dirk was.

"I have left him with the ships at Dunkirk," answered Ryk. "I was anxious to get home. In a few days I shall return and we shall finish the voyage at Amsterdam."

"Minetje and the children are well," Anna explained. "Pieter is much stronger. You will see a big difference in him. They are at your father-in-law's."

Ryk was preoccupied. Both Anna and Gerard remarked it; it seemed to them he was keeping something back.

"Did you not see Anne-Marie as you entered at the South Gate?" asked Anna. "She goes there daily to pick up any news of the fighting."

"Yes," said Ryk. "I saw her."

He was deeply moved, Anna noticed. Anthony's death must have been confirmed and he had told the child, and she could not bear to face them yet. That is it, thought Anna.

"I shall go to her," she said, and made as if to rise.

Ryk laid a restraining hand on her arm.

"No, Mother," he said. "Stay here. I should say Anne-Marie is at the South Gate still, and well content to be there. I brought Anthony Barradale home with me, you see."

Anna and Gerard started to their feet and exclaimed in one voice: "Anthony Barradale here in Delft!"

Ryk nodded. He seemed to be in a dream and there was a glow on his face as he described the rapturous lovers' meeting at the South Gate.

"Anthony saw her before I did. He was at my side and then he was not; she was standing in the gateway and then she was in his arms. They kissed and clung together. I stood beside them for a while. I touched Anthony on the shoulder and spoke to Anne-Marie, but they did not seem to realize I was there. The women who were there wept and smiled and one advised me to go home and leave the young people alone. It seemed good advice to me, so here I am."

He told them then how it was that Anthony was alive. The afternoon passed in eager conversation, and as evening drew on Ryk and Gerard went out, for Ryk wished to reach his father-in-law's farm before it was too dark to travel.

iii

The lime trees were gold-green, caught in the net of the vanishing sun. Heedless children leapt in and out of a moored barge, which, riding light, danced against the canal wall. The spires and gables of Delft caught the rosy aftermath of the sun's setting and were flushed as the face of a bride. As this thought filtered into Anna's mind it was as though Anne-Marie stood before her. But Anne-Marie was not there with her. She was walking with her Anthony under the lime trees, clinging to his arm and looking into his face, as only lovers look.

Anna thought back on her eventful life. Memories of triumph and ecstasy, of sorrow and disaster, of a love that had not withered in fulfilment, of a prince unsurpassed in his humanity and loving-kindness, were dimmed this evening because the lonely future loomed so near and overshadowed all that had gone before: Anne-Marie would leave her now and take up her life in England, and their companionship would never be the same again.

Anna sighed. Her hands had been at her sides, lightly clenched, for she had fought against a deep sense of loss. She brought them up now and crossed them over her breasts, still closed. Her eyes widened and brimmed with tears. She moved her hands slowly away from her body and slowly opened her fingers as though she released something she had hoped to hold. Thus silently and alone she took her farewell of Anne-Marie, while the twilight deepened into warm darkness that lovers blessed.

She waited long for them. When she heard them walk along the quiet street to the house she opened the door to welcome them.

iv

In the morning Anna drew Gerard aside.

"Will you remain here?" she asked him. "I wish to go to Oostermeer."

He put down what he was doing and stood for a moment regarding her. The deep love he had borne her all his life, for her and for no other, moved in his heart.

"You are going to tell Jan he has lost Anne-Marie," he said at last.

"That is it," she said. "In these affairs there is always one who is left." Her lips came together in a smile of tremulous sweetness.

BOOK THREE

THE GOLDEN AGE

PART XIV

ḦOLLAṆD

CHAPTER TWENTY-SEVEN

I T WAS MANY MONTHS BEFORE THE NEWS OF THE DESTRUCTION OF THE
Armada reached Philip in faraway Spain. When it came the
whole land mourned, for there was scarce a household of which some
beloved member had not perished in the great catastrophe. In Holland
and in England the victory bells rang joyous peals and devout services
of thanksgiving were held in every church. For a while, also, there was
an excellent understanding between these countries, delivered from the
might of Spanish sea power by their united and splendid exertions.

On the surface life flowed uneventfully on at Oostermeer. In the busy
farmhouse Anna and Gerard, Jan and his young wife, Juliana—Jan van
Braam had married Ryk van Breda's eldest daughter in the spring of
1589 a few months after Anne-Marie's wedding in the Old Church at
Delft and her departure for England—carried on with the seasonal
occupations of the farm, the cooking and the cleaning and the butter-
making, the sowing and the reaping. But, if they had wished, Anna and
Gerard could have told of strong currents of feelings of passion and
renunciation that had run in scarifying streams below the seemingly
calm surface of things. Anna and Gerard had observed much but they
did not express their thoughts even to each other; and it had been an
immense relief to both of them when the young couple had settled down
in harmony to a full life on Oostermeer.

Delft knew Ryk van Breda's family no more. He had bought himself
an imposing residence in Amsterdam. Minetje, in the seventh heaven of
delight, had installed herself and her four children in her new home and,
as Anna had correctly surmised, she was forever asking Ryk if the ancient
arms of the family might not be revived, but Ryk, none too sure of his
title to display them, had so far not fallen in with her wishes. On the one
brief visit she had paid Minetje in her opulent Amsterdam home Anna
had been fascinated beyond measure by the change in her daughter-in-
law. She seemed to have grown in stature as well as in dignity in her
changed circumstances. And Pieter also was playing a great part in his

mother's late development, for he relied on her and called out the best in her. The delicate boy showed signs of precocious intelligence, although physically he was thin and stunted. Anna was both amused and touched by Minetje's social aspirations and intended to discover what the arms of the family were and to make Minetje a present of the fruits of her heraldic research on her next visit to Amsterdam. In Holland the miller and the weaver, the sailor and the trader, the merchant and the farmer, were in the ascendant in the Dutch Republic, and if Minetje desired a place in the forefront of these ranks Anna argued that it showed that she took a sincere interest in her family and their advancement.

All these happenings were behind her on the morning of the twenty-sixth of February 1590. This was a momentous day in the annals of Dutch history, for the forces of Prince Maurice had surprised the fortress of Breda, which had fallen without the loss of a single man; and for Anna herself it was also to prove a momentous day: at eleven in the morning Juliana gave birth to a son.

In the afternoon Anna and Jan were sitting with Juliana when the infant stirred. Anna picked him up from beside his mother and carried him to the window to look at him closely. She had lived a long time, she reflected, to hold a great-grandson in her arms.

The features of the babe were minute and clear. Anna had a slight feeling of shock, as though she had unexpectedly seen her own face. This child favoured neither Jan nor Juliana, who were both heavy-featured; he was like Lourens, so long dead, and Anne-Marie, Lourens's daughter, and herself. A wave of emotion swept over her and she was so happy that tears came into her eyes. There would be a kinship between herself and this child as there had been between herself and Lourens and Anne-Marie. The void there had been in her life since Anne-Marie had gone back to England would be filled by this new life. What a strange thing heredity is, Anna thought, holding the babe very close to her breast. It was no doubt the preponderance of the Van Braam blood but the characteristics of the baron that had cropped up so plainly in each generation —sometimes once or twice—were out in this child. There was no need to look at the baby's hands, she thought as she uncovered them, for they were bound to be long and slender as her own were. When the tiny hand lay in her palm she saw it was the shape she had expected to see. She was thankful she was not very old. She felt vigorous and strong in spite of her sixty years, and she saw no reason why she should not live to see this babe a man. It was a pity, she reflected, that she knew so little about the baron. There might have been hidden good in him whether her mother would admit it or not. Well, conjecture was always amusing, she thought, and undoubtedly the stock was persistent. That debauched baron . . . he had played quite a part in her life. Anna chuckled aloud.

"Aunt Anna?" Jan said inquiringly, startled by so odd a sound in the silence of the sickroom.

Anna could think of no explanation for her mirth other than the real one, so she gave none. They would not appreciate her thoughts of the baron.

"If you and Juliana would please me, Jan," she said, "you will name this boy Lourens."

She laughed again, but inaudibly this time, and held the child very closely to her.

ii

Philip of Spain, still in pursuit of world domination, now turned his eyes on France. He claimed the succession for his daughter, and Parma was sent to further Spanish schemes in that country. This was a false move, as it gave Holland an opportunity of carrying on her warfare in easier conditions, for Parma was the leading general of his age. Prince Maurice of Orange made the most of his chance: by the summer of 1594 Groningen, the capital of Friesland, was captured, and the north was practically freed of the enemy. In the south, however, the obedient and impoverished provinces were still held in the grip of Spain.

In these full years, and in the one that followed on them, the fortunes of the Van Breda and Van Braam families flowed on in normal ways. Ryk van Breda had by now amassed a substantial fortune from the profits of the lucrative trade he carried on regularly with the Spanish dominions. The release of the Groningen properties started a period of comparative affluence at Oostermeer. Gerard, who had for some time been failing after a severe attack of pneumonia, retired to Groningen to live with his relations there, leaving the farming to Jan and two hired men. By now there were three children at Oostermeer, Lourens, Johannes, and an infant of a few weeks, Lena. Anna spent her time between Oostermeer and Groningen, tending to spend the greater part of it at Oostermeer, as Juliana needed a considerable amount of help with her increasing family. Lourens was Anna's delight and her particular charge. From the time he could speak she had taught him to address her as "my grandmother," in the endearing manner of Anne-Marie.

Anna thought often of Anne-Marie and longed to see her. They frequently exchanged letters and at Bodrugan there were also three great-grandchildren—Gilbert, Margaret, and Francis. Anne-Marie wrote voluminously to Anna, giving minute, detailed accounts of the children and the daily happenings at Bodrugan. Anne-Marie wrote that Frances Barradale had died; that she was happy that they led such a quiet life on Bodrugan, for health and vigour were returning to Anthony, and, if it had not been for the old scars of the lash on his back, she could say he had recovered from his terrible experiences on the Gold Coast. Yet, in spite of the limpid flow of Anne-Marie's letters, Anna was not satisfied. She felt there were undercurrents of disappointment and disillusionment that were never expressed. And her reason told her that something of the horrors Anthony had endured as a galley slave must remain to taint the peace of Bodrugan, and the dark time on the Gold Coast could not be eradicated from his mind as easily as from his body. If only Anne-Marie had mentioned one difficult day she would have felt happier; there was too much of peace and calm in the letters she received to satisfy her, and Anna had come to rely on her instinct where her affections were involved.

She decided that one day she would go to England and see for herself how things were with Anne-Marie. In the meantime she contented herself with writing long letters and, because sometimes there was not much news, she told Anne-Marie of the efforts of Linschoten to find the Northeast Passage to China and India, and asked her if she had read the book of his voyages which she had heard had created as much stir in England as it had in Holland.

Early in 1595 Ryk sent a message asking Anna to pay them a long visit in Amsterdam, as he had many important matters he wished to discuss with her, and they all looked forward to seeing her again. He had arranged that Dirk should call for her when next his business took him to Friesland. Ryk had set Dirk up in a coasting ship of his own, and Dirk had made such a good thing of carrying goods between Flanders and Friesland, stopping at all the ports on the way, that he had married a comely young woman in Delftshaven and had settled down to a life of peaceful trading up and down the flat coast of the Netherlands.

Accordingly one fine spring day Anna found herself on board Dirk's tiny vessel. She had Lourens with her to relieve Juliana, who had her hands full with the two younger children. Minetje had expressed a wish to see her elder grandson, so, having tethered the lively child to the bulwarks by a short length of rope in case he should fall overboard, Anna talked to Dirk, while Lourens threw small objects into the sea and laughed to see them float away.

It was a perfect day with a mild breeze blowing and the sun shining on the rippling expanse of water. It was the first holiday Anna had had for years and she felt happy and light of heart. She took off her cap and pushed it into the bosom of her gown and let the wind lift her white hair, which was still thick and wavy. And colour was in her cheeks and lips, and her eyes were beautiful with the blueness and the greyness of the sea in them.

"How the world and the times change, Dirk, and we with them," said Anna, reminiscing. "When the flood swept over Friesland and we were adrift in an open boat I never thought I should be able to look upon the sea again; and here I am gazing at it and enjoying every moment."

"I don't ever think of the sea," said Dirk stolidly. "It is my element and there is nothing exciting about it. It creates no thought in me; but when I am home in Delftshaven I am so interested in my little house and the children and the garden that I never stop thinking and planning."

"It is as well that you do the thinking, Dirk. With the twins, your wife wouldn't have the time," Anna observed.

"I see no great change in you since the day you came to Zoeterwoude."

"That was more years ago than I like to remember," said Anna, smil-

ing. "I have great-grandchildren now. Look at that one over there
tethered to the bulwarks. Ryk will be proud of him, will he not? Such a
fine lad as he is!"

Dirk said abruptly, almost unwillingly:

"He is not so very much smaller than his uncle Pieter."

"I have not seen Pieter for years. Has he not filled out then? I had so
hoped he would shake off his weakness as he grew older. Let me see, he
is eleven now."

"Pieter is a clever boy, very clever; but he does not grow in the
Amsterdam swamps. He ought to be reared in the country air. His back
is twisted and that makes him seem shorter."

"Neither Minetje nor Ryk has ever mentioned that."

"They do not like to speak of Pieter's health. I am always very careful
what I say to them. I have spoken of Pieter now so that you will be
warned that they are very sensitive."

"Is the deformity of the back very noticeable then?" asked Anna in
dismay.

"Well, he will be a little hunchback, I think," said Dirk reluctantly.
"The best physicians have been consulted, but Pieter is sickly and there
is nothing to be done."

Poor Ryk, poor Minetje, thought Anna. And Pieter their only son . . .

"I shall be very careful not to notice anything," Anna promised Dirk.
"You know I would never willingly upset Ryk and Minetje."

"Lourens is like Anne-Marie," said Dirk. "In fact he might be her
son and not Juliana's. Have you news of Anne-Marie? I have never forgotten how pleasant it used to be to take her up and down the Schie to
find out about a letter. I very nearly learned to speak English."

"Yes, I have news of her. They do well in England; but I long to see
her again. A letter, after all, is a lifeless thing."

"One day I shall take you to Falmouth," said Dirk. "I have not crossed
the North Sea in this little ship, but she is a stout vessel and will ride
out any weather."

"You are not going out on any more of Ryk's expeditions then?"

Anna had long wanted to know why Dirk and Ryk no longer sailed together. A shadow settled on Dirk's fresh open face but he gave her no
indication as to what had caused the rift.

"Marta does not wish it. I shall always fight in the Netherlands navy if
I am called out, but home waters for me otherwise," Dirk said, loyally
avoiding an explanation that would involve Ryk. "I want no more than
I have. The world is wide, and I would rather be near Delftshaven than
voyaging to foreign lands."

Anna laughed, and determined that she would find out another time.

"I like to hear you say that," she said. "So many men only come to
realize how small a thing ambition is when they have worn themselves
out chasing shadows."

"I have chased no shadows," said Dirk. "But I have no desire to be a Linschoten to be eaten by polar bears or to be the sport of walruses; nor yet do I wish to broil in the tropics and die of fever. If you do not mind, mevrou, I must help with that sail. We'll have time enough for talk as this will be a slow trip. I must put in here and there, and, if you will, we will spend two days ashore at Delftshaven."

"I should be disappointed if we were not to stop at Delftshaven," said Anna. "I wish to see your twins."

"They are fine lads," said Dirk with pride. "Like that one there. And, if I am not mistaken, Master Lourens has just this minute thrown his cap overboard."

"Ach, no!" exclaimed Anna, going forward. "And his best red one too. What will Juliana say?"

"His grandmother will have a chestful of caps for him in Amsterdam, and much else besides," Dirk prophesied. "I would not worry about the cap."

Anna thought she detected a trace of bitterness in the remark. Ryk and Minetje, wealthy and important persons in Amsterdam, were not, perhaps, the same persons Dirk had known and loved in the simple home in Delft. That might well explain why Dirk sailed alone up and down the coast.

Dirk went forward to assist with the sail and Anna, putting her thoughts behind her, picked up the child in her arms. Together they laughed as a gull screamed and wheeled above the rapidly submerging cap, while the sunlight played brightly on the clear aquamarine of the sea.

iii

The happy voyage along the coast was over. Amsterdam, the busiest and most opulent city in Europe, dwarfing in splendour the waning greatness of Genoa and Florence and Venice, reared a frieze of spires and towers against the luminous sunset sky, which grew rapidly clearer and nearer as the ship sailed up the Scheldt to the wharves.

As they drew in Dirk sprang to the assistance of the sailor, who was having difficulty with the furling of one of the patched brown sails. Anna leaned over the side and stared eagerly at the ever-nearing quay where they were to anchor.

"Do you think Ryk will be here to meet us?" she called over her shoulder to Dirk.

"Probably not, as he does not know when to expect us. I will send a man up to his house immediately we drop anchor and he will soon be here. It is not far from the house."

"We could walk there. Do not send the man."

She saw the shadow heavy on Dirk's face; he had been moody all day.

"I shall not be going to the house," he answered constrainedly, and, to Anna's great concern, he turned red as he added on a defiant note, "I shall see Ryk here. It is better for me not to leave my ship."

"The man is aboard her."

"I am no more than a rough seaman," Dirk muttered. "I have neither fine clothes nor fine manners, and I am no person to enter a great house."

"You will enter it with me, a plain Frisian countrywoman," said Anna angrily, "and, what is more, I shall carry in a child without a cap and with pitch on his clothes as any peasant might."

Dirk shook his head unhappily.

Anna forgot her quick burst of anger.

"Come with me, Dirk," she pleaded. "This is surely a foolish attitude. You have always been dear to me, and I regard you as a member of my family."

"You could have a prince on your right hand and a common man on your left, mevrou, and neither would be anything but happy and at ease," said Dirk slowly. "But then you are an exceptional person. If you will forgive me I prefer to remain in my place, which is here in the Scheldt."

"I see," said Anna, to whom much was now clear. It was time she came to Amsterdam, she reflected, for Minetje and Ryk seemed to have lost all sense of proportion.

She knew instinctively that, in some way she had yet to discover, the delicate, deformed boy, Pieter, was at the bottom of the trouble.

CHAPTER TWENTY-EIGHT

When Anna entered with the sleeping child in her arms the house was lighted up for the evening, and she stepped into a golden glow.

Minetje and Ryk had not expected her so soon. Minetje came forward with a little cry of welcome.

"Mother, you have come at last! I have so wanted you to visit us in Amsterdam."

"Friesland is quite a way off," said Anna. "And I am getting a little old for so much travelling."

"You look just the same to me," said Ryk.

But he looks older, Anna thought. He seemed careworn and not in very good health in spite of his increased weight. He was plainly but richly dressed in doublet and padded trunks.

Ryk also appraised his mother. She was wearing a long cloak which had fallen open to reveal her plain gown. Her hair lay in wavy bands under her neat cap. Her face was serene, and sweet and strong, and less lined than he had expected. Her eyes are blue as sapphire, he thought. And he felt invigorated and fresh, seeing her clearly in the golden light of the lamps. She seemed to have brought vitality to his quiet, subdued house, lending depth and colour to her surroundings. The clothes she wore were homely and simple, but she was like a princess in the room. . . .

"You have brought Lourens," said Minetje. "I wondered whether you would be able to bring him. Shall I take him?"

"He is stirring," said Anna. "When he wakens I will give him to you. It is time he was abed. And where are the children, Minetje?"

"They are upstairs. I will summon them."

At this moment Lourens sat up in Anna's arms. His face was flushed with sleep, and his fair hair was in tumbled disorder; he was a handsome child.

"What a beautiful boy!" exclaimed Minetje. "Come to your grand-mother, Lourens, my little heart."

Lourens turned to Anna, but she put him on the floor and bade him go to Minetje.

The child went forward obediently and Minetje caressed and embraced him. Ryk caught him up in his arms and made much of him. Lourens was such an exceptionally fine specimen for a boy of five it was no wonder his grandparents were delighted with him, Anna reflected, re-joicing in their pleasure.

She fancied she heard the slightest of sounds from the doorway opposite her. She glanced in that direction and saw a small, stooping boy, clad in an elaborate suit of plum-coloured velvet, watching Lourens in his father's arms. He watched with a cold, steady stare which disconcerted Anna. She started slightly, but otherwise did not betray that she had observed Pieter's entrance.

Suddenly Pieter turned his eyes and met Anna's gaze. Looking into the boy's puckered, prematurely old face, Anna's first impression of faint horror faded.

"Pieter," she said quietly, with a wealth of compassion in her voice.

Minetje and Ryk started and faced about. They all saw Pieter's face change at the tone of Anna's voice. It set in hard lines. Anna saw he would not be pitied, and she had unwittingly spoken from her heart and had touched his pride. She bit her lip in vexation. She ought to have borne in mind that he was abnormally sensitive.

The dwarfish figure approached her, bowed as he came up to her, and extended a thin hand.

"I trust you have not had too tiring a journey from Friesland, Grand-mother," said Pieter in a precise, stilted way.

"The voyage was very pleasant and we had good weather," said Anna, smiling, and wondering whether she dared kiss the child.

Pieter ignored her. He stepped to one side and watched Lourens, whom Ryk now put down upon the floor. Lourens ran at once to Anna and pressed up against her. She laid her hand on his head.

"This is your nephew Lourens, Pieter," she said, endeavouring to regain the ground she had lost with him.

"So I perceive," said the astonishing child, favouring both Anna and Lourens with a long, cool stare.

If this inhuman small boy was the result of years of governesses and tutors and exhortations to be a little gentleman, she thought nothing of the system, Anna decided with rising wrath and discomfiture. Lourens pressed closer into her skirts, Ryk and Minetje were silent and constrained. The atmosphere before Pieter's advent had been warm and loving, whereas now it was positively forbidding. Anna fought against her aversion. Pieter was no more than eleven. He could not dominate them all; the position was absurd. She held out her hand to him.

"Come to me, Pieter," she invited. "I have not yet kissed you."

She continued to hold out her hand compellingly until he came to her. She put her arm round him then and drew him to her and kissed him. His cheek was cold to her lips and she could feel him tremble. She kept her arm about him.

"You do not remember me?" she said. "We were great friends once."

"I do remember you, Grandmother."

"We will be great friends again," she said.

Suddenly Pieter pressed close against her so that she held the two children firmly to her.

"He is almost as big as I am," came in a muffled voice from Pieter. "And he is only five!"

His thin body shook with sobs. Releasing Lourens, Anna held Pieter closely in her arms.

ii

The great house in Amsterdam was lovely within and without. It was light-flooded and tasteful and sumptuously furnished. It was a quiet house now that there were only two children left in it, for Jacoba and Frederika had already married the sons of Amsterdam merchants and had gone with handsome dowries to homes of their own.

Anna had to concede that Minetje had been very clever: she had not trusted her provincial taste but had procured the services of an artist and had left the arrangement and the furnishing of the house to him. And Minetje also dressed, Anna discovered, in a style laid down by the artist, wearing rich, dark materials and simple yet costly jewellery. The house spoke of wealth in subdued undertones, but it did not shriek of it. Unfortunately Minetje, anxious not to strike a vulgar note, overdid her instructions. She and the children ordered their days to such a restrained pattern that the whole effect was lifeless, and one longed for colour and variety.

The children had been fitted into the general scheme only too well. Charlotte, a tall, plain-featured child, was much too quiet and well behaved in Anna's opinion. She had an air of breeding about her, if she lacked vitality, and Minetje had great hopes of a good match for her. Pieter was shrunken and wizened and there was an unmistakable hump on his back, which they attempted to conceal by the aid of a vast and outlandish ruff. His clothes were costly, with special padding on the shoulders. He was naturally fastidious about his appearance, and his manners were studied and stilted.

Into this precise and rich household stepped the two from the north.

Anna robustly refused to have other clothes than those she had brought with her, although Minetje gently insinuated that her modiste was at Anna's disposal. Anna had the gown she had travelled in and her best black for Sundays and holidays. However, as a great concession, Anna consented to wear the black every day, although she complained that it would probably get shiny at the back with all the sitting about.

When Ryk and his mother were alone together he asked her what she thought of the house.

"It is very beautiful," she said, "and, I must admit, a complete surprise to me. And I understand now why Dirk prefers to remain in his ship on the river."

Ryk reddened.

"It was most unfortunate," he confided in Anna. "He and I used always to walk home together after one of our voyages. I noticed he became more and more reluctant to come with me. There was an unfortunate evening when we arrived very travel-stained and weary and Minetje had the house full of the exclusive people of Amsterdam. She did not know we were coming, of course, and we did not know that she was entertaining on the scale she was or we would have slipped in quietly at the back; but as it was we walked straight in. I must say, Minetje carried it off very well, but somehow or other Dirk felt that she patronized him, and he simply would not come near again."

"Dirk is one of us," said Anna.

"I feel that also. I did the best I could. I offered him a ship of his own in the coast trade, and handed him over a few good mercantile connections to work up and let him go as he wished. I do not think I could have done more."

"In the circumstances you did all you could."

"Why were you surprised when you saw the house, Mother?"

"To put it bluntly, I had expected something more vulgar—an ostentatious display of wealth; but this house is so correct in every detail that it is a masterpiece of make-believe. And everyone in it, with the exception of yourself, perhaps, acts a part. It was very clever of Minetje: I hadn't credited her with so much acumen. And it's as insidious as it is clever. Charlotte will be found a suitable husband and she will lead the inane existence you do. And poor little Pieter—ach, poor little Pieter. I wish you would let me take him away to Friesland and let him have the benefits of country air and country food. He would develop, Ryk. He's learning more than is good for him, and you're overtaxing what little strength he has. He was much sturdier when you lived in Delft. I can see how he has gone back."

"It will kill Minetje to part with him. She sets such store by that child."

"I dislike discussing your wife with you, but I must. She does not understand her son. She insists on taking Pieter and Lourens out together, and the comparison is cruel. Pieter suffers each time and he will turn against Lourens. Do you remember the scene when I arrived?"

"Pieter often does that. He is very jealous by nature. He does not tolerate boys of his own age. He has no little friends. There were so many scenes that Minetje decided she must give up trying to make him more sociable. Obviously he is too frail to stand the strain of other children."

"At Oostermeer he would have the companionship of three children younger than himself. It would bring out the best in him to help with them, and he would get over this idea of walking alone. I am very fond of Pieter, and I think I have some influence with him. Won't you persuade Minetje to try leaving him in Friesland for a year or two?"

"There is his education. He has every advantage here in Amsterdam."

"He is very intelligent. It would not be difficult for him to make up the year or two he spends away from tutors."

Ryk rested his head in his hands. It was a gesture of weariness and despondency.

"Outwardly I have made a great success, Mother," he said. "I have a fine house and more money than I ever dreamed of; I am an esteemed figure in Amsterdam; I have my place on the City Council; my daughters have married well; my son is clever, nay, brilliant, they tell me. But there is a twist in it all, although none sees it but myself. My son is as you see him; my house as you know it; Dirk has gone his ways—and you know what Dirk was to me. There were those voyages to the Gold Coast. Twice I sailed to Guinea, twice I came away safely and the voyages were profitable, but the twist was there also. Africa had defeated me although I seemed each time to have won. Mother, I am a failure."

"No, Ryk, I do not agree."

"You do not see all I see. Nothing I have matters at all."

She did not answer but waited for him to continue.

"When I was with the Sea Beggars everyone spoke well of me. Great things were expected of me, but, again, promise never became achievement. I have always missed the essence of what I strive after. And I have not the heart to strive here. I am aware that if Pieter went to Oostermeer it would be the making of him. You and Juliana between you would do him great good. I did not even think to struggle. I told you the battle was lost."

"I might be able to persuade Minetje," said Anna. "And do not be so depressed, Ryk. I am sure you have exaggerated all these troubles."

"When I see Dirk and he will not enter my house this disgust of myself and my efforts comes over me. Each time it is the same. And in my way I have tried to do good with the money I have made—I set Dirk on his feet, I aided Linschoten and supported him each time he essayed the Northeast Passage; but there is no satisfaction in any of these things. Lately I have had an idea of what I must do to win back ease of mind. Bernard Ericks of Medenblik is going out to the Gold Coast to see whether he can establish friendly relations with the natives, and if he is successful in this a settlement is to be founded. When Ericks returns, if he goes back to the Gold Coast I shall accompany the expedition. I want to go back where I have failed and see whether, by genuine effort in difficult conditions, I can overcome whatever it is in me that causes me to miss the substance. I am always given the substitute—in full measure and running over—but it is not the same thing."

"These things happen as God wills," said Anna.

"In the beginning I wanted Liesbet," said Ryk. "I left home, and when I should have been with you and her I was away. If I was not there to cherish her I suppose I deserved to lose her."

"That is no argument. The country was at war and you were serving."

"So was Lourens. It all began there."

Anna tried for a long time to move him from his morbid obsession, with some little success, she thought. Then, after a time, he reverted to his remarks on the Gold Coast.

"Anything may happen while I am away, Mother," he said. "I am putting some few thousand guilders aside for your use. There may come a time when you will want money, and I shall not be here."

"Thank you for your thought of me, Ryk," said Anna. "From the bottom of my heart I can say you have never failed me as a son. You have had the most loving care of me. One day I shall visit Anne-Marie and use your money. Invest it for me in Amsterdam, please, because I have no knowledge of these affairs. But, my son, I beg of you, do not go to the Gold Coast. I have a dread and a horror of that country. You may never return from it. Ryk, if you will listen to me, you will be well advised to bring Pieter and come back with us to Oostermeer on Dirk's ship. The simple, quiet life is what both you and Pieter need."

"It is not as easy as that, Mother."

"Promise me you will not go, Ryk. You are rich enough."

"If I go it will not be for profit. I want to do something useful and enduring. Help found a fortress for the Netherlands in a far country, make friends with the warring tribes, do something that for once does not bring in money."

She had seen men depressed like this before and well she knew how difficult it was to lift them from their gloom. Ryk had got so into the way of wandering over seas and oceans that he grew melancholy and restless when he was shorebound. Gysbert had had just these moods, Anna remembered.

She set herself to divert him. They were laughing together when Minetje and the children returned from their outing.

For some days after their conversation Ryk seemed his normal, cheerful self. If Anna had not understood him so well she might have assumed he had settled down again; but, with her knowledge of Gysbert to guide her, she knew that he was but marking time until he could feel the planking of a ship beneath his feet again.

iii

". . . Minetje, you must see that it is more important for Pieter to build his bodily health than to lose strength by continuing his studies. When he is stronger he will pull up quickly, he is so gifted. Together we cared for him when he was an infant, and we kept him alive. Do you remember that time? Let him come back with me, Minetje."

"No, Mother, it is impossible. He has every care and attention and the most eminent physicians prescribe for him. I should live in terror if I knew he were in so isolated a spot as Oostermeer. If he were taken ill there would be no physician within several days' journey. No, I cannot even consider it."

"You always longed for a son, did you not, Minetje? Then God gave you one. Will you not do your best for him, even if it means making great sacrifices? You could close this house and bring both children and come yourself to Oostermeer. There will be room for you all."

"I do not see that it will be best for Pieter. It is what you think. We do not think the same. We do not wish to go to a farmhouse."

Minetje regretted her words immediately she had uttered them. There had been a scene with Ryk and her nerves were on edge. She was genuinely fond of Anna, and she hated herself for her stinging little speech.

"It is good enough for me and for your daughter Juliana," Anna retorted with some heat.

Twin red flags appeared in Minetje's aesthetically pale cheeks. Her hands trembled, and she could no longer control her irritation. What was wrong today? They were all at loggerheads.

"Juliana was married particularly young, and our position was different then. We lived in an obscure little city."

"Delft, it has a name," said Anna. "A great prince lived there also. But continue."

"If we'd been in Amsterdam at that time I wouldn't have considered such a match for Juliana. Jacoba and Frederika have made excellent marriages, and I'll be arranging Charlotte's next. And there's Pieter to think about. We couldn't possibly leave Amsterdam," concluded Minetje defiantly.

Anna was thoroughly angry. Minetje had never spoken thus to her.

"I have met the husbands of Jacoba and Frederika and I will tell you that I think Juliana did very well to marry Jan, even if he hasn't a sack of gold on his head!"

Minetje was suddenly too unhappy to reply. She had quarrelled with everyone lately.

"Well, Minetje," Anna went on when she saw that the fight had gone out of Minetje, "you and Ryk know your own business best. I am very anxious about Pieter's health—he is my only grandson. Will you remember that I am willing to help you at all times as I have done in the past?"

"I am sorry, Mother."

"That is all right," said Anna, feeling very weary of it all.

"I wish you could understand how changed our lives are," Minetje said. "How can one go back when one has known this?"

She extended her hands in a somewhat theatrical gesture.

"It is very magnificent," said Anna drily, "but there is a rude plenty at Oostermeer."

"Please, Mother."

"Think it over, Minetje. I shall leave you now and go to see what the children are doing."

Anna rose and went out. When she was alone Minetje sat very still for a moment, then she drooped in every line of her figure; even her lips sagged at the corners. She had had a quarrel with Ryk such as they had never had before, and it had taken the strength out of her. What was it they had said? There had been so many angry words that day. . . .

". . . I will not have that fellow in the house while my mother is here," Ryk had stormed at her. "Tell him not to come again. I met him as I came in. Fortunately she was out at the time. I told him he was unwelcome. He is not to come here again. Not now, or ever again. I have had enough of artists. We were good enough as we were. Do you understand me, Minetje?"

"What has he done?" she had faltered.

"What has he done? For years the fellow has been slinking about the place. It is Jan Bester here, Jan Bester there. Not a curtain blows or a bit of tapestry moves but I expect to see him come crawling out. When we first came I approved of him. It was his business to decorate and plan the house; but when that was done, then it was your clothes that needed his expert supervision, then how to disguise the hump on Pieter's back, then Charlotte's clothes. The only one he has not turned into a complete fop is myself, and that is only because he knew husbands were beyond his powers. I have been patient for a long time, Minetje. I have told him that his services are no longer required, so let that be an end of it."

"But, Ryk, Pieter's lessons——"

"It is mainly on account of Pieter I have come to this decision. He is a bad companion for Pieter, who is precocious enough as it is."

"You can't turn him away like that, without a reason."

"And why not? I do not think I am the only husband in Amsterdam who has had enough of young Jan Bester."

Minetje had felt her hair rise on her head in fright. What had Ryk meant by that remark? For a long while Jan Bester had been making her feel uncomfortable in his presence. Once he had touched her hand, but she, not caring whether he thought her gauche and bucolic, had snatched it away. She had often wished that they might be quit of the young man, but his taste was so exquisite that she had done nothing

about it. Well, there had been no harm in that one touch of the hand,
she thought. And she had plucked up courage to ask Ryk of what the
husbands complained.

"The expense; there is nothing but expense. He makes a fat living,
does Jan Bester, out of us merchants by foxing our fools of wives."

"Well, perhaps it is as well he is to give up helping here," she had
yielded gracefully. And she had known a feeling as of release. Jan Bester
had had such a way of attaching himself to Pieter. The two had had
hour-long conversations, and the artist was one of the few people to
whom Pieter had given his friendship. And it had been a bad thing for
Pieter. In teaching him poise and control Jan Bester had taught him to
be cold and calculating. In her adoration of Pieter, Minetje had not admitted to herself at any time that these traits were in Pieter himself and
that Jan Bester had only brought them out. It was kinder to her idea of
her son to think that they were faults that had been learned and could
be unlearned as readily. . . .

Into her thoughts Ryk's next words had fallen like a douche of ice-
cold water.

"I hope to go to the Gold Coast either this year or next," he had said.
"That is why I am getting my household in order, why I asked my
mother to come."

"Ach, Ryk, not to that country again! Ryk, no," she had cried out in
grief.

"Yes, I must go. It is no new thing for me to go on long voyages,
Minetje, so do not fret."

"Anywhere but the Gold Coast. You know from what you saved
Anthony Barradale in that cruel land."

"For the matter of that, all lands are cruel. I may meet my fate anywhere."

"But more particularly there."

"Do not be so imaginative, Minetje," he had said; but she had
expressed his own conviction.

"My dear heart, do not go," she had said impulsively, and tears had
come into her eyes.

"I must. And there is one other matter I must discuss with you:
Mother suggests that she take Pieter to Friesland. She thinks he will
improve there, and I am rather inclined to agree with her. Shall we let
him go, Minetje?"

"Ryk, I cannot let him go away from me." Her voice had been thick
with emotion. "You know what he means to me. You must not ask it
of me."

"Do not stand in his way, Minetje."

"Stand in his way! Do I not love him better than my life, do I not
lavish everything upon him, give him everything? Have I failed in my
duty as a mother?"

And, as ever where Pieter was concerned, she had become unreasonable, and she and Ryk had exchanged bitter words. They had quarrelled until he had stormed out of the room and had left her collapsed on the floor in a weeping heap. And as she lay there terror of the future had swept over her. She dreaded Ryk's sailing to the Gold Coast, dreaded having the responsibility of the house and the children, and, above all, she dreaded having to resist Jan Bester. He would insinuate himself into the house the moment Ryk had sailed, and she acknowledged to herself that she was not strong enough to control the situation.

And darker and more insistent than any of these thoughts was her conviction that peril and hardship, perhaps even death, awaited Ryk on the Gold Coast.

iv

Some weeks later, when Dirk's little ship again tied up at Amsterdam, Anna returned late one evening from a stroll to the riverside. At the gates of the house she met Pieter and a slim, elegant young man in a severely simple suit of the richest black velvet. She saw the young man had a small pointed black beard and long white hands and a languishing air. One of Pieter's innumerable tutors, she thought. Pieter and the young man were deep in earnest conversation and barely noticed her. She smiled at Pieter and passed by them and went on to the house. As she reached it Ryk came out.

"I have just come from Dirk's," said Anna.

"I am on my way there now," he said. "We will spend the evening together somewhere so you will not see me again tonight, Mother."

"I am glad. Pieter is at the gates talking to one of his tutors. It is getting a little late for lessons. Send the child in, Ryk."

"I will do so," said Ryk, and passed on to the gates.

That same evening when Anna was putting Lourens to bed she noticed bruises on his arms and thighs. She had observed them before, but now there seemed to be more purple patches on the child's white skin.

"You must take care and not run into the furniture and bruise yourself, my little heart," she told him.

Apart from wondering when he had knocked into the furniture, as he had never complained of doing so, she thought no more of the matter.

Pieter retired early and she spent an unusually pleasant evening with Minetje and Charlotte. Minetje put herself out to be entertaining and kind, striving to make amends for her odd behaviour on other occasions.

v

Next morning Anna noticed that Minetje's nerves were in such a state that she could hardly hold the cups she was washing. Like all good Dutch housewives, she attended to her own best china. She had a wooden bowl and a linen cloth and was washing the porcelain.

"Shall I help?" Anna offered.

"If you dry we will finish the sooner," said Minetje.

Anna saw that she had been crying. She could not get to the bottom of the trouble in Ryk's house. And she did not care to question either Ryk or Minetje. If they spoke of their own accord it was quite a different matter. She had no means of knowing that Ryk had told Minetje that Jan Bester and Pieter had met at the gates, and he had asked her to watch Pieter more closely. And when Minetje had defended Pieter he had lost his temper and had threatened to break every bone in Jan Bester's body if he showed his face at the house or the gates or anywhere.

The scene was domestic and pleasant and, except for Minetje's pale face and heavy eyes, there was no other sign of trouble beneath the calm surface. The two women were halfway through their task when a shrill scream came from a room on the floor above them.

Anna started.

"It sounded like Lourens," she said. "He must have hurt himself. I think he keeps bumping into the furniture and bruising himself. He must have done it again. I will go and see."

She put down the cup she had just finished wiping and went quickly up the stairs.

The two children struggling in the room with the wide-open door were too preoccupied to notice her approach. Anna stood transfixed at what she saw. Pieter, his face twisted and drawn with cold hate, had one hand firmly pressed over Louren's lips to keep back his cries, and with the other he was pinching the smaller child's arm, pulling and twisting the flesh with his sinewy fingers.

Pieter heard Anna's gasp. He looked at her. He did not release his hold on Lourens, but deliberately pinched again.

Anna ran up to them and separated them. She was frightened more than angered by the expression of naked cruelty on Pieter's face. It was as unnatural as it was unwholesome to see a look like that on the face of so young a child. In silence she gathered the sobbing Lourens to her breast.

"Hush, my little one," she said, and her voice sounded strange and unreal in her own ears. "Hush, I am with you now, Lourens."

"Why do you and he not go back to Friesland?" asked Pieter, glaring at Anna. "That is what I want. It is because of you that my friend Jan Bester does not come to the house."

"It is not," said Anna, not understanding of what he spoke.

"I told Lourens I would kill him if he told you I pinched him."

"He has not told me: I saw you."

"I like pinching him," said Pieter.

Anna did not know how to answer. She was so shocked that her brain was numb. She had always had a horror of cruelty; and suddenly there came into her mind a memory from the past. She remembered the day of Pieter's birth in Delft—he had been born on the day that the assassin of William the Silent, Balthasar Gérard, had died a terrible death.

As she connected Gérard's execution with the gloating cruelty of Pieter's expression terror overcame her. She pushed past Pieter, who tried to block the doorway, and, with Lourens in her arms, went down to Minetje.

She decided at once that Minetje must have heard a little, if not all, of the conversation in the room above, for she was standing as though rooted to the spot at the table where they had been washing the china. She still trailed one hand in the water in the wooden bowl.

"There is a question I wanted to put to you eleven years ago, Minetje," said Anna in a trembling voice. "I did not put it then because I had not the courage. But I must ask it now. When Balthasar Gérard was executed in Delft and you and your mother went out into the streets did you actually witness his execution?"

The blood drained from Minetje's face.

"Why do you ask that now?" she whispered.

"When I saw Pieter upstairs I remembered that day. Answer my question, Minetje."

"Yes. I stood very near. I witnessed Gérard's death. The accursed assassin——"

"This is terrible," said Anna. "All my life I have been opposed to torture and unnecessary cruelty; it has got me into bitter trouble many times, thinking as I do, because we live in a state of war and oppression and the worst comes out in human nature in a struggle for survival. Minetje, I have seen this naked lust to be cruel here in this house, in my own family, and I cannot bear it."

"What has Balthasar Gérard's execution to do with it, Mother?"

"What you saw that day affected the unborn, perhaps."

"What happened upstairs, Mother?"

"Pieter was ill-treating Lourens, and not in the normal way children fight and quarrel among themselves. He revelled in the pain he was inflicting; he was so cool, so calculating, so obviously enjoying himself, that I was frightened. Remember, Minetje, this is a subject on which I have never seen eye to eye with others. I am peculiarly sensitive about it, so it is possible I exaggerate the whole thing."

At this moment Pieter began to scream upstairs. Minetje started and cried out:

"Ach, he will have a fit. He has not been so upset for a long time. He has a tendency to hysteria and only Jan can calm him, and Ryk has forbidden Jan the house."

"Who is Jan Bester, Minetje?"

"He is the artist we employed."

Pieter's cries grew louder and wilder, and his shrieks rang through the house.

"I am coming, I am coming," called out Minetje distractedly, and ran out of the room, and stumbled sobbing up the stairs.

Anna set Lourens on the floor and sank down on a seat, and listened to the shrieks of the child upstairs whom Minetje had not succeeded in calming. After a time she heard someone come into the room. She turned her head and saw Ryk had entered.

"Whatever is happening, Mother?" he asked her.

Anna explained briefly what had occurred.

Ryk saw she was utterly spent. He sat down beside her and took her hand in his own. He could feel her body tremble against his.

"You have had a shock, Mother," he said quietly, gently chafing her hand.

"I cannot bear to see pain or to inflict it," she said. "It is my old weakness, Ryk. I have so often got into trouble over it. I couldn't kill Don Rodriguez, you remember, and it ought to have been such a pleasure to do so. An accursed Spaniard. Such an excellent opportunity of paying off old scores!"

"It is your strength, Mother."

"Ryk!"

"The more I see of life the more I am convinced how right you are to think as you do. I have sickened of bloodshed. I seek no quarrels outside the defence of the rights of my country and of my people."

She held tightly onto his hand.

"I wondered what was at the back of it all when you spoke to me of going to the Gold Coast to found a fortress for the Dutch and to help the inhabitants. It sounded as though the sword was to be beaten into the ploughshare."

"One must consolidate sometime."

"I understand why you must go," said Anna. "And my thoughts and my prayers will go with you. And when you have gone, Ryk, is there anything I can do for you in Amsterdam?"

"Come down sometimes from Oostermeer and see Minetje and the children. She will not leave Amsterdam or send the children from her."

"Perhaps it is better so," said Anna slowly. "It is suddenly clear to me that I should not take Pieter back home with me. I cannot change him; he was born with his strange, twisted mind, and although he may be taught self-control enough to deceive everyone but himself, be given every advantage of education and culture, you will never give him what he lacks, and that is loving-kindness."

"For some years Minetje and I have been very distressed about Pieter. He is our only son and we love him and it is but natural that we should do all in our power to help him overcome his infirmity, or, at the least, to make the best of it. Unhappily he is so self-conscious that any attempt to encourage companions of his own age to come to the house has always ended in failure. In our worst time Jan Bester showed that he could handle Pieter. But I have come to the conclusion that his association with that young man is doing Pieter no good. I arranged that Jan Bester should not come to the house again, and Pieter has been very upset in consequence. He is not always as distraught as you have seen him,

Mother. You have seen the very worst. But—and this is truly unfortunate —having taken a dislike to Lourens, Pieter will give no one in the house any peace while he is here. For that reason also it would be hopeless to take Pieter to Oostermeer."

William of Orange was in Anna's thoughts as though he were alive and she could stop and speak with him as once she had done years before. Once when she had gone to him for advice she had felt as though he had taken her by the hand and had led her to the top of a high hill and had bade her look down, and look round, and look all ways, and to think of herself not as an individual but as one of many. He had given her wise counsel—the counsel of all time. And this was a crisis in which to apply that wisdom. She saw that she must not consider the problem of Pieter as though she were working out the fate of her own grandson. She must look at the matter as a whole, remembering every single one of her large family who might be involved afterwards in what was arranged now. In her way Minetje was doing the best that could be done for the unhappy child. He had outstanding intelligence and mental capacity and promised to be shrewd enough for much money-making. He had every chance of doing very well for himself in Amsterdam. Suddenly in her mind there was a comprehensive view of the whole situation. In the future, when Pieter had the power that great wealth gives, she saw that the struggle would be between him in Amsterdam and the great-grandchildren at Oostermeer. And the north, that even in her time had stood united, would step out to meet the challenge of the south. And, as clear as crystal, she saw that her place was at Oostermeer. She must build in the north to meet the menace of the south. . . .

"Of what are you thinking, my mother?" Ryk asked her. "Your thoughts were very far away."

"I was thinking what we should do."

"For once I shall make the decision. Dirk is here and ready to sail. You and Lourens can go back with him. And do not take away with you too bad an impression of Pieter. I assure you we have not had this trouble for a long while."

"We will go back to Oostermeer then. Will I see you before you sail to the Gold Coast, Ryk?"

"I will come to Oostermeer to say good-bye to you all."

"It is arranged then," said Anna.

vi

The anchor had been weighed and they were homeward bound. As she stood on the ship watching the houses and spires and towers of Amsterdam slip by, Anna began to sort out the chaotic impressions of her visit. In the beginning she had felt very confused, with Ryk and Minetje changing their minds and their moods with bewildering rapidity. The crisis at the end had mercifully stripped them all of polite pretence, and on the last day Anna knew there had been no acting for her special benefit. She understood that Minetje's pretentiousness and her sudden bursts of irritation had their origin in her state of nervous tension; and she was no longer puzzled by Ryk's strange vacillation about Pieter and her suggestion that she take him back with her to Friesland. Pieter's parents simply did not know what to do for the best, and, when she knew that, Anna had the key to all the little mysteries that had baffled her, and the curtain had rung down on an honest exchange of opinion at the last.

As Dirk's vessel nosed her way through the lanes of shipping the great city of Amsterdam fell behind them, dwindling against the sky line, while the pointing fingers of the church spires were etherealized by distance and faded last of all.

The wind stood fair, and as they drew into open water the little ship hoisted every sail and steered for the northern ports.

PART XV

CORNISH INTERLUDE

CHAPTER TWENTY-NINE

ONE EVENING IN NOVEMBER ANNE-MARIE BARRADALE SAT ALONE IN the low, oak-panelled winter parlour of Bodrugan farmhouse, awaiting Anthony's return from Falmouth. The short day was drawing to its close, and dusk was already in the room, lit only by the blazing light of the fire and a single taper burning over the high hearth shelf.

The children were with their nurse, and there was peace in the parlour. Anne-Marie was restless, however, and in no mood to appreciate her solitude.

Someone rode up to the house. She thought it was bound to be Martin Thomas, and was not best pleased, as she did not wish to see him this evening. He had an unsettling influence on Anthony, who had come back from a visit to Plymouth with the idea of undertaking another voyage, and she felt that Martin's enthusiasm would just about clinch the matter. So she remained where she was and waited for a serving-woman to show the visitor to the parlour. She looked up when the door opened and Sir Giles Mortimer was announced.

Anne-Marie was instantly on her feet. She and Sir Giles regarded each other for a moment, he in the doorway and she at the hearth. He saw a tall, slim woman standing in the dancing red light of the fire. She wore a simple dark gown that set off to perfection the exquisite fairness of her skin and the delicate colouring of her face and hair under the French cap she wore. He thought that never in his life had he looked upon so beautiful a woman.

Anne-Marie saw a tall, handsome man, who was massively built without being stout. His hair and his eyes were brown and he had about him an air of warmth and friendliness. He was quietly dressed and she saw his clothes were a little out of the mode, the breeches not being so stuffed nor the trunk hose of the latest design. She thought how sensible he was to wear what suited his bulk instead of adding to it by adhering closely to the exaggerated fashion of the season. She had not met him before. Anthony, however, had recently given her an account of Sir Giles's circumstances. He was unmarried and lived at Herne House in Devon and was reputed to be wealthy. His father, a yeoman of Devon, had received a grant of arms in the year of the Queen's accession for services he had rendered her when Elizabeth was a girl and was in peril from her half sister Mary Tudor. In the days when Elizabeth had been in the Tower she had needed loyal and devoted friends, and when she had been made Queen she did not forget those who had served her lovingly and faithfully. On several occasions the Queen had stayed at Herne House and had gone hawking, and once she had had an elaborate pageant for her entertainment.

Anne-Marie went forward to greet him.

"You are very welcome, Sir Giles," she said.

He bowed over her hand.

"You have doubtless come to see my husband," said Anne-Marie. "He should be home at any moment now. I do not know what could have delayed him in Falmouth. Will you not draw your chair up to the fire and wait with me for him?"

"With the greatest pleasure," he answered. "I met your husband at the Pelican Inn at Plymouth. We sat looking out on the sound and the shipping and were so engrossed in our conversation that we did not observe how frequently the drawers replenished our flagons of ale!"

"Of what were you speaking so earnestly?" she asked him.

"Of the Dutchman Linschoten and the possibilities of the Northeast Passage to China and the Indies."

"The same quest that ended so disastrously for Sir Hugh Willoughby fifty years ago," said Anne-Marie. "Anthony and I also have spoken of the Northeast Passage. In her letters my grandmother in Holland has told me all that befell Linschoten on his two expeditions, and we have found the news of his adventures most enthralling. I am not so interested in the passage as in the land of sunshine and calm seas beyond it—the land of one's dreams come true."

She expressed the belief of the times that if the vast barrier of ice and snow beyond Nova Zembla could be overcome the navigator would sail into a region of hyperborean felicity, where the dwellers on the outskirts of the world lived in perpetual youth and health. And beyond that blessed land the way to China and the East lay open.

He shook his head.

"I am out of the fashion," he said. "I am a sceptic. If there were such a land, why have not the inhabitants broken through into the part of the world we know?"

"Perhaps, like us, they are trying."

"It may be; but whether such a land exists or not, the discovery of the Northeast Passage would be a wonderful event."

"What I admire about Linschoten is that he was not dismayed by two failures, and a third expedition is to be attempted. This time there will be no official support from Prince Maurice of Orange or from Jan of Olden-Barneveldt or the States-General. That is, not direct assistance; yet to prove they still have some faith in Arctic navigation they have offered a prize of twenty-five thousand florins to anyone who should discover the passage."

"Mistress Barradale, if I may express my honest opinion, I think the States-General will keep their florins."

"Did my husband tell you when you met in Plymouth that he had a mind to make the attempt?"

"Yes, he mentioned it."

He noticed that she was very agitated.

"He knows Barendz, who is one of those who has not yet given up, and he thinks of accompanying the next expedition when it sets out from Holland. I have done my best to dissuade him, but he feels he must go."

"You have relatives in Holland," he suggested. "Could they not influence him?"

"I have not mentioned the matter to them. I have been hoping that Anthony will think better of his decision, but I see that is a vain hope. In these days all men's thoughts turn to the sea. My uncle Ryk is another who cannot settle to a life ashore. My grandmother tells me he is speaking of a voyage to the Gold Coast."

"That is a country that must hold heavy memories for you," he said with a sympathy that warmed her heart.

The history of Anthony on the Gold Coast was common knowledge. Added to these tales of tragic adventures in Guinea were his natural good looks, his romantic appearance, and his lovely Dutch wife—ingredients potent enough to gain for him the first place in the brew of local gossip. And, as Anthony was somewhat reserved and uncommunicative about past events, a certain amount of surmise in the brew made it a heady compound indeed.

"I had given him up for dead," she said. "But he came back to me."

Sir Giles wished that she would say more. He had been told so much of the amazing history of Anthony Barradale that of all he had heard he wondered what was truth and what was fiction.

"I do not venture to say very much to my husband on the score of undertaking a voyage," Anne-Marie went on. She was finding it easy to talk to this kindly man, and she saw few strangers at Bodrugan, as they led a quiet life. "There are these preparations being made for an attack on Spain. The Dutch and the English are in it together, so I feel Anthony will take part in one or other of the ventures—accompany Barendz and Linschoten and search for the Northeast Passage, or join in the attack on certain of the Spanish ports. I do not know which I would rather he undertook. Both seem equally fearful to me. And there you have my principal worry."

"The war against Spain has dragged on overlong," he said. "Both expeditions, if they succeed, will finally break the power of Spain.

Linschoten's Northeast Passage will destroy her trade and take away from her the means of waging war, and the attack on Spain will carry the struggle into enemy country and they may learn to know the meaning of invasion. Whichever your husband chooses will serve our national purpose."

"Which venture will you join?"

"I have a mind for the attack on Spain."

"Then I trust Anthony makes a similar choice."

"I know we must beat the Spaniards to survive, and I am not at all sure that the Northeast Passage exists; hence my decision."

She smiled.

"I think you will always be wise and fortunate," she said. "But I like to believe in the fabled land beyond the snows and ice fields and roaring Arctic gales."

"Then we will not argue. For your sake I hope they find this land. England is fair enough country for me."

"Tell me of Herne House," said Anne-Marie. "I am told that the Queen has slept there."

"So Her Grace has, and on three separate occasions."

"When I was a girl in Holland," she said, "I saw the late Prince of Orange passing through the streets of Delft. We knew him as Father William. He was one of us; yet, for all his simple ways, he was a man of surpassing greatness and you saw it in all he did and said. In his worn-out doublet, such as a bargee might despise, he still looked a prince. I did not have speech with him, but my grandmother often spoke with him. I have described the only prince I have seen, so you tell me now, what manner of woman is Her Majesty when she is away from court?"

"She is one who is able at all times to call forth by ways only open to a woman the devotion and love of her people. To the very roots of her she is English; she is for England; she is a true queen, caring always for her people."

"You love the Queen," she said, smiling. "You speak of her as my grandmother speaks of the dead Prince of Orange. He also took loving care for the welfare of the people. On the day he was assassinated the children cried in the streets and the people of the north and the south, divided always in their loyalties and aims, were united in their grief."

He saw her eyes were misted and her thoughts were questing in some far place hidden from him. He longed to know more of her.

"Where does your grandmother live, Mistress Barradale?" he asked, trying to draw her out.

"She lives on a farm in Friesland; it is called Oostermeer."

She told him of the remote farm in Holland, of the windmill, and the black-and-white cattle, and the avenue of young poplars; told him of how the flood had swept over it; of her birth on the North Sea and her mother's death. She told it as vividly as though she were describing an actual series of scenes stretched out before her.

He loved to hear her talk. Her quiet voice flowed liquidly on, and he saw every flicker of expression on her lovely face, tinted with the glow of the fire in the hearth. He sat very still, watching her; and a passionate yearning came to him that her voice with its faintly nostalgic melancholy might always sound in his ears, that his eyes might rest on her fair face for all his days.

Thus they sat, she looking into the fire and conjuring up her memories of Oostermeer and Anna; and he looking at her with more of his longing expressed in his face than he knew.

Anthony Barradale stood for a full minute unobserved in the doorway. He heard Anne-Marie say:

". . . and now it is as though the great flood had never been. The farmhouse stands as it has stood for generations, with its graceful lines of trees and the lichen growing on the roofs of the barns."

Anthony stepped silently back; and entered again with a firm tread.

"Anthony," cried Anne-Marie with warm welcome in her voice as she heard his step. "You have come at last!"

Sir Giles Mortimer rose to his feet and was silent. To his inward consternation he found he wished that Anthony had not returned so soon, and he found he desired this with a force of resentment that shocked him, for he was in all things a quiet, moderate man.

I will get over this, Sir Giles told himself, it is no more than the firelight and her beauty and I have been bewitched for a while.

But it was an enduring enchantment as later he was to discover.

ii

It was very dark at midnight and the wind beat against the house. Anne-Marie lay in Anthony's arms and looked out from her safety and security into the dark uncertainty of the night pressing down upon the windows. This was an hour of rare contentment.

Tonight Anthony had been wholly hers; they had slipped back to the rapture of the first months of their marriage, when ecstasy had seemed a state of mind and body that could endure forever. Those first months in the golden autumn at Bodrugan had been a time of high fulfilment, with the doubts and the fears of years dispelled, and their faith and joy in each other gloriously justified. But clouds had begun to darken those happy days before the first twelve months had passed, for the surface of the initial rapture parted here and there, and glimpses of the severity of the strain which Anthony had endured for years showed through. He had been moody and irritable and unbearably depressed and for days on end he would hold himself aloof from Anne-Marie in spirit, although their lives had gone on and they had walked and talked and slept together like any other married pair. And at these times neither tears nor prayers nor passion of love had availed to lift Anthony from his dark mood. He had refused to tell too much of what had happened on the Gold Coast, telling Anne-Marie that there were events she must not seek to know. So she had schooled herself to live her life in alternating patches of light and dark, eagerly awaiting the periods when he was himself and they were happy lovers, and being philosophically resigned when he slid back into black memories of his terrible experiences. And, apart from leading a full life of comradeship and understanding one week and a starved spiritual existence with a moody man the next, she never quite knew how to behave towards him, whether to coax and cajole, or to be angry, or just loving. And her attempts to win him from his moods met with unexpected results. On this night, for instance, she had bent her head as he stripped off his garments and had kissed the scars on his back. She had felt a shiver run down his flesh; and then she had been in his arms and it had ended in lovers' bliss. But when she had done the same thing on another occasion he had moved abruptly away from her and had been cold and withdrawn for many days.

On this happy night Anne-Marie remembered none of this. She lay sleepily beside Anthony and wished the night would have no ending.

"You were very beautiful tonight, Anne-Marie," said Anthony.

"It was the gown," she murmured, rousing herself to conversation. "The new farthingale suits me well. And my grandmother taught me the trick of dark colours when all the other women are as gaudy as peacocks; and the fan collar is infinitely more becoming than the ruff."

Her voice trailed off as sleep almost overcame her.

"You are almost asleep, my darling, but you can still recite the fashion lesson you were given by Sarah," he said, laughing softly. "How you and she discussed clothes when she was last here!"

"Sarah is very handsome."

"Tonight it was you who were beautiful and you owed little to your dress. Anne-Marie, I keep you too secluded. When I have such a jewel to display it is churlish of me to keep it hidden at Bodrugan."

She was instantly wide awake. He was about to tell her that she must go to Holland and he must sail to the ends of the earth, she thought. He was preparing the ground. . . .

"I am very happy," said Anne-Marie. "We are both country-bred and used to a quiet life. I am well content."

She wished with all her heart that their relationship could be on a more open basis. They both had too many reticences. She did not tell him that she had a few plain dark gowns for economy's sake. From the little she knew of their affairs, there was no money to spare, and there were three children in the nursery now, and Anthony was too good a landlord, spending more on the improvement of the cottages and the betterment of the labourers than the farm could support. Her dowry, she thought, must all be gone. The bulk of it had been spent when they were first married to redeem the mortgage on Bodrugan. Although James Carey had conscientiously struggled to pay his share towards reducing the debt he had not made much headway against Martin's spendthrift habits. A little of the mortgage had been paid, but the farm-house and the cottages had been allowed to fall into disrepair, and Anthony had begun with a dead weight of debt and urgent calls for replacements in implements and stock and repairs of every description. In Richard Barradale's time a little privateering had brought in money and Bodrugan had never required to be self-supporting. Now, however, privateering was none too easy, as competition was keen and in any event Anthony had no ship and no means of buying one. So he had eschewed the sea and had settled down to life as a plain farmer, turning a deaf ear to Martin Thomas's plea to turn to smuggling again, as they now ran a pretty trade in silks, laces, and brandy between Falmouth and the Continent. James Carey, on whom Anthony might have relied, had himself suffered a severe setback when his timberyard was destroyed by fire, and he himself had much leeway to make up. This much of their affairs Anne-Marie understood; but she knew only too well that Anthony had a way of withholding the worst from her if it were possible, and, realizing his reservations, she was often secretly very disquieted.

"Would you not care to go to Amsterdam?" Anthony suggested. "I have been thinking that if you felt you might like a change we might ask Nan to take in the children, and you and I could go to your aunt and uncle; and we would see your grandmother."

There! It was out, and what she had anticipated. Anne-Marie stiffened, wondering how to fence until she knew more.

"I should love to see my grandmother," she said warily. "I have always been sorry that you did not have time to get to know her."

"I feel very tender towards her: you are so fond of her and she was good and kind to you. And for myself, I see in her my Anne-Marie when she is old."

"Will you still love me when I am old?" asked Anne-Marie, seeking reassurance in the manner of all lovers.

"I love you more as the years go on," he said soberly. "And desperately when the need grows for me to leave you."

"To leave me? You are not really planning to go with Linschoten, Anthony?"

"I am coming to such a pass that I must," he said. "This Bodrugan is like the bottomless pit. Money, always more money."

"I do not mind poverty, anything, so long as you do not leave me."

"If Barendz will take me with him when he essays the Northeast Passage again I will go. That is one reason why I suggested we might go to Amsterdam. We have until the spring to think about it."

"You will go," said Anne-Marie tiredly.

"I wish to very much. My imagination has been fired by all your grandmother has written of Linschoten's expeditions. And I am tired of the monotony of the farm and the seasons. I want to move about again, see men, do deeds of some importance. And finding the Northeast

Passage seems something of the first importance. Until tonight. Tonight I have thought of no one and of nothing but you, Anne-Marie."

"Then stay with me."

"I'd promise you the earth tonight, my dear, and feel bound to break every pledge in the morning," he said recklessly. "You were very beautiful sitting by the fire this evening."

She raised herself on her elbow and looked down on him. It was quite dark and she saw nothing, but the attitude seemed to express something of her astonishment. She struck him lightly on the chest.

"What is the matter, Anthony?" she demanded, half laughing. "You have seen me every day for years, and I am exactly the same woman."

"I saw you through new eyes tonight," he said. "Through another man's eyes. I prize you highly and I adore you; but I have been careless. I have even been unkind to you. I have forgotten how much I love you in thinking of other matters."

"I believe you are jealous, Anthony."

"No, only sad. You have never failed nor faltered. And the years have been hard, my love. At Pendennis I asked you to wait for me and to have faith in me. You promised me that. And you have held to it. You were very dear to me that afternoon, Anne-Marie, and you were very lovely. I remember I wanted to make wild love to you so that you should never forget me; I wanted to lay my hand upon your child's breasts; but you were so young I knew I should not. Nevertheless, I put a heavy burden upon you. It was four long years before I saw you again. You were waiting at the South Gate of Delft for me. That, I think, was the crowning moment of my life. You have given me everything, my wife; I have done so little for you. I thought this evening of another thing I had said on Pendennis. When I told you I loved you I told you also I knew I ought to leave you free to marry some more stable person. There was a man at your feet tonight who would have given you all you deserve; and I remembered what I had once said."

"On Pendennis I told you I would not have understood it if you had not told me you loved me. I loved you then; I love you now."

"When I come back from this next voyage we will be so happy, Anne-Marie."

"Oh, Anthony, that time long ago it was a voyage to Guinea. And what came of it?" she said sadly.

"This time I shall be more fortunate," he answered on a wave of optimism. "Anne-Marie, I ask you again to wait for me and to have faith in me."

"That day we parted on Pendennis the wild music of the surge was in my ears, and the wind rushed over the sea as it is rushing now about the house. I thought to myself, Whenever I hear the sea and the wind I shall be with Anthony. I thought it then, I say it now. My love, my love . . ."

iii

Afterwards Anthony slept. Anne-Marie lay sleepless beside him. In the morning she arose and bent over him. He was asleep with his own peace. His face was calm and untroubled as if no hurt could ever touch him again. She smiled down on him—a whimsical smile that was both amused and rueful, as if she were much older than he and it was her part to shelter him. After the winter it would be spring, she thought, and there would be little time for peaceful sleep.

She left him to sleep on and dressed quietly and went down the long corridor to the children in the nursery.

PART XVI

ḢOLLAND

CHAPTER THIRTY

IT WAS THE YEAR 1596. WHEN ANNA VAN BREDA LOOKED BACK ON THIS year and the year that succeeded it, she wondered how she had been able to endure the strain of knowing that two beloved members of her family had gone to the ends of the earth, it seemed, to regions most extreme, Anthony Barradale to the northern barrier of perpetual snow and ice and blizzard, Ryk to tropical Africa and heat and perennial sunshine.

Early on in this period Anne-Marie and Anthony had arrived in Holland; and a year later it had been necessary for Anna and Lourens and Anne-Marie to cross the North Sea. And Anna and young Lourens remained so long at Bodrugan that they began to make themselves understood in their broken English.

The first of the chain of voyages had been undertaken by Anne-Marie and Anthony Barradale. They had taken ship from Falmouth to Amsterdam; and from that busy city Dirk's tiny vessel had conveyed them to Oostermeer, where Anne-Marie was to remain while Anthony was away seeking the Northeast Passage.

On a day in April Anne-Marie brought Anthony to Oostermeer. They came a little sooner than they were expected because Barendz was sailing in mid-May and not at the end of that month as they had thought at one time. Dirk had concluded all the travelling arrangements for them and when they left his ship there was a high-hooded cart to convey them to the farm.

On this spring day Anna van Breda took her eldest great-grandson, Lourens, with her and went to the farthest polder to bring home a heifer and her newly born calf. They found when they reached the polder that the calf was still very weak, so that it would be a long and delightful task to bring the cattle to the farmhouse—a task well suited to the lovely day, which called for leisure to appreciate its perfection.

They went slowly homewards and, as they neared the avenue and were about to turn the heifer down in between the double row of trees, Anna saw a high-hooded cart some way off. She wondered idly who was in it and if it was coming their way. It was still too far away for her to tell.

The calf was tired and lay down in the shade of the first poplar, and his mother stood over him, sniffing anxiously. Lourens could also do with a rest, Anna thought, so she sat down on the grass and called to the child to sit beside her.

"The calf is weak and he must rest awhile," she said. "Come and sit beside me. When you are a man do you think you'd like to be a drover?"

"No. Cattle do not all think the same—the calf goes one way and the cow the other, my grandmother. And you do nothing except chase from one to the other."

"There was once a drover who was a great man," said Anna, beginning a story nearly twenty-six years old. "His name was De Ruyter, and he blew up part of the fortress of Lowenstein, killing a great number of Spaniards. There was a terrific explosion, for he had used much gunpowder."

"Had he?"

Anna nodded.

"You never have seen the castle of Lowenstein, but I have," she told him. "It is on the isle of Bommel, between the Meuse and the Waal. Many years ago it was held for the King of Spain. De Ruyter gained admittance disguised as a priest. And my son Lourens, your mother's uncle, was with him and perished with him."

And she told him all the history of that heroic happening more than a quarter of a century before. When she had finished her story Lourens the younger said with relish:

"The accursed Spaniards!"

Anna started. These sturdy Dutch babes—they imbibed hatred of the oppressor with their mothers' milk. . . ..

"You must learn to look for the good points in your enemies as well as the bad," she observed mildly. "The Spaniards are not all of them evil."

"They are our enemies."

"They are under orders. You must look higher than the soldier for the criminal. God has not blessed Philip of Spain. He sent the winds and Philip's Armada was scattered. Ach, that was a time before you were born! The galleons were as large as churches and they were driven on English and Dutch shores like broken boxes. And when the English sea dogs sent their fire ships among the anchored vessels of the Armada at Calais and they cut their cables and fled up the North Sea—ach, that was a sight."

"How the Spaniards burned. The accursed Spaniards, how they burned!" chanted Lourens, capering about with glee.

"I said a prayer for their souls even if they were misguided Catholics," said Anna severely. "I am old and I can see both sides of the story now."

"When my father goes to Cadiz to sack it and to burn the Spanish fleet he has promised to bring me a Spanish sword, and a helmet, and a fistful of silver from the spoils."

Anna sighed. Ever since Jan had announced his intention of going with the expedition to Spain in the summer there had been no repressing the child. The men and boys loved war, she thought. Only the women were never enthusiastic.

"It will be a good thing to get the war over quickly," she said. "Then, perhaps, every Spaniard will leave the Low Countries. We are free in the north, thanks to Prince Maurice; the south may also break the yoke of Spain if the attack is successful."

"God save Prince Maurice!" shouted Lourens.

"God save the Prince! God bless the House of Orange!" said Anna fervently.

She caught the spirited boy to her, and pushed him away, and rolled him over in the grass, and pretended to be Linschoten's polar bears eating him up, while Lourens screamed with laughter.

When they had had their romp Anna decided that the calf could walk again.

"The calf is rested, so we ought to be getting home," she said.

It was pleasant to think that Gerard would be at Oostermeer while Jan was away, Anna reflected. Michiel de Noot had died during the winter that was just past and only she and Gerard were left. Gerard was no longer strong, but the rest in Groningen had helped him wonderfully. The winter was always a bad time for him, as his chest was weak.

They had started the heifer and her calf and were some way down the avenue when Lourens happened to look behind him.

"There is the cart again," he cried. "Look, my grandmother, it is coming this way."

Anna turned. Sure enough, the high-hooded cart had reached the top of the avenue and was being driven down it. They turned the cattle to one side to clear the way. The cart stopped and a woman jumped down from it.

"Anne-Marie," cried Anna. "Ach, Anne-Marie!"

Tears gushed from her eyes and poured down her cheeks. She and Anne-Marie began to run towards each other, sobbing and laughing for joy as they ran.

In a maze of happy, excited conversation and explanation the four of them, Anna and Lourens, Anthony and Anne-Marie, hustled the heifer and her calf home with scant ceremony, while the driver followed at a slow pace in the high-hooded cart.

ii

The long summer days were fateful in the history of three countries, England, Holland, and Spain; and fateful also in the chronicle of Anna van Breda's descendants.

On the last day of June 1596 the combined Dutch and English fleets reached Cadiz. Under the guns of a fortress and a fortified city, and with scarcely any loss to themselves, the English and Dutch troops were landed, the fortress was seized by force of arms, and the defending Spaniards thoroughly routed. The Spanish fleet was destroyed by its own admiral rather than allow it to fall into the hands of his enemies; and the attackers gained possession of both city and citadel.

The effect of the capture of Cadiz on future military operations against Spain was of the greatest value, for, although it had been proved that the Spanish warships were no match for the English and Dutch fighting vessels, the Spanish armies had the reputation of being all-conquering. Now their prestige declined and wider and bolder schemes for the final overthrow of Philip's forces of oppression in the Netherlands began to be planned.

In the north, remote from the excitement of these great events, Anna and Anne-Marie and Juliana renewed their friendship. Anthony had sailed with Barendz on the eighteenth of May, and Jan had sailed with the expedition to Cadiz, in company with Dirk and Ryk. Gerard carried on Jan's share of the supervision at Oostermeer, but the additional labour fell to the women. However, this was not overmuch, as there was Anne-Marie's willing help to be relied on, and she could turn her hand to anything.

When the long, hard days were ended Anna and Anne-Marie sought their bed. They slept together in Anna's great bed, redolent with the odour of ripening cheeses, and there in intermittent conversation they bridged the reticences of the years they had been apart. As was her way, Anna forced no confidences. In the end Anne-Marie would tell her everything, and Anna took just pride in the faith and trust her children's children placed in her; it was a satisfying recognition of all she had striven to accomplish for their good.

One night in bed Anne-Marie said:

"I miss my children, Grandmother."

"You are bound to miss them; but you did right to fall in with Anthony's wishes and leave them at your sister-in-law's. She will care for them and it does children no good to take them on your travels. And your place is with Anthony; and, for myself, I would not have seen you if matters had not been arranged this way."

"I wanted to remain alone at Bodrugan with the children. I am accustomed to a farm and I think I could have managed somehow or other until Anthony returned; but he would not hear of it. He said it was too much responsibility and too much work. And neither of those reasons impressed me. I wondered if it was something quite different that worried him. I asked him, but he denied it."

"Men reason very strangely sometimes," said Anna soothingly, and waited for Anne-Marie to continue.

"Anthony has a friend, a Sir Giles Mortimer, whom Uncle Ryk may have met in Cadiz—Anthony asked him to look out for Sir Giles when we were in Amsterdam—and Anthony has it well fixed in his mind that Sir Giles is in love with me, and, as he thinks the expedition to Cadiz will be over sooner than the quest for the Northeast Passage, I imagine he just did not wish to leave me at Bodrugan. And this is all the sheerest nonsense because I have seen Sir Giles but half a dozen times. He is large and kind—rather like Uncle Gerard but younger and English. The children adore him when he comes. He never forgets to bring them some toy or sweetmeats, or something novel, and he romps and jests with them. At first I did not think this could be Anthony's reason; after all it is somewhat ludicrous to be needlessly jealous. I thought it might be simply because there was not enough money to leave, as he had to invest some in the ship for the Northeast Passage, and he had arranged his home affairs as economically as possible to cover the heavy expense; but there seemed to be so much money to invest in the venture that I was amazed."

"What arrangements have been made about Bodrugan?"

"Martin Thomas is to run it; and the cottagers are there and must look to him. With the house closed and the servants dismissed, money is saved there; and Martin has the stock on his place. And Nan and James keep the children for nothing. So, you see, it does save expense."

"It is always false economy to let a place run to seed," said Anna. "It is always cheaper in the long run to keep it in order all the time."

"The way of farming is different at Bodrugan," said Anne-Marie unhappily. "Here at Oostermeer, if you want a cow you save the money first and then get the cow. At Bodrugan you get half a dozen cows and then begin to think how to pay for them."

"I wouldn't understand that way of doing it; I should be very worried."

"It is on the principle of nothing venture, nothing win. I am like you, my grandmother. I would rather advance slowly but surely."

"Money could not have been so short if Anthony was able to pay his share in the Northeast Passage venture. How much did he invest in it?"

Anne-Marie told her.

"That is a great deal of money," said Anna, very much troubled.

"I cannot make sense of it, my grandmother," said Anne-Marie wretchedly. "I know that money affairs are not my province and it is silly of me to worry now when I have always left everything to Anthony; but I cannot help being troubled because nothing seems to fit. I have always tried to run the house without waste and we have lived quietly, as we both felt we must until we were richer. So you can know that I was astonished when there was suddenly all this money for the Northeast Passage. When it seemed it wasn't the question of money that lay at the back of Anthony's refusal to leave me at Bodrugan I thought it must be that he was secretly jealous of Sir Giles and ashamed to admit it; but in my heart I think the root of the evil is shortage of money."

"It is not difficult to raise money on good land," said Anna slowly. "Do you think Anthony took out another mortgage on Bodrugan?"

"He would have told me, surely," said Anne-Marie. "My grandmother, we have our little reserves, Anthony and I. We do not always speak openly to each other. He is extraordinarily sensitive and he has been through so much that I am doubly careful not to say anything to hurt him. When one loves very much, as I do, then one must often be silent."

"That is wisdom; but wisdom learned in a hard school," said Anna sadly. "I had hoped you might never have the need to learn it."

She slid her hand down along the top of the bedclothes and found Anne-Marie's hand and held it. For some minutes Anne-Marie did not speak while Anna gently caressed her arm.

"My grandmother——"

"My heart?" said Anna tenderly.

"I see now the idea about Sir Giles was so much nonsense," whispered Anne-Marie. "Anthony must have mortgaged Bodrugan, and he did not wish to alarm me by telling me, hoping the passage would be found and he could put it all right and not let me have cause to worry. There was no other way he could have raised the money. And we most certainly had not that much money; and neither James nor Martin could have lent such a sum."

"Anthony had his own reasons for not telling you if he did mortgage the place again," said Anna. "You were very wise to say nothing and to do as he wished. Have faith, and when he comes back all this will be settled."

"When he comes back!" said Anne-Marie. "That Northeast Passage is so hazardous a quest that I live in dread that he will not come back. Will they ever find that Northeast Passage? Will they ever come back? I love Anthony with all my heart. That can never change, no matter what happens."

"Do not lose hope, Anne-Marie. You must always say to yourself: He will, he *must* come back. I believe that if you have faith enough it helps them along and brings them through. Keep your faith alive, my heart."

"When you are with me I can keep my faith alive," said Anne-Marie. "Promise me you will stay with me until Anthony returns."

"Of course. I promise you."

"I wish I could see him now. I want to know he is safe. I try to imagine through what regions he is passing. I can see nothing but icebergs and snow and ferocious white bears. It is dead and frozen where he is and I cannot bear to think of it."

"Perhaps he is already through that frozen belt," said Anna. "If all has gone well they may have sailed into sunshine and calm seas. They say this land is there if they can but find the way through the icy barrier. This time they may find it. For all we know, they are being warmed by the sun as we are here at Oostermeer, with the danger behind them."

"It should be the reward of true lovers that they might be given some inner vision; time and space should not limit their sight of each other."

"True lovers do not always get what they deserve; but they have the best of life, all the same. However, like the economy of farming, life would be more comfortable for them always on an even keel," observed Anna. "Now, Anne-Marie, try to sleep. We must be up early in the morning."

Anna lay wide-eyed long after Anne-Marie had fallen asleep and was breathing evenly at her side. Later she dozed fitfully. In between waking and sleeping Anna dreamed of two phantom ships tossing on invisible waves. The icebergs drifted down upon them, and the Arctic blizzards stripped their shrouds to ribbons, and the sea froze slowly, locking them in a crushing death grip, while the dead white world grew dim and dark as the sun rose no more above the horizon.

It was a dream terrible in its vividness: Anna was thankful when the dawn came greyly into the room and she could see the first light from the open door of the high closet bed.

iii

It was in July that the ice began to close about them and, having reached a latitude which was within ten degrees of the pole, Barendz decided that they could not press on in the direction they were heading.

They had named this far frozen land on which they had turned their backs Spitsbergen. And on the night that Anna van Breda dreamed of those brave ships in the desolate wastes of ice and snow they had sailed again, manoeuvring southwards through the drifting fields of ice. Many dangers from ice and polar bears were met and overcome, until at last the expedition reached the extreme northeastern part of Nova Zembla.

Anthony was the first to see the open water ahead of them. Beyond the ice lay the sea, a blue-green gem in the crystalline purity of the scene.

"The open sea!" he cried. "The sea, the sea!"

Barendz was quickly at his side. The survivors of the expedition crowded round.

"God be thanked," said Barendz, barely able to speak for emotion. "The end of our voyage is achieved. Ahead, men, lies the passage we have sought so long."

The sails were set and trimmed to make the most of the wind, and the ships sailed on. They were full of hope that, having navigated their ships safely through the channel, they would reach the elysian seas of the Hyperboreans and gloriously achieve the end of their quest.

CHAPTER THIRTY-ONE

Before the autumn of this same year, 1596, Ryk van Breda and Dirk returned from Cadiz ahead of Jan. Ryk came from Amsterdam to Oostermeer to take his leave of his mother, for Bernard Ericks was back again with the most favourable of reports, and the project to found Dutch settlements on the Gold Coast had had the approval of the States-General. The ships were at Amsterdam, being fitted for the expedition, and expected to sail before the winter set in.

It was evening when Ryk reached Oostermeer. He was alone, for Dirk was to follow on the morrow when he had found carts to convey the gift Ryk had brought his mother from Amsterdam.

The evening was mild and mellow, and the farmhouse was bathed in the red-gold tones of the sunset. The warmth of the sky lingered on the buttressed barns with their lichened roofs. And grouped about the buildings with a nice preciseness of design were the avenue of poplars, the neat garden, and the well-kept fields. No one had observed his arrival and Ryk stood for a few moments contemplating his boyhood home. He looked on the familiar scene, barely seeing it, but hearing the waning sounds, the lost voices. It was here he had spent his golden youth with Lourens and Liesbet, here he had awaited his father's return from the sea, here he had grown to manhood with his mother ever present if he had needed her. Ryk wondered if this was the last time he would look upon quiet Oostermeer. . . .

A door slammed at the farmhouse. A voice called out:

"Grandmother, Grandmother."

Ryk walked on. Again he came upon Anne-Marie at the kitchen door. It was she who had called out. She exclaimed at the sight of him.

"Uncle Ryk, you are the first back! I will call my grandmother; she will be overjoyed."

She kissed Ryk. He embraced her and held her away from him to look at her. He noticed she was thinner and paler, and he thought the wistful fragility of her face with the dark shadows under her eyes gave to her beauty a haunting quality. If Anthony were to return he hoped it would be soon.

"Have you any news of Anthony, Uncle Ryk?" she asked.

"No, not a word has been heard of his expedition since it sailed; but Barendz is very experienced, so have no fear. It is too soon to expect them back. The end of November is the earliest time to look for their return."

"Do you think they will find the passage?"

"That is in God's hands," he said soberly. "The paths of the ocean and the sounding deeps are His. He alone knows whether there is a channel through the ice to China."

"When he comes back I hope he will never undertake another voyage."

"That will depend on what happens this time," he said. "I must find Juliana and tell her Jan is safely back. He was in a slower ship, but he ought to be home within a few days."

"There they come," said Anne-Marie. "Both my grandmother and Juliana."

They were coming from the byre. Juliana ran to Ryk when she saw him, and Anna followed behind her.

"Father!" cried Juliana. "What news of Jan?"

"He will be home in a few days, and how are the children, Juliana?"

"They are very well. And how did you leave my mother, and Pieter, and my sisters?"

"They are all very well. And here is my mother."

He was amazed when he looked at Anna. She does not grow old or weary, he thought. She was getting on in years and her face was lined, but her eyes were bright and her back straight, and she had an alert and vigorous air about her.

He was ushered into the farmhouse by the three women, who directed a stream of questions at him. Now that they had sacked Cadiz, would the Spaniards leave the Netherlands? And had the losses been heavy in men and ships? And why hadn't they pushed on to Madrid to finish the work? Ryk replied as best he could, and in the thick of it Gerard came in, and Ryk began his explanations all over again for his benefit. And finally Lourens leapt from his bed with a delighted shriek of "Grandfather!" And demanded a Spanish sword and helmet, and a fistful of silver.

Ryk tossed the boy in the air and told him his father was on his way home, burdened with all these things. How the lad grew! he thought. He was a fine specimen, this great-grandson of Anna van Breda's.

"Your father is bringing home your presents, Lourens, but I am bringing a fine large present for your great-grandmother," said Ryk.

Anna was delighted to be singled out.

"A present for me, Ryk!" she exclaimed.

"Dirk follows with it tomorrow," said Ryk mysteriously.

"What is it, Grandfather?" demanded Lourens, jigging up and down in his excitement.

"It is only meant for great-grandmothers," said Ryk. "You will see tomorrow. It is coming in three carts, and it is to be stored in the cellar under the mangers in the byre."

"We have used that cellar to store grain in for years," said Juliana. "Fortunately it is empty just now, as we are waiting for the harvest."

"It will be put to splendid use, and filled to the brim."

"But with what?" cried Lourens.

"You'll find out in the morning."

Juliana persuaded Lourens that he ought to be asleep like his brother and his sister. She and Anne-Marie went out with the child, and Gerard also disappeared. Ryk and Anna were alone.

"I have brought you some choice wine and brandy, Mother," said Ryk. "Some of the wine is from Spain. I shall be sailing for the Gold Coast very soon, and I should like to feel you had a few little comforts in the winter."

"Ryk, how thoughtful of you! The Calvinists will denounce me for a winebibber!"

"Which you are not; but a little wine sometimes in the bitter weather is a great help."

"Our remote ancestor the baron is reputed to have drunk himself to death and disgraced the family; and that is why he is never mentioned. There must be something in heredity, Ryk, for you to have had the idea of such a present; and, for my part, I thank you very much, and I shall look forward to the bitter weather."

"I have invested ten thousand guilders in Amsterdam for you. It is in your name and Minetje knows about it. It is for you in case you ever need money and I am not here to help you."

Anna was very sad. This seemed too much like a sober settling of affairs, as though Ryk had the idea that he might not return and he wished to attend to every detail before he sailed from Amsterdam. She put her hand on his arm, and he covered it with his own.

"Why do you do all this for me?" she asked. "It is almost as though you wished to make provision for my old age and did not expect to be here to care for me yourself. Must you undertake this voyage, my son?"

"Yes, for my own sake I must."

"Yes. I know it."

For so many years he had skimmed the surf of his narrow individualism and now he wanted to rise above his self-seeking and swim freely beyond the froth of petty things in the deep water. And so he must do for his soul's sake.

"I sail very happily," Ryk said. "Minetje and I understand each other and we have had our good years together. Pieter is stronger and more balanced emotionally and the life he is to lead in Amsterdam will suit him admirably. He will shape well yet, Mother. But it is Charlotte who has given me the greatest satisfaction. She has developed; she is not so long-legged and thin. She will have your height and your grace, Mother. She has been with me a great deal this year. In the spring she and I went round the market gardens on the outskirts of Amsterdam. We are taking vegetable seeds and plants and bulbs and will attempt to improve the agriculture of the Gold Coast. A few gardeners are to go with the expedition. Charlotte was engrossed. I discovered that at heart she is a country girl. She was at her best out there among the gardens. And it is not surprising when you remember that she is sprung from farmer stock on both sides."

"Would she like Oostermeer? She might spend a long time with us."

"Minetje would fret with me away and with Charlotte so far from home; but I have appeased Charlotte's passion for the land."

"How did you do that?"

"There is a farmer just outside Amsterdam, by name Daniel Schoenberg—he is a market gardener in rather a big way—and Charlotte is to visit his holding twice a week to study horticulture. Minetje thought it an unusual pursuit for a girl, but Charlotte has looked a little pale and the country air will benefit her."

Anna nodded her approval.

"Minetje and I will see something of each other while you are away,

Ryk. When Anne-Marie returns to England I will stay for a while in Amsterdam."

"That will depend on when Barendz gets back, of course."

"Do you think they will return, Ryk? Sometimes I am terrified misfortune may overtake them. It is such a perilous voyage through those frozen seas."

"I do not know what to answer, Mother. If he does not come back soon Barendz may have to face the Arctic winter; and few would survive the terrible cold."

"If they do not come back I may go to England with Anne-Marie. She cannot be left. But do not speak to her of this. Our fears may be groundless—please God they may be!—and she is troubled enough as it is. But deep down in my heart I feel we shall never see Anthony again."

"Would you rather I stayed until we know, Mother?"

"No. You have your own life to work out. And what is an old woman's premonition after all? I always was imaginative."

"I will stay if you wish it, Mother."

She longed to ask him to remain. But she had not the right, she felt. On a night when she had been tired and overwrought she had dreamed that she saw two ghostly ships entrapped in the glittering ice, and the world had darkened as the sun arose no more; the dream had left behind it an impression of disaster. For a dream's sake she could not hinder Ryk. In the last few years he had had an inner struggle and he had won a victory over himself which must not be wasted even for a few months; it should be fully exploited in the field he had chosen for his endeavour.

"I think you must go," said Anna slowly, feeling the weight of the decision she was making. "We should not torment ourselves with trying to look ahead and to read the future. What we fear may never happen. I think you must go as you have planned."

The world was wide and they must go on until each man knew his neighbour, and the earth and the rolling oceans had been charted, she thought. The men from the cities of Flanders and the Netherlands were linking up with a savage people in a tropical land, and enmity might be forgotten in the pursuit of mutual well-being. This brotherhood of man had been the gospel the Prince had preached. He had been dead for twelve years but she remembered him as though it were only yesterday that he and she had walked the streets of Delft together.

"Then we go on," said Ryk.

She smiled, and drew herself closer to him.

ii

The huge fields of ice drove down from the north and knitted themselves together in an icy unity of doom. Now there was only one ship left, and the promise of the Northeast Passage had ended in the deadly locking of the seas as the approaching winter settled on the Arctic belt.

Barendz and Heemskerk and Anthony Barradale were among the sixteen men left of the expedition when the final disaster occurred and the ship was frozen fast in the ice. The ship was firmly held and already the ice was crushing in her timber, stout as it was. In the spring it was doubtful whether she would be navigable, but the open boats could be carefully preserved and beached on the nearby shore. The survivors held a council to decide what was best to be done in the dire plight in which they found themselves, for now, ill provisioned and equipped for such an eventuality, they were called upon to face the rigours of an Arctic winter.

"I suggest we beach the ship's boats and make them as safe and secure as possible," said Barendz. "We can cross the ice to Nova Zembla and build a hut on the island. Driftwood is plentiful, and, still more important, we can hunt the bears for meat."

"I agree that we must be on land for the winter," said Heemskerk. "And we must lose no time about building a shelter, because soon the sun will rise no more."

Anthony Barradale had nothing to add to this. He felt in himself a vast inexperience, and at the same time a great pride to be where he was, in the company of brave men who faced the worst that could have happened to them with wise counsel and unshakable calm. There had been other brave men he had known. He had shared a terrible imprisonment with Lucas Mason and Roger Dunne, in which he had played the least part, and yet he alone had escaped alive from the Gold Coast. At the very end the most faithful, loyal friend a man could have had given his life for him. Of all that had happened in Guinea, of all the hell of the galleys, nothing had left so deep a scar in his mind as Tom Wilson's death. And here, given into his hand, was an opportunity of repaying some of this great debt to Tom, and Roger Dunne, and Lucas Mason, to Anne-Marie, the innocent victim of his moods and his reserves, and his bitter self-knowledge that somehow it had always been he who had survived disaster when it had overtaken others. Perhaps once or twice it had just happened that way, and he could have done nothing to alter the shape of events; but in the case of Tom it would have been as easy for him to save Tom as it had been for Tom to save him when the arrows came, but he had not lent himself to the heroic moment. As a child on Pendennis a hovering sea gull had given him an ineradicable impression of freedom which he had never attained. Here on Nova Zembla, perhaps, he would reach the realization of that never-to-be-forgotten dream.

"You may count on me," said Anthony.

If he lived up to that, there was no more to say, he thought.

Barendz, as ever, was full of courage and hope.

"We are all in this together," he said. "We are prepared to face whatever may arise. We will win through."

They set to work, the sixteen who were left. Anthony worked cheerfully and with a will. He forced himself not to be introspective and would not give way to depression. There was the fuel to be collected and stored;

the hut to be built; and caches of food to be made in places where bears and foxes would not be able to get at their meagre stores; and the ship's boats had to be beached and covered against the hard weather in case the ship was no longer serviceable after months of the grinding pressure of the ice.

Anthony fought a winning fight. By the time the winter was on them cheerfulness was no longer such an effort. And his self-mastery grew daily less fallible when it was discovered that he had quite a talent for shaping into suits the skins of the foxes they caught and ate when the bears disappeared to hibernate. It was essential to clothe themselves in furs, for their European clothing was frozen solid. And with this strange tailoring to occupy him the days passed until they shut themselves in their precarious shelter as the dreadful reality of the Arctic winter closed down upon them.

And early in November the sun rose no more above the horizon.

iii

Everywhere that winter of 1596 was a hard one. In December in Nova Zembla Barendz's small company was nearly asphyxiated. They had lighted a coal fire and had sealed all the crevices in the hut and had fallen asleep. Fortunately Anthony Barradale had awakened choking and half suffocated, and had stumbled to the door and flung it open before it was too late. In December also Gerard van Braam had again contracted pneumonia and had died at Oostermeer. Anna, grieved by the death of the last of her old friends and desperately anxious about Ryk, struggled against her sense of shock and loss for the sake of Anne-Marie, who was wearing herself to a shadow waiting for Anthony or for news of him. Occasionally letters came from England for her, to tell her that the children were well, but Anne-Marie barely read them. Her whole being was concentrated on Anthony in the frozen north. Worst of all, Jan van Braam also showed signs of strain. He was bound to have felt the death of his old father, Anna knew; but she knew also that there was more to it than that. Jan was concerned about Anne-Marie, and Anna was aware how deep the roots of Jan's affection for Anne-Marie went. Juliana watched Jan; Anna surprised her glancing from her husband to Anne-Marie with a hurt, bitter look. Anne-Marie, at the centre and heart of all these undercurrents, was oblivious of them, absorbed only in her fearful anxiety. Anna began to wonder whether it would not be wise to take the initiative and urge Anne-Marie to return to Bodrugan and to await Anthony there. It was obvious that they were all at great strain, and sooner or later one or other of them would reach breaking point; and she felt that a shattering climax must be avoided at all costs. Yet each time when she had made up her mind to persuade Anne-Marie to go back to England, she found herself remembering Anne-Marie's heart-broken cry in the dairy years before: "If I went back to Bodrugan the very stones would cry out, 'Anthony, Anthony.' " And Anna had not the heart to press her. Only the children kept the house alive. They chattered and laughed and gambolled in the old house and led an independent life of their own, in blissful ignorance of the troubles of their elders.

At Amsterdam that winter set in train a strange sequence of events. Jan Bester began to come again to Ryk's house. One afternoon Minetje came upon him comfortably installed before a blazing fire in Pieter's room. They were playing chess. He looked up and saw her and carefully moved his piece before he rose. He gave her a sly, saucy look because he knew she could not risk a scene with Pieter. She had coloured hotly but had said nothing, as he knew she must. And so it had begun and no words afterwards had the least effect. Short of asking the servants to throw Jan Bester out, there was nothing Minetje could do to prevent his coming. When he was more sure of his ground Jan Bester made covert love to Minetje, laughing when she rudely and abruptly repulsed him. Pieter, overjoyed at the return of his favourite, was ranged on Jan's side. For the first time since the urge to visit the market gardens had taken her youngest daughter, Minetje was glad that Charlotte had an interest that took her away from the house for hours on end. She encouraged the girl, who lost no time in making the most of her mother's extraordinary leniency. Minetje was very gratified to see how the girl blossomed. There was colour in her cheeks and a sparkle in her eyes, and she was gay and happy. Minetje knew that when the canals froze over she went skating with the young folk in the country, and among these young people was Julius Schoenberg, Daniel Schoenberg's only son, home on vacation from Leyden University. One evening when Charlotte returned home with her cheeks rosy with cold, and her fair hair crisp and curly, Minetje was struck by the vitality of her glowing face. The child had grown so fast that she was almost a woman. Minetje stared at Charlotte, amazed at the change in her quiet, pale daughter. The girl was radiant and there was an inward beauty that shone through her plain face and transformed it; and undoubtedly she was tall and had a lovely carriage. She was definitely marriageable, thought Minetje, instinctively running through the list of eligible young men she knew. It would be a good thing to get Charlotte married young, with Jan Bester about, she reflected. She did not trust that young man as far as she could see him. And on the very next day Minetje began to put out delicate feelers. She thought young Ruprecht Grobbelaar, whose father owned the largest weaving industry in Flanders, might make a good son-in-law. He was a presentable young man and very rich. Charlotte, unaware of these plans for her future, went gaily on her way. She had met Ruprecht Grobbelaar but once, and had not thought of him since, having no liking for successful, self-assured young men.

Charlotte skated in the hard weather in scenes which were like backgrounds to fairyland. The frozen canals were glittering ribbons of ice, and each bush and tree growing beside them was outlined in hoarfrost. The sky was blue and clear and the winter sun spangled each crystal particle on the hedges. And in this world of faëry she was not alone. Julius Schoenberg was with her every hour she could steal away. They skated and cut figures on the ice, and the exhilaration of youth and first love, unuttered as yet, was on them. In shared ecstasy the cold, tingling days went by. Charlotte van Breda, at least, was wholly happy.

The year ended; and the drama of the next year began to unfold in the spring.

CHAPTER THIRTY-TWO

The earth in the polder fell away from the ploughshare and lay in long, glistening furrows. Anna watched Jan follow the plough. When he turned and came towards her she waved to him.

"I have brought you ale and cheese," she called out.

At the end of the furrow Jan stopped the plough and came back to where she was standing, waiting for him. He threw himself down on the grass. The day was warm and there was a little breeze blowing in from the sea. From far away gulls screamed and Anna thought they must be on the meer. Light clouds chased each other across the sky, and their shadows drifted below them on the flower-studded earth.

"I wanted Anne-Marie to come with me to pick the Pentecost lilies by the windmill," said Anna. "She would not come. She is so unhappy. She will do nothing but work."

"Anthony must be lost," said Jan. "I think she is coming to realize that. No expedition to find the Northeast Passage has been away so long before."

"They may have found the passage and sailed on to China."

"We say that to console Anne-Marie; but somehow I do not think it."

"Nor I," said Anna with a deep sigh. "Jan, I have been wanting to consult you for some days past and now is a good time: I think it would be best if Anne-Marie and I went to England. If Anthony is dead she will have to move back eventually, and she might as well move now. She will not endure this waiting much longer."

"She is welcome to the shelter of my roof for as long as she wishes," said Jan.

"I am sure of that," said Anna warmly. "But she ought to be roused, taken out of herself, made to do something. Having her children round her again will be a great help."

"Perhaps you are right."

Anna stole a look at his face. He was staring at the ground and digging a broken twig into the earth. His face was stern and set and she saw he was greying at the temples. This disturbing beauty of Anne-Marie's would cause much havoc before she was an old woman, thought Anna, remembering the anxious moments she and Gerard had had when Jan and Juliana had first been married. It was time Anne-Marie went back to Bodrugan and left the family at Oostermeer to settle down into their accustomed ways.

"Juliana——" Anna began.

Jan started and looked at her. There was a sick fear in his eyes. Poor Jan, he is wondering how much I have noticed, thought Anna. She tried to keep her face expressionless; and her voice was bland as she carried smoothly on:

". . . cannot manage alone. I must go with Anne-Marie. I was thinking Charlotte might come and help Juliana. Ryk told me she liked farms and was a country lover. She might like to be at Oostermeer. I am writing to Minetje today. Shall I suggest that Charlotte come to Oostermeer while I am away in England? It would be pleasant for Juliana to have her sister."

There was relief on Jan's face. That was one rock she had skirted safely, Anna thought.

"It is a good idea. But mention it to Juliana. Hear what she thinks."

"Of course I shall. And we will leave as soon as Charlotte arrives— that is, if Minetje agrees."

It was only when she was writing to Minetje in her round, laboured hand, and reporting the conversation she had had with Jan that morning, that she found she had written, "Jan says she is welcome to the shelter of his roof." That was exactly what he had said. But Oostermeer was not Jan's; it was hers. Oostermeer was as much part of her as her own right hand was part of her. What pitfalls custom and usage laid for the feet of the unwary, thought Anna. Gerard and Jan had farmed Oostermeer for so many years that the real ownership of the place had fallen into abeyance. But Gerard had never forgotten for one moment to whom Oostermeer belonged. Dear Gerard, thought Anna with tenderness. He had had an unfailing instinct for pleasing her and he had appreciated that Oostermeer was entwined in the roots of her being. But the younger generation were apt to be a little forgetful and casual. However, Jan, and Lourens after him, were to have Oostermeer when she was gone, so what did the question of ownership matter? she asked herself. She had made a will to that effect and Jan knew about it. Nevertheless she put her quill through "his roof" and obliterated the two words. Above them she carefully wrote "Oostermeer." I am not dead yet, thought Anna. And a great deal may happen before I am dead. . . .

She lost herself in thoughts of Oostermeer. Here she had been born; here she had lived her happy life with Gysbert; here she had borne her sons; had watched and waited and suffered her sorrows. Every inch of Oostermeer was hallowed ground. Oostermeer. Oostermeer . . . How fair and pleasant it stood in the perfect spring weather.

ii

In April at Nova Zembla they saw again the open sea in the distance. Day after day they watched the ice fields break up and the great bergs crash and thunder as they struck against one another. Gradually the expanse of blue water widened and the great towers and pinnacles of ice floated away or were slowly dissolved as the sun grew stronger and the temperature rose.

The ship was almost clear of the ice. Her keel had been crushed in like an eggshell and as the steely grip of the ice slackened she began to fill with water and to settle.

The ship's boats were found to be in a good state of preservation. They had taken the precaution of moving the nautical instruments, so now they still had the means of undertaking the long voyage back to Holland in these open boats.

In the middle of June Barendz adjudged that they could begin their odyssey. He manned the boats, dividing the crews according to their strength so that the weak and the strong should be in like proportion. They were emaciated and ill-looking, having endured the extremities of an Arctic winter on scanty food and under primitive conditions.

They had not been at sea a week when disaster overtook them. Barendz, still full of hope and confidence, died of exhaustion. Now Heemskerk took upon himself the responsibility of guiding the survivors of that fatal expedition to discover the Northeast Passage across the trackless ocean to a safe haven in Holland.

PART XVII

CORNISH INTERLUDE

CHAPTER THIRTY-THREE

THEY SPILLED ASHORE AT FALMOUTH, ANNA AND ANNE-MARIE, LOURENS, Gilbert, Margaret, and Francis. Lourens had refused at the last moment to be parted from Anna and had crossed to England with them. Dirk's ship had put in at Plymouth and the Barradale children had boarded her there, and they had sailed on to Falmouth.

There had been a cheerful scene when they left Oostermeer, Anna remembered with amusement. They had been about to climb into the cart which was waiting to convey them and their belongings to the port where Dirk's ship lay, when Lourens had halted them with a demand for their clogs.

"Where are our clogs, my grandmother?" he had asked. "I don't see them, and I have pinched all the bundles and they are not there. We are not going to leave them behind, are we?"

"Why, yes, we are," Anna had said. "Don't you remember when we were in Amsterdam we wore shoes as we are wearing them now? And what a fine new pair your aunt Charlotte brought you from your grandmother in Amsterdam! In great houses and foreign lands one does not go clattering around in clogs."

"But they make such a lovely noise on deck," Lourens had protested. "Couldn't we wear them on the ship at least?"

"The farmyard at Bodrugan is like a bog in the winter when it rains," Anne-Marie had observed. "They will come in very useful on the farm. You can wear clogs just as well at Bodrugan as you can in Friesland."

And Charlotte, laughing immoderately and wishing her mother could hear the conversation, had insisted on tying up Anna's and Anne-Marie's and Lourens's clogs into yet another bundle. And, with the cart loaded to the hood, they had begun the journey.

It seemed as though the people of Falmouth had arranged to welcome them royally when they arrived. A boy, idling on the quay, had darted away like a bird as the ship dropped anchor, and in a short time women and children, and such men as there were in Falmouth who were not out with the fishing boats, came pouring out from the alleys and running down the single street to greet them.

The same question was on every lip.

"What news of Anthony Barradale?" "Did they find the Northeast Passage?" "When will he be home again?" The questions beat down upon Anne-Marie as she stood in the hot sun on the quay.

"There is no news yet, alas," she answered. "But it cannot be much longer before we have news. And, Mistress Barrow, how is your old mother? I thought of her in the winter, and wondered how she fared."

"The old lady is as sprightly as a cricket," interposed a voice before Bess Barrow, the fisherman's wife, could reply. "And doesn't Bess hear of it from her if she forgets to fill the ale jug at the inn!"

"Then she must be in better fettle than when I last saw her," said Anne-Marie. "And the Trevenna twins. Must they still wear ribbons in their hair to tell the one from the other?"

"The ribbons gave out and so did their mother's patience. You will remember that the one was Jane and the other Annie? Well, they're both called Janey-Annie and there's no difficulty!"

"And how your children have grown!" exclaimed yet another voice. "And who might the tall boy be, Mistress Barradale, that is as like Gilbert as one pea to another?"

"He is Gilbert's Dutch cousin, Lourens." Already she pronounced the name Laurence, Anna noticed, who was following the conversation with great difficulty. "And this is my grandmother, Mevrou van Breda," said Anne-Marie, drawing Anna forward.

This was the moment for the phrase she had practised so assiduously on board, Anna thought.

"Good day to you all," she said clearly.

She was not quite certain that the crowd did not cheer; but as she was nervous and the shouts of greeting were in a foreign tongue she could not be altogether sure. She was thankful she had listened to Anne-Marie and had begun to learn English at Oostermeer in the spring when she had decided that they must go to England. Lourens, who copied her in all she did, had acquired a smattering of the language in a very short time, but what with the strange-sounding words and the English habit of speaking through the top of the head and not in the throat Anna had not made much progress; but she understood a great deal more than she spoke. At this moment, when she had to use her English, she envied Dirk, who had refused to learn any foreign tongue at all, and stood mute, solid, entirely self-possessed, without a care in the world.

"You said that very well," Anne-Marie whispered in her ear. "Now say we had a good crossing. You've learned that."

"No," said Anna in hurried Dutch. "I want to say to all these good people that I thank them for the welcome they have given my grand-daughter. That is one thing you did not think to teach me on the ship, and of course, it is the only thing I want to say. All the silly things I learned! It is hot; it is cold; it is a fine day; I am very well, thank you. And not one is any use to me!"

"I will say it for you, my grandmother," said Anne-Marie; and Anna felt Anne-Marie's hand on her arm, gripping it tightly.

"My grandmother has not the English to say it," said Anne-Marie clearly, "but she wishes me to thank you for the welcome you have given us."

Anna nodded.

"Yes," she said. "Yes."

The woman they called Bess pulled at Anne-Marie's skirt.

"Do not fret, dear," she said softly to Anne-Marie. "The sea takes them for a long time, but it brings them back again. You yourself were born in the North Sea in the worst storm for generations, and here you are safe and sound on Falmouth quay. Never fear, he will return."

Anna understood most of what Bess Barrow had said. They had gathered to cheer Anne-Marie and help her over this sad home-coming. Anna looked round the circle of ruddy English faces. They laughed and jested, and Anne-Marie with them; but deep in their hearts they all knew how ill events shaped for Anne-Marie. Anna saw that Anne-Marie had her place here at Falmouth. She was home among those who had known and cared for her for most of her life.

On the long walk to Bodrugan, when the people of Falmouth had fallen away, Anna said:

"It is a wonderful thing to me to see the friendship that has grown up between the Dutch and the English races. I felt almost as though I had come home, and I have not set foot in this land before. And your children are the link between the two nations, having the blood of both in their veins. In the time to come perhaps there will be no more quarrelling among nations, no more wars."

"While there are nations there will be wars, my grandmother."

"It is a dream I shall never give up," said Anna. "But we bring the children up so badly, Anne-Marie. You have but to say the word 'Spaniard' and they put 'accursed' to it before you have closed your lips."

Halfway to Bodrugan they were met by Martin Thomas and Sarah— a Sarah grown stout and buxom and not a little grey-haired.

"We did not expect you just yet," exclaimed Sarah, kissing Anne-Marie. "But the house has been aired and the fires lighted. And there is a woman to serve you."

"I wondered if you were living at Bodrugan. You never said."

"No, we did not live there. Anthony left the matter open. We did not feel it was worth changing house for a few months; but it has been more than a year. How time flies!" said Sarah.

She talked as though she were ill at ease and wanted to cover something up, Anna thought. And Martin Thomas said nothing, and that was ominous. Anna looked steadily at him. This was the man then who had been the wild influence in Anthony Barradale's life. He looked far from wild, Anna thought, in fact he looked dejected and somewhat crestfallen. And she began immediately to wonder whether he had heard news they had not. . . .

They walked on in a sober family group, with Dirk and two other men bringing the boxes and bundles on behind them. They walked up the lane to Bodrugan and stopped of one accord as they reached the gate that led to the farmyard.

Anna did not look at Anne-Marie, nor did Anne-Marie look at her grandmother. They were too aghast at what they saw. The yard gate dragged and sagged on its broken hinges; weeds grew breast-high in the yard and nettles thrust up a luxuriant growth beside the pig troughs; no hen scratched in the yard, no beast lowed in the byre, no horse neighed in the stables. The smoke spiralling from the chimney stacks and the open windows of the house were the only signs of human activity about the place. Bodrugan lay derelict and forlorn in the setting sun. A gust of wind arose and the weeds bent and rustled before it.

When she had taken in the scene Anne-Marie turned to Martin.

"There seems to be no cowman, for I see the cottage is empty. You have the stock, Martin. We must have a cow for milk for the children."

"The stock was sold just after you left, Anne-Marie," said Martin flatly. "Did you not know it was going to be sold? There's not a hoof on this place, nor a hoof of yours on mine."

"Of course," said Anne-Marie. "I am so careless about affairs. How stupid of me to have forgotten."

"I told Martin we ought to have written and explained," said Sarah unhappily. "This must be a shock to you."

"It is a shock to see it like this," said Anne-Marie, "but Bodrugan had to be left to lie fallow while Anthony was away. There was no help for it."

"I hope you have been able to arrange with your people to help with the mortgage, Anne-Marie," said Sarah, almost in tears. "They are just waiting for news of Anthony to call in the money."

"The mortgage will be paid," said Anne-Marie haughtily; and Anna saw she was white to the lips.

Anna pushed forward until she stood beside Anne-Marie.

"Tomorrow," she said. "It will do tomorrow."

And raged inwardly at her inadequacy. If only they understood Dutch. They ought to have learned how to speak her language. The two nations divided by the North Sea had been so friendly since the destruction of the Armada that there ought not to be this stumbling block of language.

"I wish you would all come to our house," said Sarah. "I have made preparations, but you said you would rather come here. Do change your mind, Anne-Marie. Stay with us for a few days at any rate."

At last Anna and Anne-Marie dared exchange glances.

"I thank you, Sarah," said Anne-Marie, "but we will remain here."

"You will find everything you need in the house, and I will send a cow and her calf round in the morning," said Martin.

Anna left them talking and went back to Dirk, who was still coming up the lane. She wanted to make sure that a particular bundle was there. She had made up a box of some of the money Ryk had left for her and had concealed it among a miscellany of objects in a shabby bundle, thinking that if pirates or robbers waylaid them anywhere between Holland and England they would overlook such a shabby, worthless bundle. The bundle was there. She thrust her fingers into it and touched the wooden rim of the box. There was nothing here on this Bodrugan, she thought, not so much as a cow. And she touched the box again. At least there would be a little money. More than ever she understood why the people of Falmouth had been so very kind to Anne-Marie.

When the children were abed Anna and Dirk sat in the winter parlour in the golden dusk. The windows were wide open and the wind came into the room. Anne-Marie paced restlessly up and down. She had barely uttered a word since Martin and Sarah had taken their leave of her, promising to be back to see her in the morning.

"You must be dead-tired, Anne-Marie," said Anna. "Will you not sit down?"

Anne-Marie sank down on the settle. She put her head in her hands.

"I hear the sea and the wind," she said very low, as though she were speaking to herself. "Those two things—the sea and the wind."

It seemed an eternity since she had lain beside Anthony in their bed in this house, an eternity since he had said they would be so happy when he came back from this voyage—this last voyage. The night he had said that, the sounds of the sea and the wind had been in her ears, as they were now.

"He will not come," said Anne-Marie aloud. "He will never come. My love, my love . . ."

And the wind rushed up from the sea and beat against the house.

ii

He saw her first as he rode up the lane to Bodrugan farmhouse, a tall woman in clogs and a white Dutch cap. Her back was towards him and she was bending over the gate.

She heard the beat of his horse's hoofs and turned round and looked down the lane and saw him. He rode quickly up and dismounted at the gate.

His heart beat faster when he looked into the face of this aging woman. She might have been Anne-Marie with forty years added to her age.

"You are Mistress Barradale's grandmother," he said with certainty.

Anna had also been taking stock of the tall, massive stranger, who was "like Gerard, but younger and English." She liked what she saw.

This was a kind, strong man, and the Lord knew they were so defence-less that they could do with such a man to fend for them.

"And you are Sir Giles Mortimer," said Anna. "Anne-Marie has spoken of you."

"How is she?" he asked.

"She is not very well," answered Anna, marvelling that the conversation was keeping to a familiar track. "She is ill—here." She touched her breast.

"I understand. There is no news of her husband?"

"No news. I am afraid."

"It is not possible to survive the winter in those northern seas," he said sombrely.

He saw she had not understood him fully.

"I am afraid also," he said. And added: "What are you doing to the gate?"

"It is broken," said Anna.

And thought of the many matters that wanted attention at Bodrugan. They had installed a cowman in the cottage who acted as gardener and handy man, as there was only the one cow to tend. The weeds in the yard had disappeared and the place no longer looked so derelict. But the fields lay fallow. They had not been ploughed or sowed, and the autumn was coming on when the seed should be put in the ground. How was it all to be done? she asked herself for the hundredth time. She herself paid the cowman's wages and their daily expenses from her store of money, but she was always paying out, never getting in. She was horrified at the rapidity with which the money she had brought with her was dwindling. Already she was planning to write to Minetje to send more. What a blessing it was that Ryk had so thoughtfully set aside quite a small fortune for her use before he sailed—almost as though he knew she would need it here at Bodrugan. He had always been a kind, loving son, and when her mind was not occupied with Anne-Marie and affairs at Bodrugan, she fretted about him. She tried not to worry, telling herself that Anthony and Ryk had survived terrible dangers in the past and would surely come home again; but deep down in her heart she knew it would not be so easy for them this time.

"You are trying to mend the gate?" said Sir Giles wonderingly.

He glanced at her hands, stained with rust from the broken hinges.

"Yes, I was trying."

"Difficult work without tools. I will send a man."

"No," she said, shaking her head emphatically. "Not yet."

And longed to be able to open her heart to this man. There were those fields, and they ought to have cattle and horses, pigs and sheep and hens, and men to run the place.

"Is Mistress Barradale at home?" he asked.

"No, she has taken the children to the beach."

They sat on the large stones at the gate—the "Traitor's Gate" stones, as the children called them. The horse cropped the grass that sprouted from the base of the wall and round the posts of the gate. Anna forced herself to talk to Sir Giles in her halting English. He was very quick, understanding what she meant to convey even before she had said it. She wanted his advice: the untilled fields worried her, with the sowing season coming on, and she asked him what could be done about getting them ploughed and the seed in.

"You must let the empty cottages and so much land with each of them, not for money but for a share of the crops. Each man cultivates for himself and your proportion will be small, but you will bring the land under cultivation again, and that is worth a great deal. Some of the best paddocks must be kept out for pasture and you should have more cattle. If you wish I will go over the place and divide it into lots and show you which fields I think you ought to keep for pasture. If Mistress Barradale agrees, I will find tenants and help to get the scheme started. And I know where you can get half a dozen heifers cheaply to begin again."

"How much for the heifers?" asked Anna cautiously. Her bank was in her box under her bed and she wondered when the wood at the bottom was going to show through. And there was no butter money from the solitary cow, which was only a borrowed cow, as the children drank the milk and the calf was half grown. Never had she wrestled with such a deplorable situation. Her little ways of thrift and careful planning were of not the slightest good in this confusion. There had even been a threat of foreclosure, but she had dealt with James Carey and Martin Thomas and had told them they must keep the mortgage going until there was news of Anthony. She had handed them fifty guilders with the air of one who bestowed a million; and there had been no more talk of foreclosure. Of these matters Anne-Marie knew nothing. Up to the present Anna had managed to stand between her and direct financial pressure.

Sir Giles suggested a sum for the heifers. It was absurdly low, but Anna did not know that. She supposed English cattle, being inferior to the cattle of the Netherlands, cost less. Sir Giles longed to add that he would be honoured to furnish the heifers from his own herd, but he felt the offer would offend.

"Yes, we can pay for them," said Anna with relief.

"I will buy them and send them with a drover next week," he said. "And we can arrange the payment when they are delivered."

"Yes, that will do nicely. Thank you very much."

"Anthony Barradale is probably dead," he said abruptly.

"We must wait for news," said Anna, and there was a warning note in her voice, as though she advised him not to be precipitate.

"Is there anything I can do for her?" he said; and added very low, staring at the ground: "You understand there is nothing I would not do for her."

"At the moment there is nothing you can do for her. She is very unhappy and—and——" She sought through her limited vocabulary for the English equivalent of "apathetic," but gave it up. "On your way back ride to Pendennis. She is there with the children in the cove. You will see for yourself what I mean. And wait for news."

Again she stressed that.

"I will wait for news," he said. "I must wait."

She nodded; he was kind and understanding. They looked into each other's eyes and Anna felt she had eased part of her load onto another's shoulders. With this man Anne-Marie's future would be happy and secure.

iii

In the letter Barendz had written and hung up in the hut they had quitted in Nova Zembla, he had set down an account of their sojourn in that snowbound, desolate land through the long winter night, when from the twilight outside they could not tell whether they saw the light of the day or the moon shining. At the end he had written that they were putting out in open boats, committing themselves into the hands of God. To this letter each man had put his cross. Anthony Barradale had also made his mark. Although he could read and write he wished to differ in no way from the brave men who had been his associates through the dark and terrible months of the winter night.

After the death of Barendz they sailed on in the two open boats, surviving the dangers of the summer conditions in the Arctic seas by a series of divine miracles. Melting bergs and vast pieces of sea and land ice, often black with dirt and resembling floating islands, bore down upon them, towering high above the frail craft, which could make no great speed in the water, thick and sticky with the dissolving slush; and the men also were almost at the end of their strength.

There were days when there was no clarity of atmosphere; a mist overhung them and there seemed no distinction between air and sea. The crash of ice blocks striking into each other resounded in every direction.

No one lost heart. Rations were low and the Continent a long way off. They steered for the north coast of Lapland, as it was the nearest point.

Through some strange spiritual alchemy the very conditions that should have sent Anthony Barradale out of his mind had saved him. He had heard it said, and had believed it, that man could not survive an Arctic winter, for the long-continued absence of light had an unnerving effect.

Not one of the men pent up in the hut on Nova Zembla had gone mad or wandered off into the unknown interior. They had made the most of each other's company, for many days and nights had passed when blizzards or weather of terrible severity had kept them confined to their hut. It had been so cold that, although they warmed themselves at the fire, their backs had been frozen white even within the hut. On these occasions they had lost count of time.

Anthony learned Dutch and was very fluent by the time they left Nova Zembla. In the icy winter he had modelled the suits from fox furs. In the long darkness, when they had huddled round their fire to keep themselves alive, he had begun the saga of his adventures on the Gold Coast, and had laughed when he saw plainly that they did not altogether believe him. They jested and mocked him for telling tales of tropical heat and milk-warm seas when the breath from their nostrils froze on their beards.

At the end of this long time of darkness when, overwhelmed with joy, they saw the edge of the sun appear above the dazzling horizon of ice and snow for a brief moment, he knew that in the Arctic winter he had learned to turn his thoughts from himself and to think of events as they affected his fellow men. In this preoccupation with his companions he had rid himself of his introspective brooding. There was no sea gull, emblem of freedom, here in this desolate spot, but in his mind he knew the end of its flight.

In March he and Barendz had set out across the ice to the ship nipped in the frozen haven. They had seen that she would never again be sea-worthy. They knew they could not hope to survive a second winter in Arctic conditions. It was Anthony who had expressed his confidence in the future. He had said, quoting the watchword of Frobisher's expedition:

" 'Before the world, was God.' "

Barendz bowed his head.

"Amen," he said.

His head was still bowed; it was as if he prayed. After a moment he lifted it.

"We can make Europe in the boats," said Barendz with quiet confidence. "North Lapland is not so far."

"It is not so far," said Anthony.

He had been uplifted. The flight of the sea gull—the wonder of it! Man, born to strive after the unattainable, which, ever beyond his reach, beckoned him from the horizon; and by vision man lived.

And the vision of the sea gull was with Anthony. For three days and nights he lay in the bottom of the second boat in a raging fever, living through the torments of his days on the Gold Coast. He awoke to consciousness one morning to find that the mist was down like a veil and they were voyaging on through thick grey vapour. He lay still, weak from the fever and with the lassitude of weeks of privation and exhaustion weighing him down; and, perhaps because he was still a little light headed, looking up into the mist, he thought he looked into the fine, white-feathered wings of a sea gull, the wings of so vast a span they spread out in eternal watchfulness across the grey arc of the sky.

"It has come again," he muttered. "The sea gull . . . the sea gull . . ."

Heemskerk bent over him.

"Are you awake?" he asked anxiously. He had expected Anthony Barradale to die in the night; but he had held onto life. When Heemskerk put his hand on Anthony's brow it was cool to the touch. The destroying fever had left him.

Anthony struggled to sit up. Heemskerk aided him and he sat up and looked about him. He saw the grey sea and the grey sky that were blended into one grey, moving mist, out of which the leading boat loomed with a spectral vagueness; he saw the grey, haggard faces of his companions. There were four men at the oars, while another lay in the bottom of the boat.

"Have we made progress?" asked Anthony when these pictures faded. For three days and three nights he had seen pictures in his mind, and it seemed they would never cease.

"We have barely moved. Three of us cannot row, and two more are getting to the end also," said Heemskerk sadly. "I keep on changing the crews so that both boats can be kept together."

"We will all perish if the strong halt for the weak," said Anthony. "There is one way whereby we may all be saved."

There was one way. . . . Anthony looked up. The mist was so thick that the heavens seemed pressing down upon them, flattening them into the sea. There was no giant sea gull now, only the grey, choking mist.

"May God guide us," prayed Heemskerk devoutly.

"If you divide the crews differently," murmured Anthony. "Put it to the men. I, and those in my condition, or coming to it, should all be together, and the men whose strength holds out should go on with all speed while we follow as our strength permits. And the first boat home sends back help. If we do it this way there is hope for us all. If not, I think we must inevitably perish. Let the men decide."

He ceased speaking and sank back. The effort had been great. He felt he would like to put up his hand to push the sky back, so lowering and wraithlike was the mist, but when he lifted his hand it fell inertly at his side.

One night there was a storm and when daylight came it was seen that the boats had drifted apart. Anthony, in command of the boat in which he and five other men, who were too ill or too weak to do their full share of the rowing, had followed the faster boat, always keeping within sight of her, saw that they were now alone.

They had escaped shipwreck, but in the storm the few nautical instruments by which Anthony had contrived to set their course had been washed overboard. He knew the men must inevitably discover this loss, so he decided to tell them how they stood.

"The instruments went overboard in the storm," he said. "Navigators have got home before now without the aid of instruments. There are still the stars."

The shock of his announcement produced silence for a moment.

"Our fathers managed very well by the stars," said one of the men. "We can do the same."

"I suggest we drift with the current and spare our strength today," said Anthony. "Tonight we will get our bearings and set our course."

"The stars are fixed. No storm dislodges them," said another.

They had taken the bad news well, Anthony thought. And there was no apathy. They had spoken from the inward strength of high courage. He looked into their faces. They were all very ill, rapidly reaching the end of human endurance. He gave out extra rations that day. There was mercifully more warmth in the sun and they were able to dry their clothing. They must be some way southward, he thought, for it was many days since they had seen floating ice.

Where they were only God knew. They were in His hands. On several nights the sky was overcast and they were unable to steer by the stars.

By now Anthony's bodily weakness was very great. However, as his bodily strength waned, his spiritual energy waxed. He was animated by a great faith and he was able to transmit this exultation to his companions and to keep the flame of hope alive in their hearts. Anthony, having slightly increased the daily rations on the day following the storm, had kept the meagre dole to the new level, thinking that it was better to maintain strength and go on for a short while than to exist longer and be unable to do more than lie in huddled heaps of exhaustion. He did no rowing, so he kept himself on his original ration, and each day he put aside the little he had saved of his own portion for the final emergency. They caught fish sometimes and ate them. Water, however, was the principal danger. Already they were nearing the end of their supply.

On the day that his dipper scraped the bottom of the water cask Anthony Barradale first saw the lone sea gull. It was winging its way steadily above the crests of the waves.

"We are steering away from the land," said Anthony. "I have just seen a gull in flight; it will fly to land. We will follow it."

His excitement and certainty communicated themselves to the men, and they turned the boat with a will and rowed with renewed vigour.

On the second morning Anthony again exclaimed that he saw the sea gull. They looked ahead in the direction of his pointing hand and saw nothing; but they told themselves that his sight was keener than theirs and kept on their course. On this day also one of them noticed that Anthony's food and water was less than the portion of the others. He opened his mouth to protest when he was silenced by a look from Anthony. He closed his lips and bent his head, but on the third day, when Anthony again directed their course by the invisible sea gull's flight, he persuaded his fellows that he also had glimpsed the bird. He knew when a man was near death, and the signs were written on the face of the Englishman, reduced to skeleton thinness, with a flowing mane of hair and beard of a rich chestnut colour. There was a glory about this man coming so fast to the end of his life that he, and now also the others, saw; and when the grey-green eyes glinted and flashed behind the net of the long chestnut lashes and Anthony's emaciated hand pointed to the sea gull which none but he saw, their hearts were uplifted in spite of themselves and they pressed on. If death was to be the end of the quest it was as well to row on with heart and will to whatever bourne the sea gull of a dying man's vision might lead them.

They were in northern latitudes, for the Northern Lights appeared in streamers of light, leaping upwards from a rosy line above the horizon to the zenith. Long fingers played redly in the sky, edging the rippling sea.

In the next few days Anthony came to the end of the food and water. There was now only the little he had set aside from his own share for the final emergency. This he kept, and told his companions it was the last of the water and food. They rowed as usual that day, and for a part of the next day; but on the third day the languor of starvation and approaching death was on them and they huddled down in the boat and waited for the end. The boat drifted, but Anthony saw always the sea gull just ahead, and so closely at times that he could make out every detail of its wings and plumage. To add to their plight, the weather was very cold and the nights were freezing as autumn advanced.

Now there was no longer time, nor thought, nor anything but the stupor of hunger and exhaustion. Anthony fainted and lay still. Long afterwards—how long afterwards he did not know—he came to himself with the screaming of a multitude of gulls in his ears, and a down-sweeping wing brushed his cheek. He spread out his arms feebly and opened his eyes. He saw the blue sky, shredded to thin wafers between the wide white wings of the gulls, that swooped and wheeled about the boat. And the wind was strong and bore them along.

Land was near; he could smell it, and the gulls were there to lead them to it. Anthony marshalled the last shreds of his fortitude and dragged himself from man to man, giving each a little water. This was the final emergency. And when he had aroused them to the reality of the gulls and the promise that the end of the voyage was indeed in sight, they revived. These gulls were no mystic birds; they were greedy and clamorous and when each man had received his allotted portion of food he had to guard it well to keep it from the swooping sea gulls. Hope came again to them and they bent feebly to the oars, with the wind and the current to aid them. Anthony seemed to be quite certain in what direction land lay. He ordered them to alter course a little once. He did not falter or show the least sign of indecision. And for days, even weeks, there had been the miracle of the sea gull. They could not but believe.

The boat went on, and the rippling sea glittered in the sunlight.

"I want you to see that a message is sent for me when we reach land," said Anthony. "I will tell it you now so that there will be no mistake. In whatever country we land, no matter how far from England you are, you must pledge me that someone will take the message for me."

"Tell us your message. One or all of us will see that it is delivered."

They knew, as he knew, that he was dying.

"Send word to my friend, Sir Giles Mortimer of Herne House, in the county of Devon, that I am dead. Tell him the manner of my death. To my wife, Anne-Marie, I send my love. Bid Sir Giles tell her that."

He made them repeat over and over again, "Sir Giles Mortimer of Herne House, in the county of Devon," until they were word-perfect. There were no materials for writing in the boat, so that he had to rely on their memories for this last message. And when that was done his mind was quiet and he could look out for the land he knew was near.

He sighted the land first.

"Land!" he cried. He had thought he would shout the word mightily, but only a thin whisper came from between his parched lips.

They ceased rowing and looked ahead. They saw the faint green slope of distant land ahead. Oh, blessed sight!

This was the end for Anthony. He sank down in the thwarts and passed into a stupor and groaned in a dark dream. He saw Roger Dunne being blown from the mouth of the great gun on the battlements of Elmina Castle and again he lived through the agony of watching a brave man die so terribly; he was stained again with Tom's lifeblood as the body of his friend fell forward over him; he was tormented by the thought of Anne-Marie and his children, whom he had left defenceless with not a roof over their heads.

They saw he was dying, and rowed with the last reserves of their strength, and the current bore them on or they could not have done it. All through the afternoon the gulls flew about the boat, and in the evening they saw Anthony's face was quieter and he was no longer harassed by an inward distress. As the day passed the images of the hopes and the dreams that had perished fell away from him, his soul no longer sang the dirge for what had once been good and was gone, for what he had wasted of life. He saw the essential factor he had left out of his reckoning. "Before the world, was God." He had not had faith enough. He had belittled Roger Dunne and Lucas Mason and Tom Wilson by his resentment that they had given where he had not given. They had given simply and splendidly all they had to give, which was their lives; and that was the essence of living. And he belittled Anne-Marie's steadfastness and her love by his vague dread of the future; she would face whatever might arise with high courage and gather his children to her, with glory in her face and the wind in her hair as he had seen her at the South Gate of Delft. And all the while the wings of the gulls beat above his head and dispersed the mists in which he had lived for so long.

Voices spoke to him; but he heard as though from a long way off. Only the wild music of the gulls was in his ears. Then that also faded.

He opened his eyes, and again the wings of a mystic white bird spanned the heavens and sheltered him.

His eyes filmed and closed. In the frozen splendour of the frosty night he lay dying with the Northern Lights burning rosily for his passing, while his friends were borne swiftly by wind and tide, rather than by their feeble exertions, to the ever-nearing land. Anthony Barradale heard faintly, as though he were already in some far bourne beyond the stars and this was only the echo of a sound, the grating of the keel of the boat on the pebbled shores of Skye.

As he was lifted from the boat to the land he died.[1]

iv

November was a dreary month of wind and rain and fog. Bodrugan had begun to emerge from the chaos which had greeted them when they had come from Oostermeer in the spring. The cottages were occupied and the fields had been ploughed and some of them planted; and an air of order and stability was beginning to be evident about the place.

They had done well, Anna van Breda thought as she trudged home through the mist, with the hedges dark and wet with the fine rain, and her clogs sucking into the muddy track from the paddock to the farmyard. The cost of getting some semblance of order into the place had been heavy, not so much in money as in continuous strain. Anne-Marie had sunk herself in quiet grief; and from her watching and waiting for Anthony, or news of him, she would seldom rouse herself to anything that called for thought or concentration. She was content to leave the management of everything to Anna, and visits from neither Anthony's relatives nor from the kindly people of Falmouth could take her out of herself. Lately, however, she had begun to come into the room when Sir Giles Mortimer called. He had helped Anna a great deal with the farm through the summer and the autumn, and he was a great favourite with the children.

There were, however, tidings from the Gold Coast. Anna had at last had a letter from Ryk, forwarded from Amsterdam when Minetje had sent her another little box of guilders. Ryk wrote at great length and very cheerfully. They had reached the Gold Coast without untoward incident, he said, and in spite of hostility from the Portuguese they had founded their settlements and had every intention of maintaining them. All went well, wrote Ryk. Their relations with the inhabitants were very friendly, and they had already done something towards alleviating the distress the natives endured from their sicknesses. He was in good

[1]According to Elias's *Book of Polar Exploration* Barendz's expedition kept together, escaped shipwreck, and after much suffering reached the shores of Lapland, journeying from there to the Hague, where they landed in October 1597, after an absence of about eighteen months. Anthony Barradale is an imaginary character, and for the purposes of my story I have taken the liberty of deviating from the historical narrative and have split the expedition as I have described.—B.K.

health, only once having been stricken with tropical fever, but his companions had not fared so well, and he lamented that already there were several deaths to report. He hoped that Anna was well and not doing the work of everyone; he prayed her to bear in mind her age, "to be careful of yourself, my mother, as I have always striven to be careful and loving to you when I have been home." He mentioned Charlotte and was glad she was at Oostermeer; of Minetje and Pieter and his other daughters he wrote lovingly. He remembered also Anne-Marie and prayed that Anthony had returned safely from the Northeast Passage expedition. And finally he sent messages to Dirk to be given when she saw him again.

As she walked slowly back to the house Anna's thoughts were far from the muddy track and the wet hedges, and the heifer she had been looking at in the paddock. She was picturing Ryk's life on the Gold Coast and wondering what had become of Anthony and for how much longer Anne-Marie could bear the terrible strain. The rolling world went on and how little she knew of it. She thought of the mysterious North Pole as a region of snow and ice, a place for trolls and strange magic; and the Gold Coast seemed to be very much the same except that the heat was intense there and pioneers were likely to be devoured by cannibals instead of polar bears. It would have been so much easier for their womenfolk, Anna reflected, if the men of her family had settled down in comfort and security instead of sailing to unknown seas and uncharted lands. It was not always clear to their women why they endured hardships and dangers, yet the older she grew the more she realized that the exploring spirit, the frankly adventurous spirit, or the swashbuckling trader's spirit, were behind this urge for expansion and exploration. And this urge was the sign of the times they lived in, the great, grand times. And it was right that the men should fare forth or the race would lose its heritage and perish, for it is imagination and the pursuit of the ideal that add riches to life. Thinking these thoughts, Anna felt the blood stir and flow freely in her veins. Ach, life was rich and good! There had been hard years, but she had enjoyed them all. In her old age life was sweet and full and teeming with the interest of her family circle. She had pleasure in her son, her grandchildren, and her great-grandchildren. What a good thing it was I hung onto that tower in the flood, she told herself. If I had not got angry in time I might have let go, and how annoyed I should have been to have missed all this. . . .

She walked on in the dusk with her head held high and the soft, cold rain on her face.

She saw a horse was fastened to the gatepost. Sir Giles Mortimer's tall, bulky figure loomed out of the misty rain, walking towards her.

"I heard you were out in the fields and I have been waiting for you," he said. "I wanted to see you alone."

A man did not wait in the cold rain unless he had a grave reason, thought Anna; and she felt her nerves quiver and stiffen again in anticipation of some shock.

"What is it?" she said.

"Anthony Barradale is dead."

"Word has come at last," said Anna brokenly. "She knows; she has known for some time in her heart."

Her thoughts of high adventure and the lure and fascination of far places and strange climes fell away from her as though she had slipped a cloak of gold brocade off her shoulders to lie in the mud at her feet. She drew her shoulders in and shuddered in the cold, damp rain.

"How was it?" she asked.

The vitality had drained from her voice; it was flat and dead like the dreary autumnal evening.

"A Scot came down from the north to tell me. He came from the isle of Skye beyond Scotland. A boat grounded on the shores of Skye a short time ago and in the boat were six men, five of whom were alive, and the sixth died as he came ashore. When the survivors had recovered sufficiently they made this man, Angus MacDonald, understand that he must come to me, 'Sir Giles Mortimer of Herne House, in the county of Devon,' and tell me Anthony Barradale was dead. MacDonald could tell me no more than that because the Dutchmen spoke no English. They knew my name and where I lived, and Anthony's name; but that was all. MacDonald described the man who had died as they came ashore; and indeed it was Anthony Barradale he described."

He put his arm round Anna's shoulders.

"You will tell her, will you not?" he asked pityingly.

She nodded. Her voice quivered when she spoke.

"Twice in my life I will have told Anne-Marie that Anthony is dead. This time it will be true, beyond all doubt. Twice is too much."

"Shall I tell her?"

"No, she will take it best from me."

He said no more, but held her closely while she trembled against him.

"Go now," said Anna at last. "I will tell her."

Now she felt every year of her age. Three score years and ten was man's allotted span, and she was in the last decade.

Like a very tired, very old woman she went into the house.

v

All through that winter Anna could do nothing with Anne-Marie. She was a creature at bay, wild with pain. Having tried everything but a direct appeal to reason, Anna decided on plain speaking.

One evening when they were sitting in the winter parlour Anna seized her opportunity. "You will have to marry again, Anne-Marie," said she, joining battle without preamble.

Anne-Marie gazed at her in astonishment.

"Did you hear what I said?" asked Anna.

"Yes," said Anne-Marie incredulously. "But I cannot believe it."

"It is sound common sense, and you have no alternative."

Anne-Marie flushed with anger and consternation. Anna had never spoken so authoritatively before; and this was a vital matter.

"You also were left a widow, my grandmother," said Anne-Marie. "And you did not marry again."

"My circumstances were entirely different. I was forty, my children were men, and I had a house of my own even if it was under the water. There was no reason for me to marry again unless I wished. I had no young children dependent on me, in fact Ryk was helping me then as he does now, and I could work for my relations if I made my home with them. In my opinion, Anne-Marie, there is nothing you can do except to find a good man to help you rear your children."

"No," said Anne-Marie thickly. "No, no."

"Do you understand your circumstances, Anne-Marie?"

Anne-Marie's head drooped.

"I have left everything to you, my grandmother," she said at last. "It was very cowardly not to face the facts squarely. Yet now Bodrugan begins to look quite prosperous with the tenants and the cows, and the fields being tilled."

"If it were not for the mortgage, Anne-Marie, there might be a possibility of living here; but to pay that is more than I can do. As for the rest, this Bodrugan is beyond my small ideas of how to run a farm. I have done no more than put a rough patch over the worst, and already it is fraying at the sides again. And all along they have threatened to foreclose, but I have made them wait for news of Anthony. We know now that Anthony is dead, and the expedition was a total loss."

"Actually, how have you managed? It is best for me to know."

"In his extravagant fashion my dear Ryk left me very well provided for before he left. He set me up for the rest of my life in wine and brandy and guilders. The wine and brandy may go on maturing at Oostermeer, but the money I am using now. I am very glad to be able to spend this money here where it is needed because I have enough of my own to live on quietly at Oostermeer, and Ryk really left it for just such emergencies in the family. Why I have mentioned money at all is that I see everything being paid out all the time and nothing coming in, and only a fool does not pause to take stock when that happens. So I have paused."

"How much have you spent?"

"That is no concern of yours—now or in the future. The money I have used here was Ryk's gift to me, and it in no way alters my circumstances that I have spent some of it. Ryk is very wealthy and such a little sum does not affect him. There are one or two occasions in one's life when you accept the help of others, Anne-Marie, and do not talk or think of repayment. It is a rare grace in a woman to recognize these occasions and to act graciously. Be gracious, my child, to Ryk and me."

Anne-Marie stared into the fire and Anna saw she was struggling against her emotion.

"I will go on," said Anna. "I have thought and thought about your affairs, wondering what to do. The only members of the family with much money are Minetje and Ryk. The mortgage must be paid. You can expect no help from James Carey or Martin Thomas. Their families are large and they have not the means. If we put it to him Ryk would help you; but I do not think it fair to ask, as you have had your inheritance, which has been swallowed up in this same Bodrugan. And if the mortgage were paid, my heart, what of the future? You have three young children to support and to start off in the world, and you want a man to run this big farm. So there you are, up against the husband to run Bodrugan if only for no other reason."

"If I can avoid it I do not wish to marry again."

"I wondered if you could give up here and live in Holland," Anna continued remorselessly. "But there are so many factors to consider. You are Dutch by birth, but you were reared in England and in your ways you are thoroughly English. Your children are a mixture of the two races, but they are also English in their thoughts and upbringing. The transplanting would be hard on both you and your children if it were permanent—a holiday is another matter. And where would you live in Holland, and what would you do? Anne-Marie, to live and to bring up your children on the bounty of others is a hard life. I do not wish it for you. You have been a guest in your uncle Ryk's house in Amsterdam. It is not the house for young children. Minetje and Ryk would be kind to you, but it would not really suit you."

"Yes, we could not live in Amsterdam," said Anne-Marie.

"Oostermeer is my own. I should dearly love to have you and the children always with me, but I am not so young, and there are Jan and Juliana and their family to consider. Juliana is a dear, good girl and also my granddaughter. Gerard and Jan reclaimed Oostermeer for me after the flood; they brought it back from nothing while I was away in Delft for thirteen years nursing my sister-in-law. It was a time of great struggle, but we won through. In common decency I cannot expect Jan and Juliana to leave Oostermeer, although Jan now has his own land since his father died. There is not room for us all, and we would have to hire men and do some of the hard work ourselves. But, apart from these matters, there is a grave reason why you should not live at Oostermeer with us, Anne-Marie."

"What is that, Grandmother?"

How tired she is, thought Anna. How hard I am!

"Anne-Marie, you are almost broken," said Anna, too stricken to go on. "I haven't the heart to talk any more. I also didn't want to remarry."

"No, let us talk it over, now we have begun."

"Have you ever looked carefully at yourself in a mirror, Anne-Marie?"

"Why, yes," said Anne-Marie, very surprised.

"You are alarmingly beautiful, and a menace to peaceful homes wherever you go," said Anna in so forthright a fashion that Anne-Marie stared at her in amazement. "You have no hope of remaining single. You are only twenty-seven and there will be no peace until you are settled again. If I had not got you away from Oostermeer just in time I shudder to think what might not have happened."

"Grandmother!"

"You are genuinely astonished, and quite ignorant of what goes on around you. You never see anything because you are so lost in your thoughts of Anthony. Do you remember that Jan hoped to marry you if Anthony did not come back from the Gold Coast?"

"Yes, but that was a long time ago," said Anne-Marie.

"Only ten years ago, and men do not forget in ten years. Anthony came back that time, and Gerard persuaded Jan to marry Juliana, so all seemed well. However, in the first year of Jan's marriage Gerard and I had many anxious moments. Juliana is a fine woman, but she is not Anne-Marie, and men do not always take thankfully to substitutes."

"I did not dream of this."

"Not so much as a whisper has ever been heard of it until now," said Anna. "We were anxious, but we kept quiet. Lourens was born, and his brother, and his little sister, and all was well at Oostermeer. You came again to Oostermeer, Anne-Marie, and how gladly I welcomed you, my heart! Again you waited for Anthony. The same situation twice over, and don't you think Jan's thoughts turned to the first time when he hoped you would eventually be his wife? We were secretly very disturbed, Gerard and I, when Jan came back from Cadiz. As time went on I watched the look on Jan's face when he saw you, or when we mentioned you. I saw Juliana look from you to Jan and it was plain she was becoming unsettled and unhappy. Only you, Anne-Marie, knew nothing of these dangerous undercurrents at Oostermeer."

"I swear I knew nothing. Juliana and I are friends."

"You would not have been friends for much longer if you had remained at Oostermeer. And, bear in mind, with you a widow Jan is going to think about you quite often."

"I cannot be expected to change my life just because Jan van Braam chooses to think of me," said Anne-Marie. "It is not reasonable."

"Neither men nor their jealous wives are reasonable. And there was Dirk. Dirk was thoroughly unsettled when he used to take you up and down the Schie when we were in Delft. But fortunately he is very sensible, and I am sure he often congratulates himself now on not having got entangled with such a beautiful witch."

"I don't know what to make of you. You are mocking me now."

"I am really a little ashamed of myself," said Anna. "I should have left you alone. I would never mock you. I am just showing you the side of yourself we see. And there is a third man I could mention——"

"I know," said Anne-Marie.

"He mends broken gates and pays the greatest attention to an old Dutch countrywoman in clogs," pursued Anna. "He also sells me cows at far below their value and sends tenants at the right time. I asked Bess Barrow what English cattle cost because I did not want to pay too much for the heifers, and one must be careful. And I knew he asked far too little. I knew also that it would never do if he discovered how wise I had become in the matter of market prices, so I was gracious and even did a little haggling when it came to paying to make him quite comfortable in his mind. Actually I got the worst of it because he at once took ten guilders off the price, and I felt terrible!"

"You overreached yourself there," said Anne-Marie, smiling.

She knelt before the hearth and mended the fire, and held up her hands to the blaze. She said over her shoulder to Anna:

"I will not leap up and accuse you of trying to sell me to Sir Giles. I know you are only struggling to show me the way before me because you cannot help me much longer. And you are quite right: he would be very kind and good to me."

Anne-Marie had taken it so well that Anna was overcome with remorse. She fell on her knees beside her and also held out her hands to the fire.

"Look at my hand, Anne-Marie," she said, "and then look at your own. The hands are the same. In many ways we are the same; but you are kinder and more gentle than I am, like your mother was. If ever you have another daughter, call her Liesbet, to perpetuate the memory of your mother. Even when I was forty I was very vain. I delighted to have men tell me I was beautiful, and to know I had only to snap my fingers to have them at my feet. Ach, yes, I was vain, I admit it. Although I had no intention of remarrying I kept them dangling, judiciously dangling, and I did not have too dreary a widowhood. As we grew older these would-be lovers were my kind friends. But these calm friendships with men are not for you, at least not yet. If it is not Sir Giles, it will be another. You are more appealing and attractive than ever I was. With all your looks you have been a devoted wife. With your face, Anne-Marie, I would have flirted outrageously. I know it. Virtue in a plain woman is somehow expected, but in a lovely woman it is precious indeed. I admire you more than I can say for your steadfastness. I know you loved Anthony. I realize you do not wish to marry again. I have spoken hard words of sound common sense tonight. Forget them. I will ask Ryk to redeem the mortgage when he comes back. He will do it for you. And I will live here and help you, my heart, until I die."

"No. You are right. I will think this over, my grandmother. But give me time."

"I will never force you. There is no question of time. I will tell you something for your comfort, Anne-Marie. My Prince said it to me once in my dark hour and I will pass it on to you. He said, 'All passes, even pain.' It is true; I have proved it."

"I will tell you why I am so unhappy. It is not altogether because I have lost Anthony; it is what has been happening all the years since we parted and I went to Oostermeer and he to the Gold Coast. You know how we found Bodrugan. I thought it would be as we found it, although he never suggested to me what he had done. You have never said an unkind word about Anthony, and heaven knows you could justly have said a great deal when you saw how he had left me and the children."

"I know so little of Anthony, so I cannot decide why he should have left this chaos. However, one essential has always been perfectly clear to me: I spoke of it to your uncle Ryk when he came back from the Gold Coast and said Anthony had died there. Ryk said that perhaps it had all happened for the best, as Anthony was unstable and your life might have been far from easy married to him—well, as it is now. I answered that I had cause to know that you loved Anthony, and I believed that such constancy as yours was never wasted on someone unworthy of it. In spite of all the evidence to the contrary I still believe that, Anne-Marie. I am waiting to see both sides before I judge."

"Thank you, my grandmother, for that. I also have yet to see both sides, although he was my husband and we were dear to each other. He never would confide in me about those years on the Gold Coast, and he was always restless and dissatisfied about what had happened there. He would tell me nothing, but he relied on me to believe in him blindly. My feet have always been planted on the solid earth. I was the stable thing in his life. He was dreamy and imaginative and he loved me. His one cry was 'Have faith in me.' And I have had faith in him. When we came back to Bodrugan I knew I should never see him again. I was sure of it. I still did not know what was at the root of his restlessness; I was always in the dark. Now I have been told he is dead. I do not know how he died or whether he was at peace when he died. I shall probably never know what it was that had eluded him all those years. I should be happy if I knew he had arrived at some settlement of his problem. But, as it is, I can only think about him, and my thoughts are so dark."

"Keep your faith, Anne-Marie. Whatever alse you may let go, hold to that."

"I shall aways believe in Anthony," said Anne-Marie. "If only I knew he had died with a quiet mind!"

And once Ryk had tried to stem this steadfastness by burning a letter, Anna thought. Being a good Dutchman, he ought to have been wiser. The rolling sea could not be stopped with a basketful of earth, and at times even a dyke could not hold back the waters. In spite of all that had happened and might still happen, she knew it was a good thing that the flood tide of Anne-Marie's devotion had never for a moment been turned. Anne-Marie had pleaded for time. She could have a whole life-time if she desired it, for she would never urge her to a remarriage again. It was for Anne-Marie herself to shape her future.

PART XVIII

GOLD COAST INTERLUDE

IN THE VILLAGE OF THE AWOINS, IN THE CUPLIKE DEPRESSION BELOW Abrobi hill, the heat boiled up in the hollow like a cauldron of molten metal. The green jungle shrouded the swamps and crept up to the compounds, and the continuous war against its encroachment went on in the cleared spaces where the tribe dwelt. But Abrobi Hill was vividly green, covered with dense, tangled vegetation, for no foot was ever set upon its haunted slopes.

The Dutchmen sat on low stools in the compound of the Awoin Chief. The Chief himself sat on a high stool with the crown of light silver-gilt metal they had presented to him on his head. Negotiations had been opened and the palaver could begin.

The elders of the tribe were gathered about the Chief; and the fetish priests held a watching brief in the background. They drank the sweet, sticky red wine the Dutchmen had brought, and naked small boys fanned them with palm leaves.

Ryk van Breda was the spokesman for the Dutch.

"We are here, as you know, for the purpose of peaceful trade. We want no slaves and we wish that there should be no intertribal warfare to capture slaves. We will defend you against the Portuguese if necessary, even to the extent of providing arms and ammunition for your fighting men. And you have proof that these are no empty words, O Chief. We have our lodges at Mori, at Kormantin and Butri; we will not sail away in our ships and leave you to face the vengeance of the Portuguese. Your elders have visited us in our lodges. They will testify that there is every indication that we mean to remain here on the Gold Coast."

"It is as you say," replied the Chief of the Awoins. "These signs are indeed evident, and they have been reported to me."

Ryk was glad they had all made an attempt at learning the native dialect. He was quite fluent, and he had found one did better in these palavers if language was no obstacle.

"We are here to develop trade," Ryk continued. "We must have the means to support our enterprise. The most profitable trade is in gold. We have waited upon you, therefore, to discuss the reopening of the Abrobi mine."

If he had dropped an adder in their midst the consternation could not have been greater.

The elders and the fetish priests crowded round the Chief, and there was much confused and excited comment. Ryk gathered that his request had provoked a frenzied controversy. At last they seemed to reach some conclusion. The Chief waved his followers back and addressed the delegation from the lodge at Mori.

"What you ask is impossible," he said. "The Great One of the hill was not appeased. The sacrifices made were not acceptable. The sasabonsum has exacted a terrible vengeance. If he is provoked again there will be another earthquake. The land has been quiet these ten years and more. The earth and the heavens will tremble again if the sasabonsum is disturbed."

"There is a matter I must put before you," said Ryk, beginning a carefully planned and well-rehearsed scheme of persuasion. In one way he was loath to play upon the credulity and superstitious awe of the African, but as the gold trade was essential for the maintenance of their lodges on the Gold Coast, he felt there was no alternative. "I have had speech with Kwaku, Ohene of the Kormantins, on this same matter, which greatly concerns him. I will begin my palaver: in the jungle you cut a track and men walk along it, and it is a known way. Consider now the oceans and the seas where no roads are. Ponder well the miracle of the white man's ships that, with sails spread, fly before the winds of heaven, pursuing unerringly a path where no path is. The white man says, 'I shall journey to the Gold Coast.' He stands at the other end of the world when he says this. He boards his ship and sets sail. There is no track to follow, yet he reaches the Gold Coast all the same. That is the white man's navigation. There is a wizardry in this art of navigation that only the white man knows; he reads it in the stars. In the stars there are many hidden things, matters which are not always visible even to the fetish priests."

"I acknowledge the mystery of the stars," said the Chief of the Awoins. "But what have the stars and their riddles to do with the opening of the Abrobi mine?"

"I will deal now with the earthquake you mentioned," said Ryk. "My ship was lying off your shores on the night it occurred. It was on a night of most brilliant moonlight. Perhaps you can recall how bright that night was?"

There was a chorus of assent. The night of the earthquake was unforgettable in its beauty and because of the havoc that had been wrought.

"Yes," said the Chief. "We remember that night."

"On my ship all was quiet," Ryk went on sombrely. "I studied the stars, planning my homeward way. That night there was a strange design in the stars, and I did not see my course. Instead I was permitted to know that an earthquake was about to occur and to know why it would occur. If the fetish priests had but observed it the design of the sasabonsum was written in the heavens that night, but very faintly, as the moon was so bright. Only those well versed in the lore of the stars could have read the signs."

The high priest stepped out from the ranks of the fetish priests and advanced towards Ryk.

"This is a challenge," he screamed. "Is the white man's magic greater than our own?"

"I have not said it," returned Ryk. "It was just that I watched while you slept."

"Let the white man continue without interruption," said the Chief. "This is a grave matter."

"This is what I saw in the stars," Ryk went on impressively. "Three white men lay bound in the shaft of Abrobi mine, waiting till the dawn when they were to be sacrificed. They were the offering for the appeasement of the sasabonsum who had been offended by the working of the mine. As I watched at the dead of night I saw the Great One, the sasabonsum, rise up from the bowels of the red earth. So mighty was this Great One that his shadow was in the heavens. He found the offering acceptable. He bore all three sacrificial victims down with him to the depths of the earth, so that not one vestige of the men was left in the shaft—no bone, no wisp of hair, not so much as a fingernail. His wrath was appeased. All was quiet, and Abrobi Hill lay peaceful in the moonlight."

"The Great One was not appeased," broke in the high priest. "He sent an earthquake to convulse the earth."

"You slept that night," said Ryk pityingly. "I did not sleep. I saw another shadow in the heavens. It was the shadow of a monstrous injustice. The sasabonsum stirred and the earth shook. There was a very old woman in the forest and she lamented and called upon the Great One to avenge her. This woman was Aba, the aged Queen Mother of the Kormantins."

Ryk had his audience with him now. The breath of the crowd was expelled in a prolonged "Ha!"

"She was of the blood royal," said Ryk, warming to his theme, "and her tribe had turned her out. She cried that she might die and be buried according to custom, not left to perish in the jungle. The Great One heard her. He himself saw that she received death and burial according to ancient custom as befitted one of her rank and state. He led her to Abrobi Hill and there he sealed her mighty tomb and sent forth the earthquake that members of her family and her tribe should die with her and accompany her on her journey from the earth."

"Your proof," screamed the high priest. "Your proof! Did not I myself bind the cords on the three white men and leave them in Abrobi Hill? Did I not?"

He twisted and writhed in a hideous dance and appealed to his fellow priests and the priestesses of the fetish. They leapt and howled and screeched in frenzied support of their leader.

"The proof lies in Abrobi Hill," said Ryk stoutly. "There you will find only the sacred bones of Aba, the Queen Mother of the Kormantins, and you shall know that she lies there, for she will have with her her golden ornaments and the armlets of beaten gold. Now then, let us put it to the test, and, if it is not as I have said, do with me as you will. And one more thing: I have spoken of these matters with Kwaku, Ohene of the Kormantins, and he desires that the bones of his grandmother should rest in their rightful place in the tribal burial ground. And he has said that his young men will do the work of excavation if your young men are fearful. And he is even now on his way to confer with you."

"This matter will need much debating," said the Chief of the Awoins.

"There is one matter I have left to the last; and it is the reason why I have sought this palaver. Tremble, O Chief of the Awoins, for there is a warning shadow again in the stars. I have seen it, and this time I have come to you so that disaster may be averted. The shadow of the Mighty One is in the heavens. Now it is that Aba, the Queen Mother, must lie in the burial place of her tribe, so that the injustice may be finally wiped out. All this have I told Kwaku. Therefore he comes to you."

This was the moment to end the palaver, Ryk decided. He therefore requested that he and his companions might withdraw for a time to their camp in the shadow of Abrobi Hill until the Chief summoned him again.

Ryk van Breda walked with a young man, Barend Coetzee. They were often together. Ryk always made a point of discussing everything with the younger man—his present plans, and the action he thought they ought to take in the future—almost as though he were training him to deputize for him someday.

They discussed the palaver that had just ended.

"I think you risked a great deal," said Barend. "I admit you were quite sure of your ground when you said nothing of the white men would be found in the mine; but you have no guarantee that the old Queen Mother did not escape."

"Anthony was sure she did not follow them out of the mine. He saw the golden ornaments, and Kwaku gave me a good description of them. When the mine is opened up I am sure that her bones will be found, poor old woman."

"I should not have thought the story out so well," said Barend. "It sounded very convincing."

"If you are left in charge here I advise you always to put a bold face on your weakest schemes. Impressiveness counts enormously. We play upon the natural superstition of the native but we know the mine caved in because the props were ant-eaten and the shafts were badly supported.

If we can persuade the Awoins to open up the mine we must guard against accidents. We must use the soundest timber and build the main shafts solidly. The local timber is magnificent stuff. We need a sawmill. It is an industry we might well think of starting, here, near the mine. The heavier logs might be floated down to the sea in the rivers. This is a country to develop, Barend. The possibilities are infinite."

They often talked earnestly in this fashion, paving the way for the more ambitious operations they hoped to put through in the years to come.

ii

A few days later the young men of the Kormantin tribe began to hack away the dense growth of shrub and creeper on Abrobi Hill. They swung their cutlasses and sang in rhythm as they cut through the undergrowth, while the heat haze from the steaming jungle rose up about them and the stagnant vegetation threw off fetid odours as they cleared it from the red earth of the hillside. The great boulders were rolled down the slope and soon the mouth of the former shaft was discovered and the work of excavation began in earnest.

They cut into the heart of the hill and the loads of red slush and earth were poured down the hillside while a deep penetration was made. Then the time came when the young men handed over picks and shovels to the Dutchmen, and the fetish priests drew near to watch the secret of the mine laid bare. They were now working at the end of the shaft where once the galleries had branched off in many directions.

Barend Coetzee's shovel came into contact with some hard object. He fell on his knees and by the light of the flickering lamp the priests held he began to explore the crumbling earth with his fingers. He uncovered a bone. His comrades came to his assistance. Carefully they scraped away the earth, not disturbing what lay beneath it until at last they had uncovered a small human skeleton, the stained grey bones of the arms outlined with armlets of beaten gold, so dull and discoloured that it was difficult to tell of what metal they had been fashioned; and by the skeleton lay also a little pile of anklets and rings, that must have been fastened together in a corner of a piece of cloth that had long since mouldered away and left them piled up near the fleshless hand of the dead.

iii

"Until we hold this fortress there will be no end to our troubles."

Ryk van Breda uttered these words from his point of vantage on St. Jago's Hill. He lay prone upon the ground with Barend Coetzee beside him. They were concealed in the vegetation and were looking down upon the fortress of San Jorge del Mina from above.

"The fort can be carried from St. Jago's Hill," said Barend. "The weakness is here. We have said before that the castle is impregnable but I think the northeast bastion could be taken by storm."

"The States-General must be persuaded to send a small army," said Ryk. "And that they will never do while the war with Spain goes on. And we cannot follow up our successes out here without adequate military support. The opening of the Abrobi mine was a triumph. Our prestige was greatly enhanced because of that success. The Portuguese were unable to get the mine opened up; neither threats nor tortures availed them there; but we did it peacefully by guile. But how to stop these raids from the Portuguese I do not know. Now that I see Elmina I know we have no hope of stopping the mischief at its source. Our strength is not sufficient. There is nothing for it but to guard the gold convoys from Abrobi and to beat off attacks."

"We cannot storm Elmina, but I see its weaknesses. I should build a strong fort on the summit of this St. Jago's Hill, with at least four batteries and a tower. It would be the key to the castle."

"And I would make the fortress accessible to ships," said Ryk. "I would build a stone bridge, with a wooden drawbridge in its centre, across the river Benya, and cut a wide road from it to the new fort. And on this side of the fortress I would construct a battery and mount it with at least six guns, and raise a second smaller battery on that hill yonder as an additional protection to it. Stone walls would be built along the banks of the Benya so that it would be a wide canal, a narrow harbour for small vessels. They could enter and pass through the drawbridge and refit under the guns of the castle. Barend, as soon as we get back to Mori, draw a plan of these fortifications and improvements. It may come in useful sooner than we think. In any event the suggestions may prove of value to those who come after us. You are a skilled draftsman. You will be sure to set it all down? And make a note that you and I made our way to this hill to plan an attack on this fortress but came to the conclusion that we had not the strength to attack it."

"I will set it all down."

"We can at least hold our lodges here," said Ryk. "With only a little help from Holland we could be supreme out here. But it would be asking too much, as their hands are tied in the Netherlands."

"There is one thing that may hinder us from maintaining the position out here we have struggled to gain," said Barend with evident reluctance to throw a shadow on Ryk's enthusiasm. "I speak of the climate. It is our most formidable enemy, something we can neither storm nor beguile."

"No remedies seem to avail against this coast fever," Ryk admitted. "I have wondered whether, if the system gets saturated with it, in the end one does not become immune. The inhabitants seem to survive. But I must confess I feel disquieted when I hear the natives speak of Mori as the 'cemetery,' because of the numbers of our people who have died there."

"You yourself have frequent attacks. Will you not return to Holland on this next ship and come out again later when your health is better? You might be able to persuade the States-General that the conquest of Elmina is of the greatest importance. Your influence is considerable in Amsterdam. I can carry on until you return."

"I will think of it," said Ryk. "But I could not sail very soon. I want to see the mine in a really flourishing condition; and, at all costs, we must honour our obligations and defend the friendly tribes against the Portuguese. As soon as these matters are well in hand I shall sail."

Barend Coetzee refrained from further argument. It was evident that Ryk van Breda, well on in middle age, was in a low state of health. The coast fever had sapped his vitality in the past few months and his vigour had begun to fail, yet he continued his work, never giving in until he was completely prostrated. Barend registered a mental vow that, should Ryk van Breda be laid low with one of his recurrent bouts of fever when a ship was due to leave for Holland, he would take the responsibility of having him carried aboard her. The cemetery at Mori was filling up all too rapidly, and their commandant was not a man they could afford to lose. He kept his thoughts and his resolution to himself, and they did not speak for some little while as they began to worm their way back through the undergrowth on St. Jago's Hill to where a contingent of their own men and some armed Kormantins were anxiously awaiting their return.

Before they descended the other side of the hill Ryk paused on the brow of the slope and looked back at the castle of San Jorge del Mina. The massive pile stood scarred yet impregnable, with its bastions laved by the warm tide of the sea and its batteries menacing both roadstead and the jungle-covered slopes of the land. He wished, gazing down on the fortress, that it might be given him to see that proud citadel fall into their hands.

He had accomplished much; but there was the little more he longed to gain.

PART XIX

CORNISH INTERLUDE

CHAPTER THIRTY-FIVE

IN CORNWALL THE WINTER ENDED, AND SPRING CAME AND PASSED INTO early summer. Anna was still at Bodrugan, holding onto a hopeless situation with determination and grim self-mockery. Anne-Marie drifted on and there was no change in her unhappiness. Anna had begun to realize that nothing short of a miracle would bring about an adjustment in Anne-Marie's emotional affairs.

In Spain Philip lay on his deathbed. "He had aspired to universal sovereignty, and he was now passing away from all authority and all power."[1]

At this time also Heemskerk was crossing from Amsterdam to Falmouth, the same Heemskerk who had survived a winter in Nova Zembla and had navigated the Arctic seas in an open boat and was destined to become as great a scourge to Spain as Drake, the Englishman, had been. But now he was on no adventurous quest: he had a sad office to perform, a visit of condolence to Anne-Marie Barradale.

On the afternoon he arrived at Bodrugan Anna van Breda had walked to Falmouth. He had set out for the farm while she was in the hamlet, unaware of his coming, so they missed each other.

Anna took her time walking homewards. It was a clear afternoon with a blue sky. The drowsy warmth and the scents of summer were in the air. Honeysuckle bloomed in the hedges and bees droned. It was an afternoon for pleasant, nostalgic thoughts and peaceful sauntering.

As she came up the narrow lane she heard the farmyard gate open and swing to with a crash. Anne-Marie appeared at the other end of the high-hedged lane, running towards her, her arms outstretched, capless and with her hair beginning to fall about her shoulders, her face alight and radiant, and shining through her tears.

Anna stopped dead in amazement.

"Anne-Marie!" she cried.

[1] J. E. Thorold Rogers, *Holland*.

Anne-Marie came up to her sobbing, and flung her arms around her. "My grandmother!"

"Anne-Marie, what is it? What has happened?"

"He will tell you—he is there at Bodrugan in the winter parlour," said Anne-Marie wildly. "I left him and ran to find you. He—Heemskerk. He was with Barendz and Anthony in the Arctic on Nova Zembla. He came to tell me how gloriously Anthony died. Anthony died happy, my grandmother. He was at peace, satisfied. I had to know that before I could be reconciled. I am so proud. I can go on now and do my part. I could not before, but now I can be as courageous as Anthony. Anthony is dead; but I have his sons, two of them. And I shall care for them. Do my best for them. That I can do for Anthony. This money business can all be put right, and I shall pay some attention to it now. I am proud. I can do anything now. . . ."

Anne-Marie's face was transfigured. Anna was very moved. She tried to understand what had happened.

"When did Heemskerk come?" she asked.

"Not so long ago. He walked out from Falmouth ahead of you."

If only she had started a little earlier, thought Anna. This seafarer, the explorer Heemskerk, had walked her road and had wrought a miracle. . . .

"I hardly know what I am saying," cried Anne-Marie. "It has overwhelmed me. Go in to him and he will tell you. I can go on now. Before I could not live under that cloud of uncertainty. Anthony brought them to land. You will also be proud when you hear all, my grandmother."

"Will you not tell me, Anne-Marie?"

"I could not now. I want to go to Pendennis where Anthony and I often walked together. He saw the sea gull at Pendennis, and it was a sea gull that brought him home. That was a strange thing; but Heemskerk will tell you about the sea gulls. And, later on, come to Pendennis."

Anne-Marie withdrew herself from Anna's restraining hands.

"I'll wait for you at Pendennis," she said.

She began to run down the lane and slowed down to a walk at the end of it. Anna looked after her until she was out of sight. Then she turned and went quickly towards the house.

ii

Those who saw Anne-Marie Barradale walk down to Pendennis with a white radiance on her face fell back when they saw her. They wondered what had happened to send her roaming there alone, but, although they were anxious, they left her to herself. Later, when they saw her grandmother follow her, they were relieved, knowing that now all would be well.

Anna found Anne-Marie sitting on the grass on Pendennis headland. She was quiet and smiling; but Anna saw that she had wept much. The setting sun spread a broad carpet of gold over the rippling sea, and the gulls wheeled and screamed above them.

Anna sank down on the grass beside Anne-Marie. They looked into each other's eyes.

"You can be very proud, Anne-Marie," said Anna.

"I am content now," answered Anne-Marie.

They were silent then, each thinking her own thoughts.

"I will marry Sir Giles," said Anne-Marie, breaking the silence. "I will not be sacrificing myself, do not think it. I shall be happy with him and I shall not be lonely. I could not marry again until I was content about Anthony."

"I am very glad, Anne-Marie."

"I came here to listen to the wind and the sea," said Anne-Marie.

"To take your farewell of Anthony."

"How well you understand!"

They smiled at each other; and again there was a long silence between them.

At last Anne-Marie roused herself from her reverie.

"You will see Sir Giles, will you not, my grandmother? I want Bodrugan for Gilbert. But I will leave the negotiations to you."

"I will send a message and ask him to come at once," said Anna. "And this time I must be careful not to overreach myself or I shall have Herne House as well!"

Anne-Marie laughed aloud.

"Whatever should I do without you, my grandmother?" she said.

"That's better," said Anna. "That's better."

They stretched out their hands to each other, laughing and weeping together.

Years afterwards, when Anne-Marie Barradale was the wife of Sir Giles Mortimer and a great lady and the mistress of a fine mansion, the people of Falmouth would recall how she and her grandmother went home to Bodrugan together, two women of exceptional beauty. They walked from Pendennis in the golden summer's evening with their arms round each other's waists and their faces quiet and smiling.

It was a memory that lingered long in the minds of Falmouth folk.

PART XX

ḢOLLAND

THE COAST OF ENGLAND FELL BEHIND AS THE LITTLE SHIP CLOVE HER way through the North Sea and set her course for Holland. Hand in hand with Lourens, Anna had watched the shores of England fade; then she had turned her face to look across the blue waves to where home lay. Sometimes in the sixteen months she had been away she had ached with longing and loneliness for home, for the sight of four-towered gates and old bastions, and the green, flat land and the canals, and the clear light that poured from the heavens over Holland. All was well with Anne-Marie. She was married again, and her future and her children's was settled and assured. Sir Giles had placed a tenant farmer on Bodrugan until Gilbert should come of age, and Anne-Marie and her family had moved to Devon. Her work in England was done, thought Anna, and soon her longing for home would be assuaged.

Dirk had been very thoughtful. She had asked James Carey to arrange for a passage for herself and Lourens on any craft bound for Holland. However, before he had found berths for them, Dirk had put in at Plymouth. He had unloaded cargo and taken more on board for Amsterdam, but Anna felt he had arranged his business this way for her convenience. He would not be drawn into conversation. At Plymouth he had been taciturn and had avoided mention of the family, except for a brief remark that all at Oostermeer and in Amsterdam were well. Anna had asked if there was news of Ryk. He had replied briefly:

"I have not had a letter from him for a long while."

He had walked away at once and Anna had had to be content with this somewhat ambiguous statement.

Lourens wandered away to talk to a seaman coiling a length of rope. While Anna stood alone leaning over the bulwarks, Dirk came up to her.

"It was good of you to come for us," said Anna. "I am sure you arranged your cargoes so that you might take us home in your ship."

"I was very anxious that you should reach Amsterdam as soon as possible," said Dirk. "Your daughter-in-law needs you."

"What is the matter Dirk? Is it Pieter?"

"No, news of your son, mevrou."

"What of Ryk?"

A cold wind seemed to blow over the sea as she spoke. She shivered, waiting for Dirk's reply.

"I did not want to tell you in Plymouth," he said. "There were too many people. Mevrou, he is dead. He died of the fever they have on the Gold Coast the day before he was to come home."

"Dirk——"

"Minetje is very stricken," said Dirk. "It came as a great shock because she had not realized he was seriously ill. I asked her what I could do for her, and she wished me to bring you over to Amsterdam as soon as possible."

"When did he die?" asked Anna very low.

"Early in June; but we have only just heard the news."

"He was a dear son to me," said Anna.

She would miss Ryk: he had always been kind and good to her. Why could she not have died in his stead? she thought. She was an old woman and her race was almost run, while Ryk might have had many more good years. . . .

"He was my captain," said Dirk.

He left her abruptly and crossed over to the other side of the deck and busied himself with the gear to give her time to recover.

Anna wept quietly. She remembered that at Oostermeer she had felt that this might be Ryk's last voyage. He had been so punctilious in the settling of his affairs before he went to the Gold Coast, as though he had an idea that he might not return and he wished to leave everything in perfect order. He had left happily, and he had been particularly happy in his newly formed companionship with his youngest daughter, Charlotte. As she thought of Charlotte, Anna's heart warmed. She would always be the granddaughter she would associate particularly with Ryk.

She had been so near persuading him not to go, she thought sadly. Yet, in spite of her pain, she knew she had done right not to try to keep him. Holland produced sons of the sea of mighty calibre and, when one of these fell, there were others to step forward to fill the gap.

She thought back across the years and remembered her other son, Lourens. Both her sons had died, but she lived on. She could not bear her pain.

"Lourens," she called. "Lourens, come to me."

The child came to her at once.

"Give me your hand," said Anna.

With Lourens's small, firm hand in hers she recovered herself. For a moment she had forgotten him.

But only for a moment: in him now were vested many of her hopes and plans for the future.

ii

Minetje van Breda had seen them approach the house. She ran out of the door to meet them.

She and Anna embraced and wept, while Lourens stood by, a silent and amazed spectator.

Dirk followed them into the house and remained there with them for a short time. Then he took his leave of them, promising to call again on the next day.

"I am so glad you have come, Mother," said Minetje when Dirk had gone. "Dirk has been wonderful to me. He went at once to fetch you when I told him I needed you. Did it come at a bad time for you? Were Anne-Marie's affairs settled?"

"Anne-Marie has settled down," said Anna; and entered into a detailed explanation of Heemskerk's visit and Anne-Marie's second marriage and of the beautiful house she had gone to live in in Devon.

"We have no need to worry about her future, Minetje," Anna concluded. "Sir Giles Mortimer will be very good to her and her children. And what of yourself, my dear?"

"I cannot accustom myself to the thought that no ship of Ryk's will ever put in at Amsterdam and that never again will he come walking in as he used to do after his voyages. I used to look forward to his return when he was away. Sometimes in the morning I would wake up and say to myself, 'He will come today.' Sometimes it happened that he did come. Now I can wish and wish and he will never come."

"Ach, Minetje, that this should come to you too! There are too many widows in our family. It is this never-ending war with Spain that is draining away our best, and yet building up faster than it takes away. But, Minetje, how is Pieter?"

Minetje's face grew even more careworn.

"His health is much improved since you were here last," she said. "He has been very devoted to me. Now that Ryk has gone I shall need him to help me with our affairs. Fortunately he is very clever in all financial matters."

"Is he not overyoung for the responsibility?"

"I would never give him full responsibility, just talk little things over with him. He is older than his years, Mother. Jan Bester is often with him and he seems as adult as Jan in many ways."

"Jan Bester is the artist?"

"Yes," said Minetje.

She had asked Dirk to bring Anna to Amsterdam immediately because she wished to discuss this very question of Jan Bester with her. She had always regretted that she had not been more open with her mother-in-law on the occasion of her last visit to Amsterdam. She and Ryk had been in a twilight of indecision, first agreeing and then disagreeing, and not knowing in the least what to do for the best. She had often wondered what Anna had made of it all. And that scene with Lourens and Pieter. Would she ever forget it? But now she determined to keep nothing back, if only to ease her mind.

"Jan Bester advised us on the furnishing of the house," said Minetje. "Afterwards Ryk thought that his influence with Pieter was too great, and, as he thought it a harmful influence, we tried to separate Jan and Pieter. While Ryk was away Pieter seemed ailing and unhappy until Jan began his visits to the house again. So I have let him come. I do not care about this young man; but he does help my son, so I let him come to our home in spite of what Ryk wished. I do not know whether I have done right or wrong. I am hoping you will observe and advise me, Mother."

"I saw very little of Jan Bester when I was here before," said Anna. "Not enough to judge."

"Now that all the responsibility rests on me I am trying to do the right thing. I cannot blunder on foolishly and hope Ryk will come back and put it right. I am being very frank with you. I dislike Jan Bester. But there is no denying that he has helped Pieter, so I do not know whether I should let my feelings stand in Pieter's light."

"Do you think that Jan Bester helps Pieter, or does Pieter suggest he does?"

"I hardly know. Yet, wait, I do feel that Jan Bester has helped Pieter. He is almost lively when he is in Jan's company, and so depressed when he is alone."

"I shall watch them both and tell you what I think," said Anna. "I do not imagine I shall like Jan Bester when I know him better."

"I do not like him," said Minetje.

In fact she loathed him. She had had a difficult time with him, warding off his advances during Ryk's absence. He seemed impervious to snubs and open rudeness amused him. Since she had been widowed she had noticed him appraising her. Under his cool steady stare she had felt indecent, as though he saw beneath her clothes. But he had not so much as touched her hand; it was only in his looks that he degraded her. Minetje had thought to mention this to Anna but, as she turned over in her mind what she should say, the matter seemed too intangible to discuss. Therefore she kept her vague impressions to herself and Anna had no inkling of how Jan Bester's presence in the house affected Minetje personally.

"Where are they now?" asked Anna.

"He and Pieter are out in the city somewhere. They are always together. Mother, when you look into all this do not judge me too hardly. I love Pieter dearly. In a way I have set him above my other children because I gave him less at his birth, and I can never make up to him for what he loses through his continued ill-health. I have always reproached myself for not having been a little more careful before he was born. He is all the dearer to me because he is so frail. I tolerate Jan Bester only because Pieter is happy in his company."

"You must not blame yourself, my dear. These things happen."

"That is why I have struggled to give Pieter everything, even Jan Bester's companionship against my better judgment."

"Sometimes one defeats one's own ends by giving too freely. We will discuss this in a week or so, Minetje. You must be lonely, my dear."

"I will be glad to have Charlotte home. I have missed her a great deal. Lourens has grown so. He is a grandson to be proud of, Mother."

"He is a fine boy."

"I wish I lived nearer and could see more of Juliana's children."

"You must come and stay for a long time at Oostermeer. You ought also to see Anne-Marie's children. It is astonishing how alike Lourens and Gilbert Barradale are. They were great friends and Lourens was speaking good English in no time."

"Pieter is very anxious to master English," said Minetje. "He has been having conversations with the family of an English merchant here. Pieter says one must know languages. His French is very fluent, and I understand he writes Latin as well as any professor."

"He is indeed a clever boy," said Anna. "I cannot tell you what an effort it was for me to acquire even the little English I learned. I used to envy Lourens, chatting away with Anne-Marie's children as though he had spoken no other language all his life; and every now and again he would stop and put it all into Dutch so that I might understand also."

"He and Pieter must talk English," said Minetje. "It will be excellent practice for Pieter."

"Minetje, if I may advise you, I would not tell Pieter how well Lourens speaks English. There was jealousy between them last time we were here and we must be careful not to revive it."

"Ach, Pieter has quite got over those childish quarrels. It will be such a help for him to talk to Lourens."

"Pieter is sharp. He will know Lourens was bound to have learned the language while he was in England. Let him find out for himself. If you put any stress on Lourens's achievement you may raise a prejudice in Pieter's mind."

"If you really think so I will say nothing," said Minetje reluctantly.

"I do think so."

"Very well then, Mother."

It was extraordinary, thought Anna, how Lourens and Pieter seemed to come up against each other in little things. She was somewhat apprehensive. Unless Pieter had changed very much for the better she felt there might be unpleasantness in the house, as Lourens was older and very capable of taking care of himself. But Pieter had Jan Bester on his side, which would not give Lourens much chance of asserting himself.

Well, thought Anna, I am meeting trouble halfway. If any difficulty arose she could always return at once to Oostermeer.

The first week in Minetje's house was peaceful and pleasant. When Jan Bester was introduced to Anna she did not know what to make of him. He was courtesy itself, and went to great pains to please her. Pieter imitated Jan Bester in every way. He was a composed, quiet boy. He paid little attention to Lourens, but he spent hours talking earnestly to Anna. In fact he and Jan were so solicitous that Anna felt quite worn out and longed for a little time to herself. She could find no fault with either of them, but she had an uneasy suspicion that they were too clever for her and that the performance had been arranged for her special benefit. By the second week, however, Pieter had discovered Lourens's command of English and the procedure was changed. Jan Bester and Pieter and Lourens now spent hours on end in Pieter's private sitting room conversing in English. Pieter gave Lourens sweetmeats and made much of him; but Anna knew the child was not entirely at his ease. Frequently after one of these sessions in English conversation Lourens used to seek Anna out. He would not complain but he invariably slipped his hand into Anna's, which was a way he had when he was not altogether happy and felt in need of sympathy and support. Now, also, when Jan Bester put himself out to entertain her, she would sometimes surprise a look of sly amusement in his eyes, as though he knew she was there to report her impressions, and he was neatly supplying her with a roll of ready-made ones. Anna could find no fault: but she was baffled and worried all the same. She voiced her opinion to Minetje.

"You asked me to tell you what I thought," she said. "I do not know what to think. The whole matter is unreal in a sense, and it eludes me. With Jan and Pieter I am as confused as I was the last time I was here, when you and Ryk were also always play-acting. Ryk threw off the mask before he left and he was his old self when I saw him at Oostermeer before he sailed. And you are also as you used to be, my dear daughter-in-law. You still wear your beautiful clothes and your finery but there is someone I know and love in all your trappings. But Pieter and Jan Bester—words fail me. They fool me all the time. They are too clever for me. They manage me to perfection and half the time I am so bewildered by their words and their attentions that I am an easy prey. They are so polite. They are always opening and shutting doors for me, and so clever are they that they open the door when I have not even thought I wanted to go out, and out I go, and on the other side I wonder what made me go out. They bow and talk and give me no time to think. There is not one specific charge I can make, but there is something wrong although I cannot put my finger on it. I know it and Jan Bester knows I am disquieted and he laughs secretly at me the whole time. There's a sly look in his eyes, as though he enjoys enormously hoodwinking a simple old woman from Friesland. He knows that I am aware that he only hangs on here for the money he gets out of it, and he defies me to get him out of the house. He laughs at my helplessness; but his words are so smooth and his manners so perfect that I find myself wondering if after all I am not doing him an injustice."

"He has an insolent look about him," said Minetje, who understood only too well Anna's aversion to Jan Bester.

"Pieter is so much improved in every way," said Anna. "Why not suggest that he is now too old for a companion? That, I take it, is what Jan Bester is?"

"His position here has not been exactly defined," said Minetje. "He does not work for a salary. He has presents."

"But, Minetje——"

"I know it must sound reckless to you," said Minetje. "Pieter is very generous and he asks me for the money for Jan, who has been very kind to him."

"I do not like Jan Bester or the arrangements about his money," said Anna bluntly. "I am sure Ryk would not have approved. If Jan Bester must stay he ought to be paid a fixed salary. The presents might get larger and larger. He is a young man with big ideas."

"I will discuss that with Pieter. He would hate it if I went behind his back and spoke of a salary to Jan. Pieter is very sensitive."

"You are not letting him go then?"

"It will put Pieter back if I do. The improvement in Pieter is so marked when Jan is here."

"Pieter is fourteen and mentally very forward. He can begin to shape his own thoughts and actions. And Pieter will grow away from you, which would be a tragedy for you both."

Minetje burst into tears.

"He has already grown away from me," she sobbed. "Ach, Mother, he is so aloof, and no longer my loving son. And Jacoba and Frederika also complain of it. We are so devoted to Pieter. It may be better when Charlotte comes home again. She might bridge this estrangement. They are near each other in age and she has influence over him. Since she went away Pieter has grown farther away from me. And I have given him everything he has asked for—Jan Bester, and presents of money for Jan, and tutors and books, everything and anything he has expressed a wish for. I love him dearly. Charlotte must come home and Pieter will move closer to me again. I shall put off Charlotte's marriage. It has been arranged for next year; but she is young, and she can help me win Pieter back before she goes to a home of her own."

"Whom is she marrying?"

"I have not told you? No? I am so sorry. In all this rush and worry I had forgotten I had not told you. It is all arranged. The young man is Ruprecht Grobbelaar, whose father owns large weaving interests in Flanders. It will be a good match for Charlotte, and Ruprecht is very anxious to marry her."

"He has good taste. What does Charlotte say?"

"I have not yet told her about these arrangements. However, I will tell her when she comes home. There is plenty of time."

"Are you quite sure that Jan Bester is not better out of the house when Charlotte is home?"

"Ach, Mother, now you are imagining things! Jan Bester has known Charlotte since she was a little girl."

"If you won't take my advice about Jan, take it about Charlotte: arrange her marriage soon."

"Charlotte may have something to say on that score. Her father has only recently died; but she is a dear girl and we have never had the slightest trouble with Charlotte. She is happy anywhere, even among the vegetables."

"She is a nice child," said Anna.

And rather like Anne-Marie, thought Anna. She often chided herself for singling out individuals from her ever-increasing family circle for particular love. There had been Liesbet and Anne-Marie, Lourens, and now possibly Charlotte, who had endeared themselves to her. She was very fond of all the others, but they did not qualify for a special place in her affections.

Once again she was free of the responsibility of the affairs of others. There was nothing she could change, nothing she could do at all in Minetje's house, so she would be able to return to Oostermeer. Anna's heart lifted. Oostermeer was home and she longed for it.

iii

Charlotte was a nice child. She had a happy spirit and a bright, smiling face, and a slim and lovely body. The long time she had spent on the farm had been of great benefit to her. Decidedly Anna approved of her.

She sat with Anna at the fireside in the farmhouse. Anna stretched out her hands to warm them, for they had just come in from the dairy and the autumnal evenings were chilly. Juliana was with the children in another room and Jan was in the yard, putting things in order for the night.

Anna and Charlotte sat in companionable silence while the light failed. The old house creaked with age, its little protesting groans mingling delightfully with the laughing voices of the children. The silence outside the house deepened; there was no sound from the byre or from the yard, and the stars began to glimmer in the sky. It was time to light the lantern, but neither moved to perform this little task. In many ways they were akin, the young girl and the old woman; both loved the old house and were in accord with its mysterious entity, and they were both happy to sit there together, stealing five minutes from the busy day for quiet thought.

The fire blazed up suddenly and shone full on Charlotte's face, which was rapt and dreaming. She was in a golden reverie and smiling faintly.

"Who is he?" asked Anna gently, with a tenderness that was almost sisterly.

She saw the quick colour that flooded Charlotte's cheeks.

"I was thinking of Julius Schoenberg," she answered directly.

Anna started slightly. Minetje had spoken of Ruprecht Grobbelaar as Charlotte's future husband.

"You were at Mynheer Schoenberg's farm near Amsterdam," said Anna cautiously.

"Julius is his son; he is a student at Leyden."

And she told her grandmother how they had skated together, and that, as yet, there had been no word of love between them because Julius had still to complete his studies before he could think of marriage.

"But I know all the same that he feels about me as I feel about him," concluded Charlotte naïvely, obviously seeing nothing ephemeral in her romance. "Therefore I have not mentioned Julius to anyone but you."

"I should like to meet him," said Anna.

"You will someday, Grandmother," said Charlotte.

At this juncture Jan entered and the conversation was over. All that evening Anna was a little preoccupied, trying to decide what action, if any, she ought to take. She had proved in her attempt to shape Anne-Marie's affairs that she was no hand at arranging marriages. If it had not been for Heemskerk's timely arrival, Anna ruefully admitted to herself, it was highly probable that Anne-Marie would still have been a widow, with her future precarious and unsettled. Minetje, however, was well versed in matrimonial projects and had married her three elder daughters well, so she ought, perhaps, to be left to manage Charlotte's affairs without interference. And there was Charlotte herself to consider: she had a determined character and there was strength in the line of her jaw; she had all Anne-Marie's steadfastness, and with it a marked streak of realism which would pull her through a crisis where Anne-Marie, being gentler, would be most vulnerable. After further secret weighing of the matter Anna came to the conclusion that she must do precisely nothing unless Charlotte appealed to her. Charlotte and Minetje must be left to settle which husband it was to be, and, having begun to appreciate Charlotte's firm character, Anna did not really think that the girl would find herself wedded to the wrong man.

Neither of them referred to Julius Schoenberg again; but, when Charlotte was leaving for Amsterdam, Anna said to her as they embraced:

"Remember I am your best friend if ever you are in a difficulty, and Oostermeer is your other home."

"I will remember," said Charlotte.

And returned to the strange, quiet house in Amsterdam.

CHAPTER THIRTY-SEVEN

As he walked down the alleyway to his tiny cabin Dirk saw her. She was facing the lantern suspended from the ceiling and her tall figure was outlined in light. She wore a long cloak and a shawl was tied about her head. Anna van Breda in his cabin! Dirk thought he must be dreaming. He hurried down the alleyway to learn what had brought her from Friesland to Amsterdam.

The tall woman in the cloak turned at the sound of his footsteps. Dirk came to an abrupt stop in his surprise when he saw that Charlotte stood there.

"I had thought you were the mevrou, your grandmother, Anna van Breda," he said. "You looked like her from the back."

"You pay me a pretty compliment," said Charlotte with a quick smile. "My grandmother is beautiful even in her old age. Unfortunately my face does not match the figure."

"Your face is very nice," said Dirk. "You have no need to worry. But, Charlotte, is anything the matter? Why are you here alone at this hour of the night?"

"I am in trouble, Dirk, so I crept out of the house and came down to this wharf to find someone to take a message to you. I could have cried with relief when I saw your ship tied up here. I couldn't believe my eyes. I came on board and waited for you."

"What do you want of me?"

"I shall be so grateful if you will deliver a letter to Julius Schoenberg in Leyden. It means everything to me if the letter reaches him quickly."

"Leyden is not far from Delftshaven. It would be easy enough."

"Julius Schoenberg is a student at the university."

"I have only one question to ask: is it fair?"

"It is fair. You can trust me, Dirk."

"I do trust you, absolutely. I had to ask that question. I must care for your father's children and not let them do foolish things. And I can neither read nor write, so you could put down anything in your letter, and I would be none the wiser."

"At the moment I would not like to give you a full explanation, but I will someday."

"I have a piece of parchment somewhere and a quill. A bill of lading was begun at the top, but we can cut that off."

Charlotte sat with the quill in her hand. She had not come down with the idea of sending a letter at once to Julius Schoenberg. She had thought of it while she waited in Dirk's cabin. Her mother had told her that evening that it was desirable that she should marry Ruprecht Grobbelaar. She had been appalled, but she had managed to conceal her dismay and had asked for a little time in which to reflect upon the matter. And, having gained her point, she had set her mind to the problem of letting

Julius know how matters stood. She had not mentioned Julius to her mother. He had not declared himself, and it certainly put her in an awkward position. She had decided that she would write to Julius and leave the rest to him. It was perhaps a little odd that the proposal should come from her and not through their respective parents after long negotiations, but then the circumstances were somewhat unusual. Charlotte dipped her quill in the ink and wrote in careful script:

It has been suggested that I marry Ruprecht Grobbelaar. If you have other views please come to Amsterdam.

Charlotte van Breda

The next step was to come from Julius. If he cared for her he would come forthwith to Amsterdam; if he did not she had left him free to write her a letter of congratulation and that would end the matter. She had put it to the test.

Dirk watched her as she wrote. The light fell on her face. It was sweet and strong and despite its youth he saw in it the traits he so admired in her grandmother Anna. He saw her pride, her spirit, her courage, and unbreakable determination. This daughter of Ryk's would shape her life, not move meekly with its flow. His heart warmed towards her.

Charlotte waved the parchment to and fro.

"There. It is dry," she said. "Now will you deliver my letter? I shall wait anxiously for a reply, so do not be long. I am fortunate in being able to write. Pieter and I had our lessons together, but he soon outstripped me. It was as well that I was slow in learning because he was encouraged when I fell behind."

It was a tragedy that Pieter differed in so many respects from his sisters, thought Dirk. That was what overmuch care and indulgence did for one. Ryk's daughters were fine, pleasant young women. He was fond of them all, and fond of Minetje. He called regularly on her now because he saw that Ryk's death had softened her and had restored her to her senses. But Pieter was another matter altogether. He could make nothing of the lad, dressed up in fine clothes, rather grotesquely like a little frog. Dirk thought it monstrous the way he took every service rendered him as a right and battened on the affection of his sisters and his mother. . . .

Charlotte's voice broke in on his thoughts.

"Please do not mention this letter to my mother," she said. "If it is necessary I will tell her. I am quite fair, Dirk. You have no need to fear."

"I will say nothing and leave it to your judgment."

"I must go now or I shall be missed," said Charlotte.

"I shall accompany you home," said Dirk. "I will see you to the door but not come in. I will call upon your mother tomorrow."

In the street Charlotte took his arm and they walked along happily together. Charlotte's mention of the city had revived memories of Leyden and Dirk told her of how he had been responsible for delivering one of the Prince of Orange's messages to the besieged. As they walked and talked Charlotte saw the sickle moon seemingly suspended from the spire of a distant church, and the pale stars powdering the dark sky around it.

ii

He sat on the elaborately carved settle with the rich tapestry on the wall at his back. His hands were elegantly placed, one on each silk-clad knee, and he was delicately perfumed. He leaned a little forward and smiled at Minetje van Breda.

"I have come to discuss the question of marriage with you," said Jan Bester.

Minetje felt the blood rush to her head. There was a roaring in her ears and she saw the smiling face of Jan Bester through a mist. She felt she must choke and faint in the rising tide of her anger. Jan's face faded and merged with the tapestry behind him, and his supercilious voice reached her from the blur:

"Are you so surprised then? I had hoped we were good friends."

With a great effort Minetje regained command of herself.

"I have no intention of marrying again," she said coldly. "I am old enough to be your mother. I cannot overlook this presumption."

He laughed; and Minetje felt anger rising up again within her.

"Forgive me," he said affectedly, "but it is droll."

"You are behaving unpardonably," said Minetje, white to the lips. "Will you leave me, please? You are never to enter my home again."

He lounged back on the settle and regarded her with amusement he did not attempt to conceal.

"You forget Pieter," he said. "He will not hear of it."

"For once consideration of Pieter will not weigh with me. You are to leave at once."

She rose and moved towards the door. As she put her hand out to open it Jan Bester said:

"If you are thinking of calling the servants and having me put out I would suggest that you are not so rash. Permit me to explain, as I see I have failed to make myself clear. I am proposing for the hand of your daughter Charlotte. You misunderstood me, madame."

She spun round and walked up to him, and stood over him.

"Charlotte! You have the effrontery to ask me for Charlotte!"

"You will perceive that you were overquick in jumping to conclusions, madame."

He leaned negligently back, completely at his ease.

"I have no words to describe my horror," she said. "If I had permitted it you would have made ardent love to me; and now you ask me for my daughter. You are utterly base."

"I do not mind admitting that I toyed with the idea of marrying you; but when Charlotte came back from Friesland I knew that she was the one to marry. She has presence and spirit. She has slapped my face three times since she returned and I have made no headway; but I like spirited women. Besides, Pieter thinks Charlotte is the better wife for me. If we were married I should naturally control your money and Pieter would not like that."

"Have you discussed this with Pieter?"

"Of course. It is arranged down to the last guilder I should expect to receive with Charlotte."

Minetje put her hands to her throat.

"Will you go," she said in a stifled voice.

He did not move.

"This is the end," said Minetje. "Go and never set foot in this house again. I shall appeal to the burgomaster for his protection. I have influential friends in Amsterdam. I shall insist that you never come here again."

She turned away and moved again to the door. As she opened it she felt it being pushed from the other side. She came face to face with Pieter. She fell back when she saw him.

"How much have you heard, Pieter?" she said, trembling now in every limb.

Pieter pushed past her.

"I have heard too much," said Pieter. "And I wish I had heard nothing."

Minetje saw that Jan Bester was on his feet, looking pale and perturbed.

"Pieter, did you know what Jan Bester was going to say to me?" asked Minetje in anguish.

Pieter did not answer her.

"Pieter," said Minetje again, "answer me. This I must know."

"I had discussed Jan's proposed marriage with Charlotte, and we had settled what would be a fair dowry for her; but we did not mention you, Mother," said Pieter.

"Thank God for that," said Minetje. "It would have broken my heart if you had been a party to what was said this afternoon."

In spite of herself she began to weep under the strain.

"You ought not to have said what you did, Jan," said Pieter.

"I was jesting—jesting in bad taste, I must admit," Jan Bester answered nervously.

"You owe my mother an apology," said Pieter.

Jan Bester crossed the room to where Minetje wept quietly.

"Madame, allow me to express my profound regret for an ill-timed jest——"

Minetje thrust out her hand and pushed him away.

"You were not jesting," she said. "An apology is not enough. He is to leave the house, Pieter. I can never have him under this roof again."

Pieter was obviously struggling against his distress. Before he could reply Jan Bester broke in.

"It can all be put right, Pieter," he said. "I behaved badly and I am sorry. I promise you it will never happen again."

"It cannot be put right," said Minetje. "For many years I have endured the persecution of this man, Pieter. And I bore it for your sake. But now it must end. There is a young girl in the house. Charlotte is bespoken. If all goes well she will marry Ruprecht Grobbelaar in the spring."

"I was not consulted," said Pieter.

"There are some matters on which I do not need to consult you," Minetje rebuked him. "I am Charlotte's mother. It is for me and her father, if he were alive, to arrange her marriage. Charlotte did not wish the matter to be discussed yet awhile."

Pieter's lips pursed in sudden petulance. Minetje saw that she had touched his pride. He loved to be consulted. She ought to have had more tact, she told herself distractedly.

"I am not a child," said Pieter sullenly.

"We have got away from the issue in hand," said Minetje, desperately struggling to enforce her authority. "I have ordered Jan Bester to leave this house. And at once. Do you support me in this, Pieter?"

Pieter would not be pinned down to a decision.

"It is a grave matter and not to be arbitrarily settled," he said. "We will discuss it later."

"Will you go at once?" said Minetje, turning to Jan Bester. "If you do not leave I will call the servants, and there will be gossip enough to animate Amsterdam for many a long day."

"Go now, Jan," said Pieter. "I will let you know what is settled later."

"You are not to come here again," reiterated Minetje. "That you must clearly understand."

Without another word Jan Bester bowed and turned away. He glanced over his shoulder when he reached the door. Minetje saw him smile at Pieter.

iii

Minetje went to her own room. She asked a maid she met on the stairs to send Charlotte up to her as soon as she came in. Then she entered her room and bolted the door. When she was alone she paced to and fro and wept.

After a little time Pieter came to her door and knocked.

"Mother," he called.

Minetje went to the door but did not open it.

"I will come to you presently," she said.

"I would like to speak to you now. Please open the door, Mother."

"I am too upset, dear," said Minetje. "I will come later when I am calmer."

He could not persuade her to let him in so he went to his own room and waited.

Half an hour later Charlotte came. When Minetje opened the door she stood on the threshold and stared at her mother's tear-stained face. And then came quickly in and put her arms round Minetje.

"Whatever is it?" she asked compassionately. "Mother, do not weep. Why have you sent for me?"

"I am so thankful you were out of the house this afternoon," said Minetje. "Charlotte, I wished to ask you if you had thought things over and if you would care to get married at once and go out of this house. It would please me very much if you would decide to marry Ruprecht now."

"I would not mind getting married, but not to Ruprecht."

"Not to Ruprecht Grobbelaar?"

"I have been waiting to tell you about Julius Schoenberg, but a letter I have been expecting has not come. I would like to marry him and I think he wishes to marry me. I wrote him about a fortnight ago—when you spoke to me about Ruprecht—and asked him what he wished in the matter, and I am awaiting his reply."

"You ought not to have written a letter like that to a man. Such matters are for the parents to arrange, Charlotte."

"There was no other way I could find out," said Charlotte. "It seemed no more than sensible to me."

"If he wishes to marry you I cannot agree. It would not be a good marriage."

"I want no other, and I like the farm."

"I told Ryk no good would come of your going out to Mynheer Schoenberg's farm."

"Mother, when you have met Julius will you agree that we can marry?"

"You can do better than a farmer's son, Charlotte. And I had set my heart on your marrying Ruprecht Grobbelaar."

"I am the one who will have to live with him," said Charlotte flatly. "And I do not find it an entrancing prospect."

"I don't know anything about my children. They tell me nothing," exclaimed Minetje, taking refuge in a renewed storm of tears.

"What happened this afternoon to upset you, Mother?" asked Charlotte, wisely changing the conversation.

"I could not possibly tell you."

"I think you must. We ought to confide in each other. I have been secret with you, and I am sorry. But I had to be secret. Let us do better now. Mother, what did happen?"

Charlotte put her arm round Minetje and led her to a seat. They sat down side by side and Minetje told her of the interview she had had with Jan Bester that afternoon, and of how Pieter had been with them at its termination.

"I told Jan Bester to leave the house and not to return to it," Minetje concluded. "But, as he was leaving, he and Pieter exchanged glances, and I knew that I would not be obeyed. So you must leave the house, Charlotte. Go to Oostermeer if you wish and ask your grandmother to come here to me, but you cannot remain here. You have had to slap his face three times. He told me."

"Jan Bester is a slimy creature," said Charlotte. "I am quite capable of keeping him in his place. No, I will not go, nor must my grandmother come here. She is getting tired. After all, she is nearly seventy. I noticed when she came back from England that she was beginning to stoop except when she remembered and pulled herself up, and she is thinner. Let her rest. We can put this matter right ourselves. Mother, you were right in forbidding Jan Bester the house. You have ordered him out and you must insist that he stays out."

"How can I keep him out if Pieter lets him in?"

"You are in authority here."

"You do not understand my difficulties, Charlotte."

"They can all be overcome, Mother."

Minetje moved her hands in a helpless gesture.

"It has gone on too long. Pieter will not allow it."

"There is something Pieter loves more than Jan. And I do not believe he really loves Jan; it is just that Jan has this ascendancy over him."

"What does Pieter put above Jan?" Minetje put the question more to humour Charlotte than because she thought there was anything in the statement.

"Money," said Charlotte briefly.

"He is not of age and will not be for another seven years," said Minetje. "I have entire control over the money and property your father left. When Pieter is twenty-one he comes in for a certain amount, but I still keep the bulk of your father's fortune."

"You have been drained by Jan Bester for years, Mother. It is time that stopped, because his demands will become more and more outrageous unless you make a determined stand. Circumstances have arisen which justify you in never having him in the house again. You have made a stand, now abide by it. There is a way of winning Pieter over to your side."

"He loves me," said Minetje. "If only I could persuade him to give Jan up!"

"You can always bribe him," said Charlotte deliberately.

"Charlotte, how hatefully you put things!"

"We are speaking the naked truth to each other," said Charlotte. "I thought a great deal about what went on in this house when I took to visiting the farm before my father went to the Gold Coast, and at Oostermeer, away from it all, I went on thinking. And I saw clearly what was wrong. When I was a little girl and did my lessons with Pieter I was held up to ridicule if I happened to be slow, and my stupidity was always the foil to set off my brother's brilliance. I was not so very stupid; he was so very clever. But he was never taught to be kind. As long as he was pacified nothing mattered, and he was encouraged to be cruel. I helped to spoil Pieter as much as anyone, Mother. I did not complain. I let Pieter and the tutors make a mock of me, thinking that if Pieter was really happy it did not matter. But it did matter. I was helping him to be cruel. And the same thing has been happening with Jan Bester. He has been an offence and a trial to every soul in this house, but we have meekly endured his presence for Pieter's sake. Now all this must stop. I love Pieter dearly, and I do not think it is too late to make him a little more considerate. He must come to treat you better. Our father is not here to care for you so Pieter must do his share. Do you think Pieter will ever see that you have wine and little comforts in your old age like my father thoughtfully provided for his mother? Never, unless we, you and I and my sisters, begin to make him think. It is possible to change Pieter, because there is good underneath all his selfishness, if we but determine to reach it. To begin, Mother, he must realize that it is his duty to protect you and me against Jan Bester, who has been grossly insulting. Pieter is the man of the family, and it is his privilege."

"Why have you not spoken to me about all this before, Charlotte?"

"I was also selfish," confessed Charlotte. "It took the disgraceful scene this afternoon to make me see just how self-centred I was. I wanted to get away from this house and Jan Bester and marry Julius and be peaceful on a pleasant farm, and leave you and Pieter to struggle on here."

"I am glad I spoke to you."

"Pieter and I grew up together," said Charlotte. "I understand him quite well. You must appeal to him and play upon his vanity and his desire for power and never, never let him suspect that you are trying to force him along a certain path. Ask him to protect you against Jan, even weep a little if you think it will help, and then say you want his advice about your money affairs. Tell him it has occurred to you that he might be given a little capital so that he can invest it and learn his way about the money marts. Say that you had thought of this a long time ago but you feared to mention it as you gravely distrusted Jan, but that now he is out of the way, you would welcome his co-operation. Name a sum you think might be advanced for Pieter to turn over, subject always every few months to the scrutiny of yourself and your financial advisers. You must keep the whip hand there, Mother, or Jan may dip his fingers into the money. How much do you think you could advance?"

"I should have to ask my advisers, but I should say about ten thousand guilders," said Minetje, astonished beyond measure at the way Charlotte developed her scheme. And she had thought her such a child! She looked at her daughter, this strong, graceful blossom that had flowered in a neglected corner. How blind she had been, Minetje thought with a pang of compunction. Her thoughts had always been for Pieter and she had neglected her daughters except when they became marriageable and she was under the necessity of providing them with husbands. Then she enjoyed them because she loved negotiations of that sort. And suddenly she realized that it was extremely probable that Charlotte would be utterly firm about her choice of a husband. The girl was just like her grandmother, Anna van Breda. . . .

Her surprising daughter was talking again.

"That will do for the first session," said Charlotte. "Allow Pieter time to think the matter over and let him make the next move; and if there is the least sign of Jan Bester attempting to come here, or of Pieter trying to meet him, cancel the arrangement. Stress that you will call in the capital immediately he resumes the connection. But be very loving and appealing and hint that there is a great future in this idea of a Dutch East India Company. It has not yet been formed, but if he is in from the beginning there may be a fortune to be made. Be just as wise and loving as you know how to be."

"It is you who are wise, Charlotte. I had not thought of money being a weapon to my hand against Jan Bester, but I see now that it is a powerful one."

"And do not mention anything about my share in this. Let him think it all comes from you. And I will be kind and sweet to Pieter and be his companion so that he will not miss Jan too much."

"I have known practically nothing about you until now, Charlotte," said Minetje. "You astonish me."

"I began to think for myself after Father left us," said Charlotte. "He was a dear father, and I miss him very much."

"I still miss him sorely," said Minetje, covering Charlotte's hand with her own.

Minetje smiled at Charlotte. She felt safer than she had felt for a long time. In this daughter she had a wall to her back. She had lived her married life with the idea that when she really stood in need of help she could only get it from her mother-in-law, Anna van Breda. Now she saw that she need go no farther than her own home for help. Charlotte was as strong and clearheaded, as valiant and undismayed, as her grandmother. Minetje felt that some of her daughter's quiet strength had entered into her.

"I will go to Pieter now," said Minetje, rising. "I promise you I will stand firm and be as subtle as I can be."

"You will find a way, Mother. You are so fond of Pieter."

"Ach, Charlotte, I have always put Pieter above my other children. I have often reproached myself for it."

"Reproach yourself no longer. Go now and talk it over with Pieter. Between us we will keep Jan Bester out of the house. I will wait here until I hear you go down. We must dine together as though nothing has happened."

They were walking down the stairs, first Charlotte, then Pieter and Minetje, when someone knocked sharply at the door. A manservant came forward and opened the door.

Dirk and a young man walked into the hall.

Charlotte came to a dead stop almost at the end of the flight of stairs.

"I have brought the answer to your letter, Charlotte," said Dirk.

The young man's round, anxious face was pale. His eyes were fixed on Charlotte as though she were the only person in his view. They gazed into each other's eyes and Charlotte flushed and smiled.

"Will you marry me and not Ruprecht Grobbelaar?" the young man asked.

"That is for my mother to arrange," said Charlotte with dignity, drawing Minetje forward. "Mother, this is Julius Schoenberg."

Scarlet with confusion, Julius Schoenberg bowed.

"If my mother agrees," Charlotte burst out impetuously, "Julius, I will!"

She stretched out her hands to him. He crossed the space that separated them and clasped Charlotte's hands in his own.

PART XXI

ḤOLLAND

CHAPTER THIRTY-EIGHT

ONCE AGAIN DIRK WAS TO COME FOR HER, AND HE AND SHE, JAN, Juliana, and the children were to sail to Amsterdam to attend Pieter's fine wedding. He was marrying the youngest daughter of an impoverished noble house, Michèle de Romilly, thereby achieving his mother's highest ambition for him.

Anna van Breda smiled when she thought of the approaching wedding. She had been peacefully settled at Oostermeer for several years. She had uprooted herself when Charlotte had been married in Amsterdam, and now she was to do so again. Charlotte and Julius had made a handsome couple and the marriage had turned out very well. Charlotte had a son and was as contented and happy as the day was long on her farm near Amsterdam. Charlotte was a dear girl, Anna reflected. She had actually travelled all the way from Amsterdam to Oostermeer before she was married to announce the news of her betrothal to her grandmother. She had a nice sense of the fitness of things and Anna appreciated her courtesy and consideration. She found, as she grew older, that she loved being made much of, and Charlotte knew to perfection just how to acknowledge her prestige as head of the family. The girl deferred prettily, consulted Anna and sought her advice, flattering her grandmother's age and position so engagingly that Anna was enchanted. More so because, from her own observation and from what Charlotte herself had told her, she could see how shrewd and practical and kind Charlotte was. Her handling of the Jan Bester affair, for instance, had been a diplomatic achievement for one so young. Anna had at one time wondered whether, when she was dead, her mantle would fall on Minetje; but events were proving that Charlotte would automatically step into her place as head of the family.

When Charlotte had visited her to tell her that she was marrying Julius Schoenberg and not Ruprecht Grobbelaar, she had told her how it had come about that she had been allowed the choice of husband; and she had told Anna in the minutest detail of the events leading up to the departure of Jan Bester; of Pieter's acquiring certain capital on condition that he sever the connection between himself and the artist and adhered to the pact; of Pieter's breaking his promise and of how she had compelled Minetje to call in every guilder of Pieter's capital immediately; of how Minetje had restored the money when Pieter had solemnly undertaken never again to see or communicate with Jan Bester. Pieter was proving a financial genius. The times suited his ability to turn over money admirably. The Dutch trade with the Spice Isles had greatly increased, and of all Eastern produce the most generally in demand was pepper, and the Dutch had gained the monopoly of this profitable trade.

Encouraged by their Queen, the English, not to be outdone, founded an East India Company of their own. Thus the scene was set for the struggle for maritime supremacy between the Dutch and the English which was to persist for a century and more, and was to break the amity and good will that had arisen between the two races after the defeat of Philip's Armada.

Now the English Queen was dead. Anne-Marie had written to tell her of Elizabeth's passing. This year, 1603, was a memorable one. In the course of it a great queen had died, a daughter had been born to Anne-Marie Mortimer, and Pieter van Breda was to be married. Of the first and the second of these events Anne-Marie had written, and the third Anna was yet to witness.

The summer day was warm and languid. Jan had made a rustic seat against the hedge that bounded the vegetable garden so that, sitting on it, one faced the swaying poplars in the avenue. It was a favoured retreat of Anna's when the weather was fine. Today she went there. And when she was seated she drew Anne-Marie's last letter from her pocket and read portions of it again:

. . . It is a happy coincidence that my mother's name was Liesbet, which in English is Elizabeth, because I can please both you and Giles by naming our small daughter, born shortly after the Queen's death, Elizabeth, for my mother and for England's great Queen.

I am very sad sometimes that the sea divides us. I should dearly love you to see Giles's children. Rupert resembles his father, but I see Margaret in Elizabeth, so I think this babe will favour my side of the family. Gilbert and Margaret and Francis grow apace. We often speak of you and of our days at Bodrugan. I pray, my grandmother, that one day I shall be able to visit you. I am anxious not to lose touch with my relations in Holland. If my babes keep me at home I shall send Margaret on a visit to you when she is older. She and I converse in Dutch so you will be able to talk together, and wander over Oostermeer as once we talked and wandered. As I write it is spring in England, and the springing green is tender on lawn and field and tree, and flowers bloom in the hedges, and the cuckoo calls while the dew lies wet on the grass. I remember Oostermeer in the spring, and the green low land of Holland in the golden light of the sun, a fair, blond land, my grandmother.

Sometimes I hear talk of the rivalry that has sprung up between the English and the Dutch fleets of merchantmen, and there are rumours of bitter trading quarrels in the East. And all this with the menace of Spanish oppression still with you in Holland, and still threatening us here! The world is wide, and surely there is room for all nations on the earth's surface. I shall hope all these differences will soon be settled. Often when I look at my children I see in them the links that bind the Dutch and the English. But if they quarrel so I shall dream in vain.

My husband and my children send you their duty, and kind thoughts, and loving wishes for your good health. Be "careful and loving" of yourself, my grandmother.

Anne-Marie

Anna folded the letter carefully and slipped it back into her pocket. She patted the slight bulge it made affectionately.

There was no time in the march of the centuries that she would have lived in, had the choice been hers, other than her own time, Anna thought. She had seen the glorious rise of the House of Orange and had witnessed the birth of a nation in the dread struggle for freedom. William the Silent had lived among the people, inspiring them in their darkest hours by his faith and stubborn heroism, his brilliancy and determination; and when he had died he had left his sons Maurice and the young Frederick Henry to carry on the work he had so nobly begun.

England and Holland had risen side by side. It was a pleasant thought. Anna had rejoiced in the friendship between the people of both countries, and it seemed to her no less than a tragedy that amicable relations should be strained over so small a thing as the price of pepper, and, so she understood, it had been this question of pepper that had set the ships of England and Holland in opposition to each other. The one good result of this greatly augmented trading consciousness had been the draining away of Spanish influence in the far places of the world. As the far-flung tentacles of Spanish greed were hacked off one by one, so the mother body was weakened, Anna thought, and the day must dawn when Spanish tyranny would cease.

On the morrow they were setting out to Amsterdam: Anna was excited and happy at the prospect. She thought that this might well be the last time she would undertake such a journey. She was growing old and there was no peace like the peace of Oostermeer. She looked forward to her visit eagerly. There was much she wished to see for herself—Charlotte and her latest great-grandson, and what manner of farm and market-garden combined it was that Charlotte lived on; and there were her other granddaughters and their numerous children; and Minetje, who was to live alone in her great house because Pieter and his bride had an imposing residence of their own on the Heerengracht; and, above all, she wished to satisfy her restless curiosity about Jan Bester. Minetje and Charlotte appeared to have won the victory too easily to be completely satisfying.

And there was that anxiety about Pieter and Lourens to be assuaged. Minetje had written to say that Pieter had suggested that Lourens should attend the Leyden university and later enter the Amsterdam mercantile offices. The rapidly expanding business with the East made room for several of the daughters' sons. Minetje had offered to meet all the university fees and to pay the fees of a special English tutor, as Pieter had thought it would be as well for Lourens to pick up his English again. This matter of Lourens's future was in the air; it was to be settled on this visit, for the lad was thirteen and there was no time for tardiness. Anna wished to ascertain whether the old animosity persisted between Lourens and his uncle. If this strong feeling was still there she felt it would be hopeless to put Lourens into the Amsterdam business to make his way under Pieter.

As she still exercised her somewhat autocratic sway at the family councils, Anna had no intention of committing Lourens to a way of life that promised to be uncongenial. She was getting old; she knew it. She prayed each day that she might live long enough to see Lourens a man and well started on his road.

ii

They had conspired together to honour Anna on the occasion of Pieter's grand wedding. She suspected the hand of Charlotte behind the tributes of Minetje and the grandchildren and the great-grandchildren. Charlotte was ever thoughtful and, what was more, a shrewd judge of character. The presents Anna received were costly and exquisite, and months of thought must have gone into their selection, and there must have been much anxious consultation, because nothing was duplicated. Minetje gave a lovely silken gown; Jacoba and Frederika and their husbands a sandalwood casket lined with purple velvet on which rested a string of fine pearls, the gift redolent of the fragrance and the opulence of the East; Jan and Juliana gave fine linen; Charlotte and Julius brought a bouquet of perfect blooms, exquisitely arranged, and a long cloak of black velvet with a rich brocade lining of scarlet and silver, which, when Anna saw it, caused the tears to prick behind her lids, as she remembered that she had casually mentioned to Charlotte at Oostermeer that all her life she had longed to possess such a garment, having once seen a grand lady wear a similar cloak at a ceremonial gathering in Groningen when she was a girl, but she had never been able to afford the like of it in her heyday and now when she had Ryk's money she was too old. However, here it was, her dream of midnight-black velvet and scarlet and silver, most unsuitable but utterly ravishing. And more ravishing than the gorgeous gift was Charlotte's remembrance of her expressed nostalgic desire.

The great-grandchildren presented their gifts of cambric handkerchiefs, soft shoes, handsome stockings, perfume, a new Bible; and Gerard, Charlotte's infant son, held out to her in his chubby hand a long slender wineglass in which to enjoy the contents of the cellar Ryk had left well stocked at Oostermeer.

Anna was deeply touched. Even Pieter's gift, which was an elegant walking stick with a silver handle of elaborate design, did not depress her nor remind her that she was, after all, an old woman. She perceived that they loved her not so much for her virtues as for her little weaknesses. She had always been somewhat vain and she had loved to dramatize herself. She saw it was this streak of unblushing individualism which had won her the affection of her family. Their gifts, with the exception of Pieter's, were to suit not her years but her personality. Early in her life she had chosen her part and she had played it faithfully to the end. She was in the centre of the stage and would hold her place there, with their love, until the curtain came down. This recognition by her family was her moment of high reward. She had not lived her life among them in vain; she had caused the years to glow for them and for herself, keeping up their spirits and her own, inspiring them to tireless energy by making them feel they were vital participants in a stirring drama, not mere puppets to fritter their lives meanly away.

Anna found Michèle de Romilly an extraordinarily interesting study. When Anna had arrived from Friesland Michèle and Pieter had called formally upon her. Michèle had barely opened her lips, and Anna had been somewhat taken aback at the small, insignificant creature whom Pieter had decided to marry. They met again the next evening in Minetje's house at a great banquet. A hundred guests had been invited and Minetje had excelled herself. The arrangements were perfect and the affair went without a hitch. Michèle had attended with her parents, the Count and Countess de Romilly. She was splendidly dressed in a gown of pale blue silk and her mouse-coloured hair was elaborately dressed. She was finely boned, with delicate hands and feet, and a waxen skin. On her white neck gleamed the sapphires Pieter had given her as his marriage gift. The silk and the jewels were too much for her wispy personality, Anna decided, appraising the girl narrowly.

Now, two days before the marriage was to take place, Anna came unexpectedly upon Michèle, who had called alone in order to consult her future mother-in-law as to the disposal of some of the numerous wedding presents, a profusion of which had already gone to Pieter's house on the Heerengracht. Michèle, wishing to see what other things had been sent, as she had a methodical mind and loved possessions, stopped at Minetje's house on her way home from the modiste's.

She had been shown to Minetje's private sitting room on the first floor and left there while the maid went in search of her mistress.

The maid returned after a hurried tour of the house.

"Unfortunately Madame is out," she said.

Michèle was by no means disappointed. She was glad of the opportunity of inspecting her treasures alone. All her life she had been starved of luxuries and, for a time at any rate, she could not always repress her desire to gloat over the magnificent presents that continued to arrive from the wealthy merchants of Amsterdam. When she gazed upon them she was almost reconciled to having Pieter for her husband.

"That is a pity," said Michèle smoothly. "However, I know where the wedding presents are kept. I will show myself round."

"This way then, mademoiselle," said the maid, and escorted her to the library.

Anna had been in her bedroom. The maid had not disturbed her. Hearing voices, Anna decided that more of Minetje's friends had come to give advice on the final arrangements, for the wedding was to be a truly magnificent affair. She wished to avoid them and write a letter to Anne-Marie. So she slipped quietly down to the library. She was surprised to find the door ajar. She pushed it open and entered noiselessly.

She saw Michèle's slender, immature body outlined against a heavy, dark curtain that hung from the ceiling to the floor. Her face was pressed into its folds, and she had spread out her arms at shoulder height in a forlorn gesture, silhouetted in all her defencelessness against the rich maroon velvet.

"Michèle," said Anna quietly.

"Grandmère!"

Michèle had turned and faced Anna in a flash. She blinked her eyelids rapidly and tried to conceal that she had wept. She was glad it was Pieter's redoubtable grandmother who had walked in on her. She had liked the little she had seen of this fine-looking old woman, whose manner was graceful and dignified, and who had the good breeding which comes from the heart, refined into great charm from a lifetime of intercourse with a variety of persons in dissimilar walks of life.

"If you wish not to enter into this marriage with Pieter, even now at the eleventh hour, I will stand by you," said Anna gently.

Michèle was too amazed to speak.

"Why are you marrying Pieter?" asked Anna, still very gentle-voiced.

Her keen glance took in the drooping lines of the girl's figure and her white, drained face. She understood too little about this marriage. She had gleaned a certain amount from Charlotte and Minetje, but she felt she wanted to hear something about it from this sad-faced girl. That the marriage had been arranged she well knew. Michèle was the youngest of seven children, six of them girls, and the eldest the Count de Romilly's son and heir. The estates of the count were heavily encumbered, so that he had thought it expedient to marry off his dowerless daughters as speedily as possible in order to leave his property to his son. Pieter, when he came of age, would be extremely wealthy. Minetje's financial advisers had greatly increased Ryk's estate by judicious invest-ment. And Pieter, with his ability and his already large interest in the newly floated Dutch East India Company, would without doubt amass a considerable fortune. She longed to hear what Michèle thought about her marriage. The pinched, white face of the girl distressed her, and she had not the heart to see a young creature unhappy when she could mend it. Pieter was her own grandson, but she sincerely pitied the woman he took to wife. There was that cruel streak in Pieter; it was still there, and she doubted whether womanly devotion would ever remove it.

"You mistake the reason for my tears," said Michèle with a show of courage that Anna admired. "I do wish to marry your grandson. It is just that I am tired. These preparations have seemed endless. We have entertained, or have been entertained, for weeks past, and there have been visits to the dressmakers and the jewellers and the furnishers, and the lists of the guests and the wedding banquet, and the presents. I am exhausted, that is all, Grandmère."

"A society wedding is most exhausting," murmured Anna, liking her suddenly a great deal more than she had done before. This personality was not as wispy as she had thought at first.

"I hope you will forgive my tears," said Michèle.

"They are understandable, my dear."

"In a way you were right, I did feel for a moment I could not go on with it," said Michèle, speaking rapidly, as though she wished to say what she had on her mind before she repented of her candour. "I felt like that the first time my father told me I was to marry Pieter. I barely knew Pieter then, and I was unprepared. I did a foolish thing. There was a man. He was—well, it does not matter who he was, Grandmère. He was well born and he was to be executed on some charge of treason. I had never seen the man in my life, but we knew of him and his sad fate, and our sympathies were with him, as we felt he was innocent. There is an ancient law that if a maiden offers to wed a condemned man he can come down from the scaffold. I was so frightened that I thought if I married this unhappy fellow I might save his life and save myself from a marriage I did not at that time desire. I carried through with my plan, but I was greatly humiliated. The man refused my offer. He was executed. The whole affair was hushed up and, so far as I know, no one has an inkling of it. My father was furious. He spoke hard words to me and I was ashamed of myself to think I had been so foolish. Pieter was very gentle and good. I insisted that he should be told all about my escapade. My father laughed it away and put it down to a young girl's nerves. And he was quite right—just a matter of nerves. Before you came in here I gave way to my nerves, but this time it was because I am so tired."

"How old are you, Michèle?"

"I shall be seventeen in the autumn."

"I feel sure you would have heard of this from someone or other,"

Michèle went on. "I preferred to give you the true account because, if you can forgive my folly, I would like to stand well with you."

"I feel very sorry for you," said Anna, thankful that she had never arranged a marriage, not even Anne-Marie's. Michèle had shocked her deeply by her revelation. There never had been these twists and complexities save in matters that had to do with Pieter. It seemed to be his tragic lot that whatever came to him should be warped in some fashion.

"Do not be troubled, Grandmère. I feel sure Pieter and I will be very happy. I will do my best to make our marriage successful."

"I am sure you will, Michèle."

"It has been such a delight watching the magnificent presents come in," Michèle confessed naïvely. "Pieter has given me beautiful jewels. When I am alone I take them out of the casket and let them run through my fingers like coloured water. I love beautiful things. Perhaps it is because I have never had them until now that I feel sometimes as if I will wake up as from a dream and find them all gone."

"You will find this no dream. I also love beautiful things. I have had to do without them as you have, but I can assure you they are all the more lovely when you have to wait for them."

"Pieter has spared no expense in the furnishing of our house," said Michèle. "I long for you to see it."

"I hope to go tomorrow with Pieter. Did you choose the decorations, Michèle?" Anna asked, wondering what Michèle's taste would be.

"No, Pieter put the decorations and the furnishing of the house into the hands of an Amsterdam firm. The result is beyond our expectations."

"What firm was it?"

Anna had a sudden suspicion that Jan Bester might have staged an unobtrusive reappearance.

Michèle named a local firm of high repute; but Anna was not satisfied.

"They had a special man supervising the work," Michèle went on. "We never saw him, but he was always advising the workmen behind the scenes. His taste is beyond reproach. I asked one of the painters once whose directions he followed, but he was a stupid man and answered that he worked for the firm."

"I see," said Anna thoughtfully, and made a mental note that she must mention this firm of decorators to Charlotte.

"May I show you some of the presents?" Michèle asked eagerly. "I came in here to check them over and to add them to the list."

"I shall be delighted."

They walked round the long table, opening and closing boxes and cases of plate and glass and porcelain, caskets of jewels, folded piles of silks and linen. The gifts were so lovely that they took Anna's breath away. She noticed that Michèle's face grew paler and sharper with avidity and her eyes shone and her teeth gleamed between her parted lips. Anna was saddened by this unashamed exultation. The poor child must have had a hard, colourless existence to rejoice so over this array of opulent splendour. She reminded Anna of a child who, deprived of his playthings, suddenly discovers himself in the midst of more than he ever dreamed existed, and, losing himself in the wonder of it, grabs at everything within reach, fearful of missing any treasure. So it was now with Michèle.

Michèle was neither colourless nor unintelligent, Anna thought. She was also courageous. If there were surprises in the future they might well come from pale, demure Michèle.

Anna had forgotten that she had come to the library to write a letter to Anne-Marie: Michèle had proved much too interesting.

iii

When they returned from viewing Pieter's house on the Heerengracht they found Lourens with his grandmother. He had been on Charlotte's farm with the other children, but had come in with Julius for a few hours to visit Minetje.

Anna was full of praise for the lovely house on the Heerengracht. She had thought Ryk and Minetje had achieved wonders in setting up their home in Amsterdam but Pieter's house surpassed his mother's in many respects. Anna noticed that Michèle was not following what she said. The girl's eyes were fixed on Lourens, who was regaling himself on a selection of choice viands that Minetje had persuaded the head cook to serve especially for her grandson.

Pieter followed the direction of Michèle's rapt gaze and saw his nephew licking his finger so as not to lose the last morsel of the delicious confection. Lourens wished that his uncle Pieter would get married every day of the week, for never in his life had he tasted such food. Having sucked his finger, and then two other fingers for stray splashes, with diligence, he raised his eyes to his grandmother and exclaimed:

"That was good, Grandmother."

Minetje beamed adoringly upon him. She was very proud of her handsome grandson.

Michèle was murmuring in an undertone to Pieter. Anna caught her opening sentence:

"Who is this fine-looking boy?"

Anna watched Pieter and saw the muscles at the side of his head twitch; his face set. The cruel yet pathetic jealousy of one stunted and sickly for an upstanding healthy being was still there, well concealed but ever there. She could read on Pieter's face that he disliked and envied Lourens. That settles it, thought Anna, Lourens must never come to Amsterdam to serve under Pieter. . . .

"Lourens, come and be introduced to your future aunt, Michèle," said Pieter. "This is my eldest nephew, Michèle. My sister Juliana's son."

"I shall remember all the nephews and nieces one day," said Michèle. "At the moment I am very confused, there are so many."

Lourens arose and went across to Pieter and Michèle, who sat side by side on the settle. He made a little bow. He was not in the least shy. He asked Michèle how she was.

"I am very well," answered Michèle. "Come, sit beside me."

She patted the space beside her on the settle. Lourens sat down and, glancing at his uncle Pieter to see his pose, crossed one ankle over the other and clasped his hands negligently on one knee. One of Juliana's favoured admonitions was that one learned good manners by imitation. Anna, having watched Lourens's movements, smilingly wished his mother could see how he had taken her precept to heart.

"You live in Friesland, do you not?" asked Michèle.

"Yes, at Oostermeer."

"That is the family home," said Pieter. "We began there, and my grandmother lives there."

"I hope I shall visit you there, Grandmère," said Michèle politely.

"Why do you call her grandmère and not grandmother?" Lourens asked curiously.

"My father is half French," said Michèle. "We speak French a great deal in my home. It is a habit. Do you mind, Grandmère?"

"I rather like it," said Anna. "It suits my stick and my cloak and my new gown."

To the amusement of the family she had endeavoured to wear or carry the gifts they had given her in turn. This afternoon she wore Minetje's gift and the cloak, the shoes and the stockings, and carried the stick. She leaned the stick against her knee and held out her cloak on either side of her.

"Is it not beautiful?" she said to Lourens. "The colours peep out when I walk."

"It is lovely," said Lourens admiringly. "You ought to do nothing but visit in it. Go to Aunt Anne-Marie's. I would like to go again."

"I have heard of your aunt Anne-Marie; she is a great beauty," said Michèle to Lourens.

"She is a very nice woman," said Minetje. "I wish we saw more of her."

Anna saw that Pieter and Minetje smiled at each other as though they shared a secret. Minetje nodded, in confirmation of something, it seemed.

Before Anna had time to wonder what they were in league about the other members of the family arrived: Julius, Charlotte, Jan and Juliana, Jacoba and Frederika and their husbands. Wineglasses were carried in and they drank together and toasted Pieter and Michèle.

Again Minetje nodded at Pieter, who rose and crossed over to Anna.

"There is something for you to see upstairs, Grandmother," he said, offering her his arm. "Anne-Marie's and Dirk's presents were a little delayed; but they are ready upstairs. Will you come?"

"More presents," said Anna. "I had not expected this."

"The family unites to salute you, Grandmother," said Pieter.

"I wrote to Anne-Marie," Minetje explained. "I told her we wished to pay tribute to you on the occasion of Pieter's wedding, and I asked her if she would like to join in. She was delighted. It is her great regret that she and Sir Giles Mortimer are not able to be present, as she has so young a babe. As for Dirk, he lacked a little wood for the inlaying and Pieter obtained some for him from one of the warehouses, and he has been toiling to finish in time. But now all is ready. Dirk and his wife will be here tomorrow. If Ryk could have lived to see his only son married, the picture would be complete."

Anna smiled at Minetje, who had expressed her own secret thought. She took Pieter's arm and they headed the procession up the stairs.

At the twist in the stairs Anna looked behind her. They halted and gazed up at her. Pieter waited by her side. Alas, he reached not quite up to her shoulder, but as she looked down on the upturned faces her heart swelled. How fine and upstanding and kindly were her descendants, from Minetje, matronly in black, down to the fair-haired boy Lourens on the last step of all. This was a moment to remember for as many years as she yet had to live. She looked down on the bright faces below her and, as had happened once before on Falmouth quay, she had no words to express the deep feeling in her heart. There was no bar of language here to hamper her tongue, only a sense of the inadequacy of speech. She stood upright and extended an arm so that the scarlet and silver of the cloak was revealed. She said clearly:

"I will remember this. God bless you all."

Then she and Pieter went on again until they came to the door of Minetje's sitting room. Pieter turned the knob and they entered.

The golden light of the summer evening poured in through the windows. On the wall facing them hung a portrait which had not been there that morning. Anna's eyes fastened on it and she came to a dead stop. The others crowded in at the doorway and looked over her shoulder.

Anna lost all consciousness of her surroundings. She was back again in Delft, and there also it was high summer, with the heat drawing vapour from the canals and the lime trees gracious and shady. The painted face of William, Prince of Orange, gazed down upon her from the heavy frame, the high, lined forehead, the firm and kindly mouth, the large bright eyes. His humanity, his wisdom, his patience, and his loving-kindness were all portrayed there. The ruff was one she had seen him wear, the black velvet skullcap he had worn a thousand times in Delft. This was the "Father William" who had paced the shady water-ways beside her in those far-off days when life was full and questing.

Pieter saw she was overcome. He put his free hand on hers and guided her until they stood under the portrait. He spoke to give her time to recover.

"This is the portrait that is well liked," he said. "It is a copy of the portrait which Adriaen Key of Antwerp painted in '81. It hangs in most of the town halls, and it is held to be an excellent likeness. It was executed in Antwerp by an experienced copyist and was late in arriving.

And look underneath it, Grandmother. You will see Dirk's gift. That chair. He has made it himself, even to the inlaid design on the back. It is indeed a fine example of craftsmanship, and the wood was carefully selected. Dirk is as good a carpenter as he is a sailor."

"They are both beautiful," said Anna confusedly, finding her voice, and not quite certain that she had got beyond tears. "I am glad I shall see Dirk tomorrow and will be able to thank him for his fine present."

"The portrait and the chair will be carefully packed and sent to Oostermeer," said Pieter. "All arrangements have been made, and you will find the portrait will fit well into the inner wall above the settle in your living room. Jan took the measurements very exactly and the copyist was warned to get his canvas the right size so you will be able to hang it where you can see it when you sit in Dirk's chair by the fire."

"One day, Pieter, when you are burgomaster of Amsterdam, you will have your portrait painted to hang in the town hall," said Anna, giving his hand a gentle squeeze. "And I will want a copy. Do not be too long about being burgomaster, because I grow no younger."

"That is looking a long way ahead," said Pieter. "But when I am burgomaster I shall lose no time in sending you my portrait."

"I shall await its arrival confidently," said Anna, smiling.

She and Pieter drew a little aside and the others stood under the portrait, discussing it. Anna stood quietly by Pieter and felt at this moment that she was akin with him for the first time since his childhood. Perhaps, she thought, this happy day was the turning point and he would never look back on his strange and twisted years of adolescence. She prayed that it might be so. Yet she did not entirely put her trust in the impression of Pieter she had had that afternoon when he had been so understanding. She waited until she saw Charlotte alone and drew her into a corner.

"I may not have the chance of a word with you later, Charlotte, my dear," she said. "I want to tell you that I have an idea that Jan Bester may be moving behind the scenes again. Where is that man, by the way?"

"He left Amsterdam for some time; but I do not know whether he is back."

"You live here and will be on the spot to notice things," said Anna. "There is no reason at all why Pieter should not have him in his own house. If they are friends again and Michèle is at all disturbed about it, advise her to flirt with the fellow. Pieter will never stand that, and he will rid himself once and for all of Jan Bester. Michèle is intelligent. You can always rely on her to do her share."

"I feel that although Jan Bester and Pieter may have met behind our backs the friendship will not last much longer. Pieter now has his own interests, his wife, and his affairs. Jan will not be needed, and Pieter will not hesitate to thrust him off if he feels like it. So Jan Bester will just fade quietly out of our lives."

"That is quite possible. It is the way of life. Few of the queer characters one meets in the course of one's life live up to one's dark expectations. Jan Bester will probably marry some silly woman and end by being highly respectable!"

Charlotte laughed.

"It will seem rather a tame ending to all our turbulent scenes over the man," she remarked. "But it would be the best solution."

Anna put her hand on Charlotte's arm.

"Charlotte," she said, and there was a note of appeal in her voice. "When I am gone hold my dear family together. You can do it. A family is a precious thing. Turbulent, temperamental, troublesome as its members may be, hold it together."

"I hope you will be with us for a long time yet," said Charlotte. "But I will try when you are no longer with us."

This dear family of mine, Anna thought, remembering the blended tragedy and grandeur, the pathos and the humour of the years. And if she were to leave her family its members were ready now to stake their share of the future upon the energy and resilience with which, individually and collectively, they had faced the vicissitudes of the past.

There was nothing that could not be overcome: she was happy in her mind about them all.

iv

The marriage was a gorgeous affair. After the ceremony the guests, numbering three hundred, were entertained at a banquet in the home of the bride's father. She was paying for it, of course, Minetje whispered to Anna behind her fan, but that was not to be disclosed. But was it not an unforgettable scene, and worth every guilder she had expended? And did Anna think her dress was all right? It felt a little tight under the arms. She had told the modiste to let it out a trifle at the seams, but the silly woman had neglected to do so.

Michèle had made a pale but self-possessed bride. She was exquisitely dressed and bore herself well. She and her bridegroom were equal in height. Anna's heart ached when she saw Pieter stand before the altar with Michèle. If only she could have given him some of her strength and vigour, she thought. . . .

Two large saloons had been thrown into one by means of folding doors. Thirty round tables were laid in them, each accommodating ten guests. The first course of twenty-five dishes was carried in by lackeys in livery and the banquet began. A band discoursed pleasing music, wine there was in plenty, and the atmosphere soon became merry and convivial.

Anna was determined to miss nothing. She was enjoying herself hugely. What she had seen and done in this short week in Amsterdam would give her food for memories for many a long year. She might never come to Amsterdam again, so she intended to steep herself in its enjoyments. However, never coming to Amsterdam meant never leaving Oostermeer again, and that suited her well, she reflected. She foresaw many happy hours at Oostermeer. She would wander indoors in the summer and walk through the farmhouse with the golden balm of the noontide heat distilled through the wide-open windows, with brass and pewter and china and pottery reflecting the myriad reflections of indoors and out. Room after room would welcome her until she reached the peace and silence of the living room where William's portrait was to hang. There she would sit in Dirk's chair and contemplate the Prince for hours. And in the winter she would sit by the fire and look up at him. Ach, the gifts of her family had been rare indeed!

Tears threatened to overwhelm her. She thought that, perhaps, she had had too much wine and she was not used to it. She frowned austerely at her wineglass. When a flunkey, a napkin over his arm, came forward to replenish it, she waved him away.

Charlotte, sitting at another table, caught her eye. She raised her glass to her grandmother. Anna turned in her seat and beckoned to the flunkey with the wine. He came forward and filled her glass.

The wine was rich and ruby-red. She held her glass high and drank with Charlotte a silent toast to the family.

CHAPTER THIRTY-NINE

The years passed. Anna van Breda had lived to see an uneasy peace come to the war-worn land. In 1609 a truce of twelve years was signed; and also in this year the Bank of Amsterdam, in whose treasury fabulous wealth lay stored, was founded.

Anna was a year short of eighty. She lived quietly at Oostermeer. Once more it was high summer and she loved the comfort of the warm days. She got about and was still very active, but she sat down for long periods when she thought that no one was about to observe her. Today she walked down the avenue, thrusting her stick into the little thickets at the base of the poplars, seeking hens' nests, for there were several birds that had taken to laying away, and Juliana was very put out over the loss of the eggs. After a little time Anna dug her silver-mounted stick into the ground and leaned her weight on it. The stick, Pieter's gift to her, had proved most useful; and, in a way that Pieter would never have intended, it had afforded her an opportunity of indulging her taste for mild self-dramatization. It was said of her (and Lourens always kept her informed of what people said of her and her stick) that there was nothing she could not do with it—twirl it in the air and march with it like a master of the band when she was uplifted; brandish it menacingly when she was annoyed; flourish it playfully when her mood was light; and lean upon it when she wished. Once when she had walked beside a canal she had seen a child splashing in the water, in danger of drowning. She had put out the stick and the child had clutched it and she had drawn him to the bank. That was all that had happened, but the stick became famous—it was known to have saved the life of a child and it was suggested that it had on several occasions dusted the doublets of stray Spaniards; it had tapped on the marble floors of princes and had left its mark on the decks of ships crossing the North Sea, said gossip, forgetting when Anna had acquired it. The opportunity was too good for Anna to miss. When she went to Groningen, and sometimes when she was on the farm itself, she wore her cloak with the bright, rich lining, and carried the stick. She appeared always in the same garb and, as she was still able to walk upright when she pulled herself up, she used to put her shoulders back in the streets of Groningen and suffer the pains of a martyr from her rheumatism, and her cloak would swing and her stick top twinkle, and she became a legendary figure. Mothers would point her out to their children as she passed by as "that great old lady who knew William of Orange when he was alive"—a reputation greatly enhanced by her possession of William's portrait. Anna, of course, had not known the Prince as well as was supposed; but her prestige seemed to grow with each venerable year of her age. She was a remarkable old woman who had lived a remarkable life.

Lourens was her stay and her joy. His was the only arm she would lean thankfully on. He had not gone to Leyden University as had been suggested. Pieter, becoming very family-conscious after his marriage, had insisted that he should bear all the expense of the university and travelling fees. And that insistence had clinched the matter. With the animosity there was between Lourens and his uncle it would never do to force the spirited boy to be educated on Pieter's bounty. Jan and Juliana had sent the unprotesting younger boy, Johannes, to Leyden and he was intended for a position in one of Pieter's offices. Minetje had complained of her loneliness in her house in Amsterdam, so Lena had gone to live with her to learn how to be a fine lady and to make a good marriage. Only Lourens was left at home, and today and for the past ten days he had been away in Amsterdam, having travelled there to escort his second cousin, Margaret Barradale, to Oostermeer. She had been visiting in Amsterdam for more than a month and Anna and Juliana were wanting to do their share of the entertaining.

Pieter van Breda's rise to vast wealth had been accomplished in a phenomenally short space of time. He was one of the seventeen directors of the Dutch East India Company, which had unprecedented powers and, in the name of the States-General, could make war and peace, build forts and factories, enter into treaties with Indian princes. Apart from his seat on the Council of Seventeen, Pieter had been instrumental in some way in the founding of the Bank of Amsterdam. And he had married the right sort of wife for success. Michèle had a sound understanding of social matters. She entertained the right people royally. This

talent of hers, combined with Pieter's ability, had gone far towards procuring Pieter's advancement in civic affairs. Michèle also had the wit to
make .capital of Pieter's deformity and dwarf height. Was it not a
triumph that Pieter, a cripple from birth, had risen above his infirmities?
she would murmur in the ear of the most influential guest, glancing
tenderly at Pieter as she asked the question. Thus she gained admiration
and esteem for him. So far had Pieter progressed that Minetje had
written ecstatically a few months before to say that it was a moral certainty that in the not far distant future Pieter might well be the burgomaster of Amsterdam. They were an exemplary couple, Minetje had
gone on to write, and everyone thought well of them, praising Pieter
for his business acumen and his knowledge and grasp of the city's needs,
and Michèle for her devotion to her crippled husband.

There was, however, a side to Pieter's and Michèle's lives which only
Pieter and Michèle knew. In the first year of their marriage a daughter
had been born. She received the names of Hélène de Romilly van Breda.
In the years that followed Michèle was to bear two stillborn sons. Her
health was bad and the physician had advised her to have no more children. This suited Michèle very well: she could now enjoy the privileges
and possessions of her husband without having to fulfill her obligations
as his wife. The change in their intimacy fell very hard on Pieter, who
was sincerely attached to his wife, but, as Michèle's life might be endangered, he had no option but to acquiesce. He endeavoured to be more
tender and loving towards her. Michèle, unfortunately, was becoming
more rapacious the wealthier Pieter became. She masked this failing
so well that only Pieter knew of it, and he did not think her rapacious—
a little miserly, perhaps, but not rapacious. Michèle began to show him
plainly that she had married him solely because of his money, and she
deeply touched his pride when she did not trouble to conceal her delight
now that her delicate health forced them to live apart. The unfortunate
Pieter remembered that at the time of their betrothal she had gone to the
desperate expedient of seeking to wed a condemned man to escape him.
He tried by the only means in his power to win her affection, and that
was to buy her favour by lavishing gifts upon her. She always warmed
to him when he bestowed them on her, but, as her love cooled, he was
forced to bring more. Jewels were Michèle's passion. At times Pieter
poured them into her lap. It was a form of investment, he told himself.
There were coffers of jewels in the house which might well ransom a
king.

Jan Bester had begun to appear discreetly shortly after Pieter and
Michèle were installed in their own home. He had been the adviser for
the firm of decorators. He came once or twice to the house on the
Heerengracht. Michèle, who had an infallible instinct where money was
concerned, came to the conclusion that Jan Bester had expensive commissions in view. She gave Pieter no peace until he disclosed the extortionate fees the artist demanded—"presents," as Jan Bester liked to call

them. And that was the end of it. Jan Bester was far too expensive an artist for them to employ, she said; and Pieter, ever anxious to please her, finally parted from Jan.

Lourens was to stay at his grandmother's house. Margaret Barradale had spent five weeks with Pieter and Michèle, and was then to go on to Minetje's. Lourens would have preferred to stay at Charlotte's, as he wished to discuss tulip growing with his uncle Julius. Charlotte, however, was expecting her fourth child, and it had not been convenient for them to have Lourens on the farm with them.

Anna had rested long enough. She was very careful not to overtax herself. Unknown to her family, she had visited the physician on the last occasion she had been in Groningen. He had explained that her moments of pain and palpitation and shortness of breath were due to some heart trouble. He had advised her not to hurry or become excited. "Take life quietly," he had told her, "and you will live to be a hundred." She tried to act upon his advice—after all, it had cost her five guilders—but it was not always easy to remember in time. She doubted whether she would reach her century, but she wanted to live a few more years so that she could see Lourens established. She wished he would return with Margaret. She was never really happy when he was away.

She switched her mind onto the question of eggs. She straightened herself and began once more to move the sprouting poplar suckers with her stick, peering into the midst of the green leaves and grey stems. At last her search was rewarded. She found a nest with a dozen eggs in it. She knelt down and picked them up and put them one by one into the little basket she had brought with her for the purpose.

While she was kneeling she heard footsteps coming down from the top of the avenue towards her. She would know the quick, alert beat of those footsteps in a thousand. Lourens walked like that. It was too soon to expect him back. She wondered what had brought him home.

She got to her feet and gazed eagerly up the avenue. She saw Lourens's tall, stalwart form. She wanted to run to him, but just as she was beginning to do so she remembered that she must not overexert herself. . . .

"You have come home soon, Lourens," she said when he came up. "Was Margaret so popular then that they would not let her come?"

She kissed him fondly.

"Yes," he said. "And have you been careful of yourself, my grandmother, while I have been away?"

"Very careful," she said. "I am ashamed of the lazy life I lead."

"I came home sooner than I had intended because I wished to consult you," he said.

They never beat about the bush with each other. If he did not come to the point at once he was well aware that in five minutes Anna would have wormed out all she wished to know.

"What went wrong?" she asked.

"Before I tell you, there is news that will not wait. Aunt Charlotte has another son and his names are to be Gysbert Johannes. And she sent you a message. She chuckled when she gave it so perhaps it will amuse you. She said, 'Tell my grandmother that Jan Bester is married to the enormously rich and enormously stout widow of a tavernkeeper, and he paints the tavern and serves out pots of ale and hopes his wife will have heart failure at any moment. And that is how it has ended.' "

"Just as I thought!" exclaimed Anna, laughing. And, sobering up instantly, she asked: "And what was it, dear, that brought you back so soon from Amsterdam?"

"How relentless you are, when you want to know something," said Lourens, smiling and pinching her arm. "If you must know, I returned because of Margaret Barradale. There is certainly something very odd happening in Amsterdam, my grandmother."

"Go on," prompted Anna, wondering what in the world she might hear. Anything fantastic might happen in Amsterdam.

"I find it very difficult to put a name to it," said Lourens. "If I say what I think, I shall say that Uncle Pieter is in love with Margaret, and I am by no means certain that Margaret is not in love with Uncle Pieter."

"Lourens, what are you saying?" Anna's consternation showed in every line of her wrinkled face.

"I know it sounds crazy. I cannot tell you what doubts I have had, how I have puzzled my head about this. When I see them together it is obvious; when they are apart I feel I have dreamt it. I went out to Aunt Charlotte's to see whether I could talk to her about it, but she is lying in longer and it seemed wrong to trouble her. Besides, one must see to believe. I thought of mentioning it to my grandmother, but that also seemed impossible. And I am hampered by my prejudice. Pieter and I have never liked each other. It began when we were children and the feeling has grown more bitter through the years. In desperation I asked Margaret if she would come back with me and she said she had changed her mind and would not be going to Friesland for a long time. I went to Uncle Pieter in his office. I said to him, 'My grandmother has not been very well and she longs to see Margaret. I am trying to persuade Margaret to go north with me sooner than she had planned.' He gave me the strangest look. I knew then there was something in what I thought. And then Aunt Michèle looked at them with a funny twisted little smile when they were together as though she were amused by the whole thing. And Margaret. She has an expressive face. She looked like a girl who awaits her lover. Now you have it, my grandmother. And what do you make of it?"

"It seems incredible to me."

"I tried to tell myself that, because it was the easiest way out for me; but it was no good. I could not deceive myself. There was no one to ask, so I came back to you. I was in a very awkward position, my grand mother. Uncle Pieter is maintaining Johannes at the university, Lena is at her grandmother's. We are so beholden to Uncle Pieter, and I tell you I hate it. And there is really no need. There is enough on Oostermeer for us all if we live simply."

"I want to think about this, Lourens."

"Something must be done quickly, my grandmother. When I had spoken to you I was going back to say what I thought if nothing else, and to send for Aunt Anne-Marie."

"We must not be impetuous. Listen, Lourens. Do not mention a word of this to your parents. I will tell you tomorrow what we will do. I think that we will go to Amsterdam, you and I, and we will see for ourselves."

"The journey is beyond you, my grandmother. I would not like you to undertake it."

"It will not be beyond me," said Anna. "I tell you plainly I cannot credit what you have told me; but it is too serious a matter not to investigate. A visit to Amsterdam will do me no harm. I will bring Margaret back with me. Will you tell your father and your mother all the news and say that Margaret is enjoying herself altogether too much to visit Oostermeer just at present? If there is nothing in your suspicions it would be a terrible responsibility to start a hue and cry for nothing. We cannot be too careful, so we will say nothing to anyone. Do you agree?"

"Yes."

"Your relations with your uncle Pieter are not too friendly, unfortunately. He would never forgive you if you started a scandal just when he is about to be made burgomaster."

"We will say nothing. There is another thing, my grandmother, that must be discussed. And that is the growing of tulips on a large scale. I had several talks with Uncle Julius on the subject of tulips. He has already begun to cultivate the bulbs. He thinks that there may be money in the industry, and one must aim at rare colours and choice blooms. I went into it as thoroughly as time permitted. If my father is willing I should like to begin to grow tulips here on Oostermeer."

"I would never have thought of farming with tulips," said Anna. "The idea is revolutionary; but I suppose one must march with the times, and the flowers will be pretty in the spring."

"I shall tell my father exactly what tulip growing means," said Lourens. "Uncle Julius is very excited at the future the new idea may have. . . . But you will hear when I tell my father about it."

They walked to the house together, he with his arm round her, she carrying the little basket of eggs.

They found Jan and Juliana in the living room. Both were surprised to see Lourens and asked why he had not brought Margaret Barradale back with him.

"She is having too gay a time in Amsterdam," said Lourens. "My grandmother was so disappointed that she threatens to go to Amsterdam tomorrow. You must try to persuade her to stay here at Oostermeer, Mother."

"Grandmother, you must not think of it," said Juliana. "At your age the journey will be too much for you."

The mention of her age nettled Anna. She thumped her stick on the floor.

"I would like to go," she said. "But we will see in the morning."

"All the talk round about Amsterdam is about the growing of tulips, Father," said Lourens. "They go so far as to prophesy that fortunes will be made out of the bulbs."

"I heard something wild like that in Groningen," said Jan. "I paid no attention. The growing of flowers is the province of the women in the kitchen garden. On a proper farm there are important matters which need one's attention."

"We must be progressive," said Lourens.

The conversation was mainly about tulips for the rest of the day. By the evening Lourens and Jan had reached the argumentative stage. Now and again Juliana would throw her weight either on one side or the other. Anna, however, was very preoccupied: she was working out her own problem. She was well aware that Lourens was quite capable of taking care of himself and she left him to convince his father that with Oostermeer converted into a nursery for tulips their fortune would soon be made. They sat up late, well past their usual bedtime. At last, when she had decided what she must do, Anna suggested that they should all go to bed and continue the discussion the next morning.

"There is no need to continue it," said Jan. "I have no more to say. I have never in my life heard of such lunacy."

"Father, I'll convince you yet," said Lourens patiently.

"Give me your arm, Lourens," said Anna. "And help me to my bed, please."

She whispered in Lourens's ear as they ascended the stairs.

"We will go to Amsterdam tomorrow," she said very softly. "And when we come back it will be time for the tulips again."

She did not sleep very well when she had climbed the ladder to her bed and made herself comfortable in it.

Tomorrow she would go to Amsterdam and see for herself. And this, she knew, would be the last time that she would leave Oostermeer.

ii

Margaret Barradale at eighteen had her mother's beauty and her father's romanticism. She had also a very kind heart. Before she had sailed from Plymouth in the care of an elderly couple also crossing to Holland, Anne-Marie had impressed upon her that she must behave well while on this visit to her relatives, and, above all, she was to be kind to her uncle Pieter.

"I will tell you what he is like," Anne-Marie had said. "It is always a shock meeting him for the first time. You must not show the least sign that you are taken aback, even if you are. He has been extremely delicate since babyhood. He is very small, and has a hunchback, and his face is lined and seamed. He suffers great pain at times, I believe, and that is why his face is so drawn. He is very sensitive. You must appear to notice nothing and treat him as though he were an ordinary man and strong as we all are. You are to stay at your uncle Pieter's house first, so begin well, Margaret. You will hurt everyone's feelings, particularly Pieter's mother's, if you are not tactful and pleasant."

Thus, duly cautioned, Margaret Barradale arrived in Amsterdam, prepared to be especially kind to her deformed uncle Pieter.

Pieter was on the defensive, as he usually was with strangers. As the male head of the family, and a man in a high position, he felt it was his duty to take an interest in its members. When Anne-Marie had written and proposed that her elder daughter should visit them in Holland, he had written warmly, approving the idea. Michèle was interested in influential people and had no time for young girls. She had gone so far as to ask Pieter to make some excuse and put off the visit; but he had refused to do as she wished for once. In the circumstances he prepared to be gracious to cover up any deficiency there might be in Michèle's reception of Margaret.

Pieter took an instant liking to Margaret Barradale. She was young and lovely and her broken Dutch was charming. Michèle rapidly changed her front. She saw at once that she could turn Margaret's visit to her own advantage as the girl was a social asset. She issued innumerable invitations to the people of Amsterdam and began a round of entertaining. Margaret received many invitations to exclusive houses in Amsterdam, and Michèle, well pleased, accompanied her attractive relative when she dutifully toiled through her social obligations. Margaret, however, did not lose sight of her mother's admonitions in the midst of all the gaiety. She had set out to be kind to Uncle Pieter, and kind she intended to be. Her manner was natural and charming, and she sought his company whenever he entered the house and strove to entertain him, and when the three of them went out to dine or to a party she would always pay much attention to him.

Her obvious interest in him touched Pieter. He was flattered by it, as Margaret had been an instant success in Amsterdam social circles, and the young men were falling over each other for the favour of wealthy Pieter van Breda's cousin. He revealed to Margaret a side of his nature which Michèle had caught glimpses of in the first flush of their marriage. But Michèle's lack of affection had soon shrivelled Pieter's shy tenderness. Now, however, there was no check. For the first time in his life Pieter felt he could really open his heart to a woman. He was starved for affection, except maternal and sisterly love, which, having been always somewhat idolatrous, he had been inclined to push away from him. He had loved his grandmother in his early years, but she had set up Lourens in her heart, and they had lost contact with each other. He set himself to win the young girl's regard. And, with his experiences behind him, thought it must inevitably be bought.

One day he took Margaret to an expensive jeweller's.

"I wish you to choose a present to remind you of your first visit to Amsterdam," he said.

The jeweller had made his fortune out of Pieter van Breda. He hastened to lay trays of the most exquisite and costly jewels before him.

Margaret was taken by surprise. She had not expected her uncle to give her a present. She could tell at a glance that these were jewels for the adornment of a queen and that their value was beyond her imagination. She felt acutely embarrassed, feeling that Pieter should not spend so much money on her. As it was, he and Michèle had been kindness itself to her.

"Could I look round and choose?" she asked.

The jeweller smiled indulgently and humoured her. Margaret walked unhappily to and fro, wildly searching for some small thing that would not cost too much. She had almost despaired of discovering anything suitable when she came upon a collection of turquoise necklets, rings, brooches, and bracelets, in a dark corner. She sighed with relief and began to pick the ornaments up the better to see them. Her mother and her stepfather had given her a turquoise collarette for her birthday present. They had five children to provide for, so she knew they could not be lavish in their gifts. She selected a bracelet and held it up for Pieter to see.

"If I may I would love to have this," she said. "It matches my collarette. I was wearing it last night. Do you remember it?"

"Yes, I do; but will you not choose something else, Margaret?"

"I would love to have this. I have always wanted a turquoise bracelet."

"But, mademoiselle," stammered the jeweller, "something worthier. The stones in that bracelet are semiprecious; it is a trifle, not worthy of your consideration. Permit me to show you these sapphires, mademoiselle, these pearls——"

"Please, Uncle Pieter. I do want this bracelet."

The jeweller again opened his mouth to expostulate. He shut his lips firmly as Pieter nodded warningly at him to hold his peace.

"By all means. The choice is yours," he said, yielding gracefully. And to the amazed jeweller he said: "Please send the bill in in the usual way."

When he had bowed them out the jeweller stood speechlessly gaping after them. The bill . . . a mere trifle of a few guilders . . . never before had there been such an infinitesimal amount debited to the account of the wealthiest man in Amsterdam.

As soon as they reached the house Margaret put on her collarette and bracelet and came down to show them to Michèle and Pieter. She was delighted with her present. In her joy she kissed Michèle and kissed Pieter. She was so occupied in holding up her wrist to admire her new treasure that she did not notice how Michèle's lips twisted contemptuously at her obvious pleasure in her simple gift, nor did she notice how Pieter paled.

When they had left the jeweller's Pieter's emotions had been confused. He had begun to grasp that Margaret appreciated him for what he was and not for what he possessed. At the moment when she innocently kissed him he realized he was in love with her.

Now Pieter entered into the strangest and loveliest period of his life. The moment of realization was also one of renunciation. He loved Margaret, but he would never woo her; he would cherish her memory, but she must not learn to cherish his. He must not talk to her of love, so in the days that followed he showed her the secret places of his mind. He knew about artists and their paintings, sculptors and their sculpture; he had accumulated a rich store of Dutch and Flemish folklore; he had studied European politics. Margaret was young, and fresh and simple in her outlook, and she thought Pieter's conversation erudite and entrancing. From pitying him she began to be interested in him.

They held this dangerous balance for a while longer until, on an evening when they had gone to Minetje's house and it had been suggested that Margaret should move in and begin her visit there, they could hold it no longer. The thought of their impending separation was enough to upset that trembling balance. Michèle had not accompanied them. She found her mother-in-law's evenings very dull. She had pleaded an indisposition and had remained at home.

On the way home Pieter put his hand on Margaret's as it lay on his arm. They halted and stood looking at each other's faces, pale blurred patches in the half-dark. Margaret was aware of Pieter's hand trembling on hers.

"Margaret," he said hoarsely, struggling against his passionate desire to take her in his arms.

"Pieter."

Then neither could speak.

He found her other hand and held both hers in his.

"Margaret," he said at last, "do not try to think for three days. Leave everything to me to think out. I will speak to you in three days. Promise me not to think until then."

"I will try," said Margaret, so shaken that she had no clear knowledge of what she was saying.

"I will not see much of you for three days," said Pieter.

He gripped her hands convulsively before he released her.

They did not speak again until they reached Pieter's house in the Heerengracht.

Pieter suffered intensely. He was no romanticist. He saw things as they were. He might persuade Margaret to go away with him to some remote corner of Europe where they would escape from their relations and the places that knew them; this he might do and not be able to marry the girl, because he was certain Michèle would not divorce him, as she did not want a husband and it would suit her well if he gave her ample money and removed himself. She would have the satisfaction of being pitied as the deserted wife and, posing with their small daughter, would play her part perfectly. Margaret was actually his second cousin; he was an uncle by courtesy. Because of her youth and inexperience he would incur the opprobrium of all honest men for seducing her when she was in his care and far from her home and her parents. He would bring black dishonour on the family.

The financial side of the problem was the simplest. He had enough capital to invest for Michèle's support, and to live themselves he could draw on his capital at first, but he had sufficient confidence in his ability to know that he would soon succeed in re-establishing himself in business no matter where he was.

Then there was the question of Margaret herself. Was he not asking too much of her? She would ruin her life if she went away with him; her friends and her relations would forsake her; she would be completely cut off from her former associations and would have to begin again as a stranger in a foreign city. If she loved him deeply and sincerely he might demand the sacrifice of her; but did she? Was it feasible that she could love him with his deformed back and his ill-health? On her side she had the spontaneity of youth and her unspoiled beauty. It was very probable that her response to his passion sprang more from her deep sympathy than from any adult feeling. He could be sure of nothing that had to do with the state of Margaret's emotions.

One moment he decided that the world would be well lost for Margaret; in the next he saw the impossibility and the tragedy of the step he contemplated. By the end of the second day reason had prevailed and, unutterably sad, he had come to the conclusion that when he spoke it must be to tell her that she must visit his mother's and then go to Friesland. In his heart he knew that he could have been very happy with Margaret, and she also might have been happy with him, if every circumstance had not been against them. With Margaret life would be different. He would have the affection he craved, and he would come to his full stature emotionally and mentally. But it could not be. He must shut himself away from happiness.

On the third day he was still holding to his resolution. He avoided Margaret. That evening they were to go to Minetje's again. Michèle once more said she would not be able to go with them. There would be dangerous moments, Pieter saw; and steeled himself to hold to his resolution.

Margaret came down the stairs. She was dressed in a gown of filmy white and wore her turquoise collarette and the bracelet. She had the family fairness of skin and hair, and one day she would be a beautiful woman. Now she had the appeal of unspoilt youth.

She took Pieter's arm as they walked to Minetje's; they were silent as they walked; and as they neared the house, Pieter put his free hand on hers.

He had intended to say: "Tell my mother that you will come to her house tomorrow; it is a good opportunity." Instead he said:

"Shall I speak now or tomorrow?"

"Now," she said.

He could feel her body tremble against his; and her hand was cold to his touch. Suddenly he was swept back to where he had been in the beginning. He could never give her up, never, never. And there was only one way of escape open to them, and that was to give no warning of their intentions. He had not the least doubt of what would happen if anyone suspected their design. The pack of his female relatives would be on them, including his indomitable grandmother from the north, and Margaret would be taken from him. He could not stand against them. In a few days he could make the necessary financial adjustments and disappear with Margaret. He had come to the end of resistance and moral scruple. And the peace of a decision reached came to him.

He took Margaret's cold hands, turned them over, and kissed each palm.

"You know what I wish to say to you tomorrow, don't you?" he said.

"Yes," whispered Margaret faintly.

"Please think about it tonight."

"Yes," she whispered again.

"Tomorrow," he said triumphantly, "tomorrow."

In his excitement he did not notice her lack of enthusiasm. Margaret was badly frightened.

They walked on to the house and knocked at the door.

iii

A violent onslaught had been made on that same door a little earlier. Anna van Breda had walked up from the wharf as the light began to fail. When she reached Minetje's house she knocked. No one answered. Suddenly a feeling of panic assailed her. She felt ill and exhausted and did not know what might not have happened. She lifted her stick and beat peremptorily upon the door.

In a moment there were running steps and Minetje herself opened the door. Lena was close behind her. Anna caught sight of two menservants rushing down the hall.

"Mother!" exclaimed Minetje, starting back as though she had seen an apparition. She could not believe that she saw Anna on her doorstep when she ought to have been in Friesland.

"I am sorry I startled you," Anna apologized. "I knocked and no one heard. So I made a noise. I am sorry."

"Dear Mother, come in," said Minetje, drawing her into the hall and embracing her.

When they had seated themselves in the sitting room and Minetje had ordered refreshments she asked Anna what had brought her from Friesland. Were matters wrong there?

Anna looked searchingly into Minetje's face and into Lena's. Both faces were as placid and calm as usual. She began to wonder whether she had not come on a wild-goose chase.

"It is very foolish of me to travel, of course," she said, "but when Lourens returned and said Margaret would not be coming to Oostermeer just yet I took it into my head to come down and fetch her myself. I am longing for news of Anne-Marie."

"It is very wilful of you, Mother," Minetje reproved her. "At your age you ought to take things quietly."

"I know," said Anna meekly. "But I felt I had been peaceful long enough and I wanted a change. I would like to go back tomorrow and take Margaret with me, and she could visit you later, Minetje. Oostermeer is at its best in the summer."

"Pieter and Michèle and Margaret will be coming in presently," said Minetje. "Margaret is a pretty girl and has caused quite a stir in Amsterdam. Pieter also looks a great deal brighter since her arrival. She asks him to go out with them and the social life has taken him out of himself. I am very grateful to her."

"Yes," said Anna noncommittally. "Is there any news yet of the burgomastership?"

Minetje brightened.

"It is a certainty," she said with quiet satisfaction.

"Why did you come alone, Grandmother?" Lena asked.

"They are busy at Oostermeer," said Anna evasively. As it happened Lourens had left with her. She had persuaded him to disembark at Delftshaven and he had promised to wait there until she returned. She did not wish Pieter to know that Lourens had been instrumental in getting her to undertake the journey from Friesland. Lourens had gone on to Leyden from Delftshaven to visit his brother Johannes.

"There they are," said Minetje, as once again there was a knocking at the door.

They rose to their feet and looked towards the archway through which Pieter and Margaret entered.

Anna's eyes encountered Pieter's. Their glances crossed like swords. Lourens had been right; there was something between the two in the archway, Anna's nerves clamoured. She looked steadily at Pieter until he dropped his eyes. Then Anna said:

"Margaret, do you not remember me, child?"

Margaret came to her at once.

"Yes, Grandmother, of course I remember you."

Anna embraced Margaret and kept her arm protectively about her. Once again she looked at Pieter, who had not drawn any nearer.

"I understand from your mother that it is certain that you will be burgomaster," she said. "I congratulate you most heartily, Pieter."

"You haven't told me, Uncle Pieter," exclaimed Margaret.

"Nothing is certain until it happens," said Pieter, speaking for the first time since he had entered the room.

Anna's watching eyes saw a nerve twitch in his pale cheek. She drew herself erect and took her arm from Margaret's shoulders. She was wearing her black velvet cloak and there was a red-and-silver gleam as she dropped her arm to her side.

Anna turned to Lena.

"We have something to discuss, Lena," she said. "Will you and Margaret go to the little sitting room, please? We will not be long."

Lena became round-eyed with wonder. This was to have been a social evening. . . .

"If you please, Lena," said Anna again.

Lena took Margaret's hand rather sulkily, and the two girls went out of the room together. When she heard their light footsteps on the stairs Anna said:

"I have made all the arrangements for our passages to Friesland tomorrow. I wish to take Margaret back with me."

"You can't mean it, Mother," Minetje broke in. "You said that before, but I did not argue, as I wondered if you'd meant it."

"I mean it as I have never meant anything before," said Anna. "Do you agree, Pieter?"

"I think you have taken up a remarkably arbitrary stand," said Pieter.

"You know it is the right stand—the only stand," retorted Anna.

"That depends on how you look at it," said Pieter.

Minetje stared in frank bewilderment from one to the other. They appeared to know exactly what they were talking about, although she had not picked up the slightest clue to their remarks. The matter was very grave. She waited anxiously, afraid to interrupt.

Anna drew herself up. She said again sternly:

"Do you agree, Pieter?" And added: "It will be for the best."

Pieter's face darkened and set in hard and bitter lines. He made no answer.

Anna turned to Minetje.

"May Margaret sleep here tonight, Minetje?" she asked. "The ship is to sail early."

"Of course, if it is necessary," stammered Minetje.

"By God!" burst from Pieter's pale lips. "You go too far, Grandmother."

There was infinite sadness in Anna's eyes as she put the question:

"Am I too late, Pieter?"

The question seemed to hang in the tense atmosphere. Minetje put her hands on the back of her chair and pressed hard to stop herself from screaming. There was tragedy here, and drama, and she could not understand. . . .

"No," said Pieter at last.

"Then we leave tomorrow," said Anna sadly.

Some of Pieter's control left him. He was about to lose the only thing in his life that might ever have counted, the only human being who had come near understanding him. The thought tore his resistance to shreds. The loss that shattered him was apparent in his face. And she had brought it about, his grandmother, Anna van Breda. He looked into her wrinkled face, ravaged by unspeakable exhaustion; he saw her lips were bluish and he thought he saw also the signs of death in her face. Only her indomitable will had brought her there to thrust between him and his heart's desire. He thought he must hate her, but he found he loved her. And she was right. It was for the best. He dropped his head on his narrow breast. There was such grief in every line of his figure as he bent his head in mute acceptance of Anna's demand that Minetje felt tears gush from her eyes and pour unheeded down her cheeks. She wept without sound, instinctively knowing that she must not break in on this scene. Pieter kept his head bent and Anna dropped hers.

At last Anna lifted her head. She extended her hand.

"Pieter," she said, pleading for his understanding. "Pieter."

A thought occurred to him. He lifted his head.

"Lourens sent you here?" Pieter asked Anna on a hard note.

"I came of my own accord."

"You were very well informed. He was here not so long ago. Lourens is at the bottom of this."

It was obvious that Lourens must have been her informant. It was waste of time trying to keep him out of it.

"Yes," agreed Anna briefly.

"Lourens has always thwarted me. He has come between me and all I have desired," said Pieter savagely. "When he came to this house as a little boy I saw he had supplanted me in your affections. He had all I lacked: health, good looks, a straight body. Through our lives it has gone on the same way. And now this."

"And now what?" whispered Minetje, feeling that if she did not soon understand what they were talking about she would go mad.

Neither Pieter nor Anna seemed to hear her. Anna was wondering whether she should justify herself. Lourens had taken nothing away from Pieter. Her affection for Pieter had not altered. But she saw his prejudice was too great. She could batter against his bitter convictions and achieve nothing. And she had not the strength. Under her cloak she pressed her hand to her left side. Pain must not master her now. She had thought of slipping out to Charlotte in the morning, but she would go to the ship and sit on deck and do nothing, not speak, not think, until she was rested. It was a matter of the greatest urgency to get back north and plan for the future. Lourens and Pieter had always been ranged against one another, but now the enmity was open and bitter. In some way she must safeguard Lourens and set him up securely so that Pieter could not pull him down.

"Lourens," said Pieter, flinging the hated name into the silence. His hatred showed nakedly. His face was cruel and vindictive.

"You do him an injustice," said Anna.

Of what use were words? she thought. Her strength was at an end. She sank down on the settle, her hand still pressed to her side under her cloak. But she kept her eyes on Pieter. If there was more to be countered, she was ready for it.

"I am going," Pieter flung out savagely.

He turned and went out. Minetje ran out after him and her voice came to Anna, and she heard her tearfully trying to persuade Pieter not to leave the house in anger. Pieter walked out and Minetje went out after him.

After a little time the mists of pain cleared, and Anna's mind cleared. She moved her hand from her side and put it over her eyes to shield them against the light, the fingers spread open. Had Pieter been supplanted in her affections? Had the fault been hers? She did not think that it had been. In Pieter's fragile babyhood she had struggled with Minetje to preserve his life, but no strong tie above the normal affection for the small and weak had been born of that struggle. On the other hand, from the hour of his birth she had loved Lourens. She had sought to be fair to Pieter, but he had been beyond her simple methods. She had not been able to think of counter-attractions stronger than the pleasures of learning and social elegance which life in Amsterdam had fostered. However, there was one thing in her relationship with Pieter that did distress her. There had been a little fear and abhorrence poisoning her feeling for him ever since that day when he had ill-treated Lourens and she had asked Minetje if she had witnessed the execution of Balthasar Gérard. While Anna had never paid serious attention to tales of wizardry and witchcraft, she had always had a horror of unleashed cruelty, and she believed that dark forces were disseminated among those who gave way to its practice. She had striven not to allow it to influence her, but in her secret heart she had thought that Pieter had been born in an evil hour. There were dark, strange influences in his life which she could only explain in that way. He was two people—the clever, kind, man Ryk's son ought to have been, and the twisted cruel man that had been born of an evil time. Now he would always be the cruel, twisted being. But the sacrifice of Margaret was too high a price to demand of the family, and in any event Anna believed that all Pieter touched would grow black and bitter under his hand. There was nothing she could do to help him.

Nothing, thought Anna, nothing. She wept. The tears began to fall through her open fingers until she reached up her other hand and brushed them away.

When she was calm she went up to the girls in Minetje's room. Margaret came to her as she entered.

"We are going to Friesland tomorrow," said Anna, smiling.

"I am glad," said Margaret.

Her relief showed plainly on her face. She put her hand into Anna's. It was a confiding, grateful gesture.

You are no more than a frightened child, thought Anna.

iv

At Oostermeer the conversation was mainly about tulips. Which was all to the good, Anna thought. She saw that Jan and Juliana had made their reactionary stand and that, no matter what Lourens said or did, he would not be permitted to try an experiment in tulips on Oostermeer. She alone knew that Pieter, directly and indirectly, would set himself to thwart Lourens at every turn. That Lourens might be given the power to fight back was her chief concern. He was the finest of her large brood of great-grandchildren, and he should not be left defenceless. Ryk had left plenty of money, and Anne-Marie's children were secure, so she felt she could please herself about the little she owned. If Lourens wished to begin to make his life and to plant tulips, he should plant tulips. Oostermeer belonged to her. She had always refrained from pointing out this unpalatable truth to Jan and Juliana, for she liked to live in amity with her relations, but now, knowing that the great weight of Pieter's influence in the family would go on every occasion into the scales against Lourens, she hesitated no longer. She got Jan to take her to Groningen. When she had seen him disappear in the direction of the cattle market she went to the office of a man skilled in the law. She caused him to make a new will. She bequeathed Oostermeer and everything that she owned on it entirely to Lourens; and the little property she owned in Groningen to Jan and Juliana and, after them, to Lena and Johannes. Then, greatly relieved in her mind, she set herself to enjoying the last of the summer weather in the company of Lourens and Margaret.

Dirk arranged a cargo for Plymouth in time to get Margaret home in the early autumn. Anna sent her pearls to Anne-Marie by Margaret, and to Dirk she gave several pieces of jewellery, which had been her mother's, for his wife. At this time she often thought of Ryk. He had also tidied his affairs at the last when he had thought he might not return from his long voyage.

CHAPTER FORTY

On a wild autumnal night, moonless and pitch-dark, with a storm of wind and rain blowing gustily against the roof of Oostermeer, they awaited Lourens's return from Amsterdam.

Anna sat alone by the fire in the living room. The weather was so bad that she wondered whether Lourens would come until the morning. Juliana entered and sank heavily into her chair by the fire.

"Jan will be in soon, Grandmother," she observed. "The gate was swinging in the wind and he has gone out to secure it."

Juliana reached for her embroidery and began pulling her needle steadily through the fabric, following an intricate pattern with absorbed attention.

Juliana had never wasted a moment all her life, Anna thought. She wished she would fold her hands in her lap and gossip pleasantly by the fire. She had a craving for companionship this evening. Perhaps it was because Lourens had been away for three weeks, she thought, nodding her head at the portrait of William the Silent on the wall.

"How late Lourens is," Anna remarked, speaking of him on whom her thoughts were fixed. "He said he would be. back tonight, but I doubt whether he will come."

"The weather is not quite as bad as it sounds," said Juliana comfortably. "Lourens will come."

"We will have news of Johannes and Lena," said Anna.

"I trust that Lourens will not have upset Johannes. He was doing so well at his studies and someone coming from home always has a distracting influence."

At this moment Jan came in. There were drops of rain clinging to his iron-grey hair and his beard.

"Come and sit by the fire," Anna invited. "You have had a long day."

"I miss Lourens's help," said Jan.

A shadow crossed Juliana's placid face. In spite of his progressive views on agriculture Lourens was an excellent farmer. With his fine intelligence and his good appearance she had hoped for more for Lourens than the obscurity and hard work of a Frisian farm. His attachment to the soil had proved the greatest disappointment to her. Johannes, who had neither the looks nor the ability of his elder brother, had been the one to accept Pieter's generous offer and go to the university, and was later to seek advancement under his uncle Pieter, now burgomaster of Amsterdam. In her heart Juliana knew that her second son also wished to be a farmer, but she could not have both of them wasting themselves in perennial drudgery. And most certainly not Lena. She would remain in her grandmother's house in Amsterdam until a suitable marriage had been arranged for her. . . .

"I wonder what advice Pieter will have given him about the tulip growing?" said Anna, knowing quite well that Lourens had gone to thrust his head in the lion's jaws in a last attempt to get Jan and Juliana to agree to his scheme.

"I would not worry about that now, Grandmother," said Jan. "Time enough when Lourens gets back."

He thought she was looking very tired and frail. That mad journey to

Amsterdam in the summer had exhausted her. But there had been no stopping her. She was so alert and active that they were apt to forget how old she was. One was bound to wear out in the end. On the whole, Jan reflected, the years had been kind to Anna van Breda. She was well preserved and handsome still in her old age.

"My mother may have persuaded him to take a more sensible view. Growing tulips in Friesland! The idea is ridiculous. We'll be ruined," said Juliana.

"Why not let him have a polder or two for his experiment?" suggested Anna mildly. "That meadow by the windmill for instance? He will not be happy until he has tried."

"We can discuss it when he arrives," put in Jan hastily. They had argued enough about tulips in the past few months to last a long while.

"When there is no fighting men's thoughts turn to other pursuits," said Anna. "There is now a twelve years' truce, which is something after the long war. If it is only tulip growing Lourens wants you will be well advised to let him have his way. It pays to give youth its head sometimes. I have lived a long time, and I know what I am talking about."

"Now, now, Grandmother," said Juliana soothingly. "You know you do not sleep well if you get excited in the evening."

"I am not exciting myself," retorted Anna. "And I shall sleep very soundly when I know Lourens is home and this matter is settled."

"Pieter will have settled it," said Juliana, who had the greatest admiration for her brother's powers, and not the slightest idea of what had taken Anna to Amsterdam.

Anna kept her private opinion of Pieter to herself. She was well aware that at any time he was too clever by half for them all, and now, bereft of Margaret, he would create dissension and stir up strife to ruin Lourens's chances. She knew Pieter would not have given the lad a hearing, but, to satisfy Jan and Juliana, he had been compelled to go to Amsterdam to seek Pieter's advice on the tulip venture. However, she had never been one to lie and wait for things to happen; she had always preferred to go out and meet trouble, and, if Pieter was intending to go against Lourens, it was as well to know it now.

"It is getting late," said Jan, breaking the silence. He was very tired after his hard day.

"Will you not go to bed then?" asked Anna, neatly forestalling him.

"I was thinking that you needed to rest, Grandmother," he said. "If Lourens does not come soon I shall go to bed."

"I am not tired," said Anna. "I will wait with you, if you please."

She was not tired; but she was angry and a little depressed. They thought her a headstrong old woman, she knew, and tried to humour her, whereas they obstinately closed their minds against reason, she reflected. One could not stop progress. It was an irresistible force, and a healthy sign in any nation. This tulip business for instance: it was quite clear to her why there should be this craze for ornamental gardening; it followed on inevitably after the engineering triumphs of the past few years. Now that the country was at peace the Dutch had time on their hands and they had no intention of wasting it. They were no longer content merely to guard their soil from the ever-present menace of the sea; they were striving to reclaim more and more of the swampy land and the inland lakes; soon it would be seas they would struggle to make arable. And she could understand the spirit that animated her countrymen. Had she not once ploughed and sowed a field herself and been justified by a bountiful harvest? It was tulips now, not wheat, but it was the same aspiration in different guise. She might as well be dead, thought Anna, throwing up her head with vigour, as not to march with the times. If Lourens wished to plant tulips, he should plant tulips. If he was obstructed she had seen to it that he should have Oostermeer at once when she was gone. She was suddenly amused by the secret situation she had created, and she chuckled aloud. Jan and Juliana were quite accustomed to this habit of hers. She was very old, they thought, and the old always lived in the past.

Jan began to nod by the fire and Anna leaned back in her chair and fought against an inclination to fall asleep. Only Juliana worked on with inhuman industry.

At last Lourens came. The water streamed off him and he had to change his clothes in the kitchen before he could enter the living room. Anna glanced at his face and knew the battle was joined.

"What did your uncle Pieter say about the tulips?" asked Juliana when Lourens had had a meal and they had once more grouped themselves about the hearth.

"He said it was madness," Lourens answered flatly.

"What did I say?" exclaimed Juliana with ill-judged triumph. "I knew he would think nothing of your scheme. In his position he has intimate knowledge of all the neighbouring markets. You will be guided by his judgment, will you not, my son?"

Lourens did not reply. He stared moodily into the fire. He had had a miserable time in Amsterdam because Pieter had shown him plainly that he intended to oppose him at every turn. However, Lourens had no intention of giving up his project. In fact he was more set on it than before. He had spent a few pleasant days with the Schoenbergs and Julius had taken him round and they had discussed the future of the tulip industry with many market gardeners. They had one and all agreed that tulips were bound to be profitable. Lourens was silent, wondering how best to express himself with filial correctness.

"That is not to say that Pieter is always right," put in Anna tartly. "He has a business brain, but in the matter of tulips I place small value on his opinion. He has not grown so much as a pea in all his life."

Lourens smiled at her. She had an indomitable spirit, his great-grandmother! She was sitting bolt upright, and her blue eyes were sparkling with anger. How she loves a fight, he thought; it is meat and drink to her. . . .

"I made a tour of the market gardens on the outskirts of Amsterdam," said Lourens. "Uncle Julius and I spoke to many men on the subject of tulips. There they are planning ahead. They say there is a big future in the industry. The only dissentient voice was Uncle Pieter's. In the face of the verdict of so many experienced men I think we might discount Uncle Pieter's pronouncement."

"Lourens!" exclaimed his mother in horror. No one ever dreamed of going against Pieter's advice.

But Anna was well satisfied. She had purposely refrained from advising Lourens to seek counsel of Julius, who could always be relied upon to give sound and sensible advice. She had wished Lourens to work out the thing for himself. He had done so very capably. The Schoenbergs were qualified to give him the expert guidance he stood so much in need of with his parents so bitterly opposed to his scheme.

"Lourens has behaved very sensibly," Anna seconded her favourite vigorously. "He went to the right sources for his information. What stands for the Amsterdam gardeners can go for us here at Oostermeer. Let Lourens plant his tulips, Jan. I wish it. This farm is big enough. He will need only a field or two to begin with. You can always increase the acreage if the experiment justifies expansion."

"Not against Pieter's wishes," said Juliana inflexibly. "I will never agree."

"Jan," said Anna, "you are the head of this house. What do you say?"

"I will think it over," said Jan.

"That will not do, Jan," said Juliana. "We have quarrelled so over these wretched tulips that we must settle the matter. Yes or no, Jan; and remember what Pieter has advised."

"I have set my heart on trying, Father," said Lourens quietly.

Anna felt truly sorry for Jan. Pieter was a family benefactor. He was maintaining Johannes at Leyden and had hinted that Lena would not be dowerless if a good match was proposed for her. Yet was Lourens to be the sacrifice for the family ambitions? she wondered. She awaited Jan's answer with intense interest. She was no longer troubled, as she was happy in the knowledge that she had the power to make or unmake decisions.

"If it is to be yes or no," said Jan reluctantly, "I shall say no. I do not hold with these new ideas. We are making a good living on Oostermeer. Why speculate in flowers and perhaps lose it all?"

Lourens was very pale.

"Is that your last word, Father?" he asked.

"Jan, before you answer Lourens, may I say one little thing?" Anna interposed swiftly. "I have a little money invested in Amsterdam—a matter of two thousand guilders. Ryk made me a very generous present before he went to the Gold Coast. I used part of it to cover my expenses in England, and there is still that over. If I give Lourens this money, and his experiment takes nothing out of the farm, will it make a difference, Jan?"

"There are the fields given over to tulips when they ought to be carrying crops or winter roots," Juliana objected. "And Lourens's labour. Bear those things in mind, Jan."

"Sorry as I am to go against your wishes, Grandmother," said Jan, "Juliana and I had agreed that we would abide by Pieter's decision. If he says growing tulips is madness—well, it is madness, and that is good enough for us."

Lourens sprang to his feet in a white heat of rage.

"This is intolerable, Father," he cried. "Is my life to be lived in accordance with Uncle Pieter's wishes? I could wish him and his moneybags at the bottom of the Scheldt."

"And I hope it is good and muddy down there too," said Anna in hearty agreement.

"Grandmother!"

Anna's outrageous remark had shaken Juliana out of her calm. She laid her embroidery aside the better to deal with the situation.

"He is my grandson, and I shall say what I please," said Anna, working herself into a pleasurable rage. "He has a fine brain and it is God's own pity that he is so embittered that he cannot give youth a chance."

Juliana knew from past experience that Anna could be formidable when roused. She wisely ignored the reprehensible old woman and turned in displeasure to her son. And how Lourens favoured Anna! A pang went through his mother as she met another pair of flashing blue eyes and saw another outthrust chin. He has her unbreakable will as well as her looks, Juliana thought, and braced herself to oppose him.

"You are not yet twenty," she rebuked her first-born coldly. "I would have thought that was old enough to know how to address your father. And most certainly you are old enough to know that your uncle Pieter would never give expression to anything but a sound and carefully considered opinion."

"I am sorry, Mother."

Lourens dropped his hands to his sides with a despairing gesture. The same old deadlock, the same old arguments. They had not advanced one inch and he had spent that miserable time in Amsterdam trying to win Uncle Pieter to his way of thinking. Well, so much wasted effort, he thought. As he had no intention of giving up his plan there was only one thing to do, and that was to leave Oostermeer and to borrow money from his great-grandmother and set up somewhere on his own. Julius Schoenberg would help him: in fact they had discussed such a contingency.

He clenched his hands in a spasm of nervousness. From his superior height he looked down on his father, who was now also on his feet.

"This is hopeless, Father——" he began.

"Lourens!" Anna's voice rang out commandingly.

They turned to her.

"Let me counsel you," said Anna. "Let us not speak now. We are all tired and strained and we have got this affair out of proportion. Tomorrow will do."

Lourens was looking closely at her. He could have sworn that she winked her left eye at him. And, for no reason except the bright twinkle in Anna's eyes, it came to him that the day was not lost.

"We will settle it now," said Juliana, who was not going down without a struggle.

"Tomorrow is still a day," ventured Jan.

"Come now, Juliana, be reasonable," Anna urged. "You can keep Jan awake all night with your arguments, if you wish."

Lourens's lips twitched. He kept back a smile with difficulty. His great-grandmother was thoroughly out of hand tonight, and when she was in that mood there was no holding her.

"Give me your arm, Lourens," said Anna. "Help me to bed. We will all go to bed. Good night, Jan, good night, Juliana."

Juliana bowed her head to the inevitable. She began to put away her work tidily, as placid on the surface as though nothing had happened.

"Good night, Mother," said Lourens.

Juliana offered him her cheek, which Lourens dutifully kissed.

"Good night, Father."

"We will sleep on it," said Anna.

Lourens pinched her arm to her huge delight. She forgot how old she was when she had him home again. She leaned against him and they went slowly from the room. When they reached the upper landing Anna looked down the stairs. Jan was brushing the hearth while Juliana set the room to rights. Now was the moment.

"Lourens," whispered Anna, pulling his head down to her lips, "talk to me first tomorrow. There is one fact everyone has overlooked excepting myself, and that is that Oostermeer belongs to me. I am mistress here, if I wish to be. And I am far from dead yet. Grow your tulips, Lourens, here at Oostermeer. It is good land; it will reward you. Not a word now, until you have spoken with me. Now help me up my ladder, and I shall go to bed, although I know I shall not sleep a wink."

At the foot of the ladder Lourens began to laugh. She joined in and they stood clutching each other and rocking in silent mirth.

"Why did you say that about your uncle Pieter and the Scheldt?" Anna gasped at last. "It was an opening I could not resist. You led me on, Lourens. You ought to be ashamed of yourself."

"You are so old, my grandmother," he said, "and yet you confound us all. You are full of surprises. And a tower of strength always."

He held her against him, noticing with fright how frail she had become.

"Sleep well," he said. "And thank you, my grandmother."

"I shall," said Anna. "I have most blessed memories of my bed."

"What a life you must have led my great-grandfather," Lourens rallied her.

"He enjoyed it," said Anna.

She settled herself in her great bed. Before she fell asleep her mind ranged hazily and pleasantly through the many associations it conjured up for her in the darkness. Everything that had been important at the time, or had been important afterwards, had begun in this bed. Her marriage, her children. Gysbert had shared its warmth with her; Don Rodriguez d'Esquerdes had slept in it; Anne-Marie and she had reached friendship in it; and now it was left to her great-grandson to crack ribald jests with her at the foot of the ladder that led to it. And she could stretch her limbs in voluptuous feather mattresses and smell the all-pervading and comforting odour of rich cheeses, and know that in the little cupboard to her hand was some of the rare brandy Ryk had thoughtfully provided for her—not that she drank very much of it, but it was satisfying to know that it was there, and that Ryk had had such tender thought of her. Yes, to write my epitaph one would need to know the history of this bed, she thought, drowsily wondering who would write of her when she was dead.

And drifted from her thoughts into refreshing sleep.

ii

They sat in the autumn sunshine of an afternoon, fine after the storm. The sun poured down on the rustic seat against the hedge and gilded the bare branches of the poplar trees in the avenue before them.

". . . Now, have I made myself clear?" Anna asked.

"Perfectly, Grandmother."

"Repeat what I have said. We must have this precisely understood, Lourens."

"My aunt Anne-Marie had her portion left in England, and everything you possess in Friesland ought by rights to have gone to my grandfather, who is dead, and died a wealthy man. You feel, therefore, that you may please yourself as to whom you bequeath Oostermeer. You have left it to me in your will and I have made you a solemn promise that I will at all times help my brother Johannes, who you think may have a difficult time in Amsterdam."

"That is right so far," said Anna. "I feel strongly that you and Johannes will have to make a stand against Pieter at some future time. I cannot explain this feeling: it is instinctive. My instinct is sure, Lourens, so do not discount this as the rambling notion of an old woman. Now go on."

"My father and my mother are to have your properties in Groningen."

"Be good to your parents, Lourens. They are good souls, both of them; but your uncle Pieter's influence is too strong for them. You must work against him."

"With all the pleasure in the world, my grandmother."

"You will own Oostermeer, Lourens. You must see that you are the master here."

"There also there will be no difficulty," he said.

Anna nodded.

"I must burden you with yet a little more tedious advice," she said. "If the tulips fail, promise me you will revise the position thoroughly. If you see you have miscalculated the advantages be man enough to admit your error and make good your losses by hard work; if you have been no more than unlucky go on again and show the courage of your convictions."

"I promise you that."

"There is a little thing, Lourens, still to ask you. Let one of the fields for your experiment be the meadow by the windmill. It is a matter of sentiment with me. Once I ploughed and sowed that selfsame meadow with the aid of your grandfather. If you begin there I am superstitious enough to feel that you will succeed."

"The soil in that meadow is exceptionally rich," said Lourens. "It will be an excellent place to start."

"For the last, keep your eyes open and find yourself a nice wife. And now go down to the meadow by the windmill, Lourens, and come back and tell me how it appears to you. I should like to go there myself, but I doubt whether I could walk that distance. Be my eyes, Lourens, and come back quickly and tell me. I shall wait here in the sun for you, and when you come back we will return to the house together."

Lourens left her. He turned and waved to her as he struck away from the avenue across to the meadow. Anna raised her hand to him in farewell. She watched his tall figure until he was out of sight. When she could no longer see him she leaned back and closed her eyes.

The autumn sun shone strongly down upon her, bathing her in its warmth. She dozed, for she was very tired.

iii

She began at once to dream, a neat dream where event succeeded event in orderly sequence. Her mind followed the march of time with dazzling clarity:

This truce, she saw, was not to endure. The age of war in which she had lived would not end with her life, but Lourens in late middle age would see the faithful accomplishment of the task to which William the Silent, Prince of Orange, had dedicated himself. There would be peace in Holland only after eighty years of intermittent strife; but it would be a glorious peace and of the tremendous panoply of Spanish might, invested in the persons of Alva and Parma, nothing would remain.

A divine purpose ruled out fate: the land turned to the sun again.

The years that lay not too far ahead were clear to her: she saw the zenith of Holland's Golden Age, and the country flashed before her in bright pictures—the tulip fields, the gorgeous mansions mirrored in the busy grachts; and all the while the work of peaceful reclamation went on. The waters were subdued in low-lying lands and in the marshes. In her vision Anna saw that in the course of centuries the Zuider Zee would be dry land, and over it the ripening corn would ripple in golden waves. She saw the comfort of Dutch life, and the wealth and splendour of the cities of the Netherlands.

The people passed her in the cavalcade of the centuries: there were stately burgesses and sturdy peasants, sober soldiers and daring sailors. The future was with the people. No fear, no weariness could stop them. There was a host of Dutchmen to sail the seas, to voyage to Africa and the fabulous Indies, to penetrate to strange, far lands.

In the ranks that passed her Anna could single out the men and the women of her blood. She saw Gysbert, her father and her mother, her grandfather, and—her heart beat thickly with excitement—she saw the baron and knew for certain that she and Anne-Marie, Charlotte and Lourens, were bone of his bone and flesh of his flesh. She saw Anne-Marie with her children and they were always together in England. Lourens was very close to her in her dream. She saw without surprise that Johannes was to be the husbandman and Lourens was to finish Ryk's work in a tropical land she had not beheld until now. As the Dutch flag broke above a scarred grey fortress Ryk touched her on the arm, and she turned and smiled at him, and saw his brother Lourens and Liesbet close behind him. She saw with sorrow that Pieter and Michèle had not lived to be old and their daughter, Hélène de Romilly van Breda, was left mistress of a fortune so vast that she did not know what exactly she possessed. And Hélène loved Lourens as deeply as her father had hated him; but Lourens loved a Frisian girl and married her and had a son. Anna's last sight of Hélène was when she left the surging company and locked herself in a chamber, in which were open coffers of jewels; and she picked up ropes of emeralds and pearls, sapphires and rubies, and let them slip like rainbow-hued water through her fingers, looking at them with empty eyes. Anna saw that she died unwed, and the strange twisted stock perished. Always the strength in the family was to flow at Oostermeer, where Johannes reigned while Lourens made a great name for himself in a foreign land. Anna longed to call out to her especially beloved ones, Anne-Marie and Lourens, but there was a long rattle coming up in her throat and she could not speak, although she confused the sound with the roll of drums. She saw two members of her family, of a generation as yet unborn, descendants of Anne-Marie and Lourens, and they struggled in mortal conflict. They were of the same blood, but they strove in bitterness, for the Dutch and the English were at war and fighting for the mastery of the seas.

Here she saw that her country had entered upon a disastrous period in her history. Anna smiled to see that once more the dykes were cut and wide areas of fertile country were submerged. The enemy hated the sea, and again there was peace. So strangely did the whirligig of national fortune twist about that a descendant of her beloved Prince sat upon the throne of England. And her own descendants were friends again. Anna saw that the bitterness had been transient and that all things readjusted themselves in the fulness of time. In the East, in the Indies, in Africa, in America, and in Europe her descendants seemed to meet. Sometimes they knew they had a common ancestress, sometimes they did not; sometimes they quarrelled, but more often they worked together in harmony.

And now time was running out, and the story of the struggle for freedom she had known was staged against a modern background. A new, tragic, and ruinous conflict arose in a time that was centuries ahead of her. In their lives of simple faith and quiet duty the people of Holland had sought to maintain inviolate the ramparts of freedom; they had striven by conscientious effort to develop a state of friendship between themselves and the nations and peoples of the world. They deemed they had achieved a measure of success until, without warning, the black tide of wanton aggression was rolled down upon them, and the jack boots of the invader marched across their borders, while the mighty armaments of a ruthless vandal razed their fair and prosperous cities to the ground. As ever in her darkest hour Holland was to know the record of a free and shining spirit: a Queen of the House of Orange spoke to her people, flinging the gage into the dark sea of battle:

"At this immensely grave moment in the history of mankind black, silent night has settled on yet another corner of this earth.

"Over free Holland the lights have gone out. The wheels of industry and the ploughs of the field that worked only for the happiness of a peace-loving people have come to a stop or are turned to the horrible uses of a death-dealing conqueror. The voices of freedom, charity, tolerance and religion have been stifled.

"Only one hope lives amid the smoking ruins, the hope and faith of a God-fearing people which no human power, however evil, can extinguish —faith in the all-conquering might of divine justice; faith sustained by the proud memory of earlier ordeals manfully endured and successfully overcome in the end; faith founded on the unshakable belief that such injustice as the people of Holland have suffered cannot endure. . . .

". . . It was the same four centuries ago when religious freedom was in peril. The world knows how the people of the Netherlands then regained their voice—the voice that through the centuries has helped to spread Christianity and the gospel of freedom, tolerance, enterprise and human dignity and all the things that make man worthy of his stay on earth.

". . . To keep aloft the banner, unseen yet ever present for those who have lost their voice but neither hope nor vision;

"To speak for Holland to the world, not of the justice of its cause, which needs no advocacy in the eyes of honest men, not of the unspeakable horrors and infamous stratagems imposed on its brave army and innocent population—but of the values, ideals, of Christian civilization, that Holland is defending at the side of the allies against the onslaught of barbarism;

"To remain true to the motto of Orange, of Holland, of all that immense part of the world that is fighting for that which is infinitely more precious than life:

"Je maintiendrai—I shall maintain."[1]

The voice of the Queen was still in her ears when she saw that other powers besides England were fighting for freedom. America, "the new world, with all its power and might, was stepping forth to the rescue and the liberation of the old";[2] and from the vast steppes of Russia brave millions were streaming to the conflict; in the East the Chinese had raised the banner of freedom. Tears forced themselves beneath Anna's closed lids because it was too vast and panoramic a picture for her mind to encompass.

When she could see again there was a man coming towards her. There was a white dog at his heels, and he stopped and spoke with the children who played by the canal where the slow barges drifted. He came up to her and stood at her side and together they saw on the faces of the people their resilience in misfortune; they saw that they had attained the full stature of their ancient greatness where the unity of free men was an irresistible force; and also they saw, reflecting the glorious martyrdom of Rotterdam, the lights of victory shining clear on the horizon.

Anna's wrinkled hands moved in a gesture as of release. They did not move again.

iv

"Grandmother, Grandmother," Juliana called from the house.

No answer came to her.

"She is asleep, and the sun is sinking," Juliana grumbled to herself. "I will find a shawl and take it to her."

Lourens returned from the meadow by the windmill. He saw Anna lying back in the seat. It was getting late: he would help her in, he thought. He quickened his pace.

She was lying so still that his heart misgave him. He picked up her limp hand.

"Grandmother," he said. "My grandmother."

And knew that she would never speak again.

He pulled off his woollen cap and fell upon his knees beside her. As one other had done before him, and he a Spaniard, he pressed his lips to the hem of the black gown that trailed in the dust of Oostermeer.

[1]Philip Paneth, *Queen Wilhelmina.*
[2]From one of Mr. Churchill's speeches.